good book!

~ Acclaim for Sharon Struth ~

"This writer is exceptional, and the way you get to know all her characters so completely is outstanding. She showed how people can overcome life's obstacles and begin to live again. I really enjoyed this story." 4 1/2 STARS

—It's Raining Books

"If you're looking for a book that will keep you intrigued, then I recommend *The Hourglass*. It's a book you will read cover to cover and then think about after you're done." 4 STARS

—Long and Short Reviews

"Debut author Sharon Struth has created characters who are smart and sexy, honest and forgiving—a total breath of fresh air. It was hard to turn that last page and say goodbye."

—Dixie Lee Brown, Bestselling romantic suspense author

The Hourglass

Sharon Struth

etopia
press

Etopia Press
1643 Warwick Ave., #124
Warwick, RI 02889
http://www.etopia-press.net

THE HOURGLASS

Edited by Julian Smith

Print ISBN: 978-1-940223-23-0
Digital ISBN: 978-1-939194-96-1

First Etopia Press electronic publication: April 2013

First Etopia Press print publication: July 2013

~ Dedication ~

For my dear husband, Bill, and Linda Chiara, mentor and friend.

Thank you for believing in me.

Chapter One

Damn it, Jack!

Brenda McAllister took a deep breath, twisted the knob, and popped her head outside the hotel room door. She followed the gold-patterned carpet to the elevator, hopped inside, and pressed the button for the lobby.

Brenda caught her reflection in the mirrored elevator wall. She'd thrown on jeans and a clean T-shirt for the quick latte trip, but had forgotten to brush her hair. She did her best with her fingers, but a few rogue strands stuck out from her head like pieces of straw. The puffiness beneath her lower lashes, beyond repair at the moment, reminded her of car airbags. In college, she could roll out of bed and look halfway decent. Thirty years had changed a lot.

Damn him for not being there to make the coffee run!

Brenda closed her eyes and willed her tense jaw to relax. The elevator doors parted. She scurried out into the quiet hallway toward the lobby, eager to enjoy the first frothy sips of her drink and return to her room for a long, hot shower. Last night when she arrived, the area had bustled with activity from crews arranging vendor tables for the first day of the conference, sponsored by the New York State Writers Guild. Sessions featured authors in fiction, nonfiction, poetry, and screen writing. This morning, tables held stacks of books with posters propped nearby to market each author.

At the end of the hallway, Brenda passed a table containing her own books. A cardboard poster read "Brenda McAllister, Psy. D. *Life in the Middle Ages: A New Generation*." On the other end of the table stood a similar poster announcing her new release, *Sex in the Middle Ages: A Baby Boomer's Guide in the Bedroom*. Looking at the tangible results of her hard work laid out on the table made Brenda swell with satisfaction. Her best friend and agent, Reggie, had practically dragged her to this event, but now that she was here, she was glad she had come.

Brenda hurried through the quiet lobby, relieved nobody else lurked around at this early hour, and picked up her pace when she spotted an arrow pointing to The Market, a place the hotel pamphlet in her room described as self-serve room service without the wait.

A member of the hotel staff approached. Conscious of her ungroomed appearance, Brenda lowered her head, gaze trained on the marble floor. She rounded the corner, her mouth watering in anticipation.

Bam! A force slammed against her. The impact sent her wobbling back a step with the movement of a crash test dummy. Stunned, she reached for the nearby doorjamb to regain her footing and looked up into the face of a tall, sturdy man. He stared back at her in openmouthed horror.

His venti-sized cup flew in one direction, the lid in the opposite. The strong Colombian brew soaked the front of his starched white shirt. Several boiling drops seared Brenda's forearm and she quickly wiped them off. The stranger grabbed the front of his shirt and yanked it away from his body.

"Jesus Christ! What the—" He looked up at Brenda, his eyes wide with disbelief, shaking the fabric away from his skin.

Brenda stared back, too stunned to speak. He examined

stray coffee drops dotting a camel-colored sports coat flung over his arm. The remainder trailed down his hand and drenched the packet of papers he held. When his gaze fell on the wet papers, he lifted his head and glared at her through angry slits.

The icy stare hit her like a blast of arctic air on a hot August day, jolting her awake more completely than even the strongest coffee could have. "Oh my God. I didn't see you!"

"Didn't see me? Of course you didn't," yelled the man. "You weren't even looking." He held the papers away from his body as liquid streamed from the pages and trickled to the floor.

"I'm so sorry."

"Sorry isn't going to help." The red in his cheeks deepened. "I'm meeting Lenard Gaudet in fifteen minutes to discuss a movie deal. I was about to grab a cab." He waved the papers and coffee drops frantically jumped off them, as if sensing impending danger. "To sign this contract."

The well-known film producer's name caught Brenda's attention. A movie deal with Lenard Gaudet was big. She studied the stranger. Where had she seen this guy before? The tickler file in her mind worked overtime as she took in his features—close-shaved head, strong, commanding face softened by salt-and-pepper facial hair.

With equal curiosity, he looked her up and down, scrutinizing her from head to toe. The heat of humiliation crept up her cheeks. Her mission to grab a latte and sneak back to her room unnoticed became an official failure. At that moment, Brenda would have considered a deal with Satan if it meant she could evaporate with the spattered coffee on the floor.

"Please, let me buy you a new shirt. Maybe we can clean up that jacket." She brushed past him and fumbled with a napkin from a nearby dispenser, then dabbed at the sports coat on his arm.

He pulled away. "It's not necessary. If you want to help,

watch where you're going next time." Before storming off, he cast one last glare in her direction. A member of the hotel staff rushed to his side. "Mr. Morrison, let me help you."

Morrison. CJ Morrison? The recognition brought further humiliation. Every morsel of bravado Brenda had mustered to attend the conference and face the world disappeared. It was obvious now why the hotel staff fussed over the man.

Brenda wanted desperately to flee but her feet froze, as if stuck in dried cement. The thick lump in her throat and burn in the back of her eyes told her she was one step from spilling tears. If she cried now, over something as silly as this careless accident, the dam would burst and all the anger and hurt of the past year would come rushing out. She used all her strength to hurry toward the elevator, her legs trembling.

* * *

The desk clerk handed CJ a cloth napkin, then sent a bellhop for club soda and towels. "Let me take the jacket for you, sir. I'll send it to be cleaned and it'll be back in your room before dinner."

"Thank you." CJ dried his hands, annoyance still smoldering over the abrupt shift in his plans.

Regret stepped in the second he glanced over at the woman who'd slammed into him. CJ watched her step into an elevator and give the button an impatient slap. Before the doors closed she raised a hand and wiped under her lower eyelid. Had he made her cry?

CJ's mother used to say his temper resembled a forest fire: swift, unyielding, unpredictable. Just like his father. Not a comparison CJ appreciated.

Today's meeting with Lenny Gaudet, who wanted to turn CJ's novel into a movie, meant everything to him. The French producer had to catch a flight out of JFK, leaving only a brief morning time slot, but had agreed to meet with CJ and his agent. Although they'd Skyped and e-mailed many times, they all deemed a face-to-face meeting critical before signing the contract. CJ examined the soggy papers on the reception counter and tried not to let them dampen his hopes.

The clerk behind the desk seemed to read his mind. "Someone's on their way with towels." The clerk was a short man in his early fifties, with a full head of sandy hair laced with thin strands of gray. His name tag read Marco.

"Thanks." CJ stood quite a few inches taller than the man, but he would have gladly traded several inches of height in order to have maintained his thick head of hair.

CJ checked his watch. He'd be a few minutes late if he changed, but wasn't about to have this important meeting wearing a coffee-stained shirt. Autumn had been sound asleep when he'd slipped out earlier. With any luck he could run to the room, change clothes, and make a quick escape without a conversation.

"Don't worry about the towels. I need to get a clean shirt." CJ lifted the dripping document.

"Sir, I'll take it." The clerk reached for the sopping papers. "I'll clean them off…that is, if you don't mind."

"Mind?" He handed them over. "No. I'd be grateful. I don't have time to reprint them."

Every so often, being a celebrity paid off. Before the success of his novels and screenplays, CJ never received this type of treatment. He would mention Marco's attentive service to the manager.

On his way through the lobby, he took out his cell phone. "Lenny? CJ here. I'm running late. Sorry. Be there in about fifteen."

Irritation over the delay nipped at him as he boarded the elevator. Any lingering remorse he'd had for the way he spoke to the blonde disappeared. Maybe next time she'd watch where she was going.

He hit the button for his floor, then took a deep breath to ease his frazzled nerves. A saturated spot on his slacks grazed his leg. The other time he'd had to clean himself off after meeting a woman was the day he met his wife, Carla. Her response to his ornery actions had been to dump a dressing-coated salad on his lap. He'd deserved the treatment and apologized right away. He wanted to chuckle, recalling her spunk, wanted to warm at the remembrance of their good times, wanted to see her understanding smile—the one that told him she believed she'd married a good man. But he was well-practiced at blocking fond memories of Carla, and he was left feeling only sorrow at her absence.

The elevator opened and he rushed down the hall, key card in hand. He slipped the card into the slot in the door and pushed.

Clunk. The door opened only a few inches before it was stopped by the metal security latch. The sound of running water from the bathroom, combined with familiar singing, meant Autumn had woken and decided to shower.

He banged on the door and raised his voice. "Autumn."

No response. He banged again and yelled his girlfriend's name, louder this time. The bathroom fan hummed along with her musical number. CJ glanced both ways. At six fifty in the morning, he worried about waking other guests. Or spotting a headline in tomorrow's *National Enquirer* announcing "NY Times Best-selling Author Locked Out by Girlfriend."

The minutes ticked by. When she stopped singing, he banged again and called her name. Still no reply. He paced the hallway a few steps in each direction, never far from the door. Jesus, how long did it take for a woman to shower?

A slow stream of resentment surged through CJ, aimed right

at the sleepy stranger who'd created this mess. Was she attending the conference too? Remembering his high blood pressure, he counted to ten and hoped he didn't run into her again during his stay.

* * *

The ding of the lobby elevator sounded. Brenda rushed in, thankful for a way to avoid the conference hallway and flee to her room. Tears clamored on the edges of her eyelids.

Jabbing the button for the third floor several times, she remembered the napkin clutched in her hand and wiped a few escapees from under her lower lashes. The doors banged shut and the elevator lifted her away from the awkward moment, although her damaged dignity followed her like a shadow. She swallowed to hold back further tears. Once in the safety of her room, she plopped on the bed and the tears let loose.

It had only been a year, and a residue of pain still lingered from Jack's suicide. Since then, other than appointments with patients and an occasional dinner with those close to her, Brenda had spent her time in the solitude of her home, where she dwelled on the self-pitying notion that she could no longer fulfill her role as a reputable relationship and sex counselor. Sure, the success of her first book gave her credibility in the field, but after Jack died, the success seemed as deceitful as a credit card scam.

She had lost her spouse and the father of their children, but she had lost something else too. Every night she went to sleep wondering why she hadn't been able to save the man she loved from himself. Fixing relationships was her job. It wasn't exactly a case of the shoemaker's children going barefoot — it was more like the shoemaker following those kids around trying to shove shoes on their feet and them running away.

After a five-minute cry, she stopped and blew her nose. Whenever they used to travel, Jack had always made it his mission to seek out their early morning cup of coffee. He would quietly slip out while she showered and, upon his return, he would bestow the beverage upon her with the pride of a knight who'd located the Holy Grail. It seemed every day she'd turn a corner and find an unexpected reminder of him.

The coffeemaker on the vanity held renewed interest. While she filled it with water, she stole a glance at a copy of her second book perched on the hotel dresser. It was completed just before Jack's death. After his death, even edits were difficult to handle, making her thankful for its completion before her horrible loss.

Brenda poured a packet each of nondairy creamer and sugar into the cardboard cup, then took a sip. Her nose crinkled at the taste, but it would have to do. She went to the window and pushed aside the heavy curtains. The normally busy city, never quite asleep, seemed solemn and subdued at this early hour.

For at least the tenth time that morning, Brenda asked herself why she'd come to the conference at all. The answer was always the same: she had no choice. Reggie had made that clear two months earlier when she showed up one night without warning and delivered her tough-love speech.

"You've heard the expression, 'when you find yourself in a hole, stop digging?'" Reggie asked that evening. "Guess what, honey? The hole is about a foot above your head. Pretty soon we'll need a crane to lift you out."

Although the friendship started in Miss Young's third grade class because of a common link—their blonde hair—it evolved into so much more. Even in their childhood, Reggie never held back when she believed Brenda needed the truth. Brenda valued her honesty as much as she did their friendship.

"I know. You're right." Maybe it was time for her hibernation to come to an end, time she peeked out from beneath the blanket of shame, time she faced the judgmental stares of others. "Doesn't my book make me look like a hypocrite though?

I'm forty-nine, single, and haven't had sex in over a year. Who'd want to read anything about coping with sexuality later in life written by me? I mean, if I'm going to talk the talk, shouldn't I walk the walk?"

"Come on, a year isn't very long."

"Easy for you to say. Your husband crawls into bed next to you every night."

Reggie shook her head with obvious disappointment, the flipped ends bouncing in double-time near her shoulders. "Well, my friend, this book isn't about your prowess in the sack, although feel free to write about that next time."

"I don't have enough material. Besides, the timing of this book stinks."

"Would you stop it? Your credentials speak for themselves. Do you think Dr. Ruth runs around doing 'it' all day?"

"She might. By the way, thanks for the visual."

With reluctance, Brenda had agreed to attend the conference where she now sat in her hotel room with her crappy coffee. She hadn't left her problems behind.

Jack's last words always remained close at hand, spoken to her the day he died. She'd been leaving for work, pulling her coat from the closet, ten minutes behind schedule, to make her first appointment of the day. Jack approached her in the hallway, a gloomy energy surrounding him. Then he said in a quiet, peculiar voice, "Sometimes people are forced to make choices and do things they never thought they'd do."

After all the times she'd begged him to discuss his problems, dumping this as she ran out the door fueled rage she'd kept bottled inside for years. Brenda snapped at him about how she was late and they'd have to discuss it when she got home.

That discussion never happened.

Even now, remorse made a crash entry, pressed its weight against her chest, made her wish she could alter the past.

She went to the sink and dumped the remainder of the vile coffee. She'd had enough of punishing herself with bad beverages, avoidance, and pity.

The first day keynote address would begin at nine, a motivational speaker she looked forward to hearing. Then her workshop started at ten thirty. Day two of the conference would kick off with an address by CJ Morrison. For a split second, she considered skipping it; then it hit her how silly that sounded. A famous guy like CJ wasn't sitting around thinking about her. She'd be long forgotten by tomorrow, if she wasn't already.

On her way to the shower, her husband's cry for help still tugged at her conscience and injected a heavy dose of regret into her heart. Her voice disrupted the silence in the still room. "Jesus, Jack. What the hell were you trying to tell me?"

* * *

Brenda peeked at her watch. 10:28. Two minutes until showtime. She smiled to a new arrival, then surveyed the crowd, many of whom looked as tired as she had felt not too long ago. A steamy shower and a few dabs of under-eye cream had gone a long way. Hopefully that, along with the new taupe suit and cream silk blouse, hid the fact she'd been a wreck just a couple of hours earlier.

She pushed aside thoughts of the unanticipated morning mess. With any luck, she wouldn't run into CJ Morrison again. The two-day conference appeared to be well attended based on the advance reservation workshops, so even if she crossed paths with the best-selling author of political thrillers, she should blend in with the large crowd. Brenda fidgeted with her gold pendant necklace, which suddenly seemed heavier than it had in the store.

The big hand hit the half hour mark.

"Good morning. I'm Brenda McAllister." She pointed to the

screen behind her where the title appeared on a white screen hung against a cherry-paneled wall. "This session is called 'How to Parlay Your Day Job into a Writing Career.'

"If you're here, you might do something for a living which you believe worthy of sharing with the world. Or maybe the session next door, 'Polishing your Pitch,' is full."

She received a few sleepy chuckles. The thirty or so attendees had no place to look other than at her in the windowless conference room.

"The idea for a book developed by accident when my best friend's husband shared a story about how their fifteen-year-old son taught him stunts on the skateboard." Several attendees seemed to wake with the subject change. "My friend reminded him she had her keys ready for a trip to the emergency room and that he looked ridiculous. His response caught my attention." She paused. "He said 'Who cares how I look? Isn't forty the new thirty? Nobody ever told Tony Hawk to get off his board, and he's no youngster.'"

The bob of heads from the middle-aged audience members gave her confidence to continue. "Many of my patients have struggled with their identity and relationships as they've gotten older. The societal boundaries that used to define age-appropriate behavior no longer exist. Written material on this topic was hard to find."

The slide presentation stopped at a picture of her book, *Life in the Middle Ages: A New Generation*. "Three years after that conversation, my first book was published." She launched into her presentation.

An hour later, the low hum of voices in the hallway indicated the end of the session. A messy-haired twenty-something conference helper walked in and waited for her to finish. He led her to the table she'd seen with her books. Nearby, other vendors and authors lined the hallway while participants shuffled between them.

The young man pointed to a nearby table. "If you need anything, I'll be over there."

She got comfortable and looked forward to the rest of the day. This was her first signing in over a year. She had avoided them since the idea of promoting her book always left her with the fear someone might raise the question, "What kind of psychologist are you? Your husband committed suicide."

It would have been a fair enough question, one which pursued her thoughts like a bloodhound following a scent. It was one she couldn't answer, but Brenda still believed the answer to Jack's problems lay elsewhere—somewhere just out of her reach.

Her phone's message reminder tinkled through the air. She flipped it open. A text from Reggie, who should have been here by now. "Held up @ wk. Dinner @ 7 Ballroom. Save u a seat. Have surprise."

A surprise? Her surprises were either great or bad, never in between. Brenda started to reply but stopped. A low buzz of excitement hummed throughout the crowd. Heads turned and necks strained as the sea of bodies parted. She stood to see why.

CJ Morrison worked his way through the crowd.

Crap. Brenda's pulse skyrocketed. A man stopped CJ and said something, causing the author to smile. Brenda relaxed. He'd no doubt calmed down since that morning. If he recognized her, she'd pour on the charm with an affable grin and a clever remark like "fancy bumping into you again." He moved down the hall, closer to her table.

In the morning calamity, Brenda hadn't paid close attention to his appearance. Now fully awake, she studied him with more thought. In person, he looked better than in the pictures of him on the Internet. The photos were often accompanied by a sensational headline—"Author Morrison dating top model,

Monique Le Sexy" — or something along those lines. Brenda skipped that kind of article with disgust, not sure why gossip qualified as newsworthy.

CJ appeared to be in his early fifties. He carried the popular shaved head style for men quite well, the effect softened by a subtle shadow where hair would have grown. Under different circumstances, she'd have described him as downright handsome. Her attention fell to his dark brows, then followed the hard lines of his face, a bit weathered but carrying a strong, regal manner. The neat trim of his modified goatee and a simple mustache rounded out the overall impression, rendering him quite desirable.

Strutting with the confidence of Zeus, he'd changed into a blue sports coat and striped shirt. After being so close to him this morning, she knew he stood quite a bit taller than her, and she was a notch above average. His wide shoulders and fit chest explained why their contact earlier hadn't felt like bumping into the Pillsbury Doughboy.

A female fan yelled to him. He beamed back. The rugged lines of his features and sturdy jaw softened. Charisma radiated through the twinkle in his eyes while he spoke to the fan, the complete opposite of what Brenda had seen earlier. She no longer questioned why Monique Le Sexy, or any woman, ogled him, although she'd caution them about spilling coffee on the guy. He had a quick temper. It didn't take a doctorate in psychology to recognize the signs. What did it mask?

While a blazer had hung off his arm this morning, now he had something else draped there. A succulent specimen by any man's standards, no less than twenty years his junior, looped her arm through his. Brenda couldn't decide whether he'd chosen her as pure eye candy to play up his image or whether she was an actual girlfriend. Either way, she played her part to perfection. Her dark straight hair swayed as she took in the crowd and swaggered with her prize.

Men who chose to date out of their age bracket hit Brenda's nerves worse than the sharp scrape of metal being dragged on a road surface. Many of her female clients approaching their forties and fifties complained the disregard made them feel invisible. She agreed.

Brenda's furtive assessment screeched to a halt. CJ, now close by, stared straight at her. Remembering her earlier positive attitude, she attempted to ignore the nervous flurry in her stomach. Her mouth curled into a smile and the words "fancy bumping into you again" were poised on the tip of her tongue, waiting to launch.

His vision shifted away. She exhaled her relief a moment too soon. His stare returned and his brows scrunched close. In a nanosecond, the slow drop of his lower lip made it clear he recognized her.

"Not you again!" He leaned toward the young beauty latched to his arm, tipping his head in Brenda's direction. "*That's* the lady who knocked my coffee all over me."

The beauty viewed her with indifference.

An unexpected gravitational pull swelled Brenda's anger. Her cute quip ran into hiding. She no longer cared about winning this man's favor. His rudeness left her feeling as if *she'd* been doused with hot coffee this time. Brenda clenched her fists. A year of internal browbeating over Jack's suicide had left her easily irritated.

Brenda gripped the frail edges of her self-control. "I *once again* offer my apologies for the *accident*, by definition an unplanned event with lack of intent." He looked down his sturdy, Grecian nose at her, so she put her hands on her hips. "Shouldn't you, as a writer, know that?"

Every line on his face tensed. "I could do without your sarcasm." He leaned closer. "Thanks to you, I missed my meeting. Maybe tomorrow morning you could get room service."

The brunette unleashed a tight smirk. CJ motioned for them to move on.

Brenda fumbled for a good retort. As he stepped away, the last word went with him. The same way Jack had the last word in their life together. A silent explosion went off inside Brenda's head and propelled her anger forward.

"Mr. Morrison?" She raised her voice to be heard above the crowd.

He looked over his shoulder and arched a questioning eyebrow.

Brenda crossed her arms and fixed a phony smile as she nodded toward his companion. "It's so nice of you to bring your daughter to the conference."

Chapter Two

The large ballroom buzzed with the excitement of conference attendees seated at tables or gathered in clumps with heads together in conversation. As Brenda panned the room, her stomach growled, bombarded by delicious aromas drifting from the kitchen. However, all she cared about was finding Reggie and avoiding CJ Morrison.

Brenda had relished the bright crimson glow in his cheeks that her remark had caused, akin to a stove top set to high. He'd been about to reply when she turned and walked straight to the ladies' room, savoring every scrumptious morsel of the delicious last word. Yet almost immediately after the snarky comment, her insides shriveled with regret. Before Jack's death, Brenda would never have behaved in such a way, especially out in a professional capacity.

Regret took another swipe, and this time she didn't even bother to duck. Many years ago, her son, Devin, then in middle school, complained Tommy Carrington put chewed bubble gum on his seat before science. Devin sat right in the gooey pile and arrived home with threats of payback. Brenda had pitched the "two wrongs don't make a right" logic. Thank God her son hadn't witnessed her behavior today.

"Yoo-hoo…Brenda." Weaving between chairs and waving

an arm above her head, Reggie stood out amid the sea of earth-toned fabrics worn by the other guests. Like a human-sized bumblebee, she wore a bright yellow silk scarf wrapped multiple times around her neck and a black jacket with slacks. The flip at the ends of her long, ash-blonde hair bounced with her movements. Dark rectangular-framed glasses hung precariously from her perky nose. Reggie dazzled the world in an offbeat kind of way. From their first meeting in elementary school, Brenda found her friend's contagious energy hard to resist.

"I saw you when you came in but didn't want to yell from across the room." Reggie got closer. "We're sitting over there."

They hugged and Brenda followed her through the table maze.

"Sorry I didn't get here sooner." Reggie talked over her shoulder and almost walked into a table. She laughed it off. "A huge deal almost fell through this afternoon, but now we're all good."

"Great." Brenda itched to fill her in on what had happened earlier. "I've had a helluva day, too."

"Tell me later. There's someone I want you to meet."

Brenda settled into a seat next to Reggie at a large round table.

"Brenda." Reggie motioned to a man with thin, wire-framed glasses, a lean build, and mousy hair trimmed neat with orderly waves who sat across from them. "I'd like you to meet Dale Ellsworth, one of the partners at my firm."

"Nice to finally meet you." His voice had a relaxed, languid pace. A broad stretch of the "i" in "nice" had the sound of a tempered southern accent. "I have a client who's interested in meeting you. He stepped away for a minute but..." Dale glanced around the room. "Good. Here he comes now."

Brenda followed his gaze. Her breath stalled. She hoped, for a moment, that Dale meant the lanky man behind CJ, but then the famous author stopped at the empty chair on Dale's side and put a drink on the table. Heat accelerated at warp speed along Brenda's cheeks and topped out along the crest of her skull.

"This is CJ Morrison." Dale held out his palm, like the model on *The Price is Right*. "CJ, this is who we've been telling you about, Brenda McAllister."

CJ stared, coldly. The only hint of life in his face was a noticeable pink hue to his throat.

Dale continued. "In fact, Brenda, we were just talking about you."

She swallowed hard before speaking. "Oh, well, uh, we—"

"About helping with a project." CJ sat next to Dale and his dark chestnut eyes continued to bore into her.

"A project?" She turned to Reggie.

"Ta da! My surprise." Reggie opened her palms toward CJ. "Guess who's looking for a psychologist to help him with his latest book? He needs assistance with a character profile. Dale asked me if I knew anybody, and here you are."

CJ peered at her over the rim of a whiskey glass. His young beauty had joined him but scanned the room, uninterested in their conversation. Her slinky dress left little to the imagination and exposed a fair amount of cleavage. Brenda reached to her collarbone, all of a sudden feeling as if she was wearing high-necked flannel pajamas, not her V-necked sleeveless black dress.

CJ cleared his throat. He'd been watching her study the young woman. "This is Autumn." He offered no official title.

Brenda nodded and tried not to gawk at her chest as she pondered the real-or-fake question. The sultry sex object brushed close to CJ. Her silky dark hair dropped and hid her profile. She whispered in his ear and he nodded. Autumn left without a good-bye. CJ examined Brenda and gripped his drink as if bandits might swipe it from him.

"Bren, after Dale looked at your books, he felt you were

perfect," said Reggie. "I do too."

"Th-there must be somebody more qualified," Brenda stammered.

"Honey, you're becoming a relationship guru."

"Jeez, Reg, you can spin anything. Isn't someone like Dr. Laura available?"

CJ guffawed. A ridiculous sneer plastered across his face.

Brenda felt herself about to draw her verbal sword but managed to keep it sheathed.

"Sales on this second book have already surpassed your first one, and guess what? I got a call this afternoon from your publicist. She's been trying to find you all day. CNN wants to include you on a panel."

Brenda's cell battery had died during the book signing and she'd forgotten to recharge it back in the room. "CNN?"

"Your name's getting out there." Reggie pointed at Brenda with her index finger. "Working with CJ would be a boost. I'm sure you've seen or read his Ken Blair books or gone to one of the movies." Reggie's head bobbed, nodding the "yes" for her.

"Of course." Brenda hadn't. "This is a bit overwhelming."

CJ downed the last of his drink and let the glass land on the white linen tabletop with a thud. "We're not asking you to write the damn book."

Brenda glared in his direction. He didn't flinch.

Dale nudged CJ with an elbow. "Brenda, you'd be doing us a huge favor if you helped. The time commitment shouldn't be more than a few meetings. We'll set up a fair contract to compensate you for your time."

Brenda avoided CJ's stare, fixing her gaze instead on his thick fingers, with their perfect crescent nails, as they wrapped around his emptied glass. The veins on his hands were pulled taut from his grip. Could she stand even one meeting with someone so ornery? Brenda caught herself biting down on her lower lip, a habit she'd had since childhood when absorbed in thought. She tried to avoid doing it while in her professional shoes, and she let the lip slide slowly back to its rightful position. "I'm sure you'd be fair, Dale. The money isn't the issue, it's—"

"Brenda?" The edge on CJ's expression disappeared and his deep tone sounded close to congenial. It was as if Dale's poke had flipped a switch. His tight lips remained straight, a forced rise at each corner forming a bitter smile. He swallowed, and his Adam's apple gently rolled. Did he regret what had happened earlier? Brenda wanted to know more. Could CJ be a man reacting to the course of his life rather than someone who charted his course? Was she crazy to care?

"Yes?"

He released the glass and spread his palms face down on either side of it. "You come highly recommended and I could use someone with your expertise."

Everyone stared in her direction. Like the fox in a hunt, Brenda saw no way out.

* * *

Groove-Rider, a DJ straight from the 1970s, raised the music volume and people swarmed to the dance floor. After dinner, everyone had left the table to mingle. Brenda waited at the bar for Reggie to return from a conversation with a client.

While KC and the Sunshine Band suggested she get down tonight, a man seated near the far end of the bar caught her eye. A loose curl of hair near his temple reminded her of Jack, whose dark locks were the first thing she had noticed when they met in college. The stranger glanced her way, the impact hitting her like flint against steel and igniting a spark inside her that had been dead for some time. Panicked, Brenda dropped her vision to the rich wood bar top and swirled her Grand Marnier with a subtle twist of her wrist, unsure how to play the bar game these days.

Unlike Monopoly, she figured the rules had changed.

Her attention focused on the rows of bottles lined up in front of a mirrored wall behind the bar. In the mirror's reflection, she caught CJ surrounded by a small crowd. His confident posturing seemed to be captivating to his informal audience. This time a different spark flared. She was just glad that dinner was over. A sip of the citrus-scented drink paved a warm path to her chest, a momentary pacifier after the uncomfortable meal.

Conversation at their table had been sociable enough, but the hostile undercurrent between her and her newfound nemesis had persisted throughout the dinner. He'd directed questions to the others but hadn't asked her one thing. Several times she'd inquired about his work, but each time he responded with a short, polite answer and then immediately switched his focus to someone else.

Throughout the meal, Brenda stole furtive glances in his direction, but he never so much as ventured a single peek her way. On three separate occasions, female fans approached CJ. He spoke to them with sincerity and interest, as if nobody else existed in the room. He listened with the rapt attention of someone receiving instructions on disarming a bomb. He dazzled them with his charm. This all reminded Brenda how much she craved a man's attention herself. His restrained disregard toward her made her livid.

By dessert, she'd decided he was uppity and his flirtations phony. How would she manage to work on a project with this egomaniac? The credential would look good, but was it worth tolerating him for several hours? Jack used to tell Brenda he admired her for never backing down from a challenge. God knew CJ Morrison presented a challenge.

A second swallow of the amber drink took its warm path down her throat and she glanced again at the guy at the end of the bar, now absorbed in a conversation with another attendee.

Maybe the time had come to quit obsessing about the stuck-up author. If their work arrangement came to pass, she'd treat him with professional indifference, add the high-profile job to her résumé, and hope the credential wiped away any tarnish on her work reputation caused by her husband's suicide. Her professional profile would shine with new life.

Her shoulders stiffened when she caught CJ in her peripheral vision striding up to the bar a few feet away. Keeping her new mantra of professional indifference in mind, Brenda remained silent, but she wished he'd at least say hello. She needed to get a grip. Maybe the problem at dinner had been her oversensitivity, a reaction to the day's events. It wouldn't be the first time in her life that had happened.

CJ waited for the bartender, who was busy at the far end serving two women. He had removed his sports jacket, which revealed his wide shoulders and fit waist, obvious even though hidden beneath a tailored dress shirt. He glanced to his side and their eyes met. Offering a near-imperceptible nod, he shifted his stance to face the bartender.

The view of his back sent a strong message. The needle measuring her anger inched upward.

Brenda bit back her natural impulse to lambaste him. Whenever her anger exploded, she possessed all the finesse of a sumo wrestler performing ballet. Jack used to say, "Uh-oh, here comes Sugar Ray Brenda," when she lunged at him with a verbal assault after holding something in for too long. Sometimes the pun cast a spotlight on her behavior and she settled down. Other times he wasn't so lucky.

Her leg jiggled on the stool as she grew more and more angry with each passing second. Her new mantra kicked in. She repeated the silent phrase over and over in her mind, but on the third chant of "professional indifference" instinct won out over intellect. "Cat got your tongue?" Brenda's jumpy leg stilled.

CJ slowly turned to face her. "What?"

"Isn't 'hello' in your repertoire?" Brenda's fingers marched in place on the wood bar top.

"I nodded."

"Hmpf." Aware of her fidgetiness, she stopped her fingers, wrapped both hands around her drink, and peered into the glass.

"What did you want me to say?" His deep voice elevated.

"Hey. Howdy. *Hola. Buongiorno.* I'm flexible." The power of his stare penetrated, yet she refused to look in his direction.

"Are you always this upset when people don't acknowledge you to your satisfaction?"

"I'm not upset." Her head swung around. "It's awkward to have dinner with someone and then be ignored when you stand two feet away."

"My dear," he said, in a gentle voice usually reserved for five-year-olds, "in man-speak, a nod means hello."

The tips of her ears burned as if touched by the flame of a match. "Man-speak? What's that?"

"How men say in one word what women say in ten."

"Hmmm." She took a long sip of her drink. "You should get that checked."

"Get what checked?"

"Your attitude." She gritted her teeth.

CJ's expression hardened. He waved to the bartender, who indicated he'd be right over. "What do you *really* want from me?" He raised a single brow, and the repressed curl of his lip reminded Brenda of the way a parent viewed a child caught in a lie. She played with her bracelet, studying the links as if she was seeing them for the first time. There *was* something she wanted from CJ, but exactly what it was remained unclear.

Rubbing a single finger along the polished silver bangle, she regrouped. "How about a thank-you? At least I didn't turn down your offer of work by telling Dale how rude you were to me this afternoon."

"What?" CJ's eyes opened wide and his jaw fell, quickly followed by an indignant glare. "First off, Dale's not my father. He's my agent."

Brenda waved a dismissive hand. "Whatever."

"Second, keeping our history quiet served us both quite well."

"You're kidding, right?" She leaned forward on the stool. "I didn't do anything for which I haven't already apologized."

The bartender arrived. CJ blew out a loud gust. "Yes, I'll have two cognacs, please." He shifted several inches away from her, then leaned both elbows on the bar and stared straight ahead.

Somehow her goal of indifference toward this man had gone into hiding. Determined to fix the added damage she'd just done, she straightened her shoulders, softened her tone, and smiled. "Double-fisted drinker, huh?"

He cut his eyes in her direction and evaluated her with suspicion. "One's for Autumn."

Brenda chortled out loud as a Shirley Temple-drink wisecrack jumped from her brain to the tip of her tongue. About to open her mouth, she halted the comment when CJ narrowed his gaze.

"Listen." Brenda's tone became more affable. "We'll have to work together pretty soon. I'm thinking we should clear the air."

"Really? Well, I'd say you're itching for a fight."

For a brief second, she pondered the notion that he might be right. Had CJ's earlier grumpiness offered an excuse to funnel untapped anger over Jack's abrupt departure? Anger she'd kept bottled inside for the past year? "No. Just conversation." She used as much sincerity as she could muster.

He surveyed her, then shook his head. "My Aussie

grandmother used to call me a larrikin when I acted like you."

"What's a larrikin?"

"Depends on how it's used." He cast a scorn-laden glance in her direction.

The bartender placed two cognacs in front of CJ, who pulled a twenty from his pocket and handed it to him.

"You didn't answer my question."

The bartender returned with his change.

"Look it up." CJ pocketed the bills, then lifted the drinks. His mouth curved into an I-got-the-last-word-this-time smirk and he walked away.

After stewing for several minutes over the disconcerting remark, Brenda reached into her handbag, dug out a bank slip and a pen, then scribbled "larrikin" on the back. She tucked the note into the bag's side pocket while scanning the bar area. At the end, the guy who reminded her of Jack seemed preoccupied, talking to another man. Her gaze paused on him; then he glanced up and smiled.

Before she could react, Reggie flew in with her usual strong gust of energy.

"Were you talking to CJ?" She hoisted herself onto the tall bar stool.

"I sure was."

"Great. So you two are hitting it off?"

"In a manner of speaking." Brenda twirled her stool toward Reggie. "What's a larrikin?"

"I have no idea. Why?"

"Never mind. Here's your drink." Brenda pushed the martini glass toward Reggie. "I thought dinner would never end."

"Why were you so quiet? Does it bother you that CJ's a celebrity?"

"Not at all." Brenda shook her head. "In fact, I bumped into him earlier today."

"Oh? Who introduced you?"

"Nobody. I mean I *literally* bumped into him. Like, head-on. Early this morning I rolled out of bed and went to the lobby to grab a latte. I wasn't looking and slammed right into him. Coffee went all over his clothes as he was on his way to a meeting."

"Oh my God." Reggie started laughing. "Did he get angry?"

"Remember the 'mad as hell' speech from the movie *Network*?"

"Oh, come on. You're exaggerating."

Brenda grinned. "I wish. Before he stormed off, I apologized and tried to help him clean himself off."

"You tried to clean him off?" Reggie's nose crinkled. "Care to go into details?"

"Use your imagination. At least I didn't do the mom-wetting-a-napkin-with-her-tongue thing."

"Well, by dinner he seemed over it."

"Oh, no." Brenda crossed her legs and leaned on the bar. "You've only heard part one of our fun-filled day." Brenda recapped their second meeting and Reggie almost choked on her drink when she heard the daughter comment.

"Jesus, that's something I'd say. You're usually a bit nicer than me."

"My patience for people seems to be diminishing with age."

"I hear you, sister." She studied Brenda then rested a hand on her forearm. "We haven't signed anything yet. Do you want Dale to find someone else?"

Brenda focused on the corner of the room and Reggie followed her gaze.

CJ stood within a small circle of people. The men observed with admiration while he spoke, and the women stared with adoration. His girlfriend, hooked to his arm, glowed by his side.

"Why's Autumn always holding his arm?" asked Brenda.

"Do you think she's legally blind?"

"No, wise-ass. She is nauseating, though. Do you want me to talk to Dale?"

Brenda took a second. "No. I can handle him."

"OK. He's all yours. In spite of the CJ incidents, you're doing all right for your first foray back into the world of the living. Don't you think?"

"Sure. My session was great, and being out feels good. I even checked out a guy earlier." Brenda waggled her eyebrows. "Guess some parts are still in working order."

"Good to hear. You know we haven't been out at a bar like this since our girls' weekend for my fortieth birthday."

They reminisced about the outing on Cape Cod with a few other college friends ten years earlier, falling into fits of giggles over the memory of the two relentless suitors reminiscent of the "wild and crazy guys" portrayed years ago on *Saturday Night Live*.

"Excuse me." The man from the bar with the hair like Jack's stood before Brenda. "Brenda McAllister, right? I've read both your books."

"Oh. Thank you." She worked hard not to be swayed by his ruffled, cinnamon-colored hair and the perfect shape of his lips.

"I'm Nate Walker." He extended a hand.

Reggie hopped off the stool and grabbed her drink. "I see someone I need to catch up with. Back in a bit."

She took off before Brenda could object and left her staring into the face of the handsome stranger.

Chapter Three

Alone, at a quiet corner table in the back of the hotel's banquet room the next morning, Brenda inventoried her selection from the breakfast buffet. She ignored the bland scrambled eggs and overripe cut fruit, dutifully taken as healthy choices. Her sweet tooth struggled between the icing-laced cinnamon bun and the apricot Danish, taking up half her plate. Guilt didn't enter into the equation.

After Jack died, Brenda dropped a clothing size without even trying and inched closer to her wedding-day weight. Until their move many years ago from upstate New York to Greenwich, Connecticut, she'd never questioned her average-sized curves. Once living in the prosperous Connecticut community, however, the grocery stores and PTA meetings were flooded with more size zeros than you'd find at Anorexics Anonymous.

Jack loved her curves, even with a few extra pounds rounding them out over time. One morning while lying in bed, shortly after they got married, his hand and appreciative eye smoothed the side of her body. He stopped short at her hip and, with a twisted smile, whispered, "Your sexy curves remind me of a bold red wine, a real Marilyn Merlot."

She'd burst out laughing, but the amorous gleam in his gaze

had made her feel like a *Cosmo* model.

She shut her eyes for a brief moment and savored the memory with sadness. Sometimes the happier slices from a past life were almost harder to swallow than the difficult moments of recent years.

"Brenda?" The unmistakable soft, squeaky pitch of Patricia Dupont pulled her back to the conference. Round-eyed with a circular face and ruffled dark hair, Patricia was a darn close match to the ditsy cartoon character Betty Boop, albeit an intelligent and classy version. She looked anything but ditsy today dressed in a tailored red suit with gold buttons, with a leather portfolio tucked under her arm. "What a coincidence. I was going to call you this week."

"Patricia. How nice to see you." Brenda stood and they hugged. The moody scent of Patricia's Chanel No. 5 mingled with the room's breakfast aroma. She'd have bet anything her call had to do with the unanswered fiftieth birthday invitation for her husband, sitting at the bottom of a pile on Brenda's kitchen counter. The file of excuses stored for moments like this worked overtime, searching for a way to get out of the party. "Are you attending the conference or just staying at the hotel?"

"The conference. I've started writing again and a friend in my critique group suggested I come. She's upstairs getting ready. You're coming to Bertrand's party, right?"

Brenda had refused many invitations over the past twelve months, some of those from Patricia. The hope-filled smile on Patricia's ruby lips made Brenda cry uncle. "Yes. Of course I'll be there. Sorry I didn't respond yet."

"Oh good. He'll be glad. We've missed seeing you." She glanced at the empty table. "Mind if I sit?"

"No. I'd love to catch up."

Reggie's push into the world of the living had shoved Brenda a little further than she wanted to go. No turning back now.

Patricia dropped her Gucci snakeskin bag on the table, leaving Brenda to contemplate how many snakes a bag that size required. "Be right back." She headed off to the buffet table.

The sweet pastries on Brenda's plate lost their appeal. Since Jack's funeral, she hadn't spoken to anyone from his employer, Global Business Systems. Patricia's husband, Bertrand Dupont, was a transplant from Montpellier, France, where GBS's European corporate headquarters were located. He now served as the vice president of marketing at the Stamford offices. As chief financial officer for GBS, Jack had worked closely with Bertrand. The social part of their friendship evolved after a company function at which Brenda had hit it off with Patricia.

Brenda almost wished she'd ditched the pastries when the petite woman returned with a bowl of oatmeal and a side of fruit. They caught up on the kids and work, and then Patricia lowered her voice. "Have you heard what's going on at GBS?"

"No. I haven't spoken to anybody from there since…" Brenda swallowed. "Since Jack's funeral." Her hermit-like behavior of the past year left her a bit embarrassed, but she didn't bother to explain.

"Of course." Patricia rested a well-manicured hand on Brenda's forearm. She bent her brows in thought and dropped her gaze to the table for a second. Then she looked up at Brenda again. "Something's brewing there. Last weekend, when Luc and Aimee came over, the men whispered about it. Luc said something about calling you."

Brenda's cheeks got unbearably hot at the mention of the other couple, and she willed herself not to flinch. Luc and Aimee were part of a small posse of close friends she and Jack had developed through his office. The idea of seeing Luc was one of the reasons she'd avoided the party RSVP.

"Why would anything about GBS matter to me?" Brenda

asked.

"Well, between us, when Aimee and I walked into the room, the two men clammed up." Patricia lifted a spoonful of oatmeal but stopped short of her small mouth, her dark brows aloft. "I caught enough snippets to get the idea that whatever is going on" — her tone dropped to just above a whisper — "involves Jack."

Brenda had spent the past year certain Jack had withheld something. A year without a single clue as to why he took his life. A year blaming herself for his death. Patricia's comment pointed a floodlight on what she'd always believed but couldn't prove: that work was at the root of his stress and depression.

Brenda leaned across the table, so close that the overdone Chanel would probably stick to her all day. "Did you get *any* details?"

Patricia shook her head, her curly locks moving a little. "I asked Bertrand about the conversation later on. I even mentioned Jack. He didn't look too happy but said Luc might contact you and I should stay out of it."

On Brenda's list of things to avoid, Luc ranked one, two, and three. "Oh. Well he hasn't called yet. Will he and Aimee be at the party?"

"Of course. Luc and Bertrand were friends back in France. Luc can't wait to torment him about turning fifty." Her mouth formed a devious grin. Then she chuckled. "He's been keeping that horrible novelty store at the mall in business buying gag gifts."

Brenda joined Patricia in the laugh but wasn't laughing inside.

Jack's silence about what ailed him, even when directly asked, always left Brenda feeling as if she'd tripped and fallen at the start of a race. Yet Patricia's comment was like the blast of a starting horn at a new race where, maybe this time, Brenda stood a chance. Some long-overdue answers about Jack's work life would be good. The fact that they would be coming from Luc, however, was not so good.

"More coffee, ma'am?" A ponytailed waitress stood with a carafe and waited.

"Yes, please." Brenda leaned back and the waitress poured. In the few short seconds it took for the waitress to fill her cup, she'd decided there had to be a way to get answers without Luc and without violating Patricia's trust.

* * *

Click.

Autumn closed the bathroom door and the latch snapped shut. Several seconds later, the shower started. CJ rolled onto his back and breathed a sigh of relief. Her bubbly persona in the morning had been endearing at first. After three months of dating, the appeal had disappeared.

His temples pulsed, a reminder that he'd had one too many drinks at the banquet. After crawling out from under the covers, he threw on a thick terry cloth robe and tightened the belt. At the window, he pushed apart the heavy curtains to check the weather. The sun's glare greeted him by way of a daggerlike pain piercing his skull. He jerked the curtain shut again.

His body couldn't handle overindulgences like last night's anymore. Right after Carla died he had woken most days with a throbbing head and cottony mouth. Those mornings hadn't been due to social overimbibing. That had been more like survival drinking. Dale put a stop to them, though. He'd pulled CJ from his nightmare and kept him from swerving off the road of success he had achieved with his first two books.

CJ took a moment to be grateful for his friend. Without Dale's friendship, where would he have ended up? Without Dale's intervention, he never would have written his most

successful book, *The Hourglass*. A big hit seven years ago in the
US and Europe, the current foreign movie offer had come out of
nowhere. A movie presence overseas would be a further career
boost. If only he had met with the producer and signed the
contract. The reminder kicked off leftover frustration from
yesterday morning, which trickled with the slow drip of an IV
through his system. Lenny had indicated he'd be in touch, so
perhaps the deal wasn't a fait accompli.

CJ went to the desk and opened his laptop, hopeful that he
would find an e-mail about the potential project. He pushed the
power button and waited. Yesterday resembled a comedy of
errors, although he found little humor in what had happened.
The coffee accident should have been a sign to get on a train and
head home to Chappaqua. Brenda's remark in the lobby had
rattled him, and the discovery that Dale's search for a
psychologist had landed on Brenda McAllister was like
something out of the *Twilight Zone*.

Autumn hummed a pop tune in the shower, one that had
played two days earlier on the radio and she claimed was her
favorite. He admitted he'd never heard the song before and an
expression reminiscent of how teens looked at their uncool
parents crossed her face. She told him the name of the group too,
but he had never heard of them. Their interests were miles apart.

When the laptop finally powered up, CJ logged in and
waited again. Brenda's remark yesterday afternoon about
Autumn still irked him. A few years back, he would have
ignored the comment as a middle-aged woman's jealousy of a
man's May-September romance. He sure as hell didn't need her
pointing out their obvious age difference. But Brenda's comment
brought back a question he'd been asking himself all too often
these days. Why the hell did he keep dating these younger
women? Her outspoken insult yesterday had struck a nerve.
Damn her!

His shoulders tensed. He could almost hear his doctor say, "Remember to breathe." CJ inhaled deeply, then slowly let the air escape, the tension in his shoulders diminishing as his lungs gradually emptied.

He bypassed e-mail and opened his notes for this morning's address. Today would be the first time he'd used the speech about last year's Mount Everest climb. The trip did more than inspire his writing and feed his soul. Climbing the twenty-nine thousand feet had helped him gain perspective on the lonely journey he'd traveled since Carla's death ten years earlier. Adjusting his day-to-day outlook to reflect the insights gained on the spiritual journey, however, was even more difficult than the ascent had been.

CJ ignored the speech document and instead Googled Brenda's name, scanned the results, and found her Web site. Her picture popped up on her home page. A sunny smile greeted him. She was leaning against the edge of a large mahogany desk with crossed arms. He guessed her to be close to his age, perhaps a bit younger. A slight tilt of her head, combined with a confident aura, suggested that if you had a problem, she could fix it. Her crystal blue eyes showed a starburst of creases near the edges. The rest of the page told about her two books.

A second picture, on the bio page, showed her with a scruffy gray-and-black dog, posed by her side with perfect posture. The caption read, "Brenda McAllister is a psychologist whose practice specializes in individual and couples' relationship counseling as well as sex therapy in her Greenwich, Connecticut, office. With a master's degree and doctorate in clinical psychology from the University of Hartford, Brenda sits on the board of the Fairfield County Psychology Association. Aside from her work and writing, Brenda likes to hike, travel, and play tennis."

CJ knew Greenwich, the affluent community where she

practiced. Close to Manhattan and sitting on the shores of the Long Island Sound, aka Connecticut's Gold Coast, houses there cost a bundle. In fact, the director of one of his films lived there and had invited him over for dinner a couple of times. Did she live there too?

CJ couldn't find mention of a significant other. Who was the man he'd seen her with at the bar last evening? They'd talked for a while, even hit the dance floor.

The shower stopped, but his curiosity about Brenda still needed to be fed. He located her Facebook page, but instead clicked on an article that had appeared two months earlier in the *Stamford Advocate*. He scanned it until he spotted a paragraph that mentioned her husband had passed away unexpectedly a year earlier. The article also said her children were grown.

The bathroom door opened and he quickly exited the article. Autumn stepped out in a white terry cloth robe, a towel wrapped around her hair. "Mornin'! I'm glad you're up. You'd better hurry if you want breakfast before you go on."

"Can you order room service while I'm in the shower?" The throb in CJ's temples increased. He shut the computer and walked toward the bathroom. "I'll have oatmeal and coffee. Please."

"Sure thing, honey."

Her agreeableness annoyed him, yet it didn't stop him from admiring her sway as she walked to pick up the room service menu. A stab of shame forced him to admit that his involvement with her had started and continued for all the wrong reasons.

He turned on the shower, popped two Tylenol, then stepped into the steamy enclosure. Within minutes, the dwindling pain in his head subsided to a tolerable level. Brenda crept back into his thoughts. Besides her nasty comment, there was a second, more irritating reason that he couldn't get her out of his head: Brenda was precisely the type of woman he'd been trying to avoid for the past ten years.

* * *

At nine a.m. sharp, Brenda slipped into the crowded ballroom, just as the event coordinator ushered CJ to the podium. She spotted several empty seats against the back wall and took one, adjusting her fitted skirt to her knees, then crossing her ankles. Based on the near-capacity crowd, CJ had quite a following. Their work relationship justified the purchase of at least one book in the Ken Blair series.

Brenda searched the crowd. A surge of excitement pumped through her at the prospect of finding the object of her desire: Professor Nathaniel Walker, who preferred to be called Nate, or as Reggie had nicknamed him in a text that morning, "Professor Charming, as in Prince." Brenda felt a twinge of disappointment when she failed to locate him in the crowd.

Last night, Nate had talked, danced, and participated in some serious flirting with her for two hours. A divorced college professor with no children, he had come to the conference to pitch a philosophy book. Brenda figured many of the young women at the private college where he taught were smitten with him. She knew she certainly was.

By the time they parted, she'd fantasized about running her fingers through his thick sandy hair and kissing his full lips. He had a killer grin, yet even a frown on his boyish facade would have kept her attention. The way he surveyed her while they danced had an effect on her like a motorcycle being kick-started. Brenda fell asleep satisfied in the knowledge that she was still functional in the libido department. She glanced at the empty seat beside her and hoped it remained that way in case he came in late.

After an introduction extolling CJ's credentials, the author stepped forward to thunderous applause.

"Good morning." His husky voice rumbled through the microphone. The tan sports coat she'd spilled on yesterday morning had been cleaned and was now being worn with a black crew-neck shirt tucked into a pair of black dress slacks.

Holding both sides of the podium, CJ leaned into the microphone. "A good friend asked me to do something two years ago. It appealed to me on many levels. The task required commitment. Not just my time. There were physical demands to be met. A true challenge to even the most fit among us. Now, anybody who knows me well would say I don't shy away from challenges." Soft laughter from the crowd reminded Brenda of the news clips she'd seen over the years highlighting his escapades, including skydiving and race car driving.

"So, I balanced my options," CJ went on. "Nothing required me to say yes. I have a nice low-risk job. Carpal tunnel and eyestrain are my primary occupational hazards." More chuckles from around the room. He hadn't been this witty at dinner.

"Hi." Nate dropped onto the chair next to Brenda, a twinkle radiating from his fawn-colored pupils. "I hoped we'd run into each other."

Brenda's heart leaped in high-five joy. "Me too."

They turned their attention to CJ.

"I knew a blind man and a fifteen-year-old had successfully accomplished this feat, but I also knew that one hundred and seventy-nine people had died attempting it over the years." Anxious silence hovered above the crowd. "One question stopped me from saying no right away." A second pause held the suspense. "Will doing this enhance my writing?" There were many nods among the sea of heads. "I knew the answer to that. So when Edgar Christy called me again to ask if I'd fly with him to Tibet and climb Mount Everest, I couldn't refuse."

CJ lifted the microphone and paced with a confident stride as he told the story about the months of preparation leading up to his journey. At times during the climb, he questioned why he had agreed to go. It drained his physical and emotional strength in unforeseen ways, yet perseverance paid off. Standing on top of the world empowered him in unimaginable ways.

His story approached its climax, but his voice suddenly quieted. His gaze dropped to the floor for several long seconds. Then he surveyed the audience. His gaze was steady, but something somber lay beneath. His voice lowered and stayed flat. He detailed how the physically wrenching climb had awakened him to the idea that the approach he had taken to his mountain journey could also be used to conquer his personal struggles. Brenda noted a contradiction between his inspiring words and the sadness hidden in his face. It was the type of red flag she looked for when working with her patients. CJ picked up speed and his voice rose, again strong and determined. With the skill of an expert guide, he led the attentive crowd back to the craft of writing, showing them how to apply the lessons of Everest to their own work.

The speech ended to deafening applause.

Another side of CJ had emerged. This wasn't the same man who had screamed about spilled coffee, who had barely tolerated her presence during dinner, who made petty comments that stung like paper cuts. Why did he date someone like Autumn, half his age and with no obvious conversation skills? Why was he so ready to lash out, with only the slightest provocation? Why, with his career success and money, did something seem amiss? The answer, she believed, lay in whatever had gone on in his thoughts during the secret, somber moment she had just witnessed.

Nate leaned close to her ear. "I love this guy's books." He always spoke with an even keel, but there was something alluring about his voice. It was probably his class lecture style. "Are you a fan too?"

"Not really." She liked how it felt to have him so close, their shoulders brushing. "I did enjoy listening to him, though."

"There were autographed books of his for sale yesterday. I didn't see them out there today, though."

"Maybe I can get you one. I had dinner with CJ last night." She didn't want to sound like a name-dropper. "He's represented through the same agency as I am."

"I noticed you talking to him." Nate's gaze softened, his tone teetering at the edge of flirtation. "So even though your beauty drew me to you, it turns out you're well connected, too."

"My beauty? Not because you read my books, like you said at the bar?"

Nate's mischievous grin held her captive. "The truth is, when we first glanced at each other, I knew I had to meet you."

Last night's thoughts of kissing this stranger returned. Brenda glanced at CJ and his entourage as they shuffled past. CJ stared at Nate. Then his gaze shifted and hovered on her. Yesterday's antagonism had disappeared from his expression, replaced by intensity in his eyes that came close to resembling longing. Before Brenda could say hello, he looked away. The blow to her ego felt like a bad book review.

"Care to join me later for lunch?" Nate asked. "I have to drive back to New Jersey this afternoon."

"I'd love to." She brushed off her irritation at CJ's snub, annoyed with herself that his opinion even seemed to matter.

Chapter Four

CJ now regretted last night's hasty decision. He stared out the cab window as the car flew down Lexington Avenue toward the offices of the Wallace and Ellsworth Literary Group for his meeting with Dale. There had to be a face-saving way to get out of working with Brenda.

In a rush to resolve his manuscript issue, the second their dinner had ended, he pulled Dale aside and requested they hammer out a contract today for the consulting job. This morning had changed everything, though. After the keynote address, CJ left the podium with his head surrounded by the fog of his thoughts and desperate to escape emotions that had haunted him for the past ten years. Delivering the speech had been difficult. Revealing his true private thoughts had required more emotional strength than he'd anticipated, although he'd regrouped in front of the crowd quickly enough.

A second blow had come as he neared the ballroom doors to leave. Brenda's desirous gaze at the guy she'd been with at the bar the night before caused CJ's gut to harden. Avoiding any woman who reminded him of Carla and his devastating loss had become easy over the years. All that had changed yesterday.

Rather than catch up with some friends for lunch, CJ had returned to his room to work, thankful that Autumn had gone shopping. In spite of his best efforts to stay focused on his writing, his mind wandered to the attractive psychologist. He replayed the various encounters with her the day before. Before he could stop himself, his fingers wandered the keyboard and he pulled up some Internet reviews on Brenda's books. The reviews were decent, but his opinion of the cover was that it didn't look very serious.

The cab driver leaned on the horn and cursed at another car, jarring CJ back to his problem. Maybe he'd simply tell Dale the truth. Dale had been there when CJ had lost his wife and knew firsthand what it had done to him. Dale knew CJ better than anybody. Better than he knew himself. CJ dismissed the idea with a shake of his head. Dale would probe for details, and CJ didn't feel like talking about it.

The cab turned down a tree-lined street and pulled to a stop in front of a red brick building, two blocks from the historic center of Gramercy Park. The driver, whose dashboard ID read Khondokar Haq, mumbled the fare. CJ glanced at the meter to confirm what he'd heard, paid, and hopped out.

Fourteen years earlier, during his search for an agent, CJ's submission to the midsized literary agency had landed on the desk of their newest employee, Dale Ellsworth. After more than twenty-five rejections, Dale was the first to respond with an interest in CJ's manuscript. When they met, it became clear to the author that his earlier rejections might have been a gift incognito. Right away, CJ recognized that Dale provided the yin to his yang. Beneath Dale's easygoing manner hid a no-nonsense man who could get the job done. The book's success helped launch the careers of both men. Now Dale was a partner, and the agency was staffed with seven agents and a sizeable support team.

By the time CJ reached the second floor entrance to the agency's suite, he had accepted the idea that he was stuck moving ahead with the arrangement with Brenda. He opened the glass doors and entered the upscale offices. Glossy hardwood floors and fresh white walls hung with vibrant modern artwork hid all signs of the building's age.

"Hello, Jennifer."

The young receptionist's long curls and round wire-rimmed glasses reminded him of someone who might have attended Woodstock, not a product of the post-Gen X population.

"Hey, Mr. Morrison. He's expecting you. Go right in."

CJ headed down a short hallway to Dale's office and stepped inside.

Despite the large volume of books, spanning various styles and sizes, Dale's office proved to be the very model of organization. CJ's own office was a disaster zone, at least compared to the librarian-like efficiency of his friend. Once Dale had organized CJ's home book collection after trying to locate a book he wanted to borrow and not being able to find it in the haphazard system.

Dale's slim fingers wove through his wavy hair and his elbows rested on the desktop as he concentrated on the manuscript in front of him. He was dressed impeccably, as always. Today he wore a starched white shirt and red silk tie, which made CJ conscious of his own casual attire. He still wore the sports jacket and black T-shirt from this morning's speech, but had changed into comfortable jeans for the trip home. It was a dressy outfit by his own standards, considering most of his days were spent in front of a computer wearing sweatpants.

"Any good?"

Dale lifted his head. "Hey. Yeah. This one has promise."

A native of Georgia, Dale's accent had faded over time, yet his soft voice carried hints as to where he had been raised. Nothing ever ruffled Dale's mild-mannered exterior, making him easy to work with. His calm presence often reminded CJ to rein in his own temper. The elbow tap the other night at dinner had been one of those times.

CJ took a seat on the other side of the large teak desk, where tidy stacks of mail covered every spare inch.

Dale pushed aside a pile and handed CJ a packet. "How'd everything go this morning?"

"Great. I used the Everest speech. The audience feedback was good."

"Good." Dale tipped his chin toward the papers. "Here's your preliminary contract with Brenda McAllister. It's the same format we've used before when we've acted as brokers to these types of arrangements. Make changes as you see fit."

CJ reached into his attaché and retrieved his reading glasses.

Dale picked up his coffee mug, then paused. "After meeting Brenda, I think working with her could be good for you."

CJ almost asked what he meant, but instead slipped on his glasses and tipped his chin to peer at Dale over the frames. "That remains to be seen."

CJ buried his nose in the contract details to avoid further discussion. After a minute, he said, "I don't like the restriction on total hours. The work may take longer and I don't want to be left hanging if it does."

"OK." Dale scribbled on his copy.

"I also want to add a stipulation that we meet at my place. I work better at home."

"Consider it done." Dale jotted a short note.

He continued his review and flipped back to the first page. "Isn't this hourly rate a little steep?"

"Reggie said Brenda requested that rate." His words flowed at a slow, measured pace. "She has a doctorate degree."

"Hmmm. Fine." CJ removed his glasses and placed the document on Dale's desk. "Other than those few items, it looks good. After she signs, shoot me a copy, and I'll sign too."

"There's a chance Brenda will stop by later this afternoon when she's through at the conference. If not, I'll fax it to her. Are you staying another night in the city?"

"No. I'm heading back to Chappaqua soon."

"I'll fax the revisions to your home then."

"Great. Have you known Brenda's agent long?"

"Reggie? I'd guess six or seven years now. Why?"

"You're comfortable with her recommendation of Brenda?"

"Absolutely."

A sharp *beep-beep-beep* sounded from CJ's watch. He reached down and shut off the alarm. "I'm meeting Autumn soon. I think my days with her are numbered."

Dale started to say something but stopped.

"What?"

"Never mind." Dale raised a dismissive hand. "I've already put in my two cents on your dating life."

"Yes, you have. The words of a jealous, married man." CJ flashed a grin and Dale laughed. They'd had this conversation before.

Dale stood and came around his desk. "Come on. Am I jealous or a sensible friend?"

"You *are* a good friend." CJ patted Dale's back. "I got your message."

CJ grabbed his briefcase and Dale followed him to the door. They walked together down the hallway.

CJ was suddenly pounded by a reminder of how vulnerable he'd felt that morning when he'd seen Brenda. He stopped just outside the reception area and turned to Dale. "On the psychologist thing, should we have checked around more?"

"Why?"

"I looked at Brenda's books. They seem kind of like a flaky, pop-psychology effort."

"Flaky?" Dale snorted. "They've been flying off the

bookshelves. Reviewers have called them approachable and several top psychologists provided reviews for her too. Don't judge a book by its cover. She's more than qualified." He tipped his head and grinned slyly. "Besides, like I said before, working with someone like her would be good for you."

CJ ignored the innuendo. "She didn't seem to want to work with me."

"Jeez, I can't imagine why." Dale's brows rose in a knowing salute. "You weren't very polite when she first joined us. Something else going on here?"

"Not at all," he quickly replied. "I just thought she showed a little attitude."

"She'll need a lot of attitude to deal with you." Dale grinned and patted CJ's shoulder.

The exaggerated clearing of Jennifer's throat made them look in her direction. She tilted her head toward the corner, then fussed with the papers on her desk.

Both men stepped into the reception area. Brenda sat on the love seat, her arms banded tight across her chest. The vibrant flush of her cheeks and tight clamp of her lips told CJ that she'd heard everything.

CJ's mind whirled. What exactly had he said? The word "flaky" sprang to mind. Maybe this was a blessing in disguise. She might be angry enough to walk away from the job, and Dale would be none the wiser about CJ's true feelings.

"Brenda." He nodded curtly.

She only returned his nod.

Last night's clash with her at the bar when he didn't say hello returned to his thoughts. Their banter had elicited a strange reaction in him. He'd accused her of itching for a fight, but maybe he had wanted one too. Or maybe he just wanted a conversation that made his blood pump, that gave him a reason to give a damn about something.

CJ stopped at the door and turned around. She raised her brows and gave him a glassy stare. Just how tough was Brenda? Tough enough to handle him?

He cleared his throat. "By the way, Brenda, we went through the contract. If you have any problems, work them out with Dale."

Her flush deepened. He pulled open the door and walked out. He proceeded down the hall, satisfied that she'd probably rip the contract in half the second Dale took it out. Maybe then these feelings he had around her—the same ones he used to feel around Carla—would disappear.

Another part of him regretted his curt remark, but he hurried down the stairs and pushed her from his mind.

* * *

At the age of thirteen, Brenda learned the meaning of the word tenacious. Her father had returned home from a two-day business trip, during which her mother, home with the kids, drank herself to an incapable state both nights he'd been gone. Thirteen-year-old Brenda fended for herself and her sister, three years younger. She found rides to after-school activities, cooked dinner, and did a load of laundry. When Brenda's father found out, he didn't storm off to the bedroom where his wife slept to start a fight; he just shook his head and rubbed his throat while he digested the fact, his dismay obvious.

"Thanks for helping out, honey." He wrapped Brenda in a hug. "Good thing you got the tenacious gene from my side of the family." He frowned deep and bitter as he stared at the staircase leading to the bedroom. "You'll need it with her as your mother."

Thankful for the show of support, she hadn't asked what tenacious meant, but later looked up the meaning. Back then, the primary reason for her tenacity was making sure outsiders didn't find out about her dysfunctional family life. That morning's discussion with Patricia had reawakened some of those old feelings. The idea of outsiders discussing her husband's problems made her feel uneasy in a way that was all too familiar. During those times when her mother hadn't been able to man the home front, the looks of pity from the neighborhood moms had filled Brenda with shame for their family.

The same feeling of shame filled her now. If Luc and Bertrand were discussing Jack, others were too.

After getting Georgie, her miniature schnauzer, from the neighbors, Brenda tried to forget about CJ Morrison's snub and concentrate on how to research GBS. Everything was on the Internet these days. At the long pine kitchen table, she opened her laptop, grabbed pad and pen, and typed "Global Business Systems" into Google. In addition to the company Web site, she found a great deal of information in *Forbes*, the *New York Times*, *Bloomberg*, and *Business Week*. Mostly the articles were about stock prices, new prototypes, and other business matters with no meaning to her. She stumbled on several articles in which Jack had been quoted about earnings, but the details would have worked better than an Ambien. Still, she scribbled a few notes about the topics he discussed.

She added "Chief Financial Officer," Jack's title, to her search. Several stories popped up about his unexpected death. Pain throbbed in her chest as she scanned each one, but she soldiered on. One headline read, "Global Business Systems Appoints a New CFO." The piece discussed Roger Chapel, the thirty-five-year-old who replaced Jack. His background at a large public accounting firm was impressive, but Brenda thought him relatively young to be appointed to such a high-ranking position, considering Jack had been over forty when he started the job.

A small picture next to the article showed Roger. His long neck, short side-parted hair, and black-rimmed glasses made him look like the spokesperson for Accountants R Us. A quote from Bob Manning, the firm's CEO, stated, "We're proud to have Roger on board. He brings a great deal of experience to the firm."

Jack hadn't been fond of Bob, but tolerated his boss, as all good employees should. Brenda had met him at Christmas parties and company picnics each year. He always ignored her, even when they stood in a group together, which always made her uncomfortable.

Georgie nudged Brenda's knee, her cold, wet nose pressing through Brenda's pantyhose. She scratched underneath the dog's wiry chin. "Hungry, girl?"

Salt-and-pepper fur surrounded Georgie's round, dark eyes, which pleaded "yes." Or at least that's what Brenda figured. The computer screen showed it was five thirty, meaning she'd been on the computer for almost two hours, still in the clothes she'd worn today at the conference. Probably time to throw on some sweatpants.

Halfway out of her seat, Brenda plopped back down and typed "Bob Manning, GBS" into Google. Several hits popped up from the same publications she'd read earlier. The last entry on the page was from *Connecticut Lives*, a cultural and philanthropic magazine featuring residents of Fairfield County. She clicked it open. A picture from a fundraiser two years ago showed two tuxedo-clad men, both with graying hair and the same *Mad Men* corporate haircuts—short and parted on the side.

A caption read, "GBS CEO Bob Manning with wife, Jessica; GBS Chairman of the Board Donald Wainscott with wife, Mary." Wainscott, a stout and chubby man, pressed shoulders with his age-appropriate wife. Manning, taller and with a broad chest, had an arm looped around the waist of a younger woman, perhaps close to forty, with blonde hair, a clingy gown, and a bronze, metallic tan. A real trophy wife.

CJ's girlfriend flitted into Brenda's mind, along with a dose of disgust toward men in general. Just once, she'd like to see some graying female executive with a boy toy at her side during a philanthropic fund-raiser. The picture probably wouldn't even make the paper.

She refocused. If Patricia's comment this morning at breakfast had any merit, it raised questions. What was creeping out of the woodwork now? Did Jack's boss know about it when her husband was still alive? She stared at the photo of Bob and willed it to give her an answer.

Brenda went upstairs to change her clothes. Each step dragged her down with the heavy weight of her disappointment. She'd hoped the Internet search would provide a lead about the problems at GBS, or maybe spark a memory of a conversation with Jack that might have contained some clue about what was going on at the company. Instead it felt like one big, confusing dead end with no other streets in sight. Unfortunately, the one road with answers was the one she wanted to avoid the most — the road to Luc Pelletier.

Chapter Five

Brenda grabbed the cordless phone off her kitchen wall and punched Reggie's work number in a little harder than necessary. She dropped the fax she'd just received from Dale on the kitchen island and plopped down on a tall stool, her fingers hopping a nervous jig on the granite countertop while waiting for an answer. This one last request from the arrogant author was the last straw.

Two days had passed since meeting with Dale at his office. So far she'd agreed to every minor detail CJ's agent had requested, even though one or two things annoyed her. She'd agreed to meet at his place, notwithstanding the near thirty-five minute drive, over an hour's travel both ways with no mileage allowance. She'd even agreed to not contact him directly, only through his agent.

In fact, she'd decided to be the bigger person and ignore his haughty display at Dale's office, even though his attitude bothered her like bad sunburn. When it first happened, she was stunned that he had stood a few feet away and discounted her credentials as well as her books. Then his suggestion that she "work out the details with Dale" further rubbed salt into a fresh wound. If she started an entry in *Wikipedia* under "Egotist" and threw in his picture as an example, it'd serve him right.

Only one thing had kept her from jumping off the sofa in Dale's waiting area, scurrying down the hallway, and putting up her dukes. Her comment about his girlfriend from the Mickey Mouse Club seemed to have bruised CJ's ego. His attitude reeked of masculine one-upmanship.

Now they were even. Which was why she couldn't ignore this latest ridiculous demand.

On the fifth ring, Reggie's assistant answered. "Reggie Lang's office."

"Hi, Cindy. It's Brenda McAllister. Is she around?"

"Sure. Hold on."

A minute later, Reggie picked up. "Hey, Bren. You got the addendum?" Her quick, breathy sound, almost always present, came across as if she'd just warmed up for a race.

"Oh, I got it, all right. What type of person is rude enough to put a clause in a contract which allows them to cancel a prearranged meeting with just half an hour's notice? Who does he think he is, Madonna?"

"Sorry, sweetie. Rank has its privileges. Dale said CJ's got a lot going on and, in case something unexpected comes up, wants flexibility."

"I'll agree to two hours' notice. Jeesh. I'm Penny Punctual. With his clause, there's a good chance I'll be on my way over and he'll cancel. He may get a glimpse of my not-so-lovely side if that happens."

"You mean the side he saw at the conference?"

"Exactly. Tell Dale two hours or it's a deal breaker."

"Are you serious?"

"Yes."

"Will do." Reggie paused. "What else is wrong? You sound off."

Reggie possessed the homing abilities of a pigeon, at times annoying. This time, Brenda was glad she'd asked. "You know that thing I told you at lunch—what Patricia said about some buzz at GBS having to do with Jack?"

"The one I told you to ignore since she's prone to exaggeration?"

"Yeah, that one." Reggie's statement held a truth that Brenda chose to overlook. "I've been doing some research but can't find anything. You know I can't ignore any possible clues as to why Jack was so desperate that he'd take his own life."

"But Bren, answers won't change anything. Let's move forward, not back. Isn't your lunch with Professor Prince Charming today?"

The day after the conference, Nate Walker had sent Brenda an e-mail saying how much he had loved spending time together at the conference. The message ended with an invitation to meet him for lunch halfway between her home in Connecticut and his in New Jersey.

"It sure is."

"Nervous?"

"A little, but it's not a blind date. Besides, he's been divorced for seven years and, with his looks, should've had plenty of dates. If I make an idiot of myself, let's hope he can pick up the pieces."

"What are you wearing?"

"Black jeans tucked into boots with a print tunic top."

"The silky one you bought when we went to the outlets last month? With the plunging neckline and fitted bodice?"

"Yup. With a camisole underneath, I'm shooting for the accidentally-on-purpose glimpse of cleavage. He won't know if I want him to see more or if the damn shirt just slipped, but I'll bet he looks."

"I have a love/hate relationship with those things. A man must have designed them. Just tug it up every now and then. You don't want to appear desperate."

"You mean like I am?" A sarcastic tone slipped through, but Brenda was thankful for Reggie's push in a better direction. She shifted the conversation to work. "If CJ agrees to the revision, fax it over, and I'll get it back to you right away. Feel free to have Dale pass along my threat to Mr. Morrison. I wouldn't want him to think I'm a complete pushover."

"Oh, I doubt CJ would ever think that about you."

* * *

Five minutes early, Brenda scanned the parking lot in the southern Westchester County restaurant for a silver Saab, but there wasn't one. La Paella, located in a small strip mall, had wrought-iron gates on either side of the entrance. She got out of her car, leaned against the side, and enjoyed the warm sun. It did little to lessen the nerve-bending concern which emerged on the drive over—that in the bright of day she and Nate might realize that this was a horrible mistake.

A silver car pulled in next to Brenda's, and she pushed aside her worries. Nate stepped out looking every morsel the part of a sexy professor—corduroy jacket, button-down shirt, jeans, and loafers—and aimed a charming grin right at her. Back in her younger days, a teacher like him would have warranted a major crush. She tried to still the wild scamper of her heart.

"Hope you haven't been waiting long."

"No. I'm always a little early." How on earth did a guy with his handsome face and personality remain single?

"This place is great. It's a tapas restaurant. Have you ever eaten in one before?"

She shook her head.

"You're in for a treat. A friend who lives nearby took me here once."

Inside, her eyes adjusted to the darker lighting. Black iron chandeliers cast a dim glow against the golden walls of the rustic room. After they were seated in a booth, Nate chatted about the restaurant. Brenda studied him in the amber glow, noticing a little gray around his temples and miniscule creases surfacing near his eyes when he laughed.

The tapas experience, sharing appetizer-sized portions of a variety of dishes, brought intimacy to their meal. Food arrived piecemeal, at an unhurried pace. They split each culinary treat, savoring and dissecting ingredients, divulging their favorites and making comparisons to the previous dishes. It set the tone for a laid-back flow to their conversation.

Nate's anecdotes about college life made them both laugh throughout their meal. When the conversation shifted to a more serious discussion on the philosophy of politics, his words were balanced, leaving Brenda wondering which party he voted for.

Just as their coffee arrived, Nate started to say something, then hesitated.

"What?"

He waited for the waitress to leave. "You mentioned at the conference your husband passed away. How long ago?"

"A little over a year." Suddenly awkward, Brenda reached to her chest and tugged up her camisole, as if it would prevent too much from being revealed.

"Had he been ill?"

"No. His death was unexpected." The bruise on her heart, always tender to any touch, throbbed. She blinked, hoping to hide the developing moisture.

Nate's hand slipped over hers. "I'm sorry. We don't have to talk about this."

"Don't be sorry." The protective warmth of his touch made her feel safer. She took in a deep breath. "My husband committed suicide."

Nate's expression held the same pity she'd witnessed the countless times she'd shared the news. She always got the feeling that something unspoken lay behind the sympathetic expressions. The suicide changed the way others saw her, much like when a teenager's wrongdoings caused others to judge the parents.

"I'm so sorry." Nate sandwiched her hand between his. "It must have been horrible for you."

She nodded. "Horrible to lose a spouse. Guilt because I'm a therapist and couldn't see the signs."

"You can't blame yourself."

"I know. I'm working on it." Even to her own ears she didn't sound convincing.

A while later they left the restaurant. The bright sun had a blinding effect after the dark inside. Nate's hand rested on Brenda's lower back again, a reminder of how much she missed a man's touch. At her car, they stopped and faced each other.

He reached out and played with a strand of her hair. "Since you're new to dating in this millennium, there's a recent rule I'll share."

"Oh?" His closeness created heat in places untouched for far too long.

He traced a finger along her cheek and softened his voice. "It's safe to have a parting kiss if both parties agree to a second date."

"Really?" She fingered soft waves near his temple. "Sounds made-up to me."

He pouted. "After I wowed you with my deep philosophical thinking, you think I'd do that?"

"Even if I did, I'd still vote yes on the second date."

Nate leaned close and sampled her lips with the same care he'd given to the dishes served during their meal. Brenda pressed herself to him, deepening the kiss, breathing in every detail—tender lips caressing hers, a hint of lingering coffee, the soft brush of his shaven cheeks.

He pulled back and whispered, "So it seems a second date is unanimous."

* * *

CJ stood on the redwood deck outside his home office, rested his elbows on the railing, and inhaled the fresh air. He hated this time of year. The tree buds had popped up out of nowhere two weeks ago. Many even had full-blown leaves. He shut his eyes, turned his head upward to the sun and let its warmth settle on his skin.

Spring. Always a reminder of the approaching anniversary date. The day one bad decision changed his entire world. The sun's heat disappeared and CJ's eyelids slowly opened. A thick gray cloud had moved in front of the sun, shutting off its power in an instant. The cloud inched across the sky, prodded along by a slight breeze, and eventually the heat returned to his skin. He wished the agony inside him could pass so easily. Plopping on a cushioned cedar lounge chair in the corner of the deck, CJ stretched out his legs. Before he could get comfortable, the phone in his office rang.

He sprang from the chair, hoping the caller was Dale. They had been involved in a game of phone tag all day. On the third ring, he found the cordless phone underneath a pile of scattered papers on his desk and answered.

"CJ. It's Dale. We finally connect. Listen, I got the addendum back from Reggie this morning. Is this a good time to discuss it?"

"Sure."

"First, Brenda wants two hours' notice for cancellations. Oh, and in case you're on the other end making a sour face, it's a deal breaker."

"A deal breaker?" CJ chose to ignore the sour-face remark. He'd had these work arrangements before and most professionals agreed to his terms. "A bit of an overreaction, don't you think?"

"Not after what I heard. Reggie told me dinner at the conference wasn't the first meeting between you two."

"So?" Even with Dale, he wasn't about to show his hand.

"So? I'm hearing you were your usual ornery self with her."

"Jesus Christ," CJ muttered. "Did Brenda tell everybody what happened?"

"No. She told Reggie. Reggie told me. Brenda had second thoughts about agreeing to work with you once your contract demands started to roll in. I can't say I'm surprised, especially after I heard about your first fun-filled day together. You could've given me a heads-up, buddy."

"Didn't seem important at the time."

"My point is a small concession on your part would go a long way."

Brenda's willingness to break the deal was a gutsy move on her part. She stood to gain from their working together too. She was showing him she wasn't afraid of him, even after how he behaved when they ran into each other at Dale's office. He liked that in a woman. "All right."

"I have one more request." Dale paused. CJ suspected it wasn't going to be something he'd like. "When you meet with her, an apology would be in order."

"An apology?" CJ's annoyance flared. He paced toward the glass doors. "Her sarcastic insult stooped to a new low. Did you hear what she said to me?"

"No. And I don't want to. We've been friends for close to fifteen years. You probably deserved what she said. I've seen you when someone pushes the wrong button."

"Fine. I'll find a way to make amends." He went to his desk and sat again, shuffling papers to locate his calendar.

"I appreciate it. How's the first draft coming along?"

"Good, but I'm itching to get working on the psychological

profile. I can't get past this issue with the character." The calendar hid beneath several issues of *Horse Illustrated*, needed for research on a new character, a horse breeder.

"Reggie said Brenda could meet with you as early as next Wednesday."

CJ located a pair of reading glasses on the desk, slipped them on, and flipped open his calendar. Six days away. Longer than he'd wanted, but after the deal-breaker comment he'd cut her some slack.

"Wednesday any time after ten thirty should be fine. Let Brenda pick the time so she thinks I'm being accommodating."

"That's the spirit." Dale sounded pleased. "Jennifer will contact her right away and get back to you with a time."

CJ scribbled the tentative meeting in his calendar, then returned to the deck, again settling into the lounge chair. An undertow of unsettled emotions tugged at him. It was worse than a bad song that wouldn't leave his head. He tried to concentrate on a new plot slant. The persistent bad feeling grumbled in the background and tripped every thought. Then Brenda McAllister made an appearance in his mind.

Yes. She was the reason he couldn't concentrate.

He couldn't shake the memory of seeing her as he left his keynote address. The flirtatious tension between her and her suitor screamed to him from across the room. He'd been pulled toward Brenda's expression of longing, even though it was not directed at him. Then, bam! A pang of jealousy struck without warning. Worse, she had caught him gawking. Had she detected his jealousy? Even as he turned away, he had known it was rude, but his embarrassment had left him no choice.

Why he felt this way at all, about a woman who'd probably argue with a red light that she didn't have to stop, required some deeper thinking. Watching other men receive adoring looks always annoyed him; it was usually him who garnered this kind of reaction from women. Maybe that was the reason. Or was it more?

During his Everest climb, he had begun to tackle his past. Climbing held a meditative quality — the attention to his breathing, the importance of every step, the respect for nature. The trip shook him awake, made him admit that for nine straight years Carla's death had locked him in an emotionless cocoon. He still wrestled with the awakening and, even a year later, couldn't seem to pin it to the mat.

Brenda's appearance in his life made him want the match to end.

Her comments left him furious, yet he respected her for them. The thin line between love and hate always intrigued CJ. Both caused strong reactions. Both meant you cared. Neither were rational.

Brenda's arrival swept in like an unexpected tornado. He liked surprises. She was intelligent, articulate, and witty. With her, a challenge waited around every turn. At one time, these were the exact qualities he had searched for in a woman.

A single thought kept running through his mind, one he couldn't ignore: she reminded him of the only woman in his life who was able to handle him. Lately, for the first time in years, being with a woman like her mattered.

Chapter Six

The expression about April showers seemed to be true. Brenda sipped her coffee by the French doors in her kitchen and stared out at her soggy garden beds, the ones she planned to weed today. Rain, predicted for all day Saturday and well into Sunday, ensured a crappy weekend. For once, the weather guy had hit the bull's-eye.

Her computer finished booting. Brenda shimmied onto the tall stool next to the kitchen peninsula. First stop, check a week's worth of ignored personal e-mails, then hunt for a recipe from a cooking show she'd watched two nights ago. After this past year by herself, she considered writing a book called *Dating Yourself: How to Make Time Alone Special*. The recipe for Spicy Thai Lobster Soup didn't seem like much, but it took her mind off the solitude.

Fifteen minutes later, e-mail checked, recipe bookmarked, and gardening no longer an option, she shifted to the next item on her to-do list: finish CJ's first Ken Blair book in the series and start the last one.

Their meeting was five days away. She'd never get through the entire series and was worried the touchy novelist might throw some kind of tantrum if he found out. Luck knocked on her door. She remembered Reggie's comment about movies made of the popular series. A quick hunt through Netflix yielded some easily downloaded results. She'd fooled Mrs. Pritchard in eleventh grade English with an essay on *To Kill a Mockingbird* having only read the Cliff Notes. Got a B plus. If she could fool Mrs. Pritchard, tricking CJ would be easy.

The legal pad, where she'd jotted some possible paths to explore on Jack's company, still sat on the marble countertop. Prior research hadn't shown anything significant, but Patricia's remark about GBS gnawed at her subconscious. The place she'd been avoiding for the past year might yield some answers: Jack's home office.

The office door had been closed on the day he died and had seldom been opened since. She had quarantined the room, as if it contained radiation from a bomb. Her emotional state had always been too fragile to open that door. But now, encouraged by her success in facing the conference, she vowed to try.

After a quick scan of her written research, mostly quotes from Jack that she had found online, she headed for his office. As she approached the dreaded inside garage door, a chill formed along her nape and gradually crept up her scalp. The gateway to the two-car garage sometimes kicked off memories of the day Jack died. It was the door through which the grim reaper had entered her home and changed her life.

Details of the moment she discovered Jack's body came flooding back, as if they had happened yesterday. Unlike in a movie, in which dark clouds might have foreshadowed the discovery, a warm sun had beamed down on her that day as she drove home from work. As soon as she pulled into the driveway, a sixth sense told her something was wrong. She hit the car remote and the large outside garage door opened like a stage curtain. Jack's black Lexus, which should have been at the office, sat inside, Jack's silhouette slouched in the driver's seat.

A slow awareness of the scene took hold. Adrenaline

coursed through her veins. Brenda flew from the car and rushed into the garage. The smoggy stench of exhaust fumes overwhelmed her senses. She covered her nose and mouth with her palm as she struggled with the car door. Jack sat motionless, dressed as she'd left him that morning. She reached over his lifeless body, fumbling with the keys, and finally shut off the engine. She grabbed Jack's shoulders and shook him — shook him over and over and over with frenzied strength. *Jack! Jack! Wake up!* Her screams sounded muted to her ears.

He remained still. Any hope that his eyes would fly open and the unreal moment would pass, disappeared. Her hands trembled as she ran inside and dialed 911. "I just found my husband in the garage. His car was running. Please hurry."

She hung up and ran back to the car. Jack hadn't moved, so she shook him several more times; although, by now, numbness had taken over and her arms had lost their strength. Time froze. Each second seemed like an hour. Each thought started with "Why, Jack? Why?"

And then an awful possibility occurred to her. Did he know what she'd done with Luc?

Sirens blared as EMS vehicles screeched into her driveway, temporarily disrupting her inner concerns. Two workers checked Jack's vitals. She prayed they could revive him, her prayers all she had left to give. Ten minutes later, they lifted Jack's body from his car and carried him out on a stretcher. Alone in the garage, she leaned against the car that had become Jack's coffin, unable to stop crying.

She ran a hand across the leather of the empty driver's seat. A bittersweet feeling surfaced, one which filled her with shame. Relief. The unfixable problem she'd lived with, Jack's drinking and his silence about why, had finally disappeared. Heavy boulders, carried on her shoulders for the past five years, rolled off and crashed into pieces. For the second time in her life, the death of a loved one eased the weight she carried. The first time was after her mother's fatal accident—a drunken slip in the shower.

Brenda tried to forget the memories of that day, forcing herself past the entrance to the garage and along the hallway to Jack's office. The bravado she'd felt moments ago now seemed weaker and unsure. She stopped and stared at the door, the memories returning once again. This had been her next stop that day, right after they removed Jack's body. The officer had come out to the garage to ask her where her husband might have left a suicide note. She wandered to this room, the most logical place.

Officer Rodriguez, who up until then she'd barely noticed, followed her into the office. His dark eyes filled with sorrow and he pressed his lips tight. "Are you OK, ma'am?"

She nodded, then stood in the center of the room. She wanted to tell the officer about the time Jack and Devon worked in this room on the model '64 Chevy Impala, still displayed on the built-in bookshelf. Or the time Shannon's boyfriend broke up with her and Brenda came home to find her sitting across from Jack sniffling, but smiling, as Jack said a better guy would appreciate all her beauty and brains.

Jack was a perfect father. When Brenda glanced at Officer Rodriguez, he averted his gaze to the ground, offering her privacy. The desktop revealed nothing. She opened Jack's top drawer and pushed aside some items. The effort only lasted a few minutes before she collapsed in the chair, sobbing.

"Ma'am, a note would have been left for someone to find, not hidden in drawers. How about we check the kitchen?" He helped her from the room and shut the door behind them. From that day on, each time she had contemplated a more detailed cleaning, the day's horrors returned. Now she couldn't remember the last time she'd gone into that office.

She faced the white four-paneled door and tried to summon

the same courage she'd found to attend the conference. Instead, a drawn-out, dull pain hit her. It was like pulling a scab off a slow-healing wound. Brenda pressed her back against the hallway wall, slid down to the wood floor and hugged her knees. This time she didn't cry.

No way in hell was she ready to tackle Jack's past today.

* * *

The secluded dirt road didn't appear to go anyplace but into deep woods. Brenda's GPS had led her here from the main route through Chappaqua, New York. She glared at the device with suspicion.

Pulling over to search for clues, she finally spotted a large tree with the brass figures "151" stacked vertically on the trunk. CJ's house number. Maybe the GPS was right after all. She followed the road, and the sun disappeared behind a canopy of trees. The dirt entrance changed to smooth pavement, making for an easier ride on the long, curvy driveway.

Six days ago she'd received the signed contract from Reggie, an agreement to perform consulting services. After reading two of his books and watching two movies made from the ones she didn't read, Brenda was hell-bent on proving him wrong about her own work. She prayed this encounter would go better than their first few. CJ's willingness to let her pick the time of the meeting showed he was capable of compromise.

At a clearing, the sun materialized, and a large contemporary house greeted Brenda. Set amid woods, its natural stain siding and linear design reminded her of a grown-up tree house. A balcony jutted out from the second story, furnished with cedar lounge chairs.

Brenda parked her Audi next to a sporty Mercedes and a shimmering red Porsche. Was Autumn here too?

A mild breeze carried the aroma of a nearby lilac bush to her open car window. A male robin chirped loudly from a nearby branch, expanding its tail feathers and lifting them in the air. Brenda enjoyed the sign of spring love and, once again, indulged herself in memories of Nate's tender kisses a few days earlier. She had been on two dates with him, and his interest ignited a giddy high, like an injection of dopamine coursing through her veins. After twenty-five years of marriage and a year of isolation, the rush of infatuation felt damn good.

Her pesky nerves, having made some intermittent appearances on the way over, resumed their abdominal jig. She headed toward the front door, releasing her jitters with a deep breath. She'd treat this like any other business venture. If CJ acted miserably, she'd ignore his antics and act professional. She didn't need him anyway. He needed her.

Brenda rang the bell and prayed Autumn had disappeared for their meeting. At dinner, CJ's girlfriend had proved to be quite vacant in the conversation department. Autumn provided living proof that God must divide skills among us. He'd given her an ample bosom and stunning looks to ensure the opposite sex wanted her, but no personality.

Something still bugged her about an eligible man her own age dating this hot young thing. Brenda had issues with the Victoria's Secret Angels who invaded her mailbox and slinky *Cosmo* models who taunted her at the supermarket checkout lines. "Normal" women her age blended into the background like they didn't exist.

Brenda pressed the bell again. She smoothed the edges of her knit top and brushed a dog hair off her black slacks. She nearly jumped when the door swung open.

CJ held a phone to his ear. Black half-frame reading glasses were perched on the end of his nose. He motioned for her to come in, indicating he'd be a moment. Then he went down the hallway to finish his call.

Brenda peeked beyond the foyer toward a great room and wandered in as CJ's voice faded in the distance. Tall windows and a high ceiling planked with golden cedar lent warmth to the ice-white walls. Large oil paintings added vibrant color to the room.

Brenda scanned the contents of CJ's built-in shelving units. He had a ton of books, including a wide array of popular fiction, many stepping out of the genre CJ wrote. In a section devoted to nonfiction paperbacks, one title caught her attention: *The Portable Curmudgeon*. She pulled the book from the shelf. The well-worn front cover described its contents as quotes and stories about world-class grouches. The inside cover had an inscription: "CJ, To my very own curmudgeon on his fortieth birthday…All my love. Carla." Brenda replaced the book. Carla, whoever she was, must be a connoisseur of castigation.

The next section, devoted to travel, included *The Snow Leopard*, by Peter Matthiessen. CJ had spoken of this book with high praise during his conference address, explaining how Matthiessen's journey into the Himalayas had reinforced his own decision to climb Everest. Brenda pulled it from the shelf.

A minute later the sound of footsteps disrupted her reading.

"I apologize for making you wait." CJ came toward her. "I had an overseas conference call. The time difference makes scheduling tough. Dealing with a foreign film production company is more complicated than I would have thought."

"Is the movie for one of your books?"

"Yes. *The Hourglass*."

She nodded and went to return the book to the shelf.

"What are you looking at?"

Brenda held it up, glad she wasn't still browsing through the curmudgeon book. "What you said in your address left me curious. Based on the first two pages, I see why you were inspired."

"Borrow it, if you'd like."

"Oh." Brenda was surprised. This couldn't be the same man she'd spilled coffee on at the Hyatt. "Thank you."

"No problem."

She dug deep for small talk. "Your home is nice."

"Thanks. I like the privacy."

"Is Autumn here?"

"No. Why?"

"I noticed two cars in front."

"They're both mine. The Porsche is primarily used for racing."

"Oh, right. I read racing is one of your hobbies."

His stare told her everything. It was clear to him that she'd read up on him.

He shifted to a businesslike tone. "Before we get started, I think we need to discuss something." He paused, glancing away with a slight look of uneasiness. "About our incident at the hotel."

Brenda shriveled inside, fearful they were about to drag race down the same road as their last meeting.

CJ continued as if he hadn't noticed. "The morning we had our unfortunate encounter, I'd been on my way to meet with a French investor for this film. He had a short window to meet with me before a flight at JFK. The coffee added a layer of stress to an extremely important meeting. I guess I didn't show you my best side...then or later when we met up again."

Brenda suspected the word "sorry" would never exit his mouth; however, a backhanded apology was better than none at all. "I appreciate the explanation." She chose her response carefully. "My own reaction didn't present my best side either."

"No need to dwell on it." CJ waved a dismissive hand. "I'm looking forward to working with you and want the issue behind us."

"Me too."

"Good. Then let's sit and get down to work." He motioned to a contemporary sofa while he went to a leather club chair across from her.

She removed a pad and pen from her tote, then rested the tote on a solid burgundy area rug beneath her feet.

CJ propped his ankle on the opposite knee, exposing his sockless loafers. His attire—blue jeans and a dark, fitted T-shirt—suited him. Brenda admired his muscular arms, which hadn't been as obvious in his business clothes. Eyeglasses, slipping down his nose when he opened the door, were now pushed atop his head, giving a quirky twist to his commanding presence. Her attention fell on the heavy five o'clock shadow on his scalp, making her wonder how much maintenance was required to maintain such a style. He seemed meticulous enough to take care of it, since his squared beard and attached mustache always seemed perfectly trimmed.

A persistent thought niggled in the recesses of her mind. If today marked the first time she'd met CJ, would she want him to like her? Not just as a psychologist or fellow writer, but as a woman?

The answer was a resounding yes. She was either going crazy or influenced by the carryover effect from the recent dose of dopamine that Nate had triggered.

After an amiable discussion about the success of Brenda's first book and a mini job interview about her psychology credentials, CJ asked, "Have you read any of the books in the Ken Blair series?"

"In preparation for our meeting, I read the first one and the last one and scanned the others."

"Oh? Just for our meeting?" The corners of his mouth bowed upward.

"Yes." Was he teasing or mocking her? "Something funny?"

"You're amusing. Most people would have just said yes." He studied her, his face now unreadable. "Something tells me you're not like others."

"What's that supposed to mean?"

"I'd define it to mean you have qualities setting you apart from the crowd."

"Gee thanks, Mr. Webster." She chuckled. "I deserved that. I meant to say, do you consider the quality good or bad?"

"Ah, so you *do* care what I think about you." His expression brightened with the same sparkle she'd seen when he spoke to a female fan at the conference.

"I could ask you the same question." She tried to sound playful, no repeats of the conference malice. "You seem quite concerned with the reason I read your books. Is being a fan a requirement for this job?"

"*You* were the one who brought up the reason you read them."

Tongue-tied, she attempted a poker face. His obvious delight showed her failure.

"Advantage Morrison." She barely gave in to the moment with a tight-lipped grin. "Guess I've been served an ace."

"It takes a big person to admit defeat. Besides, I'm not egotistical enough to think everyone I meet is a fan."

"Did I say that?"

"No." He paused. "I wouldn't want you to think so later, though."

"Aha." This time she launched a fully committed smile. "So you do care what *I* think about you?"

"It's conceivable." The glint in his gaze was the sparkle of a brilliant gem.

Brenda couldn't move her eyes from his, trapped by their power. She couldn't remember why he annoyed her so much only a week earlier. Now their conversation felt like a delightful dance.

"By the way, I enjoyed your presentation," she said. "I wanted to tell you afterward, but you walked right past me."

"I saw you." He waited a beat. "You were busy talking."

A subtle shift of his expression hinted that more rested behind the comment. Without knowing him better, though, she couldn't figure out what.

Before she could respond, he switched gears. "Since you read the two books, can you tell me how you view the hero, Ken Blair?"

"Sure." The sudden shift to work came as a surprise, but she was on his dime. "Ken seems intelligent. The strong, silent type. He has keen observation skills which serve him well as a CIA agent. He's fearless, as I suppose all agents should be, confident, loyal, and he accepts his assignments without question."

"A fair assessment." CJ nodded. "Anything else?"

"His fastidiousness is an asset in his line of work; yet it carries into his personal life and becomes a drawback. Especially in the last novel."

"How so?"

"Well, in the first book he's an obvious player." She leaned back and crossed her legs.

CJ's gaze fell to her pointy-toed black pumps.

"Charming guy. Lands a sexy beauty in his bed whenever he desires. Every man's fantasy."

He met her gaze. "Do you always editorialize?"

"Only when necessary."

CJ stroked his chin. "Go on."

"Your character didn't want commitment in book one. Still, I got a sense he connected with his conquests. True?"

"True."

"I also noticed, by the last book, the way he selected and responded to women had completely changed. He picked women with obvious flaws, then dwelled on the things he hated about them. He used those shortcomings to push them away."

"Any idea why?" CJ dropped his foot to the floor and leaned toward her, placing both forearms on his thighs.

"He mentions the loss of someone. A love interest. My take is that he no longer believed he deserved the type of woman he wanted." She studied CJ closely for a reaction, to determine if the story came from personal experience. He didn't flinch and kept any thoughts private. "At least that's one theory." Brenda shrugged.

"Do you think Ken wants love?" CJ's tone was soft, as if the words escaped by mistake.

"Doesn't everybody?"

He clamped his mouth tight for a moment. "Then you do believe it's what he's after?"

"Why don't you tell me?"

"Because" — CJ folded his hands — "I want to know how *you* see him."

"As a therapist, this would be more productive for me if I understood the character as *you* see him."

"Aren't I paying for your expertise?" CJ's voice carried the same edge as when they first met.

Firmly, yet in the most nonthreatening voice she could muster, Brenda said, "My expertise would be more useful if you clued me in on your thoughts."

CJ sighed. "This journey with you might be the next feat I can add to my list of accomplishments." He stood. "I'm going to get a bottle of water. Would you like one?"

"Sure. Thanks."

He walked off.

She'd jabbed him a little, but wasn't sure why, since this type of egging on was usually reserved for those closer to her. She rose from the sofa and followed him to the kitchen. Leaning against the doorjamb, she crossed her arms.

He reached into the refrigerator.

"CJ?"

He pulled out the bottles and glanced over. "I would have brought it to you."

"I know. Listen, I've never done anything like this before. My role in this project is a little unclear to me."

"We'll figure this out."

"What if we can't? I tend to be direct. Maybe you'd rather find someone more accommodating. I sure don't want to be added to your list of challenges."

He moved toward her and stopped, just a little too close. Brenda couldn't move, trapped by dark chestnut irises that silently commanded her attention. The room seemed to pulse around them. Brenda's breath bottlenecked at her throat.

"You won't." His answer carried quiet confidence. The smooth baritone timbre of his voice grew soft. "Something tells me you'll be on a list all your own. The way you are is fine. I'd like it if you'd stay."

Brenda's breath vanished. Who was this man? It certainly wasn't the same CJ she had met at the conference. "All right," she mumbled.

"Besides," CJ continued, sporting a grin capable of making a nun reconsider her vows, "I climbed Mount Everest. I'm pretty sure I can handle you."

He handed over a bottle of water. She wanted to twist off the cap and splash some on her face, just to be certain this new and improved version of CJ wasn't a dream.

* * *

While Brenda returned to her seat, CJ admired her curves, well-outlined in black slacks and a fitted sweater. Her closeness had left him undone, and he had barely been able to regain his footing. The same directness she displayed at the conference, which had made him crazy, drove him crazy in another way this afternoon.

"How about I tell you how Ken Blair came to life?" CJ said. A focus on work would help him recuperate.

"Perfect." Brenda leaned back.

For a solid twenty minutes, he rambled on about his series, pausing whenever she asked a question. While she scribbled notes, he observed her every move. Soft, wheat-colored hair brushed her shoulders. A gentle part of her perfect lips occurred right before she lowered her pen to the pad, like a thought was about to exit them but was written instead. Sometimes she twirled her hair while she reread notes, then tucked the strands behind her ear, displaying more of her creamy complexion.

"Have any of the novels discussed Ken's upbringing? Childhood is the root for so much of our adult behavior." Her hands moved when she spoke, conducting the thought, as though the sentence would have been unintelligible without their movement.

"Yes. I've written a total of five books in the series. In the second book we find out he lost both his parents at a young age. They were in a plane crash. An aunt raised him. The loss contributes to his emotional distance from women."

She bit her bottom lip while she wrote, then stopped both. "That's the reason he's so focused on sex rather than romance, I suppose?"

"Not at all. Ken's romantic. For men, sex is a way to express their feelings toward a woman. It's more obvious in the third book, when he falls in love." She wrote and he wished he knew what she'd put down. "Besides, my target demographic is men. Most men don't typically read romance novels and I don't write them."

"I know what sex means to men." Her gaze shifted from the

paper to him. "My practice includes sex counseling. I just wanted to see how you'd respond." Brenda flashed the welcoming smile he'd seen in her Web site photo, making it difficult to be annoyed at her slight manipulation. "You know how we little larrikins can misbehave." Her eyebrows arched in a good-natured manner.

He chuckled. "I'd forgotten about that."

"Well I sure didn't. If I remember correctly, the definition is a nonconformist or mischievous person. However, in Australia, where your grandmother came from, it's slang for a hoodlum. Care to tell me which one you meant when you called me that at the conference?"

"I'd rather let you decide."

"Chicken." She shook her head. "Trust me. Your use wasn't used as a term of endearment."

"No, I suppose it wasn't." He was shocked that she had bothered to research the answer. "I wouldn't call you one today."

"We're not finished yet." Her warm tone held humor.

At least his name-calling at the bar hadn't caused offense. His relief surprised him. In fact, today was turning out to be full of surprises.

"Let's discuss the third book," she said, "where I believe the character changes the most."

"I thought you only scanned that one?"

A guilty smile wavered on her lips. "Caught me. I rented the movie."

He stifled a grin. "In book three, Ken meets a woman. The second they meet, he knows she's special. A strong connection. Unlike any he's ever experienced."

"Does she feel the same way?"

He nodded. "She does. Their passion surpasses physical intimacy."

Brenda's blue eyes penetrated his, the natural light from outside making them glisten like the sun's reflection against clear water.

A wave of sentiment stirred inside him. He leaned back and tried to ignore the feeling. "Anyway, they fall in love. Ken's a changed man. Then someone trying to kill Ken hits her by mistake. She dies."

"So, it's guilt?" Her usual smooth, confident voice quieted.

"Yes. He was the target. The way Ken is able to get through the day is to shut off the valve to his heart." CJ stood and walked to the sliding doors to stare outside, mostly to avoid Brenda's gaze. "At first, he's driven by the need to avenge her death. Unable to satisfy it, he turns to reckless behavior, no longer caring about his life. Ken's soul is lost."

He sensed her watching him. The silence hovered for a long minute, then he turned around, thinking she was taking notes or had left the room. She stared back, the strain of her thoughts obvious, her lips parted to speak but no sound came out.

"Anyway," CJ continued in a matter-of-fact tone, "he needs to regain the lost piece of himself. It's time." He shoved his hands in his jeans pockets but couldn't hide his growing discomfort over the topic. "But I don't know how to make it happen. That's why I need your help."

"Does Ken's dilemma bother you?"

"Of course. I wrote it years ago. This isn't new to me."

"I suppose not." She bit her lower lip again. Brenda's pen tapped against her pad. The sound filled the still room, like the beat of a warning drum, hinting that a surprise might come at any moment.

The beat stopped. "What struggles have you had to tackle?" Brenda asked.

"We're talking about the book." CJ walked closer to her and stopped.

"I know. As the author, shouldn't understanding ways you've coped with problems help you develop this part of the character?"

"I didn't hire you to analyze me."

"No, you didn't. However, in your Everest speech, you mentioned how the climb made you think of your struggles." Her pen wobbled between two fingers. "Something was missing from your words."

He admired her observation about his speech. That line had carried great meaning for him. "A good writer conveys his message using as few words as possible."

"An excellent writer communicates the full message."

During their difficult conversations when they first met, Brenda had only seemed equipped with a transmission which pushed her in one direction: forward. This conversation confirmed his notion. "Are you always so...so contrary?"

"I can be. Do you always avoid answering revealing questions?"

The phone rang. CJ started to walk over to answer but stopped next to her.

She lifted her chin and gazed at him.

"Are you going to help me solve this character's problem?"

Her voice softened. "Of course I will."

"Thank you." He continued toward the ringing phone.

"Guess you were saved by the bell, huh?"

He peered over his shoulder and, once again, was left powerless by the way she looked at him. "Me? Maybe you're the one saved."

However, in the short hour with this woman, CJ had no doubt it was him.

Chapter Seven

Georgie's head moved back and forth to Brenda's movements as if she were watching a match at Wimbledon. Brenda scratched the dog's head. "It can't be this exciting watching me put on sweatpants." Georgie's short tail wagged.

Finished, Brenda bounced down the stairs to the kitchen with the salt-and-pepper dog half a step behind. It reminded her of the way baby ducks imprinted with their mothers.

The week had been an exhausting one. In addition to her normal patient schedule, she'd spent her midweek day off at CJ's, then shifted her Thursday schedule to accommodate a trip into CNN's Manhattan studio to participate in a panel discussion on the aging baby-boomer population.

After sorting through the mail, she popped a frozen entrée into the microwave and poured herself a glass of chilled chardonnay, then took a long sip. She remembered when Friday nights were fun. Pizza, a movie, anticipation of the weekend plans. A glance at the microwave showed fifty-nine seconds until she had to stir and turn. Life had taken a pitiful turn, starting with this lackluster meal.

Countless times over the years she'd grumbled while fixing a dinner after a long day at the office, especially at the end of a long workweek like this one. Tonight she missed the commotion. Or did she simply miss the companionship? Two days ago, when she returned home after a few hours at CJ's, it struck her how quiet her life had become.

With a tray, she carried dinner to her desk in the dark family room and flipped the wall switch. A Tiffany floor lamp cast a warm glow on the beige walls. This was her favorite room. French doors led to a patio and flat backyard. In daylight, Brenda enjoyed the yard's mature trees and untamed garden plots of wild flowers, planted by the previous owners. In order to make the inside close to the nature outdoors, Brenda had decorated with a floral, well-cushioned sofa and large overstuffed leather chairs. A heavy pine desk faced the gardens. In years past, one corner had held a toy box, the contents often scattered all over the floor. The box long gone, a wrought-iron étagère loaded to the gills with photos of family memories stood in its place.

She sat at the desk, put the food aside, and logged into her e-mail account. Twenty messages appeared, at least ten of them screaming sales pitches from her favorite stores and one offering to sell her Viagra. An e-mail from "Luc0220" stopped her cold.

Last Saturday night, almost a week ago, was the party at the Duponts'. Dressed to go, she'd called their house a half hour before the start. After an apology for the last-minute call, she feigned a stomach bug. Patricia politely bought the story, even though Brenda was certain she suspected a lie. The truth was that seeing Luc with Aimee would be too much for her right now.

The last e-mail she'd received from Luc Pelletier had arrived a week after Jack's funeral. She hadn't responded, having already asked him to respect her space. Since the ignored correspondence, he'd never tried again.

Jack and Luc had worked together for four years. With Jack

as chief financial officer of North American and European operations, Luc's transfer from their France office as senior vice president of technology put them in constant contact.

They'd hit it off right away, often traveling together for work. The friendship deepened on the basketball court. Jack had played in both high school and college, his tall, lean physique making him a natural. Luc joined Jack's local men's league, a bunch of middle-aged guys looking for an excuse to hang out. Over time, the friendship grew to encompass spouses.

Brenda groaned the first time Jack had suggested the four of them go out. He'd walked in the door from work, excited about the double-date prospect.

"He's so...French." Brenda crinkled her nose.

"What does that mean?"

"They can be arrogant." She threw a handful of cherry tomatoes into a large salad for dinner. "Besides, don't they hate Americans?"

"You're being ridiculous. You like Bertrand and he's from France."

"Mmmm. Well, he's lived here for twenty years. Practically American."

Jack loosened his tie, gave her a peck on the cheek, then stole a cherry tomato from the wooden bowl. "Do you think I'd like an arrogant person?"

"I guess not."

Jack pulled a face. "We'll go out once. If you have a bad time, we won't go out again."

On Saturday, they met Luc and his wife, Aimee, at a local restaurant.

Aimee epitomized every French woman Brenda had ever seen in a film; she was attractive and she carried sexy the way most women carried a handbag. Her aloof tone made for limited conversation, yet her words were never wasted. What she didn't say meant as much as what she did. She wasn't quite Brenda's drink of choice, but Brenda did her best around her.

At first glance, she had pegged Luc as a typical Frenchman—average height, not an ounce of noticeable fat on his body, and side-parted, sable-colored hair worn a little long on top in harried disarray. However, once he started to speak, he more than made up for his wife's shortcomings. In addition to his heart-shaped face and sexy accent, his world travels offered a never-ending stream of delightful tales. Upbeat and positive, his eyes held a shine which glowed bright from behind his tortoise-rimmed glasses. Topped off with a dollop of charm and a quick sense of humor, Brenda found it impossible to not like the guy.

Georgie scratched and the clang of the metal tags on her collar sounded like an alarm, a warning to Brenda to suspend any further fond memories of Luc. She took a sip of her wine and enjoyed the feeling of warmth as it slipped down her center, providing the boost needed to open Luc's e-mail.

Hello Brenda —

You asked me not to contact you anymore, but something has come up and we must speak. It is related to a problem Jack had before he died. I should not put this in writing and do not want you to find out someplace else. Can we meet?
I hoped you'd be at the Duponts' party. Bertrand was truly surprised. Hope you are feeling better. You are still in my thoughts.

Luc

Everything she'd done wrong remained hidden behind his last sentence, pointing the ugly finger of guilt in her direction. She turned away from the monitor and stared out the window into the black night.

The last conversation she had with Luc occurred the night of Jack's funeral. He wasn't too happy with the way their talk ended. But an answer to Jack's problems might help heal her family. Help heal her too. She typed a reply then reread her response.

I think of you, too. Let me know where and when you want to meet.

Brenda hit Send.

* * *

Brenda hung up the phone after talking to her son, feeling fragile and exhausted. The day Jack died, a crack had formed in the bond Brenda once shared with Devin. The fault in their relationship widened each time he begged for an answer about how his father could have committed suicide under her watch. Every conversation with him revived her guilt about Jack's death, like fertilizer on a dying plant. This morning's regular Saturday phone call was no exception.

Mother Nature had scooped her ladle into the same gene pool and handed her two children with such different traits. Shannon, logical and pragmatic with the tall, slender physique and dark hair of her dad. Devin, sensitive and idealistic, with his mother's average height and fairer features.

The phone rang again. Brenda wasn't surprised to spot Shannon's name on the caller ID. Both kids understood the year had been lonely for their mother. Their weekly calls had become a ritual since Jack's death. She picked up the cordless phone, wandered into the family room, and plopped on the sofa.

"Hi, Mom. How are you doing?"

"Good. I just spoke to your brother." Brenda relayed the details of his latest adventure while enrolled in an MBA program in Rome—a trip to Ostia Antica, the ruins of an old

Roman seaport. Shannon, a middle-school teacher, shared a few escapades from her classroom with the preteen set.

At a pause, Brenda said, "Since I've told Devin this, I want to let you know too. I've been out on an official date. Actually a few. All with the same guy."

"Hallelujah! About time. With one of Aunt Reggie's fix-ups?"

"God, no. They've all been disasters. With a man I met at the writer's conference. He's a philosophy professor."

"Cool. How'd Devin take the news?" Shannon's sarcastic tone indicated she already knew the answer.

"As only Devin would. It was hard for him to hear."

"Sometimes I think he blames you for what happened."

"He might. Give him time."

They spoke for another ten minutes, then hung up. The kids' phone calls were meant to alleviate her loneliness, yet afterward the emptiness in her life seemed more obvious than before. She'd never say anything to ruin their good intentions.

Georgie followed Brenda upstairs. The silence in the large colonial was oppressive, each footstep on the hardwood staircase magnified by the quiet. Brenda went to her room and made the king-size bed. Jack's side remained neat. Combined with the kids' sympathy calls, the vacated bed space where Jack had slept only deepened her sense of loneliness.

She threw the last colorful throw pillow against the wrought-iron headboard. How many times had she and Jack stood on each side of this bed, dismantled the pillows before climbing in, and then reassembled them in a joint effort to remake it the next morning? She stared at the space where he used to stand, tying a knot in his tie, buttoning his sleeves, telling her he'd be home late that night.

Jack still lived in these walls. He'd painted them their creamy ivory color. He'd helped her select the purple-toned, diamond-patterned quilt on a vacation in Pennsylvania. The week they moved in, he was at her side to rip up horrible wall-to-wall carpeting and scrub clean the hardwood floor beneath. An involuntary shiver coursed through Brenda.

Jack died in this house, too.

Some days the thought jumped out of nowhere and yelled "boo." Well-intentioned friends suggested she move, an idea holding some merit. Only after Devin returned from overseas, though. Selling his childhood home before he could see it again seemed wrong. Besides, why give him another reason to criticize, another reason for blame?

Finished with the bed, she wiped down the bathroom vanity. Like the bed, the double-sink layout was easier to clean minus one adult.

Her son's well-being nibbled at her subconscious. Devin hadn't handled Jack's problems well, but he'd brought to her attention a telltale sign that Jack's drinking was getting worse. Regret swelled as she wished for a do-over on the actions she took the week of that conversation.

Devin, in his senior year at the University of Connecticut, had called her early one morning. "Mom, Dad sent me an e-mail late last night. It was weird. Was he drinking again?"

Jack *had* been drinking the previous night. After several weeks incident-free, he'd come home from work distracted. Without even a hello, he had disappeared into his office. Brenda had immediately knocked on the door and, when he didn't say "come in," she barged in anyway. An open bottle sat on his desk. He glared at her.

"What's wrong?" Her stomach had contorted into a jumble, just like it had after countless encounters with her mother's drunken episodes.

"Get the hell out." Jack's voice was dark, almost threatening. He'd never spoken to her in such a manner. She retreated.

Brenda didn't share those details with her son. "Yes, Devin. He was drinking last night," was all she said. "What did his e-mail say?"

"He babbled on about a bunch of stuff he loved doing with me when I was little, and how life was hard for adults at times. He's scaring me."

It scared Brenda too. "Could you forward the e-mail to me?"

"Sure. What are you going to do?"

"I plan on talking to him again today."

"Mom, he needs a doctor. Maybe he's depressed and needs medication."

"Honey, I've begged him to go to a doctor. Even recommended a few." Brenda held back her tears. "I'm doing everything I can."

"I called Father Reynolds," Devin blurted out.

"Oh?"

"Yes. I told him Dad was having problems."

"Devin, our lives are personal." She bit her tongue. Devin had always embraced religion, much like his father in his happier days. "I'm sorry. I'm not sure if Dad would want that."

"Well, Father Reynolds said you two should talk to him."

Brenda adored the Episcopal pastor. Sunday mornings he stood at the pulpit and always delivered a thoughtful, positive message. Family church attendance had always been at Jack's insistence, but through Father Reynolds Brenda had begun to relate to God in a way she'd never thought possible and allowed faith to become part of her life. But Jack's interest waned with his increased issues, and so did the rest of the family's. As Jack's problems worsened, Brenda didn't feel close to anybody, including God. As she lost control of everything around her, faith meant giving up even more control to something intangible. Instead she found solace in the logic she had always embraced in psychology.

"I don't know, Devin. I'll mention the idea to Dad."

"Should I come home this weekend? Maybe I can get through to him."

"No. You have midterms next week. After I talk to him, I'll call you, but I'm certain he won't want you leaving campus for this."

Her confrontation with Jack later in the day wasn't pretty. His animosity, directed at her, was still at its peak. He remained close-lipped and Brenda worried. Only one thing she'd done would provoke such fury. Yet she didn't think he'd found out and didn't dare ask.

His very last words to her a week later, spoken offhandedly as she tried to leave for work, remained a mystery: "Sometimes people are forced to make choices. Do things they never thought they'd do."

Halfway out the door, his cryptic comment stopped her. Already late, she asked if they could discuss his problem later.

Later never happened. During the day, he took his life.

Jack's funeral had been her last visit to their church. She'd sat in the wooden pew, head bowed in prayer, paying her respects to the good man she'd married. Nobody there would have guessed, as she paid homage to her deceased husband, that she believed God looked down at her exposed soul and judged what she'd done.

She'd been a far from perfect wife.

* * *

The bedroom in order, Brenda shed her sweatpants and pulled on new Levi low-cut, prewashed jeans. She half considered leaving on the comfortable Mickey Mouse sweatshirt she'd put on after her morning shower. The chances were slim she'd run into anybody she knew on the train ride into Manhattan. But then she remembered that she had hadn't expected to meet anyone on the morning of her ill-fated coffee run at the Hyatt either, so she tugged off the Disney garb and opted for a long-sleeved silk pullover and blazer to dress up the denim bottoms. Heading for the doorway, she stopped at her dresser to grab some earrings from an old double-drawer mahogany box that had belonged to her mother. She opened the lid and trailed a hand over the necklaces dangling from hooks. When she reached a Celtic cross Jack and the kids had given her for Mother's Day many years ago, she lifted it, the chain still attached. Her finger smoothed the brushed silver, and she remembered how little faith she'd had before meeting Jack. He'd opened the door for her.

The Celtic cross meant a great deal to Brenda. Her parents had only attended church on major holidays. The first time she and Jack ever discussed religion, he'd shared how the church sanctuary had been his place of refuge as a child. His father was a nonexistent person in his life, and his small, upstate New York community often stood in obvious judgment of his unwed mother. The church was a place where he could go without fear of judgment, where he felt equal to others.

Why then did he turn to the bottle instead of God at the end of his life? What could have been so bad? Brenda would never know. She carried a long list of doubts about how she had handled her life in recent years. The two top things on the list kept her from ever reentering the big red doors at St. Mark's church: her unrelenting guilt about Jack and shame at her actions with Luc.

She let the cross drop from her fingers, grabbed a pair of dangling pearl earrings, and pushed the lid shut.

Chapter Eight

"That grouch flirted with you?" Reggie's jaw dropped. On the way to their monthly Saturday tennis game, Brenda was about to mention Luc's e-mail from the night before when Reggie interrupted to probe for details on her meeting at CJ's house.

"I said he *may* have been." Brenda adjusted the strap of her tennis bag. "He was really nice."

"Nice? That's not flirting, honey. I realize it's been a while."

"He wasn't grouchy this time. I'm telling you, this was flirting." They'd just left Reggie's apartment and were walking along the shaded city street toward the Upper East Side Tennis Club. "Isn't playful repartee and comments with a suggestive undercurrent considered flirting? It was in the movies with Rock Hudson and Doris Day."

"You watch too many old movies."

Over the past few days, Brenda had caught herself rehashing the details of her time with CJ so often the syndication fees would've left her broke. Their contact at his house had been laced with sexual tension, at least in her mind. She squinted into the sun as they rounded a corner of the crowded main avenue and slipped on her sunglasses.

"Don't think I'm crazy, but I flirted back." The encounter

had roused deep and unexpected emotion in Brenda. Deeper than she felt for Nate. After Reggie's "grouch" reference though, she'd use care in what details she shared.

Reggie looked over, not even attempting to remain judgment free. "What about Professor Nate?"

"We're not going steady. We've gone on two dates. Besides, he seems busy, and it's difficult to find days to go out. Both times we did, we met halfway between our homes." Brenda shrugged. "He probably dates other women as well."

"Maybe. But really, Brenda." Reggie wrinkled her nose. "CJ? I mean, I admire the guy as a professional, but his personal life makes me wonder about him."

"He has good qualities."

"Besides the fact that Dale, a man I respect, seems very close to him, can you name any?"

"First, at the risk of sounding shallow, he isn't too tough to look at."

"I won't disagree. Still, he acted rude to you at the conference."

"Everyone can have a bad day. He's quite smart and an excellent writer."

"Keep going." Reggie's tone remained skeptical.

"There's an unexpected depth. He shows passion about certain things. Plus, I enjoyed our conversation. He challenged me. In a good way."

They stopped with the crowd, at the corner of Fifth Avenue and 47th Street. While they waited for the light to change, Reggie studied Brenda. "Are you sure you went to the right house?"

"Yes. I'm sure he didn't slip anything in my water either."

"Doesn't his taste in the young, hot, and vacant-upstairs department bother you?" Reggie raised her voice over a beeping car horn nearby.

"A little." It bothered her more than she let on.

"Be careful. He might be a Casanova."

"Hey, my charm might have swayed him, too. You know, I liked being noticed by a man."

"Sounds like Nate notices you."

"Jeesh, what are you…my mother?"

"Try the voice of reason." The light changed and they crossed. "How'd the work go?"

"Great. I always thought his books were for guys, all government plots and guns. I was surprised by the depth of the main character. I'm enjoying the process of picking him apart, looking for a way into his head."

"Whose? CJ's or the fictional character's?"

"You're a riot. Leno should book you."

"Sorry." She rubbed Brenda's back. "I worry about you."

"Thanks, but why are you acting like I analyze everyone?"

Reggie cocked a skeptical brow.

"OK. Guess it explains my career choice."

"Exactly." Reggie nodded her satisfaction. "It wouldn't be the first time you've gravitated toward a complicated man. God knows you've always liked a challenge. CJ fits the bill."

On Brenda's way home from CJ's house, she'd stopped and purchased the third novel of the five books in the Ken Blair series. The movie had told her the basics, but it had clearly been a turning point for the character, and Brenda hoped the written material would offer a hint into CJ's psyche. The book's dedication had jumped out at her: *In memory of Carla. My love and my light. I will always miss you.*

"I researched him on the Internet," Brenda said as they arrived at the tennis club.

"Why am I not shocked?" Reggie pulled open the glass door. "Let's hear the lowdown."

"CJ stands for Charles James. He's fifty-two and was born and raised in Maryland. Attended military academy and served in the army." She paused as Reggie flashed her membership card at the front desk clerk, then signed in.

"After he got out, he worked in Washington as a CIA weapons analyst. He married, moved north, and pursued his love of writing. His wife's name was Carla."

"Divorced?"

"No, she died. It didn't say how. I stopped nosing around. At some point, Internet research crosses a line to creepy."

"Want me to ask Dale?"

"No way. That's too junior high, and if CJ ever found out..." Brenda rolled her eyes.

They reached the busy locker room. Reggie's skepticism, always offered with a strong dose of opinion, had a way of making Brenda second-guess herself. It always had.

Now she had doubts about mentioning Luc's e-mail. Reggie knew how close Brenda and Luc had become before Jack's death. The idea of mentioning his recent contact might raise unwanted questions. No. She wouldn't share their reconnection with anybody right now. Like their brief affair, she would keep this quiet.

* * *

"Thanks for joining me in a match. This contract was a good excuse to get together." Tom Mendelson, CJ's entertainment attorney since his first novel, opened his leather attaché and slipped in the agreement for the foreign film investors.

There was a point in the past ten years when CJ would have turned down an invitation to the tennis club. Tennis reminded him of Carla. During their courtship, she had pushed the blue-blooded sport on him as an activity they could do together. He had always preferred more manly athletic endeavors. Still, he had played to make her happy and grew to enjoy the game.

"I should be thanking you. Not every lawyer will meet on a

Saturday." While Tom signed the credit card slip for their lunch tab, CJ noted how his lawyer's black hair stayed remarkably free of any graying, even though they were close in age. Probably hair dye. "We haven't been on the courts in a while. Back in the day, seems we got out a few times a year."

"From the way you were returning those balls, I'd never have known." Tom tapped his heavily padded midsection, well hidden underneath his roomy polo shirt. "I'm trying to get out here more. Work on the winter weight gain. You still running?"

"Three days a week." CJ removed his glasses and tucked them away. "Not like when I trained for my climb."

They picked up their gym bags and left the Sports Club Café. At the lobby's reception desk, CJ waited by the huge windows overlooking the tennis courts while Tom booked a court for later in the week.

He recognized a woman with a bright blond ponytail and dark-rimmed glasses serving the ball on the second court. It was the agent he'd met at the Hyatt. The one who worked with Dale. Reggie. She slammed the returned ball back over the net.

Then CJ saw who Reggie's partner was, and his breath caught. Brenda dived to the left and smashed the ball, returning to center court and bouncing on her toes.

CJ's heart fluttered. His cheeks burned. He glanced both ways, as if someone else might have heard the noise of his emotions. What was wrong with him? Brenda's skin glistened with perspiration, her face nearly as bright as her pink tennis dress.

Since their meeting on Wednesday, he'd been having visions of her. They came upon him without warning—while editing of his manuscript, while corresponding about his movie deal, and even during dinner with Autumn the night before she had to leave on an assignment. Since Wednesday he had been playing an uncontrollable game of hide-and-seek with Brenda inside his head; however, he wasn't sure if he played the hider or seeker.

Tom appeared at his side. "You headed to Grand Central?"

"Uh-huh, but my train doesn't leave for another fifty minutes. Some friends are down there. I think I'll watch their match."

"OK. I'll be in touch." The two men shook hands and Tom left.

CJ placed his bag next to a cushioned chair overlooking the indoor arena and sat. Brenda's forehand was strong. She moved toward every shot with gusto, a competitive approach. It didn't surprise him. The spirited verbal game during their work session had shown the same edge. The pair had easily engaged with one another, each holding their trump card until just the right moment in conversation to catch the other off guard. He'd enjoyed himself, more than he had with any woman in a long time.

In fact, since the first day they met, he had been uncomfortably aware of the impact she had made on him. The dig about Autumn's age had reminded him of how his wife used to confront him—with the courage of a matador in the bull ring. Early on, while dating Carla, she'd called him stubborn, suggesting bluntness would be the one way to get him to listen. Even when he slipped on his gruff exterior, she never backed down.

Brenda smashed her opponent's lob. The ball bumped the top of the net and returned to her side of the court. She threw her hands in the air, then looked up to the heavens for an answer.

He liked her directness and found her easy to talk to and quite smart. She was also sexy, in an unassuming way. Her presence magnified the poor choices he'd made in women since his wife died. He had chosen each of them for one reason—they didn't remind him of Carla.

He checked the time. He could still catch the express train. Just as he lifted his bag, Brenda and Reggie headed off the court and started to pack up their rackets. What were the chances of running into her again? He hurried down the stairs to the lower level.

* * *

The second Brenda spotted CJ, she felt goose bumps rise across her skin. She instantly felt the same electric energy that she had felt in CJ's kitchen, when he had stood close to her and asked her to stay. Since then, she had often replayed that moment in her head — the way he'd moved so close she'd felt him without touching, the way he had asked her to stay, his soft request as intimate as a caress.

Standing at Reggie's side, she attempted to pull herself together as CJ approached. She kept silent while Reggie carried the conversation, discussing an agency matter. But then CJ turned to Brenda.

"It's nice to see you." His gentle smile, and the dark sparkle in his eyes, charmed her. "I've wanted to call you."

"Oh?" Her cheeks flushed.

"Yes." His brows rose, then a grin escaped. "To follow up from our meeting."

"Oh yes, of course. Our meeting." Brenda nodded, feeling like an idiot. "Yes, I've been meaning to call you too. Why don't you join us for lunch and we can talk?"

Reggie's eyes widened but Brenda didn't care. The unplanned invite seemed like the only face-saving way out of her embarrassment. Besides, the idea of some time with him held great appeal.

CJ hesitated. A wave of disappointment made her suddenly regret the offer. Reggie was probably right. This guy was a showman, used to turning on the charm to lure female fans.

Why was her skill at reading people good in the office but gone around this guy?

He finally said, "Sure, I'd love to join you. I just ate lunch with my lawyer, but could use another cup of coffee."

"Great." She feigned a comfortable smile. "We'll change and meet you in the club's café."

Brenda hurried off to the locker room with Reggie at her heels. The second they were safely behind closed doors, she turned around.

Reggie stared back, not even bothering to hide her amusement. "Girlfriend, you're in deep. Let's see if he can sway my opinion of him at lunch."

"I'm not in deep, but I am in. You'll see. He's not so bad." As she hurried off to the shower a realization settled in. Her inability to read CJ had more to do with a failure to understand her own emotions when he was around.

* * *

An hour later, Reggie took the last bite of her food and pushed back her plate. "I don't mean to eat and run, but Ted wants to go to an afternoon movie." She took her bag and searched for her wallet.

"I've got it." CJ held up a hand. "I enjoyed the company. Brenda, I'm heading over to Grand Central too. If you're not in a hurry, we can have another cup of coffee and then walk over together." His eyes softened, full of hope.

Brenda wanted to jump at the chance, but she hesitated. It would be stupid to allow herself to get any closer to this man, who had already demonstrated himself to be volatile and rude. But then, was that assessment fair? Everyone had bad days, and she had also seen his gentler side by now. Besides, experience had shown Brenda that behind every rough exterior lay an issue that could be fixed. Could be fixed, that is, if the owner wanted it fixed.

"Sounds leisurely. I'm in," Brenda said, at last.

Reggie flung her purse and racquet case over her shoulder. "CJ, thanks for lunch. Nice seeing you again." She leaned over to hug Brenda and whispered, "Call me later."

The café noise had died down since their arrival with only two small groups at tables and a few stragglers at the juice bar.

CJ motioned to the waiter and pointed to his empty coffee cup. "Have you known Reggie long?"

"BFFs since third grade." Brenda pushed the sleeves of her purple silk top to her elbows, thankful she hadn't kept on her early morning Disney-designed attire.

"Bee-eff what?" His brows huddled in confusion.

"Best friends forever."

"Oh." He shook his head. "My ability to keep up with this new slang ended with L-O-L."

"I'm not as hip as I seem. A thirteen-year-old neighbor comes over to play with my dog. Besides knowing the latest pop star, I've practically learned another language."

"You seemed pretty hip on *CNN*."

"You saw me?" She groaned. "Must've been a slow TV night."

"I wondered if you'd razz anybody on the *CNN* panel." His grin teased, revealing a playful side she'd never have guessed existed when they first met.

"What? Who else do I razz?"

"Why don't you tell me?" His eyes held a good-natured gleam.

"Hmmm. Well, my razzing days are over."

"Over?" CJ took on a lighthearted tone. "I guess they weren't through when you brought me to my knees with your simple observation about my companion at the conference."

"Brought you to your knees?" Brenda waved a dismissive

hand. "I wish. You did look pretty ticked off, though."

He laughed. "Yes, well sometimes that's not too hard for anybody to do."

Jack had often ignored his own flaws. CJ's admission about his anger showed an introspective side to his personality. Brenda rested her forearms on the table and her hands flopped together in a small pile. "Actually, the show went better than I expected."

"You were worried?"

She shrugged. "My first book did well, but this type of national coverage is intimidating."

The waiter arrived and offered Brenda more coffee, which she refused, but CJ accepted a refill.

"They'll get easier," CJ said.

"Don't the personal questions bother you?"

"No." He reached for a sugar packet. "I only answer what I want."

"Well, my deer-in-the-headlights look is tough to recover from."

"It didn't show during your interview."

"Thanks. I'd prepared some. Guess when you write about delicate topics, readers wonder how it relates to you."

"That's what happens when you're a writer." He dumped sugar into his cup. "People get my reality intermingled with my characters'. Actors deal with that all the time too."

"I suppose, but I'm not my case studies. The book is clinical to me. As an expert on relationships, I'm speaking to generalities, not personal experience."

"You said on the program you were married." He lifted a spoon. "I'd say you qualify as having relationship experience."

"Guess you did pay attention."

Brenda sipped her water and studied him while he stirred his coffee. The gray-and-black speckled trim of his beard and mustache formed a straight, tidy square from his upper lip to his chin, leaving his cheeks smooth. A shadow of his former hair was visible on his scalp, a bit darker than last time she'd seen him. She resisted an urge to reach out and graze her fingertips across the contrasting textures. His strong cheekbones added a rugged edge to his profile. Dressed in a gold, washed oxford shirt tucked neatly into his jeans, all he needed was a Labrador at his side and a shotgun to pose for the Orvis catalog cover. Brenda had to admit, he was extremely appealing. Different from most of the men she'd been with in her lifetime.

"Being single again takes getting used to. You'll do fine." CJ's gaze locked onto hers with seriousness, but his tone remained casual. "Your gentleman friend at the conference seemed quite interested in you."

"Oh? I didn't realize I was under observation."

"Most people don't." CJ sipped his coffee. "Watching helps my writing."

"There were a lot of people in the ballroom besides me."

"Who's to say I didn't scrutinize others too?"

"How come you're always vague?"

"I'm building suspense." He said it seriously, with a straight face, but there was a mischievous twinkle in his eye. "Isn't some mystery fun?"

"Sure, when I can skip to the last page for the answer."

"Hmmm." CJ rested his elbows on the table and leaned forward. "You're one of *those* people."

"Patience is an overhyped virtue."

"You may find conversations with me a disappointment."

"Why?"

"I don't give anything away." His expression stayed neutral.

"Tell me something I don't know." She raised a brow and the corner of his lip curled. "I doubt your conversations will disappoint me, though." She leaned in, lowering her voice as if telling a secret. "I seldom leave a mystery unsolved."

Neither moved. The undertow of his charismatic gaze gripped her, doused her ability to think straight.

His voice turned quiet. "Are you involved with him?"

"The man from the conference?" The question had surprised her. CJ nodded. "We've gone out a few times. Why?"

CJ leaned back and stroked his chin. "You leave me curious, I guess. A sentiment I try to avoid."

"Why would you avoid a wonderful trait like curiosity?"

"One of my favorite quotes is from Dorothy Parker. She wrote, 'Four be the things I am wiser to know: idleness, sorrow, a friend, and a foe. Four be the things I'd been better without: love, curiosity, freckles, and doubt.' I'm inclined to agree with Miss Parker on all accounts."

"A bit of a cynic, aren't you? Experiencing love and curiosity make life exciting."

The muscle of his jaw flexed. "You think so? Even when things don't go as planned?" CJ dropped his gaze to the tabletop, but not before Brenda caught a shadow of pain crossing his face.

She picked up her napkin and twisted the end with her thumb and index finger, curious what could have caused his reaction. Rather than probe, she chose a clinical answer: "Especially when they don't go as planned. That's how we learn."

Brenda's adult life sure hadn't gone as she had expected. Whenever Jack got drunk, Brenda's childhood memories of her mother's alcoholism floated nearby like apparitions— transparent, surreal, and powerfully haunting. The past year she'd realized something: alcoholism had railroaded her life.

CJ slowly met her eyes, and suddenly all the pain was gone and they were back to the lightheartedness of earlier. "Then should I pursue my curiosities about you?"

"Please. Go for it." Brenda dropped the spiraled napkin and

it fell open partway. She'd tell CJ anything. Almost anything.

CJ drummed his fingers on the table but watched her while he thought. "Favorite book?"

"Just one? That's hard to answer. Hey, wait a second — is this a set-up like the lie detector operators do before throwing out a zinger?"

"I don't have any plans but make no promises." His serious expression contradicted his playful tone. "I told you curiosity has its drawbacks."

She ignored his comment. "I read all types of current fiction. As far as the classics, well I guess I've always been an Austen and Brontë sisters kind of gal."

"Care to elaborate?"

"No." She attempted a tight smile, playful yet with the uncertainty of Mona Lisa's facade. "I figure you're entitled to some mystery."

He tapped his lip with an index finger, although it didn't hide the start of a grin. "Where are you from originally?"

"Upstate New York, near Albany. My dad worked for GE."

He nodded and studied her for a few seconds. "So, you were married until a year ago?" CJ took a long sip from the cup, but his rich chestnut eyes never left hers.

"Yes. My husband died." She paused and let her breath catch up. "He committed suicide."

CJ's face stayed static. Not the pity she saw from others. In fact, he almost appeared immune to her pain. Yet years of experience drew her to the place where sorrow hid behind the expression.

"I'm sorry. It must have been difficult."

"Yes." She could have shared how Jack's complete desperation slipped under her radar. How in the last five or so years of their marriage there were days he acted like the same sweet guy she had married, but at other times a cloud of despair hovered over him. She didn't.

CJ examined her, a question mark on his face, like he'd read her mind. "Have you always wanted to be a psychologist?"

"No. I fell into it. Growing up, my parents' marriage wasn't good. By college, I needed counseling. It surprised me, made me feel less abnormal. I'd never realized the power we have over our minds. I switched my major to psychology. The relationship counseling came later. My parents' pitiful marriage was an ideal lead-in."

"Yours had no problems then?"

Taken aback by his directness, Brenda contemplated her answer. Of their twenty-five years together, Jack's drinking only consumed the last five. The sadness always manifested itself at the end of a workday...a long stretch of time when she had no clue who or what he was dealing with. She speculated that the cause might be work issues, another woman, or even a midlife crisis.

"Early on everything seemed fine. When I think back, there are things I ignored. The last few years were mixed. Jack had problems he never discussed."

Even in better days, Jack hadn't exactly offered up his innermost thoughts on a platter. His moments with the bottle signaled that he wanted solitude. When probed, he grumbled about a tough workday, then closed his office door, the click of the lock a symbol of his unwillingness to discuss the source of his pain.

"People change." She shrugged. "Not everything can be fixed."

The topic left her uneasy. For Brenda, every time the signs appeared — slurred words, a shift in his demeanor or the odor of liquor on his breath — the old wounds of her childhood reawakened. A crater of angst would swell in her gut while her inner soul waited in the same gloomy place as Jack's until he returned to normal. She pressed her lips tight, unwilling to say more.

CJ's jaw tensed and, even though he looked at her, it seemed his mind wandered deep in his own life. He replied quietly, "You're right. Not everything can be fixed."

Sadness filled the space between them. An emptiness in CJ's expression left Brenda wanting to know more.

Before she could ask anything, the waiter appeared. "Can I get you anything else?"

"Just the check." CJ's face relaxed as he abandoned the painful place he'd just visited. "If you're not in a hurry, would you like to detour and take care of an errand with me before we go to the train station?"

"If I say yes, can I question you?"

"Another negotiation?" He shook his head and she almost heard the silent *tsk*. "If I say no, is it a deal breaker like the last one?"

"Not this time."

"Either answer gets me your company, right?"

Brenda lifted her purse off the floor. She was filled with more curiosity than ever about CJ, about what he'd thought a moment ago. "I'll take that as a yes," she said.

Chapter Nine

Brenda had forgotten all about the midweek erotic dream, at least until CJ placed his hand on her lower back as they exited the tennis club. Then the details hit her with the same startling force as the bright sunlight.

It had happened two mornings earlier. The shrill beep of her alarm yelled *wake up*. She did, but couldn't move. The dream had left her numb, flushed, and recuperating from a nighttime encounter with CJ.

Brenda dreamed she stood alone in a windowless room, surrounded by stark white walls. Sadness, as stifling as a humid day, hung in the air. CJ appeared from nowhere. The walls closed in, pushed him close until they were separated by mere inches. His palm grazed her bare shoulder. It cupped her breast and took gentle liberties. He continued, possessively, to the curve of her waist, easing to her backside. He drew her tight to his pelvis then tipped his head, aiming right for her lips. Sexual eagerness replaced the prior sadness. Need made her press her thighs together for relief. His lips floated above hers, not quite touching. Anxious, Brenda stretched up to get closer. *Beep! Beep! Beep!* She woke…disoriented, disappointed, and desiring a man's touch—CJ's touch.

Now even the light touch of his hand against her back,

guiding her through the crowded street, left her squirming with need. He removed his hand as they blended with the crowd. It did little to ease the turmoil inside her.

She could think of nothing from her psychology background to explain this sudden attraction. Somehow, in just a short time, CJ had sunk his hook deep into her. A smart fish would fight it. Her post-Jack life had just begun to change. She was out again, doing normal things. She'd had a casual date. Even gotten some possible answers about why she lost Jack.

CJ was too much, too soon.

Feeling a need to regain a little control, Brenda took advantage of her turn to ask questions. She learned he loved strawberries and had no favorite color. When asked the top rock band of all time, he didn't hesitate to say Queen, claiming their 1980 Madison Square Garden concert had provided him with a near-religious experience. She'd also attended day two of the weekend-long concert and the band still remained one of her favorites. He beamed at the news, more pleased than she'd ever seen him. Perhaps because most women he currently spent time with were in diapers when Freddie Mercury had pranced around the stage.

They passed an electronics store with a camera pointed out to the street. She and CJ appeared on a television monitor in the storefront window. His tweed driving cap and leather jacket made her think of Jack.

"That cap and jacket look good on you." She looked at them paired together on the monitor and enjoyed seeing him at her side.

"Thanks."

Even though her Internet search provided the answer, she plowed forward with her next question. "So, I talked about my marriage. How about you?" From the TV monitor, he turned to look at her. "Ever been married?"

"I was." He touched her arm and tipped his head. "Let's go."

They walked together, slow and so close her hand brushed his. "Divorced?"

"No. My wife died, too. Ten years ago." Hurt spread across his profile, so obvious it stood out like a fresh coat of paint.

"I'm sorry." She'd hit the nail but had second thoughts about pounding any further. They stopped at the corner to wait for the light to change. "So, did you enjoy working with me the other day?"

His brows rose as if surprised by the question. "I did."

"Me too. What'd you like most?"

He leaned in and lowered his voice. "How you say things I never anticipate."

"Oh? Then you'll love this next question."

"At least I've been warned."

They shuffled through the crosswalk with a small group.

"Do you remember the day I went to sign our contract with Dale?"

He nodded.

"Did you know I overheard you talking about me while I waited in the reception area?"

He nodded again and didn't flinch.

"Why'd you treat me that way?"

"My treatment bothered you?"

"It's my turn to ask questions, remember? And yes, your conduct put me off."

"Yet you still agreed to work with me."

"Oh my God!" She stopped walking and threw her hands up while the crowd swarmed around her. "After a conversation with you, Sigmund Freud would change careers." She picked up her steps. "Is it asking too much to get a straight answer?"

"Of course not. Afterward, I regretted the way I treated

you."

"Uh-huh. And the reason?"

"There were two." He hesitated. "One I won't share."

She sighed. "Let's hear the other."

"I always wonder what people will do when they're pushed. So, I pushed you."

Brenda almost couldn't believe the answer, but gave him a checkmark for honesty. She stopped short of asking again about the item he wouldn't share, although the comment left her curious. "Care to elaborate?"

"If you backed out, you weren't right for the job. If you didn't, I'd have learned something else about you." Despite CJ's confident tone, his lips twitched. "I've been told pulling those games isn't my best quality."

"I'd agree." The intentional lilt to her voice was the kind of subtle reprimand she sprung on her kids. She almost asked who it was who had told him this, but figured it must have been his wife.

They waited for another light and she stepped over to a nearby shop window to peer at the shoe selection. In the glass reflection, CJ watched her.

Brenda turned to look at him, and their eyes met. "What?"

"Guess I'm lucky you didn't toss me aside."

The switch to an apologetic tone hit a tender spot in her heart, but she wasn't going to let him off that easily. "You'd never get so lucky. In truth, I couldn't stand to let you have the last word."

He chuckled as the light changed and they crossed the street. "Here's our stop."

They entered Barnes and Noble on Fifth Avenue and wandered into a section with new fiction. A short minute into browsing titles, Brenda picked up a book by one of her favorite authors and studied the back cover.

CJ came up behind her, close enough to her shoulder to hear the faint pattern of his breath.

"Anything good?" His smooth, soft tone and sudden nearness felt like a caress.

The damn dream returned. "Uh-huh."

"What's it about?"

"Sssh. I'm trying to read this, you know."

"Really?" His voice inched closer. "You know, it's not every day I get shushed."

Brenda dared to glance over her shoulder. A got-you-to-look smile frolicked on CJ's lips. She rolled her eyes but a grin slipped through. She tried to concentrate on the book jacket again, but his presence surrounded her like a low fog reaching a shoreline. Daring to twist her neck and look, his face had moved closer. The impact of it rendered her breathless, and she waited for his touch.

"Mr. Morrison?" A male voice came from near the aisle end cap. "I'm Liam." A skinny young man with a buzz cut stepped out from a small group of employees and offered his hand. "We met the last time you were here for a book signing."

"Hello, Liam." The two shook hands. "Sure, I remember."

"A few of the others wanted to meet you."

The staff gushed over CJ. He took their praise modestly and gave them all a conversation they'd never forget. He introduced Brenda and mentioned her books. They nodded with mild interest; after all, hers hadn't been made into movies.

When the staff returned to work, Brenda turned to CJ. "Hey, I want to look at the cookbooks. Should we split up and meet back at the registers?"

"OK." CJ glanced at his watch. "At three?"

"Sure. Hope I don't find you over by your books spying on potential buyers."

"You won't. It's too painful when a customer picks one up

and then puts it back."

"Sounds like the voice of experience."

"Only had to happen once." He gave a tilt of his brow then walked off.

A half hour later, they reconvened in the checkout line. He examined the books in her arms.

"Are you trying to win my favor?" CJ reached over and removed her copy of *The Hourglass*. "Didn't we establish you're not a fan and I don't expect everyone I meet to be one?"

"I'm still not a fan." She forced a straight face. "When you and Reggie were talking about the movie, I realized the storyline sounded different than the Ken Blair stories."

"It is."

He flipped the book around and they both examined an earlier picture of CJ with a full head of hair and the beginnings of a receding hairline, barely discernible against his dark waves. He was still eye-catching, but the hair gave him an altogether different, equally appealing, appearance.

He studied the picture with a troubled frown.

"What's wrong?"

"A few years ago I heard a comedian say it's not about hair loss, it's about face gain."

She laughed. "For you that's quite an optimistic statement."

"I didn't say I agreed. I simply found it interesting that someone found humor in this sad condition."

"Come on, CJ. We all age."

"If you met this guy" — he pointed to the picture — "or me at a party, which one would you want to give your phone number to? Be honest."

"That's easy."

"The guy with the hair, right?" His certain nod suggested he knew how all women thought.

"No."

His forehead jumped in surprise.

The cashier called out, "May I help you?"

Brenda, next in line, moved forward, then stopped. She turned to him. "I'd pick the man who left me the most intrigued... The way you leave me."

His eyes softened, suddenly possessing the power to make butter sizzle, to make metal bend, to make knees buckle.

Brenda strolled off with legs as fragile as Jell-O, thankful to reach the cashier and lean on the counter.

What was she doing? This man, in a single glance, had walloped her with the force of a quake registering ten on the Richter scale. Why would she let this happen? All she wanted after the drama with Jack was to get back on her feet and go on some noncommittal dates, maybe even try her hand at the sport of casual sex. Based on his behavior at the conference and his evasiveness during their first meeting, she guessed that CJ came standard with a set of built-in problems. That was the last thing she needed right now.

She handed her credit card to the cashier, then peeked back at CJ as he waited in line. He smiled and the effect hit her like an aftershock.

Had she just opened a can of worms? Who was she kidding? The can had opened the day they worked at his house. Now the quiet critters were beginning to crawl out. She'd better keep a close eye on them.

Chapter Ten

A clear blue sky stippled with cotton clouds provided a perfect day to head to the motor club. CJ shifted the red Porsche 911 GT3, easing onto Route 17. The management at the private race facility often reminded members that the isolated stretch of highway leading there might tempt them to speed, but to hold off until they reached the track.

He pressed the gas pedal. The Porsche burst forward. A gust of cool air swept through the open window, releasing an electrifying charge over him at the anticipation of this afternoon's outing on the four miles of race-grade asphalt. He slowed the vehicle, mindful not to speed.

This was exactly the distraction he needed today.

The afternoon spent with Brenda had confirmed several suspicions he'd had about her. Yet only after parting had he realized the true effect she'd had on him: Brenda had crossed into his defensive line.

Your defensive line was the fastest path around a turn, and following this line made it difficult for another driver to pass. This was how CJ had chosen to deal with women for the past ten years. Yet somehow, in a single afternoon, his defensive line had been violated without warning.

How did he let it happen? On the train ride from the city to

Chappaqua, after they left the bookstore, he figured out that the answer was in front of him all afternoon. Brenda's intense, sapphire eyes held him hostage. Her unexpected teasing charmed him, leaving him curious to know what might happen next.

In short, he liked her.

Once home, he tried to concentrate on a new book while eating Chinese food, but his conversations with Brenda crept into his mind, causing the words on the paper to lose all meaning. Around nine, when an action movie on cable only led to provocative images of Brenda's curvy hips and appealing rounded bottom, which he'd covertly examined more than once, he retrieved a twelve-year-aged bottle of Elijah Craig bourbon from his bar and poured a neat glass. Even the comforting smolder of the drink didn't stop the flashbacks to Brenda.

The next morning, he woke with the image of her lustful gaze at the checkout line in his head. A gentle stirring under his covers forced him to get up and run two miles.

Now that he was behind the wheel of his Porsche, he felt more like himself again. He enjoyed the gentle roar of his car's engine. A day at the track should take his mind off her. A glance at the speedometer showed his speed to be slightly over the legal limit. A moment later, a minivan breezed past him.

CJ upped the volume on a Rolling Stones CD, just as Mick Jagger belted out a reminder about how he might not always get what he wanted. Yesterday with Brenda, he had surrendered himself to the kind of desire that he had so scrupulously avoided in his post-Carla relationships.

He had also realized what he didn't want any longer: Autumn. Their time apart had proved to him that they never should have started dating. With this admission, his shoulders relaxed into the leather bucket seat. Yes, admitting this meant he could remove the mask he'd worn for ten long years. He'd never truly been himself when dating younger women. The minute Autumn returned from her assignment, he vowed to end their relationship.

Three months ago, the twenty-eight-year-old model had pursued CJ. At first he wasn't interested. He'd always joked he'd never date anybody less than thirty or older than thirty-five. However, Autumn's amazing looks and doting attention played to every part of his ego. Any red-blooded man would have found her difficult to refuse. At the outset, their inability to hold a conversation was easy to overlook.

Now it mattered. He'd wasted ten years of his life with bad choices.

A barbell of regret rolled across his chest. He accelerated, and the Porsche stirred to life. Switching lanes to get around several cars in his path, CJ no longer gave a damn if he violated the speed limit. He finally slowed in the right lane and glanced in his rearview mirror. No signs of the police. The weighted feeling gone, he inhaled a deep breath. Would his past problems ever fall behind so easily?

Ten minutes later, CJ pulled up to the valet at the Jefferson County Motor Club and tossed his keys to the attendant. "I'll be on the track after lunch."

The eager young man nodded, the message understood. CJ's car would be prepped and waiting when he was ready for his drive.

CJ bounded up the outside stairs toward the restaurant. The smell of burned rubber and the distant roar of a car engine slammed his senses. The familiar rush cast aside his earlier concerns.

The impressive upscale off-track facility, nestled in the middle of wooded surroundings, had a top-story restaurant with enormous windows providing 360-degree views of the course layout. The restaurant was designed for men, with dark walnut woodwork set against white walls and contemporary, no-nonsense furniture. He scanned the small crowd. Only a third of the tables were occupied. Outside the large window, which overlooked the track, very little traffic appeared on the black road surface.

He spotted Larry Chambers who, due to his height, always stuck out in any room. To his side sat Hugh Schmidt, an old college buddy of CJ's who'd also settled in the Northeast after graduation.

"Hey, guys." CJ approached them. "Hope you weren't waiting long."

"Good to see you." Hugh offered an extended hand. "We just got seated."

Larry stretched a lanky arm across the table to shake too. "Hugh and I were wondering why you weren't here two weeks ago when they reopened."

"I don't know about you guys, but I have this little thing I do in my spare time." He slipped into a chair facing the window. "I call it work."

"Starting with the early retirement digs already, huh?" Larry, a forty-eight-year-old, semiretired computer industry millionaire, still carried the look of someone who'd been a member of the math club in high school, but the look was now tempered with graying temples.

"Listen, we're both a little jealous of you," chimed in Hugh, partner at a large law firm in Manhattan. "I've been swamped lately."

"At least your salary paves the way for days like this." Larry grinned.

"Good point." CJ never forgot his writing success was the reason he could afford the $50,000 club membership fee and annual dues of $10,000.

A saucy brunette waitress arrived to take their orders. She

smiled more than necessary and laughed too long at a corny joke Larry made. No doubt a tip booster.

When she left, Hugh nudged CJ's elbow. "I'm taking out the Ford GT today. Maybe I'll whip your ass for a change."

The club's owner, Tom Maier, allowed rentals of special race cars to qualified drivers. Hugh's driving had improved since joining the club, but Tom's offer still surprised CJ. A skilled negotiator in the courtroom, Hugh must have worked his magic.

"It's not only the car, my friend." CJ tapped the side of his head. "Driving is as much about what's going on up here. That said, I accept your challenge."

CJ drove for the thrill of speed. After Carla died, driving fast became an outlet for his anger. Anger at himself. Behind the wheel, he drove in reckless harmony with death, never afraid of what might happen; however, time had had a mellowing effect. A race today with Hugh would be about the sport and safety.

Larry looked at Hugh. "Shooting for the two hundred miles per hour club with that car?"

"Depends on the headwinds." The stocky lawyer grinned.

"Which GT did Tom give you to drive?" CJ leaned his elbows on the table and cupped his chin.

"The yellow one."

"Hmmm." CJ slowly nodded and tried to look concerned. "Not the red?"

"Why?" Hugh's eyes opened wide. "What's wrong with the yellow?"

CJ did his best to look wary. "I think the red one goes faster."

Hugh reddened and they all enjoyed a laugh at his expense. Their food arrived. They ate quietly and quickly, watching the few cars on the track zip by and making some commentary. A short while later they were on their way out the door and headed for the track entrance.

The cry of a distant engine indicated a car was being driven on the back part of the track, and within seconds the thunderous sound neared. A white Corvette sped by. CJ inhaled the burning fumes. The smell seemed to sharpen his senses.

The staff positioned the men's cars near the start. CJ got into his. The dashboard was wiped clean and his gas tank registered full. With a click, the seat belt hugged him like a familiar friend. He tugged at the wrists of his leather gloves, pulling them taut, and grabbed the wheel.

A track marshal gave the signal to head out. He inched toward the start, accelerated, and hit 100 mph in a short time. He took it easy, circled the track a few times, and refreshed his memory on visuals where there were turns. Once he got comfortable, he navigated the course by recall alone, like a blind man familiar with the layout of his own home.

On his eighth trip around, he shifted and gained speed in a straightaway. A car flew by him, but he paced himself. CJ melted into his seat, one with the car. After two more laps, he spotted Hugh waiting for him at the start and slowed to his side. They gave each other a nod. The flags were dropped.

CJ took the lead with ease. He maintained the position through eighteen of the track's twenty hairpin turns, the yellow GT always close behind. His conscious thoughts faded away as the line separating man from machine became indistinguishable. He rounded a turn and accelerated on a straightaway.

The sudden drift of his attention came without warning. Visions of Carla appeared, a distant lighthouse in the fog of his memory blinking for his attention. He lost all concentration as memories of his past blinded clear thought.

God, he missed his wife.

A great sadness slammed into the center of his chest. He struggled to breathe. As he passed the large metal pole of a track light, it reminded him of his race. The pulse in his neck throbbed at a frenzied pace, and he felt himself lose control of the car.

He gripped the steering wheel and squeezed, willing himself back to reality. Brenda appeared in his mind. He opened his mouth and sucked in a gulp of dry air. His foot slipped off the gas pedal.

From the rearview mirror, the nanosecond of delay allowed Hugh to gain on him. CJ's foot slammed on the accelerator. The speedometer needle tipped to 180 mph. He approached the last turn and slowed, still ahead of his friend. CJ entered the turn, then cut in close to the inside edge. A second glance in the mirror showed Hugh still behind, braking for the challenging corner.

What the hell happened back there? With the thought, his grip on reality slipped once more, like water through his fingers. Carla's sweet voice ascended from the recesses of his mind: "CJ, stop torturing yourself. Move on."

The words pierced his heart and sent a sharp pain to his chest. His foot slid off the gas pedal. Hugh flew past him and gained the lead on the final turn. CJ fumbled to recover. He shifted gears, trying to catch up to Hugh, able to maintain a steady speed behind him.

Carla's voice still floated around him.

* * *

A supersized seagull dropped onto the wet sand and pecked the ground for morsels left behind by the departing tide of the Long Island Sound.

Nate pointed at it. "He's huge. Think he's the boss?"

"He'd better be." Brenda watched Nate while he stared at the choppy water. "If he's not, I don't want to see who is."

Nate grinned, then inhaled deeply. "Ah, there's nothing like the ocean air. Makes me wish I didn't live in a landlocked town."

"That's one of the reasons we moved here. Now my house is

too big for just one person, but I hate the idea of leaving Greenwich." Brenda pushed up the sleeves of her Martha's Vineyard sweatshirt, then lifted a handful of sand. The granules funneled through her palm into a small pile, each grain at home in its new place. She wished it were so easy for her to move on.

"What about looking for a condo in town?"

"I might. One day at a time." She looked at him. "Are you glad I invited you to my place for our date instead of meeting halfway?"

"I sure am." His gaze swam in hers, capturing her in its whirlpool effect.

Two little boys ran close by and broke the current. Nate watched them for a second and then squinted into the bright sun, which swathed them in warmth on the midspring day. A few residents lingered on the outskirts of the water. Nothing like the crowds of the summer months.

Nate's hair ruffled in the gentle breeze. Even though she wanted to comb her fingers through the disheveled softness, she found herself comparing him to CJ for the third time on this date. CJ didn't have any hair to wave in a breeze, yet she still wanted to let her fingers climb the crests of his strong shoulders and wrap them around his muscular neck. He somehow caused the logic Brenda typically applied to dilemmas to flutter out the window. A business colleague who had a girlfriend shouldn't be invading her thoughts in this way.

But she loved how he had listened to her—really listened, like he anticipated the unexpected. His responses often seemed laced with hidden meaning, a maddening, though alluring quality. She sometimes said things that would have left other men speechless, but he responded without wavering. When he chose to, he oozed charm. Charming men always made her wary.

In short, CJ both provoked and enticed her.

A different measure of satisfaction came from the engaging man with her now. Smart, handsome, and attentive, nothing Nate did irked her like CJ. She was ready to kick herself for making the comparison.

Nate pushed up the sleeves of his baggy cable-knit sweater, which he wore with a faded pair of jeans. She rested a hand on his visible forearm and he smiled.

"I have a philosophy joke for you." She smoothed his skin with her palm.

"Is it funny?"

"Is that a typical philosopher response? Always in search of deeper answers?"

He laid his hand over hers and returned a slow caress. "What's the joke?"

"What's the difference between a philosopher and an engineer?"

"About eighty thousand per year." His face remained deadpan.

"Aw, you've heard it."

"That's an old one."

"New to me." Brenda frowned.

"Here's one for you." Nate tipped his head, the same way he probably did when posing a question to his students. "How many philosophers does it take to change a lightbulb?"

"Define lightbulb."

Nate's face brightened. "I'm rubbing off on you."

"No. I found it surfing the Web. The great time waster. At the bookstore the other day, I even scanned through the philosophy section to impress you."

"I'm not seeing you because I want to talk about philosophy."

"I *knew* you had other motives." She narrowed her eyes, and Nate laughed. "Seriously, though, I did take a college philosophy course about a hundred years ago. Right after I switched to psychology."

"Did you enjoy the class?"

"All I remember is a theory I disagreed with and the professor arguing with me."

"You argued with a professor? About what?"

"Hmmm." She searched back many years, remembering the middle-aged professor, whose mismatched clothes suggested his concern for intellectual thinking precluded any notion of fashion sense. "Ah, yes...it was the idea that every event is determined by prior occurrences."

"Determinism."

"If you say so."

"What'd you disagree with?"

"At first the concept had merit. In psychology we try to find events from the past that might have caused a reaction. But the philosophy instructor took the logic a step further. He claimed everything that happens is the only possible outcome. If I believed that, I would've given up on my major." She wiggled her bare toes in the sand. "In fact, I'm not sure I'd get up in the morning if I believed I had no say in the outcome of my day."

"In many ways you don't."

"Sure. Shit happens, but nothing stops us from taking action to change outcomes."

"I'm tempted to play devil's advocate."

"I warn you to proceed at your own risk."

He laughed. "Professors love students like you." He traced her cheek, his index finger taking a lingering journey on her receptive skin. "Makes class lively."

Nate's delicate touch stilled her. He brought his lips to hers and she wilted under their soft strokes. His hand slid around her back and pulled her closer, deepening their kiss and fanning the sparks created by his touch. She ran her fingers through his hair, the way she had wanted to earlier.

He pulled away. "Should we head back to your place?"

She nodded. Would today end her long sabbatical from sex?

They walked back to the car, hands together like a couple. Once they were on their way, they made small talk. A few days earlier, Brenda had picked up condoms at the local drugstore, just in case. She'd felt ridiculous since her tubes were tied years ago. However, the world had changed.

Nate pulled into a gas station with a convenience mart. "I need to fill up and run inside. Do you want anything?"

"No thanks."

"Be right back." He went to the gas pump.

A knot tightened in her belly. She hardly knew Nate. Was allowing a near-stranger into her bedroom smart?

Over her shoulder, she watched him fiddle with the gas nozzle. He appeared honest. He caught her looking and winked, then set the pump to automatic before trotting into the convenience mart. His simple gesture warmed Brenda to the core. Yes. It had been way too long since she had had any fun.

Her sex life with Jack had been good. Many evenings he had rolled close and touched her, giving her little hints of his desire, and had sparked the same craving in her. That stopped when his drinking worsened. Yet their last intimate act wasn't like any of those nights.

It happened two days after he'd sent Devin the strange e-mail. Two days after he'd acted unusually angry toward her and hid away in his office. She'd never forgotten their conversation, or what followed.

Jack had returned home from work around eight that night. She cornered him in their bedroom while he changed out of his work clothes, demanded they deal with his problem. Jack didn't play along. His words were clouded by unexplained anger. He tossed handfuls of defensive, irrational comments her way.

When she cried, so did he. An hour later, he still wouldn't tell her why he'd been angry, although he agreed to seek help.

In the calm exhaustion that followed the argument, they had lain together on their bed, Brenda spooning Jack's side. His arms circled her, loosely, as if he'd understand if she needed an escape. Neither spoke, although the words of the fight hung above their heads. Brenda rolled over and studied his face. His lashes glistened with wetness. The man she loved for so many years — still the same on the outside, yet inside he'd become damaged, filled with pain.

Using his fingertips, he wiped away a wet spot on her cheek. He pressed his lips to the spot and followed a trail to her mouth. The deep kiss carried salt from their tears, but also a tenderness that triggered an immediate need in both of them. They pushed aside no more than the necessary clothing. Jack rolled on top of her while she wrapped her limbs around him tight, as if holding together the pieces of their broken marriage. Each movement was full of love and sorrow.

When they were finished, they lay quiet for some time. Brenda moved to get up. Jack pulled her to him and hugged her tight. "I will always love you," he whispered in her ear.

The gas hose clicked off and made Brenda jump. She pushed the memory back into the past as the buzz of Nate's cell phone startled her a second time. The phone rested in the console between the two front seats. Through the store window, Nate leaned over to look at something at the end of an aisle. The phone rang again. A brightened display announced "Home" calling.

Home?

Nate lived alone. He was divorced, without children. A warning flag rose.

How well did she really know this man?

The ringing stopped. She stared at the quiet phone.

The driver's side door flew open. Nate slid in and dropped a pack of gum into the console next to the phone. He buckled his seat belt and started the car. "Turn right on Route One and then where?"

"Stay straight for a mile." Brenda's heartbeat marched to a nervous beat as she pondered her next move. "Your phone rang while you were inside." She nodded toward the console.

He lifted the device, glanced at it quickly, and pushed a button before dropping it back on the console. Pulling onto the street, he shifted in his seat. "Just a friend. A buddy from my college days." He rubbed the back of his neck as if it was stiff. "He's in town visiting so I let him stay at my place. I'll give him a call later." Nate flashed a smile—fast, overconfident, toothy.

Brenda could always spot a liar. Up until then she had just missed the signs.

Chapter Eleven

A trained psychologist can learn to spot a liar, but no one is better at spotting a liar than another liar.

In her teenage years, hiding the truth became a specialty of Brenda's. When friends invited her to a movie or the mall, she'd often find her mother passed out or drunk, unable to grant permission, so Brenda would make up excuses — she had a dentist appointment, she had to clean her messy room, or her mom was sick. If an adult showed up at the front door asking for her mother, Brenda fabricated a story about her whereabouts.

It didn't feel like she was being dishonest. She employed lies like a shield, allowing her family to save face. In public, or when company visited, Mom behaved like a test-tube clone of genes obtained from Martha Stewart and June Cleaver. None of her friends would have guessed the drama that occurred during this woman's downtime. Daughterly duty forced Brenda to stand by the facade. But in college, away from her family at last, she began to wear honesty like a badge. She never wanted to feel the guilt of her childhood lies again.

The only time she had slipped into the old habit since then was toward the end of her marriage to Jack, and that was for reasons beyond her control. Or at least that's what she told herself every time she found herself with Luc.

During the drive home, Brenda analyzed how Nate's behavior had changed since she had mentioned the phone call—the uncomfortable shift in his seat, the delayed and vague explanation, the overexaggerated gleam of assurance. Sure, it was possible a friend was staying at his house. Was it probable, though?

They pulled into her driveway. He reached for the key and she touched his arm. "We need to talk."

"OK." He leaned back and kept his fingers wrapped around the steering wheel.

"I had a great time today."

"Me too."

"I'm not ready to invite you in, though."

His jaw flexed tight. "You were back there on the beach."

She hunched her shoulders. "Sorry if I misled you."

He let go of the wheel and cupped her face in his hands. "Are you sure I can't change your mind?"

Before she could reply, he leaned closed and pressed his lips against hers. She allowed his kiss to go on longer than seemed right.

Nate pulled back. "Well?" He blinked, appearing anxious. Had he learned of Reggie's nickname and started to believe he really *was* Professor Prince Charming?

"Sorry. I'm sure."

Clamping his mouth tight, he stayed silent for a few seconds. "If that's what you want, I understand."

He drove off a little too fast. Through the window, his expression looked like that of a hitchhiker who'd been jilted by a slowing driver.

She hurried inside and, after Georgie's enthusiastic greeting, poured a glass of wine. What the hell just happened? Was Nate up to something or had she used the strange call as an excuse to put her energy into CJ?

She leaned against the countertop, and took a long sip of crisp pinot grigio. The step from solitude to socializing had sure changed her days. She tried to make sense of everything that had happened over the last few weeks. Sorting the facts into tidy compartments always soothed her nervous mind.

Nate, attractive and agreeable, was a good kisser and enjoyable company. On a five-star rating system, he had been approaching a four—at least until the phone call and his strange reaction. Some sniffing on the Internet could change his score. It was something she should have done earlier.

CJ, attractive and charismatic, possessed an edgy mystery. They were so simpatico together. Her heart jittered when he was near, she became light-headed, and her fingers yearned to touch. Possible five-star material.

Love life aside, Brenda's other nagging concern was Patricia's comment about GBS. The upcoming lunch with Luc filled her with the same sort of dread as a root canal. She wanted their past to stay put. Was there another way to get information on the firm without talking to Luc?

Think. Think. Think.

A solution, so obvious she'd almost missed it, surfaced. Reggie's husband worked for a brokerage firm. He might have some information. Imagine Luc's shock if she called him and announced that she already knew what he was going to tell her.

She dialed Reggie's home number. Nobody answered. Then she remembered Reggie and Ted had taken the kids to upstate New York to visit her sister. She toyed with calling her cell, but decided against it. Too pushy, especially given what she needed to discuss. When the tone beeped, she said, "It's Brenda. Call me when you have a minute. Thanks."

Georgie followed her to the family room computer where Brenda undertook an Internet game of hide-and-seek with Nathaniel Walker. Her only ways to contact him were a cell number and university e-mail address. Neither said much about his personal life. The first search on his name yielded over a million hits, including a plumber, an exchange student, and a minister. On the second page was a link to a paper published through a philosophy society, most likely the Nate Walker she wanted, but she wasn't interested in his work. She added the words "address" and "New Jersey" and tried again.

When a search service appeared, she went to their site and entered a few more pieces of data. Listings for three Nathaniel Walkers in New Jersey materialized, complete with age and town details. Only one was Nate's age—forty-nine.

To the far right, the report listed relatives. A Tina Barnes showed as his wife, age forty. His first wife? No. He claimed to have divorced his high school sweetheart. Was Tina his current wife?

She clicked on the woman's name and the system gave her an option to buy a report on him for $19.95. Included in the data were searches on records for property, death, birth, marriage, and divorce. That covered it all, and it seemed a small price to pay for peace of mind. She grabbed a credit card and finished the transaction. The report would be e-mailed to her within one business day.

Brenda copied the link to Nate's entry and opened a new e-mail to Reggie. She pasted the link and typed, "Check this out...am I paranoid? Do me a favor. Ask Ted if he's heard any talk about GBS lately...in case Patricia's comment is true. Thx. Call me. B" She hit Send.

Farther down in her inbox was a reply from Luc, but she didn't open it. A silent wince, some combination of embarrassment and disgust, made her wish she hadn't said yes to their get-together. Why couldn't he simply give her the information over the phone? This secrecy seemed ridiculous. Was it just a way to get her to see him again?

She got up and took Georgie outside, then decided to throw a chicken in the oven. After Jack's death, avoidance had become a familiar technique for dealing with discomfort. She soon forgot about the e-mail, but an hour later, caught up in a romantic comedy on HBO, she was reminded of it when the male lead caught the female lead with another man—or at least, so it appeared to him. Brenda only wished her marital fling had been filled with such amusing antics. She took her glass of wine from the coffee table, settled into the leather office chair by her desk, and logged onto the computer.

She hadn't seen Luc since Jack's funeral. Just knowing that he would be there had added an overwhelming guilt to her sorrow at losing her husband. But Luc had been indispensable at the funeral.

Brenda had woken in a fog that day. The limousine drove her and the kids to St. Mark's Church. When the driver opened the door, Brenda remained slumped in her seat, hoping that if she blinked, all this would disappear and fade away like a horrible nightmare. Then she spotted Luc at the top of the steps and, to her surprise, she found comfort in his presence.

He approached the limousine with reassuring calm. "Come." His voice was soft. He took her hand, guiding her out with the same encouragement you'd give a frightened animal. "It will be over soon. I am here."

He hugged the kids, hugged her. Most of all, he acted as if their rendezvous had never happened. He acted like the good friend she needed.

He had watched her throughout the service, ready to catch her in case she fell apart. From the pew, bitterness toward Jack for doing this reared its spiteful head, replaced seconds later by sorrow after a glimpse of his photo on the casket. Her concentration rested on insignificant things. The most minute details captured her attention—the scent of the floral arrangements, Father Reynolds's wingtip shoes, the organist's short hairstyle—anything to distract herself from Shannon's tight grip on her arm, or the limpness of Devin's body next to hers, his soul so overpowered by grief he couldn't seem to hold on. And all the while Luc maintained a steady watch in her direction.

Somehow, she made it to the cemetery. While she stared down at the large hole, waiting for Jack's casket to be lowered into it, she worried her knees would give out and she'd crumble on top of the fresh dirt.

A hand pressed against her back. "Do not worry. I will not leave." Luc stood close and quietly spoke into her ear.

She acted indifferent, but she didn't reject his much-needed support.

"That is what friends are for," he added, his voice quieter.

She looked up into his slack expression and wanted to smile but couldn't force her lips to move. In the background, her vision landed on his wife standing near Patricia and Bertrand. Her face was inscrutable as she watched her husband. Brenda felt renewed guilt, like a slap across the face.

He had been so kind to her that day, but his every gesture was a reminder of her mistakes. Shame lay in wait, beneath her skin, a blister waiting to pop. Three months earlier, she'd all but given up on Jack and she had filled the void by spending time with his best friend. He had made her feel special and needed. He and Aimee had troubles too. Brenda and Luc both needed a distraction.

There were times when she rationalized the whole thing. After all, they had never actually broken their wedding vows. But she knew this was nothing but a feeble attempt at diminishing her guilt. The lines of infidelity were always blurry—a flirtatious suggestion in an e-mail or an attempt at the new sexting craze. If you stopped short of actually sleeping together, were you safe from judgment? Brenda knew deep down that there were many ways to cheat.

Even a year later, a lump lodged in Brenda's throat as she thought about it. She lifted her wineglass and swallowed a big gulp, but the lump remained.

With a few clicks and a deep breath she opened Luc's e-mail. He'd selected a place away from Greenwich and Stamford, claiming he didn't want to run into anybody from the office.

His covert approach worried her. Jack's work office had been emptied of his personal belongings almost immediately after he died. In fact, Jack's assistant, Rosie, had visited to retrieve Jack's office key from Brenda the very next day. Even in Brenda's distracted state, the sudden request seemed strange and inappropriate.

She confirmed the Tuesday meeting and prayed for answers. Maybe Tuesday would give her some insight into why Jack had taken his life.

A rock-hard knot developed in Brenda's stomach. Tuesday might also be the day Luc uttered the four words she hoped she would never hear: *Jack knew about us.*

* * *

"Two marriages minus one divorce equals still married." Brenda balanced a coffee cup in one hand, the search report in the other, and wedged the phone on her shoulder between her shoulder and her cheek. The report had arrived late Monday night. Once again, the miracles of technology left her awestruck.

"Wasn't that an SAT question?" asked Reggie.

"It should be." Brenda dropped the paper on the kitchen peninsula and sipped her coffee.

Still stewing, she rescanned the facts. Nate's first marriage, to a woman named Maria, lasted from 1984 until 1996. Another marriage took place in 2006 to Tina Barnes, the name appearing as a relative under Brenda's original search.

On the other end of the line, Reggie mumbled to one of her kids to finish breakfast. "Maybe he's separated."

"Then why wouldn't he say so?" The word hypocrite dangled in front of Brenda. She chastised Nate for dating behind his wife's back, yet she'd done the very same thing with Luc. Brandishing a confession-is-good-for-the-soul attitude, Brenda decided to tell Reggie about Luc.

"You're right. He should have said so." Reggie made a sarcastic chortle. "Man, I must be naive. He seemed so damn sweet at the conference. I'd never have pegged him to be a lying two-timer."

"*Alleged* lying two-timer. You know, I'm not defending Nate, but there are any number of reasons why people have affairs."

"Bren, he's not your patient. Don't make excuses for him before you have facts."

Brenda remained silent. Reggie's strong opinions sometimes made it hard to confide in her.

Reggie snorted a chuckle. "Jesus, by comparison, CJ looks better and better."

"He's not up for grabs. Remember the young, beautiful, and restless Autumn?" Brenda pulled her bathrobe more securely and tightened the belt, hiding her aging body behind the flannel from the mere mention of the young model. "Besides, CJ's a work associate."

"So? You dated your boss when you worked at Baskin-Robbins the summer between freshman and sophomore year of college."

"That was different."

"My point is, you can't play the 'working together' card. CJ's dating, not married. Even *I'm* convinced you should give him a second look. God, he gushed over you when he met us at the courts, in case you hadn't noticed."

"He was nice, but gushing? CJ doesn't seem like the gushing type."

"Well, if you only consider him a work associate, I think he's in violation of some sexual harassment laws."

Brenda smiled. "After all our sleepovers as kids, I don't remember you being this funny early in the morning." She stood and removed her popped toast, inhaling the homey smell, good enough to be a Yankee Candle scent.

"He could've said he couldn't join us, or left when I did."

Brenda grabbed a jar of strawberry preserves and returned to her seat. "True. When we said good-bye at Grand Central, I asked him why he wasn't with Autumn. He told me she was on an extended photo shoot out of the country. Then he offered, of his own accord, the fact that they hadn't been dating long and it wasn't serious."

"See? I was right. He wants you to know. I can tell you're smitten with him too."

"I enjoy being with him."

"Brenda, you *enjoy* tea with your grandmother. I saw you two at the club. A bit more than tea with Granny."

"OK." Brenda chuckled. Since they were kids, Reggie's dose-of-reality assertions were hard for Brenda to deny. "CJ hits every button there is to hit, the good and the bad. In fact, Saturday he had a field day with the good buttons."

"I rest my case."

Brenda could almost see Reggie's satisfied chest-puff over the phone. "You're a regular Clarence Darrow, my friend."

"CJ must like sarcastic women. Back to Nate. Has he done anything else to make you think he's married?"

"In hindsight, he has. He's met me on odd days; midweek for lunch and a Sunday afternoon. Not the typical date times. Plus, he's only given me a cell number. Claims he doesn't have a landline." She picked up the report. "This report suggests otherwise. It says 'Residence Phone Number.'"

"What else is in there?"

"Properties he's owned over the years. They're consistent with the places he's told me he's lived. Oh, listen to this — there's a birth record showing a child born in 2006. Same year as the marriage."

"You said he doesn't have children."

"Because that's what he told me."

"Jesus, what kind of person lies about this stuff?"

Brenda knew exactly what kind of person lied about stuff like that. Guilt pounded at her like a silent jackhammer. "Sometimes things just happen. Stop being so judgmental." The release valve on her conscience begged to be twisted, to release some pressure. If Reggie knew about her past, and why she had taken solace in Luc, she'd lay off the critical remarks. "It's not always so black-and-white." She took a breath. "Three months before Jack—"

"Hold on. What, Ted?" Reggie yelled away from the mouthpiece.

Ted yelled in the background that the kids needed help and he was about to leave.

"Sorry, Bren, I've gotta run. Oh, Ted says he hasn't heard anything about GBS, but he'll ask around. I'll call you later."

"Bye." The phone clicked in Brenda's ear. She stared at the paper in front of her. Still holding the cordless handset, she punched in the phone number to the residence listing on the report.

Chapter Twelve

"Everything you need to know about trauma but were afraid to ask."

Brenda stopped reading the recent issue of *Psychology Today* and glanced at the doorway. Dr. Stephanie Greco, one of five psychologists in the small group with whom Brenda shared her work space, stood there holding out a thick manila folder.

She smiled at the petite brunette. "Already? You're fast."

Stephanie approached the desk and handed Brenda the folder. "You lucked out. I had two patients cancel last minute this morning."

Brenda liked all her officemates, but had formed a friendship with Stephanie, who plopped down on a nearby love seat and crossed her legs. "This for a new patient?"

"Kind of." She pushed aside the magazine.

Her colleague barely reached the five-foot mark. Since Brenda had met her, she'd worn her hair styled in a pixie cut and would have required only the green tights and tunic to pull off the role of Peter Pan.

"He's fictional."

Stephanie's well-plucked brows jumped. "You're helping pretend people now? Not enough real ones to go around?"

As Brenda described the unusual work arrangement, her colleague's skepticism faded into wide-eyed awe. "CJ Morrison? My husband loves his books. Hey, if I picked up one at the bookstore, would you get it autographed for Don? His birthday's next month."

"Sure. I'm meeting with CJ at the end of the week. Drop it off by Friday morning."

They chatted for several minutes about an attendance issue with the new employee in billing, then Stephanie left. A quick check of the clock told Brenda her lunch date with Luc neared.

Luc — her little secret so dirty even an industrial-strength cleaner couldn't scrub away the grime. A knot tightened in her gut. Today's secretive meeting reminded her of old times, but not in a good, nostalgic way.

Their relationship had evolved innocently over their mutual concern about Jack. Luc phoned her one afternoon at the office to discuss Jack's worsening behavior. The following week, after Jack had disappeared into the abyss of yet another bottle the day before, she called Luc.

By pure coincidence, they ran into each other after work a few days later, while browsing ties in the men's department at Macy's. They wandered up to the food court and talked for an hour at a corner table for two, far from others. The next week they made a lunch date. The e-mails soon became more personal, laced with suggestive overtones from both parties. The diversion from problems at home and overdue attention from a man made Brenda glow inside, in a way she hadn't in many years.

The next time they met for lunch, Luc told her that he found her attractive and hoped that they would become closer. When the waiter offered them coffee after their meal, Luc rested his hand over hers and in a tender voice asked, *"Mon amour, do you want anything else?"* Yes, she did. It wasn't anything on the menu.

Two days later, Luc e-mailed and suggested they meet at a location several towns over for a drink after work. She lied to Jack about adding a couple of evening patients to her schedule and drove to the unfamiliar restaurant. After a cocktail, they scooted out to his car and kissed for a while.

Over the next two months, they met in secret places. Their passion heightened, each craving more. Brenda always pulled back before things could go any further. However, one cold afternoon, everything changed...

Her phone's shrill ring pulled her from the uncomfortable memory and she hoped Luc wouldn't mention the incident today. Brenda answered, scheduled an appointment with a returning client, and decided to leave a few minutes early for her lunch date. She pulled on her blazer, grabbed her purse, and went to a mirror behind her door to reapply her lipstick. The white silk blouse and black slacks should send a signal that their meeting was business, not personal. On her way out, the receptionist reminded her about a two o'clock appointment.

Music from a local rock station blared during the drive, but Brenda scarcely listened, the nervous churn in her stomach taking precedence. Twenty minutes later, she arrived at the parking lot of Franco's Bistro. Luc's suggested meeting place, far from his Stamford office, was across the state border in Rye Brook, New York. His BMW was parked in the front of the lot. She pulled into a spot on the other side, in case anybody recognized their cars.

Inside the quiet restaurant, low voices and the clink of glasses disturbed the still air. Nobody manned the foyer, so she entered the dining room. Dark walnut paneling and heavy red curtains didn't do anything to take away from the size of the large room. Only a few tables were filled. Art deco paintings, antique mirrors, and an eclectic mix of knickknacks gave the place a European aura. Luc sat in the back corner. He waved and stood.

Luc had a strong chin and an angled nose, all set on a long face with fashionable tortoise-rimmed glasses. His dark brown hair, short and parted on the side, always looked as if he'd applied Brylcreem, but then allowed some woman to muss it with her fingers. Still fit and fashionable in a nicely tailored suit, Brenda's mouth went dry. He looked good. Damn good.

"Brenda." His sincere smile showed no signs of nervousness. Luc, the quintessential showman, was always at his best, even with a small audience. He opened his arms. "It's good to see you."

"You too." She'd forgotten the thickness of his accent, his pronunciation of "it's" sounding like "eets."

She stepped into his embrace, careful to maintain a safe distance, but he drew her close, tight to his chest as if to reattach their shared history. With his gentle hold, the familiar scent of vanilla Pinaud Clubman aftershave and cigarette remnants folded around her, reminding her of their times alone.

"You look beautiful," he whispered.

"Thank you." She loosened their hug and stepped back. "You look good too."

He pulled out her chair for her and then took his.

Brenda mentioned that she needed to be back at the office by two, so they ordered right away.

New gray spots laced Luc's hair in all the right places. He brushed aside several strands, hiding his forehead, reminding her how silky and soft the strands were to the touch.

"How's Aimee?"

He didn't flinch. "Fine. She's in France visiting family." Maybe things between them had improved.

They talked about the kids, her book, and Bertrand's surprise party. Elbows on the table, he leaned close, resting his chin between his index finger and thumb. His slender hands always appeared well manicured, flawless, like they'd never seen a dirty day.

He cleared his throat. "You must be curious about my reason for contacting you."

"Curious would be putting it mildly."

He took a deep breath, the first sign of discomfort she'd seen since her arrival. "A complaint has been filed by the Securities and Exchange Commission against GBS, accusing us of earnings manipulation."

"What's that?"

"The firm has been under a lot of pressure, for several years now, to show results with sales figures. Ever since their big growth spurt in early 2002, pressure has been on to keep stock prices high. Analysts were always hyping the company stock. As CEO, it is Bob Manning's responsibility to produce the figures. In fact, he's obsessed about it." Luc sat back and lifted his spoon. He rotated the utensil in his hands but kept it close to his torso, as if it were a shield. "There are ways, accounting tricks, to make earnings seem better than they are."

A sick wave washed over Brenda. Two short weeks ago, Patricia Dupont told her something was going on at GBS that might involve Jack. As chief number-cruncher for the firm, he'd know more accounting tricks than anybody. It didn't make sense, though. Jack had spent the first part of his career as a public accounting auditor working to stop guys like Bob from manipulating data.

"So, Bob fudged numbers to make the firm seem better than reality?" She wrapped her fingers around the edge of the table to brace herself for his answer.

"Not Bob." Luc drew in a deep breath. His gaze dropped to the table. "Jack."

The sick wave pulled Brenda under again, this time stealing the wind from her lungs. A thousand thoughts spun in wild disarray. She searched for a reason to not believe him, but her nerves teetered on the brink of stone-cold panic. "What makes you think Jack would do that?"

"It's the firm's accusation, not mine. Bob Manning's accusation."

The pieces began to come together. A hot rush sped through Brenda from scalp to toe. Her hand flew to her mouth to bottle the anguish about to boil over.

"There's more." Luc lowered the spoon. "Do you need a minute?"

She swallowed to force the bottled-up emotion downward and lowered her arm. "No." She didn't recognize her own voice. "Go on."

"After Jack died, I learned that Bob asked his secretary to remove Jack's personal belongings but leave everything else alone. I think she asked you for Jack's key?"

Brenda nodded.

"A suspicious move on his part." Luc snorted. "Anyway, late last week, Bob met with the senior executives and told us charges would more than likely be filed this week. In the meeting, he announced Jack was fully responsible for the problem. The way he acted right after Jack died came back to me, and I wondered if Jack may have kept something to incriminate his boss."

"So they're trying to pin this entirely on Jack?"

He nodded. "When I got in this morning, auditors had taken over. Several of them had already made a home in Jack's old office."

Brenda rubbed her temples but was so numb she could barely feel her fingertips.

"This might make the nightly business news. I'm sure tomorrow the local papers will carry the story. I suggested to Bob that he contact you."

"What'd he say?"

"That he had no intention of doing so." Luc shrugged and threw up his hands, a reminder that he was only the messenger.

"What an arrogant ass!" Brenda's anger hit DEFCON one. Jack had often described Bob as a phony, rich snob who spent more time entertaining and schmoozing with other big shots on his yacht than running the company. Pure, unfiltered hatred toward the CEO coursed through her veins. Brenda knew one thing: Jack would never have done these things on his own.

The waiter brought over their iced teas, and Brenda could barely mumble thanks through her clenched jaw. She thought about driving to the GBS corporate offices and tracking down Manning, but didn't trust herself to behave with dignity.

Brenda poured two sugar packets into her tea and stirred. Luc stared at his beverage and said nothing. Many times, she'd asked Luc if a problem existed at the office. He'd always said no.

She narrowed her gaze. "Did Jack ever talk with you about this?"

Luc, about to take a sip of his drink, stopped and shrugged but avoided actually looking back. "Does it matter now?"

"Yes. Did he?"

Luc's chin dipped to his chest and his posture slumped. "Sometimes." His gaze shifted up. "When he'd drank too much."

"You *knew* he had work problems?"

"Brenda, we were all under stress. Men sometimes talk."

"You should have told me." Her voice went quiet.

"He asked me not to repeat it."

"How often did I tell you I worried Jack's work problems had to do with his drinking? His changes around the house?" Her volume rose alongside her anger. "You lied to me."

He opened his mouth to speak but stopped when the waiter arrived with their salads.

After the waiter left, Brenda pushed the plate aside. "Why'd you lie?"

"I did not lie. I just did not say anything. How could I betray Jack's confidence?"

She leaned across the table. "You betrayed him in other ways without a problem." His jaw tensed, so rigid she half expected to see a crack form. "I don't believe this." Brenda smacked the tabletop with her palm. A man sitting at the corner table glanced over. Brenda lowered her voice. "I could have helped him."

Luc's shoulders rose, quick and dismissive. "I did what I believed right."

Brenda pushed back her chair and stood.

"Where are you going?"

"The ladies' room."

The reality of the SEC charges, the idea that her husband committed an illegal act and that he wasn't here to defend his actions, pushed her one step closer to tears. She crossed the room but couldn't feel the floor. Once behind the ladies' room door, she fell against it and the tears escaped.

In spite of the horrible news, she felt some relief. At least Luc hadn't said what she most dreaded: that Jack knew of their hidden personal liaison. Would Jack have killed himself over a work problem, though? Why wouldn't he have come to her? Gone to the authorities? There had to be more to the story.

Whenever she'd tried to help him, he had pushed her away. This news, though, filled her with pity for her husband. Jack's way out seemed utterly ridiculous and plausible at the same time. A million details clunked around in her head, like marbles in a bag rolling into an unmanageable pile.

Her instincts always taught her that when life was going in a bad direction, she should grab the reins and drive the horse. Right now, her most important concern was her children. She'd contact them immediately so they wouldn't be shocked to find their father's name dragged through the mud.

The man she'd married, who possessed a strong moral and ethical code when it came to his line of work, had to be innocent. How could she defend him against these accusations? She went to the sink and wiped mascara smudges from under her lower lashes. As she splashed water on her cheeks, a thought whispered in her mind: had Luc only kept Jack's confidence in the hopes that her marriage would worsen and she'd turn to him?

Brenda waved her hand under the paper towel dispenser three times before a carefully measured piece appeared, as if it had to consider the matter carefully before making its decision. Dabbing her damp cheeks, she decided that Luc would never go that far.

On the way back to the table, Luc's anxious expression shouted from across the room. "Brenda, I'm sorry," he blurted as she neared the table.

"Let's drop it." She sat, and the worry lines near his eyes faded. "I guess you had to keep your word to Jack." She watched Luc closely for his next reaction. "In your gut, do you believe Jack acted alone?"

"No." He didn't blink. "Of that, I am certain."

"Why?"

"Jack told me pressure from above forced him to do these things over time. It went back at least five years. Small things at first, ones which distorted the line between legal and illegal." Luc focused on a spot directly behind Brenda. "As pressure from the shareholders increased, the demands from above became even more brazen. He would not say who pressured him, but the possibilities are limited." His lips drew in, as if to stop himself from saying more.

"Bob?"

"He is one of them."

"No wonder Jack wasn't himself. He must have felt like there was no way out of this mess."

"Perhaps." Luc stroked the fleshy area under his chin. "When you cleaned Jack's home office, did you find anything that might have something to do with this? Something he may have saved to cover himself, show he was pushed?"

Brenda thought about the unsuccessful attempt she'd recently made to hunt through Jack's private study. The soft drum of Luc's long fingers on the table made her gaze shift to them. "I haven't touched a thing in Jack's office since he died."

"I understand." Luc's sympathetic voice brought back memories.

"Maybe it's time." She looked up.

"Maybe." His warm palm slid over her hand. "Can I help?"

Brenda forced herself to stay put. "No thanks. I'll do it. When I'm ready." Then she slowly pulled back her arm and freed herself from his touch. Lifting her fork, she poked at her salad. "You understand, right?"

"Of course." He followed her lead and pushed his salad around the plate too, but his unflinching stare remained on her. "Brenda?"

"Yes?"

Luc leaned back, drew his lips into a straight line, more uncomfortable than she'd ever seen him. "If you find anything suspicious, you will call me, right?"

"Sure." She speared a piece of lettuce, but in his question she heard a thin layer of desperation. "Soon. This weekend." Brenda attempted her best we're-in-this-together smile.

"Good." The word came out at an unnaturally high pitch. He stared several seconds longer than comfort dictated, then returned to his salad.

* * *

The overstuffed chair in Brenda's office was positioned so that, with a negligible shift of her vision, she could see the clock on the built-in bookshelf behind her patient. The digit flipped to 4:29, indicating the session had come to an end. The bomb Luc had dropped on her during lunch had left her exhausted. She'd finally get some time alone to digest what he had said, and consider the impact on her family and her husband's reputation.

"Mary, during the week, think about what you gain and what you lose by letting Scott back into your life." Brenda took out her appointment book to signal the end had arrived.

The thirty-five-year-old mother of two, who'd been dealing with the aftermath of her husband's extramarital affair, nodded, and her long, tight curls bounced with the motion. "Sounds like a good idea."

"Most major decisions aren't black-and-white, as some people in your life are suggesting. We'll discuss what you come up with next week."

"Thanks, Dr. McAllister. I'm acting off pure emotion right now."

"Emotion over his request is normal." Brenda checked her calendar. "However, you don't want to let your emotions dictate your decision. Same time next week still good?"

Mary nodded, put on her jacket, and left.

Given the dips and crests of her own emotional roller coaster today, Brenda almost laughed at her advice. She felt as if she were standing on the edge of a cliff, peering into a dark chasm. She knew it was bad down there but couldn't tell how bad.

Infidelity seemed to be the topic du jour. That morning she'd called the home phone number listed in Nate's personal data. After four rings, a woman had answered.

"Uh, hi. Is Nate Walker there?"

"No, I'm sorry. He's at work. This is his wife. Can I help

you?"

"I'm not sure I'm even calling the right Nate Walker. The one I'm looking for is a professor at Chapman College."

"That's my husband. And you are...?"

"Brenda McAllister. I met Nate at a writers' conference not too long ago. Would you mind passing along a message I called?"

Brenda had hung up and sat for a long moment in disbelief. Nate had lied. She hoped once he realized his cover was busted, he'd scurry away like a little rat. The multiple messages during the day, however, suggested otherwise. She ignored them in order to deal with the more important matter of Luc and his lunchtime revelations.

The flash of her message light caught her attention. She pressed the button to listen. Nate again. This time his words reeked of such desperation she smelled them over the phone. The handset banged loud when she hung up.

"Are you busy?" Stephanie stood at Brenda's doorway.

"No. Come on in."

"At lunch, I picked up CJ Morrison's book for Don's birthday." Stephanie waved a book in the air. "He'll be shocked when I give him a signed copy." She flipped to the back cover. "Good picture of the author on the jacket. He's a nice-looking guy." She handed it to Brenda, picture-side-up.

A close-up photo of CJ covered the entire back cover. His rich brown leather bomber jacket hung open, over a stonewashed oxford shirt, collar splayed to reveal a few speckled gray hairs on his chest that almost matched the coloring of his tidy facial hair. Light hit the rough grooves of his cheekbones, highlighting his masculine features. His expression held an air of ambiguity; a thin smile suggested he possessed a secret. The photo lured Brenda in, much the way he had on Saturday.

"You're right. Great picture. He looks that good in person

too."

"The bio didn't say anything about a wife." Stephanie shrugged. "I mean, since you're on the market again."

Brenda tore off a paper from a small notepad. "Well, for the record, it's true that he's unmarried, and your observation is duly noted. How do you want this signed?"

"Dear Don...Happy 45th birthday. I'm just saying, sometimes things land in front of you for a reason. Now you guys work together. Later, who knows?"

"Believe me. He hasn't gone unnoticed." Brenda scribbled the note and stuck it on the inside cover. "At least I can say I've gotten my first date in over twenty-five years out of the way."

"Right, the guy from the conference. How was it?"

"A day ago I would have said great. Today I found out he's married."

"Really?"

"Yep. He stone-cold lied and said he was single."

"Being in a bad marriage can cause people to do very strange things."

Brenda nodded. She wasn't sure what motivated Nate to lie, but she understood the gradual drifting from a spouse, how problems in a marriage could consume you like quicksand. "Ever have any moments with Don where you wondered if your marriage was in the right place?"

"Once. Reality can eat away at things you once believed in. Around the seven-year mark, I went through a thing. The seven-year itch." Stephanie dropped her gaze for an instant as if ashamed by the admission. "I found myself flirting or fantasizing about other men. After some soul searching, I realized we'd let our relationship get stale. Once I focused on spicing things up, my itch stopped." She grinned and winked. "I'll still indulge in fantasyland, though. What about you?"

"At the height of Jack's problems, I'd be lying if I said other men didn't have appeal. I never stopped loving him, but he made it hard to *like* him some days."

The office receptionist stuck her shaggy blonde head in through the doorway. "Stephanie, your five o'clock is here."

"Thanks. Lunch tomorrow?"

"Sounds good."

Brenda got up and shut the office door after Stephanie left. Once back at her desk, she grabbed her cell phone, dialed a number, and waited for an answer.

On the second ring, Nate picked up. "I'm glad you called me back. I thought you might not."

"You thought right."

"Brenda, I'm so sorry. There were so many times I wanted to tell you."

"Why didn't you when we met?"

"Would you have gone out with me?"

"Of course not."

"Exactly."

"Nate. You lied. Not about your weight or how much you could bench press. Your marital status. Why?"

"I'm not sure." All defensiveness left his voice. He now sounded defeated and confused. "Being at the conference alone reminded me of my single days. You caught my attention. Then, after we talked, well, I really liked you."

"Uh-huh. Why weren't you wearing your wedding ring?"

"I, uh, slipped it off right before I came over to you."

"Sounds premeditated to me, Nate." She snapped his name.

"Brenda, my wife and I have been having problems and —"

"You decided an unknowing victim in your troubled life might make things better?"

"No." His voice quieted, now less defensive. "I wanted to be with someone who didn't want to fight or hassle me about being a better husband." He let out a long, deep sigh. "Talking to you reminded me of when I first started dating my wife."

Brenda remained silent, unsure how to respond. It would have been easier if Nate announced he needed variety in his sex life, or admitted his status and power as a handsome professor had gotten the better of him, causing him to pursue casual affairs without much forethought — then hating would have come easy.

"Listen, I understand about your marriage, but don't think an affair will fix your life. Decide if what you have matters. If it does, work on it."

"Please, Brenda. I—"

"Please, Nate. Don't call me again."

He agreed and she hung up. Her gaze landed on a family photo propped on the corner of her desk, taken during a family trip to Disney World eight years earlier. Jack's arm wrapped her shoulders; the kids huddled close. Everyone was hot and tired but in high spirits. The picture of happier times made her wish someone had doled out similar guidance before she had gone down the wrong path. Brenda felt tears forming.

Her affair had ended close to the end of Jack's life. Too late to fix her marriage and too late to forgive herself.

Chapter Thirteen

Bob Manning swaggered, with the kind of confidence that commands respect, toward a tall brunette in black spandex short-shorts and a hot pink exercise bra. She slowed her pace on the elliptical. From Brenda's viewpoint, covertly watching from behind the window in the lobby, she couldn't tell if the interruption was welcome or not.

This was a crazy way to spend her day off.

"May I help you?"

Startled by the unfamiliar male voice, Brenda turned and peered at a short, muscular young man whose name tag read Rick.

"No thanks. I'm waiting for a friend. She's in the locker room." This fellow's emergence might have some advantages during her secret operation. "I've been looking for a Pilates class. Do you offer them here?"

"We do. Let me get you a list of our class schedules."

He went behind the reception desk, his return delayed by the ringing telephone. Brenda continued her watch of Jack's former boss. Bob's hungry leer at his co-member suggested that he was untroubled by his quote in today's newspapers, one which added more wreckage to Brenda's already damaged life. Her jaw clenched tighter than an angry fist.

The GBS executive's square face carried the signs of age pretty well for a man in his late fifties. His full head of short silver hair, however, made him appear older. Nylon gym shorts and a baggy T-shirt didn't hide his spreading midsection, thicker than she remembered. He hung onto the sides of a hand towel dangling around his neck. The elliptical babe gazed at him as if he were Elvis, probably due to the combination of his bank account and status in the business world. It certainly wasn't due to his looks.

Bob chattered away, his wanton gaze raking the young woman while she pedaled. Brenda studied the woman's firm posterior. Maybe she'd buy an elliptical. Brenda tried to read Bob's lips as he spoke. He must have said something good, because the shapely exerciser stopped and beamed at her admirer. His superior expression melted away, replaced with such saccharine sweetness that Brenda half expected ants to stampede the room and head straight for him. At Jack's work functions, Brenda had witnessed Bob's chameleon personality switch from dazzling to don't-you-dare in a matter of seconds.

"Here you go." Rick's return almost made her jump. A job with the CIA was not in her future.

She glanced at the sheet, feigning interest. "Is membership needed to attend?"

"Classes alone only require a partial membership. The prices are on there. If you have any other questions, let me know."

Brenda thanked him. Her attention returned to the workout area. Bob disappeared into the locker room. She went to the juice bar in the establishment's small café, ordered a Perrier, and took a seat in the corner where she'd see him come out. The manner in which she approached him would make or break this conversation.

The hunt for Bob Manning might have been the most ridiculous use of her midweek day off since she'd started taking them during the writing of her first book. It had begun early that morning, while she munched on her cereal and scanned the Internet news posts. Reports of GBS and its fraud held the stage everywhere, from local television news to the front page of her AOL account. Thanks to Luc's disclosure, she'd buckled down for the impending storm. Still, its arrival pounded the walls and loosened her hinges.

The detailed articles in the *New York Times* and *Wall Street Journal* about the SEC's investigation each carried the same quote from Bob: "Global Business Systems is shocked by the SEC's accusation. We believe the fraudulent deeds were initiated and administered at the direction of Jack McAllister, the CFO of our North American and European operations. Unfortunately, Mr. McAllister's suicide a year ago leads us to speculate the cause of his death may be related to the actions he took while employed here. In light of what the SEC has uncovered, I'm not surprised Mr. McAllister searched for a way out. We are cooperating fully with the auditors and the government."

Right away, she phoned her kids again to let them know the news had gone public. She then paced the house, sipping her coffee and brainstorming ways to manage the problem. Twice, she stood in the hallway outside Jack's office and considered doing what Luc had asked her to do. Both times ended with her frozen in place outside the door, paralyzed by memories of Jack waiting in every dusty shelf and cobwebbed corner. Maybe Reggie could help her look.

After much thought, she'd found no solutions but arrived at one conclusion. Like the three hundred Spartan soldiers who stood up to the mighty Persian army, she would fight the corporate giant, beginning with Bob Manning.

At ten, she had called Manning's office. His secretary took a message. By the time the clock struck two, he hadn't responded. She placed a second call. This time, Brenda demanded to speak to him today. By five thirty there was still no reply. She grabbed her handbag and walked out the door. Since Bob wouldn't come to the mountain, she'd lift the damn mountain and bring it to him.

Brenda drove to the GBS office complex. Hidden in the far corner of a half-empty employee parking lot, she backed into a spot and kept a vigil on the front entrance as employees left for the night. Her gaze stayed glued to Bob's Jaguar. At seven, he finally exited the building, threw his briefcase on the passenger seat, and left.

Her heart thumped against her ribs, but she followed several cars behind and reviewed her loosely thought-out plan; if he went any place besides home, she'd pretend she happened to run into him. If he headed home, she didn't know what she'd do. His drive straight to the fitness club seemed the luck of the Irish, which hadn't graced the McAllister name in far too long.

With the Perrier bottle tipped to her mouth, Brenda tried to look relaxed and read the handout on the Pilates class. A few minutes later, Bob emerged wearing his suit and white shirt, without the tie, and carrying a gym bag. She rested her bottle on the bar top and waited until he reached the entrance doorway, then trotted out behind him.

Once outside, she yelled, "Bob?" Her voice squeaked a bit higher than she'd expected.

He stopped and glanced back, his surprise obvious. "Hello, Brenda. It's been a while." His jawbone flexed. "Are you a member here?"

"No. Just came to get information on a class." She waved the sheets Rick handed her in the air as proof, thankful now that she'd asked for them.

"Oh. Well, nice to see you." He continued to his car.

She glided alongside and kept up with his strides. "Funny I'd run into you tonight. I left you two messages today."

"We have nothing to discuss."

"I disagree."

Bob's pace quickened. The moment she'd waited for all day had finally arrived. The pulse in her neck pounded, tapping like Morse code and sending a clear message: proceed at your own risk.

She swallowed. "Don't you think a heads-up about your accusations against Jack would have been appropriate?"

He stopped and faced her, puckering his mouth as if he were about to scream. Instead, the muscles of his face gained control. "Your husband acted in a criminal capacity. I'm under no obligation to discuss anything with you."

"Obligation? This isn't about your obligation. It's about human decency." Brenda quieted as another gym member walked past and waited until the man had stepped far enough away. "Jack was a loyal employee. You can't possibly believe he acted on his own. There must be someone else involved or another reason Jack would have done those things…if he even did."

Bob blinked several times. "I've been advised by my attorney not to discuss this with anybody while it's under investigation." He took another step away from her.

She stuck to his side and kept pace. "So, you're telling me Jack came up with these illegal things alone?"

"Exactly."

"Strange."

"What's strange?"

"Jack always told me you were very hands-on. I find it hard to believe a CEO who's hands-on could lose such control over the finances."

Bob stopped short. The parking lot lights highlighted the steel glare of his pupils. "Is it a coincidence we've run in to each other tonight, or do I need to contact my attorney to take out a restraining order on the disgruntled wife of a criminal?"

The threat stunned her, like a bird flying into a sliding glass door, leaving her speechless. A quick reminder that this might help Jack gave her the courage to fight back. "Listen, Bob. My husband had high principles when it came to his work. He'd never do those things on his own."

Bob moved in close. So close Brenda could've sworn she felt the heat of his reddened cheeks. "Just who do you think you're dealing with?" His voice lowered. "If I were you, I'd tread very lightly around this issue. I'd better not ever run into you" — he raised his fingers in air quotes — "'accidentally' again or you *will* be sorry."

He stomped away. Brenda didn't follow. She stood in place, her knees wobbling. She did recognize one thing: Bob's threats were rooted in fear.

Chapter Fourteen

The Friday evening 6:22 express train screeched to a stop at Bedford Hills, New York, right on time. Passengers exited the commuter rail while the orange sun crawled toward the horizon. Reggie and her husband, Ted, finally appeared on the platform. Brenda tooted the horn and waved.

Reggie's black gauze skirt sashayed with her perky gait, swooshing the tops of knee-high, pointy-toed boots. A tight leather jacket and bright fuchsia top all but yelled to onlookers, "I'm here." Brenda's outfits were so Ann Taylorish compared to Reggie's urban flair that, at her friend's side, she often felt like the words "The Connecticut Friend" were plastered on her forehead. Today's leggings, worn with an oversize belted shirt and flats, proved the point. Ted's presence only amplified Reggie's loud appearance. His short hair, cotton oxford shirt tucked into plain jeans, and delicate wire-frame glasses gave him a gentle appearance, which didn't scream of anything. A style befitting a man who worked at a brokerage firm.

Brenda stepped from the car and her friends embraced her with comforting hugs.

"How are you holding up?" Ted asked. "I couldn't believe what I heard on the news yesterday."

"I'm tired. There isn't much I can do to stop GBS." Brenda

almost told them about the conversation with Luc, but Ted had never liked him, so she held her tongue. "My gut tells me Jack would never have done those things on his own."

"No." The word flowed from Ted's mouth like a lone, sad note. "Not the Jack I knew."

Brenda sometimes forgot that, although the two men only spent time together due to spousal intervention, a deep friendship had developed between them. The wilted muscles of Ted's face were a reminder that he still hurt from Jack's loss.

Brenda gave Ted an extra hug. "All I can do is hope the SEC gets to the bottom of it. That damn Bob Manning never bothered to tell me he planned to throw Jack's reputation into the gutter."

"Doesn't surprise me." Ted shook his head. "He's about running his business first, people second. Jack said that enough times."

Reggie looked at Ted. "Guess it's paid off for him. Didn't you say his name appeared on a list of top earning CEOs in Forbes?"

"Close to the top. He sure has plenty of motives for earnings to look good. A couple of guys at the office were talking about him today."

Reggie looped her arm through Ted's. "Let's get going and talk on the way. Dale's expecting us soon."

At the car, Reggie hopped into the front seat, leaving the back for Ted, far from the crossfire of their girl talk.

Brenda pulled out of the parking lot. She glanced at Reggie as she accelerated onto the main road. "You're still in some trouble with me."

"A dinner out won't kill you."

Ted stuck his head between the front seats. "A smart man wouldn't ask this, but what's going on with you two now?"

"Nothing horrible." Reggie pulled a mirror and tube of lipstick from her purse. "I called Brenda and asked if she wanted to have dinner with me Friday. When she said yes, I told her the meal would be at Dale's to celebrate his birthday along with a few other people."

Brenda thumbed toward Reggie, who applied the pink shimmer tube. "I reminded yenta, the village matchmaker, why I'm gun-shy about her invites."

Twice in recent months, Brenda had been invited to Reggie and Ted's for dinner with some mutual acquaintances. Each time, a single and age-appropriate male was among the attendees. Since the other guests were all couples, the two loners stuck out like whale hunters at a Greenpeace meeting.

Reggie drew in her upper and lower lips to spread the sparkly gloss. "What was wrong with the high school basketball coach?" Her voice suddenly possessed a mousy squeak. "The kids love him."

"He spent the entire evening chatting about sports with the guys. If you'd introduced me as Michael Jordan, I might have stood a chance."

Reggie remained too quiet, a tip-off that Brenda should brace herself for the next pitch.

"Hmpf. I still think Stan Harvey, the newly divorced man in my building, is a nice guy."

"He was nice. But when he realized what I did for a living, our conversation evolved into a long therapy session. I learned more about him than many of my regular patients."

Reggie put away her cosmetics. "I guess that could be a turn-off."

"Thanks for trying, but you might let me do this on my own, unless I ask for help."

"Fine. But about tonight—you can't deny that once I drag you someplace, you always end up having a great time. Like the writers conference."

"Most of the time, yes. Not always."

In truth, Brenda had always been glad to have Reggie coaxing her out the door during middle and high school. In those days, her mother's drinking had taken a downward turn. Brenda often avoided going out for fear of what she'd find upon her return. In hindsight, staying in didn't always ensure peace at home either.

"Dale came up with the idea to invite you, anyway." Reggie was known to pulverize an already dead horse. "If I'd told you the truth up front, would you have come?"

Brenda shrugged, not really sure what she'd have said. The recent news about Jack left her mentally spent.

"Anyway, the night isn't about your love life." Reggie pointed to a street not far away. "Make a right there."

"Good." Brenda took the turn. "You were right about going to the conference. I might have said yes to tonight without the manipulation."

"Sorry." Reggie pouted. "I worry about you."

Brenda reached over and squeezed her friend's hand. "I appreciate that."

Reggie's lips retreated inward, as if cornered by a thought. "So, to be clear, the times I invited you over for dinner with those two guys—the problem was that you didn't know them, right?"

Brenda tilted her head toward Reggie.

From the back seat, Ted muttered, "Uh-oh."

"If an unmarried guy you already knew showed up at a dinner, would it be OK?"

"Who's coming?" Brenda already had her suspicions.

"Dale might have invited CJ."

"So? Won't his leggy girlfriend be there too?"

"Maybe." Reggie twisted her entire body to see Ted. "You never finished telling us what the guys at your office said about Bob Manning."

"Smooth topic change, honey." Ted acted as if he hadn't caught the annoyed glance from his wife. "As a matter of fact, there was something. Word on the street is people higher up in the firm were involved. Bob's on the short list."

"I figured. Explains why, when I nabbed him at his health club and called him a liar, he reacted the way he did."

Ted's head appeared again between the seats. "You did *what?*"

Brenda launched into details about the run-in at the health club. Ted stayed in his position, resting a hand on the front bucket seat, his mouth agape the entire time.

When she had finished, a look of concern crossed Ted's face and he slumped back in his seat. "You'd better be careful. Bob Manning may not have written the book on being ruthless, but I'm pretty sure he's read it."

"I don't care. All I care about is Jack's reputation."

"Me too. If I hear anything else, you're my first call."

"Thanks." Brenda caught his concerned eyes in the rearview mirror. For the first time since all this came out, a scary reality took hold. Her husband might have faced some pretty dark demons at the office each day. Demons she'd have to face if she was going to help him.

* * *

Dale's antique colonial sat on two acres of sprawling lawn surrounded by mature trees, one of which had a tire swing hanging off a strong branch. Inside the large country kitchen, the last of the daylight filtered in through tall casement windows above the sink. Dale's wife, Vivian, stood in front of a stainless steel industrial stove and sautéed Swiss chard in fresh garlic. Brenda's mouth watered during their introduction.

"Nice to finally meet you, Brenda." Vivian's voice held the same relaxing drawl as her husband's. The petite blonde lowered her fork and pushed aside her wispy bangs with the back of her small hand. "Dale's told me so much about you. You know Arthur, right?"

She motioned to Arthur Wallace, who co-owned the agency with Dale, and sat on a tall stool next to a large granite-topped kitchen island.

"Of course." Brenda went over and hugged Arthur, whom she'd met many times. Seventy-one years old, he carried a soft spread through his midsection and had full, puffy red cheeks. The overhead lights reflected a shimmer off his tall forehead, which extended nearly to the crown of his head, before his thick gray curly hair began. Brenda also hugged his wife, Kay, a slender woman with shoulder-length gray hair tied back into a low ponytail.

While they discussed Brenda's latest book, Dale and Vivian's sons came running into the kitchen, asking for some cookies. A proud mother's beam surrounded Vivian's round face as she introduced eleven-year-old Kevin and his brother Jared, four years younger. Treats received, they ran back to their video game.

The doorbell rang. Vivian wiped her hands on a dish towel and stepped away to answer. Brenda leaned against the counter and took advantage of her clear view to the foyer. The front door swung open. CJ entered...minus the girlfriend.

He embraced Vivian, but midhug he spotted Brenda. The lift of his brows suggested surprise, at once replaced by a warm glow which gave off a spark that landed right at Brenda's feet. He released the hug and handed Vivian a bottle of wine.

Brenda leaned close to Reggie. "Guess who's definitely coming to dinner?"

"Mmmm, Sidney Poitier?"

Brenda tipped her head. "Always a wise comeback, huh?"

"Oh well." Reggie's mouth turned upward into a satisfied

expression. "It's not a fix-up."

"Your mother always said you should've been a lawyer," Brenda mumbled as CJ entered the room.

His gaze homed in on Brenda and lingered, well past the normal zone of comfort. The same carnal craving she had experienced five days earlier at the bookstore nearly immobilized her again. Her face warmed but she hoped the others thought it from the Chardonnay. Somehow, she managed to exchange a proper greeting.

Once the welcoming exchanges were finished, Arthur launched into a rant about a rumored sports trade. CJ jumped in with his own strong opinions on the matter, only stopped by the boys' shouts of delight as they ran into the room, their footsteps carrying the sound of a small army.

"Uncle CJ!" Dale's sons circled him. "Come try our new Xbox game. It's awesome."

"Aw, come on boys." Dale sent an apologetic glance toward CJ. "Give him a chance to talk to the adults for a little while."

CJ smiled and held up a palm at Dale. "I'm a man who never passes up on anything described as awesome."

The kids each took a hand and dragged CJ away. On his way out, his gaze caught Brenda's and he winked. She flushed, its power whooshing through her like a hot summer breeze.

She joined in on the conversation, which turned from sports and to politics. She hoped that nobody would bring up the recent news about the fraud at Jack's firm or the accusations against him.

Every now and then a disappointed "aaawww" or a roar of delight came from the family room. Curious, Brenda finished the last of her wine and walked down a long hallway toward the sounds. Leaning against the doorjamb, she observed CJ and the boys at play.

CJ's sports jacket was flung over the sofa arm. He sat Indian-style on the carpeted floor in front of a flat-screen TV, dressed comfortably in faded blue jeans and a crisp dress shirt, sandwiched between the two boys. All three gripped their remotes as if the electronic weapons possessed lifesaving powers.

"OK. Now hit that one." Jared, the younger boy, pointed to one of the objects. "You get extra points."

CJ zapped it and his score rose. He and Jared slapped their palms in a high five. Another object appeared from the side of the screen.

"What are those things?" CJ pointed at a squiggly creature.

"Don't let them hit you or you'll die," Kevin warned in a tone so serious only a fool would ignore the warning. CJ swerved his character.

Footsteps made Brenda turn.

"Those boys love CJ." Vivian said as she approached. She stopped at a closet in the hallway and opened the door. "He's Kevin's godfather."

A quick calculation told Brenda that Dale and his wife must have been friends with CJ for more than eleven years, which meant CJ's wife was alive when he'd been named godfather; Vivian must have known Carla.

Brenda stepped away from the family room opening. "He seems to enjoy them, too. Can I help you with anything?"

"Sure." Vivian reached for a large ceramic platter. She handed the dish to Brenda and stretched toward the top shelf. "Dale's glad you and CJ are working so well together." She took down a bowl and hugged it to her chest. "They're quite close. I shouldn't admit this, but I think Dale had other motives for inviting you both here tonight, even though he wouldn't tell me." Her smile forced a few minor wrinkles at the corners of her eyes, set against otherwise peach-perfect skin.

Brenda chuckled. "Yes. Reggie too." She gave a short pause.

"You said CJ is Kevin's godfather." Even though CJ was far enough away, she lowered her voice. "You must have known his wife."

Vivian nodded and refocused her efforts in the closet. Her cheeks sank as the happiness vanished. "Yes. We all miss her." A breathiness in Vivian's voice spoke of great sadness. She glanced toward the family room and the despair on her face was replaced with a let's-not-discuss-this-here look. She handed a small platter and bowl to Brenda. "Could you put those in the kitchen? How about after dinner I give you a tour of the house?"

"Sure." Brenda walked down the hall. Maybe later tonight Vivian would provide an answer to the question CJ seemed unwilling to answer himself.

* * *

With ten minutes until dinner, Brenda wandered Vivian's backyard gardens, located off a large patio. Both women shared a love of gardening. The flat area contained layers of flower beds connected through a variety of arched trellises, adding mystery and depth to the outdoor space.

Brenda thought about how CJ had behaved around the boys — another unexpected layer to this complicated man.

A warmer-than-usual April day disappeared as the sun hovered at the horizon and dusk delivered a chill to the air. Brenda followed a bluestone walkway flanked on both sides by shrubbery. Many of the shrubs had kept their green leaves during the cold winter months and others were beginning to bud in the warm spring temperatures. Underneath weatherworn woodchips, summer perennials were just becoming visible, offering a promise of vibrant color. Once the bright red tulips and cheery daffodils finished their act, they'd get their turn to shine.

Although Brenda would never admit it to Reggie, CJ's

arrival earlier had made her feel like she was glowing. His presence drew her out of the dark place she'd retreated to after losing Jack. Jack had affected her much the same way when they had met in college. He had offered her a bright light after the gloom of her childhood, his own dark history bonding them in a strange way.

CJ had a past too. Brenda sensed he searched for a light, something to help him move beyond whatever it was that troubled him.

At a bend in the path, Brenda discovered a welcoming alcove where a wooden bench faced a dry pond. She sat and enjoyed the chirping birds in their chatty quest to hunker down before sunset. Two chubby cherubs sitting on a rock with the inscription "Love grows here" faced the bench seat. Their serious and thoughtful expressions were aimed in her direction.

Would she have come if she had known that CJ was going to be there? Brenda wasn't sure. When they were younger, Reggie's gentle coercion often kept her from shying away from social situations. Reggie chided Brenda's lack of spontaneity. While Brenda pursued her graduate degree, she learned that children who grew up in alcoholic households often had difficulty having fun, taking themselves too seriously. As she grew up, the pendulum in her household swung from somber and sad one day to normal, even enjoyable, the next. By middle school the pendulum had slowed with more bad days than good. The good ones weren't great, just less threatening. Reggie's interference had helped her social life become normal.

The patio door opened and footsteps tapped lightly on the walkway. CJ rounded the corner. "Vivian said you were outside." His husky voice filled the quiet, crisp air. "Thought I'd say hello, away from the commotion."

"I'm glad you did." Brenda scooted over and patted the bench. "Have a seat."

In the tight space, his leg touched hers but neither moved. The smell of soap mixed with sandalwood made her want to cozy up to his neck and breathe him in at close range.

"I didn't know you'd be here tonight." He turned his head and met her gaze. "It was a pleasant surprise."

"I found out about you on the way over. Maybe we're the unwitting victims of a conspiracy."

"Wouldn't be the first time." His lips tumbled into a shy smile. "It's not always good…but this time it is."

The comment threw her off guard. He was blatantly flirting. But what of his sexy girlfriend? Why would he tempt her when he wasn't available?

"These days, Reggie's pastime has been introducing me to unsuspecting single men." Brenda said. "Then again, you're attached so this doesn't count."

"Autumn and I aren't serious."

"Really?" She remembered Autumn hanging off his arm at the conference and bet that she thought otherwise. "Well, I wouldn't think you'd need the help anyway. Not with the vast array of young beauties at your fingertips." Brenda couldn't stop herself from sniping at him. "At least based on the Internet pictures I've seen."

He raised his dark brows but said nothing.

Brenda gathered her pettiness into a huddle for a reality check. "I mean, well, you don't seem to have trouble finding female companions."

"They're not relationships, just dates. Big difference. Besides, Dale's views on most of my choices are similar to yours, only he tells me more gently."

"I knew I liked Dale." She hoped the joke would help smooth things over.

They sat for a moment, surrounded by silence. Even the slightest movement was noticeable. CJ leaned forward, placing his palms on his knees. His warm thigh pressed against hers. She inspected his hands, sturdy with thick knuckles but well groomed. How would they feel against the soft skin of her cheek or caressing the curve of her waist? Brenda shifted her attention to the garden cherubs, almost daring the figurine to use its magic.

Suddenly CJ sat upright. "What if we hadn't met before tonight and this was our first time?" His expression glowed, like he'd just discovered a hundred-dollar bill in his pocket after spending his last dime. "Say our friends introduced us."

"If we're playing truth, I'll take the dare."

"My dare could be worse."

"I might ask you the same question. Why don't you answer first?"

"OK." His fingers smoothed his chin. "Well, let me see…" His head moved as he inspected her, taking her in from top to toe.

"Oh, for heaven's sake. You act like you're buying a horse. Next you'll want to check my teeth."

A grin slipped through his focused scrutiny. "Hmm…if my friends introduced me to a woman as pretty, intelligent, and engaging as you, I'd be wondering what the best way would be to thank them for introducing us."

Brenda laughed. "You're so smooth I'll bet your middle name is butter."

"I'm not trying to be smooth." His words were even. "Just honest."

"OK. If we're being honest, I wouldn't be disappointed with you either."

He stared at her with satisfaction.

Her voice softened. "I enjoyed our time together in the city."

His expression shifted to a longing that gripped her with surprising force. The slight part of his full lower lip caught her attention, a beckoning and suggestive gesture, prompting her mind to run amok with curiosity as to how his lips would feel pressed against hers.

The sound of laughter from inside the house brought her back to reality. She glanced at the brightly lit kitchen through the tree branches, a reminder that others were nearby. "So, did you enjoy the Xbox game?"

"I sure did. I love coming over here. Playing with the boys makes me feel young again."

"You don't have any kids of your own?"

"No."

She wondered why, but changed the subject. "Remember when the first video game came out? The black screen with the moving cursor and two paddles. It amused me for hours. I can't remember the name."

"Pong." He nodded. "My favorite too. Along with Pac-Man and Frogger. Today kids would call them all lame." He chuckled, but his next words carried a sarcastic bite. "I'm pretty sure Autumn would call it lame too."

"I wish you wouldn't bait me." She grinned. "Haven't you noticed I do well enough on my own?"

An amused sparkle radiated from his eyes. "Yes. You certainly do."

"My kids' pediatric dentist had Ms. Pac-Man in the waiting room. I always hoped the dentist would run late so we could play."

"A pediatric dentist?" CJ's forehead wrinkled in confusion as if she'd spoken another language.

"They're the new thing. Disneyland for dental work. Taking the fear out of dentistry for children by letting them stare at a cartoon while their tooth is being filled." She shrugged. "Hey, if I could've pulled off being under eighteen, I'd have been a patient."

"Jesus, what next?" CJ shook his head, the dismay obvious. "Childbirth in the Caribbean? Get a tan and have a piña colada while you deliver?"

"Now you're getting the idea."

"We're such an overindulged society."

Brenda noted his cynical comment, but after seeing this side of him emerge a few times, she had begun to find it endearing. The curmudgeon book she'd seen at his house, and the inscription from his wife, now made sense. A chilly breeze rustled through the bushes and Brenda rubbed her arms.

CJ watched her. "Cold?"

"A little."

Without hesitation, he reached behind her back. His warm hand landed on her shoulder, then rubbed with slow movement, warming her in places besides her upper arm.

Embraced in his secure hold, Brenda's desire to kiss him returned. She dared to look up. CJ gazed at her. She watched for a signal but, like a rusty baseball pitcher who'd been benched for a long time, the catcher's gestures no longer held meaning. The wrong pitch could make them both feel foolish. His lips parted slightly, and hers did the same. The movement of her chest with each breath seemed magnified.

"Hey, you guys." Vivian shouted from the direction of the house. "Dinner's on."

CJ cleared his throat and removed his arm. "Ready to head inside?"

"Sure." She shook off the moment of unsteady anticipation, but she wished for just one more minute alone with CJ.

He stood and extended his bent arm. She raised a quizzical brow, surprised by the chivalrous gesture. Jack had never been the most gallant guy in the world, and this type of treatment was foreign.

"After four years of ROTC in high school, I've never

forgotten how to treat a lady. Or would you prefer this?" CJ launched into a poor British accent. "It occurs to me, Mrs. McAllister, your attire is not proper for these cold temperatures. However, you appear quite pleasing to my eye." He arched one brow for emphasis. "May I escort you to the building?"

Brenda stifled a laugh. "Who's that supposed to be?"

"Hugh Grant from one of those period pieces." He gave her a lopsided grin. "You told me you liked those eighteenth-century female authors."

"Oh. Are you sure it wasn't Cary Grant?"

He resumed the accent along with the act. "Your mocking behavior reminds me a bit of a most disagreeable woman I met at a conference not terribly long ago. Although I will sadly admit, she left me wanting for more of her." He moved his arm closer, the tone of his voice gentle and caring. "May I?"

She stood and placed her hand on his forearm. They strolled together along the darkened walkway to where the patio light brightened the space. When they reached the door, she stopped.

"Well, Hugh or Cary, or whoever you are...I'm glad to see you again tonight."

He opened the door and waved a hand for her to enter. Resuming his normal voice, he said, "Guess that makes two of us."

Chapter Fifteen

Procrastination nagged at Brenda.

After a busy Saturday running errands, two things remained on her to-do list for this weekend: finish CJ's book, *The Hourglass*, before they met on Monday, and begin her hunt through Jack's office for evidence of his innocence.

Four days had passed since the conversation with Luc. The chances that Jack had buried important documents at home seemed slim, especially since he hadn't even left a suicide note. A dull pain pounded her chest as Brenda found herself once again dragged into the hollow sadness of Jack's hidden world. The details offered by Luc about GBS made the doors to Jack's study even scarier than usual, as if once she entered that room, she might never escape.

The novel won. Tomorrow she'd tackle the office.

Armed with patterns revealed in CJ's other characters, patterns she speculated might be CJ's own, Brenda dived in. Her conversation last night with Vivian had given her more ammunition in her quest to analyze the fictional Ken Blair.

After dinner, Vivian had offered Brenda a tour of the house. In the second-floor Laura Ashley-decorated guest bedroom, Vivian turned to her. "Are you enjoying your work with CJ?"

"So far." Vivian motioned them down the hall and Brenda

followed. "He's different than I expected. We got off to a rough start."

Vivian nodded, as if the news didn't come as a shock. "CJ's bark is worse than his bite." Vivian's tone became solemn. "He changed when he lost his wife."

"So you knew her?"

"Yes." Vivian stared straight ahead. "She was a friend of mine. A lovely woman."

"I'm sorry."

"Thank you." She stopped and met Brenda's gaze. "It was rough on CJ."

"Yes. Losing a spouse is hard."

Vivian laid a hand on Brenda's arm. "Oh, I'm sorry. Of course you know. I'm sure it's been a tough year for you too."

"Thanks." Brenda searched for the right words to pursue her curiosity—less clinical, more caring. "The circumstances around Carla's death must have been difficult. I still see his pain."

Vivian's mouth twisted. "Yes. Difficult." More softly, she added, "Regrettable."

The word hung between them, a million possibilities rambling through Brenda's mind.

"Things got better when he started to write again—" Vivian stopped, interrupted by a small stampede of footsteps pounding on the stairs.

Her sons ran down the hallway and announced that Dad had sent them upstairs to brush their teeth and get to bed.

The word "regrettable" hung in the air, intangible but stifling, like intense humidity. Their conversation on the topic had ended.

Brenda popped a bag of microwave popcorn, grabbed *The Hourglass*, and went straight to the family room. She sank into the soft cushions of the floral sofa, pulled her legs to the side, and tucked her feet close. Georgie waited. When Brenda was settled, the small dog curled into a ball next to her.

A quick glance at the back cover showed a photograph of CJ, perhaps in his late thirties, with a head full of hair but no beard or mustache. He stared into the camera, his dark chestnut gaze still drawing her in, much like the photo on the book Stephanie had purchased for her husband.

Longing for him burst in her chest, an unexpected and deep sensation. Last night at Dale's, a line had been crossed while they talked in the garden. Vivian's call for dinner had interrupted what seemed like an imminent kiss, a moment she'd replayed too many times to count. Was CJ thinking about that moment too? On this Saturday night with Autumn out of town, was he alone or with another woman?

She opened to her place, well into his novel, and eager to finish. The novel wasn't about the Ken Blair character, for which she'd been hired to do a profile, yet she'd learned from Dale that it was the first book CJ wrote after Carla died.

Three hours later, she'd finished. This novel was worth her time.

The Hourglass, a dark thriller, centered on Detective Mark Saunders. Saunders was on the trail of a twisted serial killer who played a demented game. After kidnapping his victims, he contacted the distraught family. He doled out three questions, one at a time, which would lead them to the victim, who he assured them was still alive. They had an hour to try to solve each question, beginning when the killer flipped an old wooden hourglass. After the third clue, if the mystery remained unsolved, he told them they were "out." Usually the murdered bodies were found within weeks.

Detective Saunders got closer to the killer's identity, nearly catching him, infuriating the psychotic madman. Two weeks later, the detective's wife went missing. Soon Saunders learned it was retribution for the near-catch as he became the new focal point of the lunatic's madness. He couldn't save his wife. After her death, hunting down this assassin consumed every waking moment. In the end, he found the lunatic, who pulled a gun on himself—a bittersweet ending. Saunders knew that it did nothing to return his prior life to him.

The gruesome nature of the story wasn't the type of thing Brenda enjoyed, but two facts stood out in the books, so clear they might as well have been bolded, italicized, and underlined: Detective Saunders and Ken Blair both believed they were responsible for the death of a person they loved and neither was able to forgive himself for it.

Did CJ feel responsible for his wife's death?

An unexpected smack on the forehead walloped Brenda, the kind you got when you were looking for the mayonnaise in the fridge and, after several minutes, you realized it was sitting on a shelf in front of you the entire time. For the past year she'd stood in the same shoes as the fictional characters. The idea of self-forgiveness had been pushed from her vocabulary. Not a day passed when she was able to let go of her culpability in Jack's death.

This work with CJ and his character's issues might help her too. Maybe her absolution would begin with tomorrow's search of the office, with helping her husband, who no longer had a voice.

The bottomless ache of CJ's expression the day he revealed to her that his wife had died returned to her. Her professional gut read told her his characters' pain mirrored his own. The theme wasn't a coincidence. The answer to one question would reveal much about CJ and his fictional alter egos: how had Carla Morrison died?

* * *

As a treat that night, Brenda drove to a local restaurant and picked up an early Sunday supper of thin-crust pizza with goat cheese, sundried tomatoes, and extra mozzarella. Food, the quintessential stress reducer, wouldn't eliminate anxiety over Jack's office search, but at least her taste buds would experience a feel-good moment. When she couldn't force down another bite, she thanked God for the band on her sweatpants, cleaned up, and trudged down the hallway to the office.

Bravado made her push open the door quickly, before she could chicken out. Darkness welcomed her. She flipped the light switch and a table and floor lamp both came on. The room remained untouched. Jack could have walked right in and picked up where he'd left off. A large oak desk, given to them by Jack's parents after they purchased the house, held a leather cup of pens and pencils, Post-it notes, and a stapler. Two thick books were stacked in the desk's center.

Brenda crossed the room slowly, as if the hardwood floor had been wired with land mines. She reached the desk and lowered herself into the high-backed leather chair, its anguished creak suggesting it preferred to be vacant. She traced her index finger along the edge of the desk, unsettling particles from a thin layer of dust. Georgie's wet nose nudged her dangling hand, but Brenda scooted her away.

This room had been labeled as Jack's since the first day they moved into the overpriced four-bedroom colonial in the wealthy New York City suburb. Anywhere else in the country, the house would have sold for half the price they paid. Yet the move to this affluent community in particular signaled a step up in the world, which mattered to Jack, even though she'd have been happy anywhere. On moving day, he'd passed her in the hallway, hauling a large box toward the stairs.

He stopped. "Hey, babe, I don't care how you decorate the rest of the house, but I want one room just for me." With his head, he motioned to the office. "This one."

"Will it be like your old apartment?" She crinkled her nose. "If you think for a minute—"

"It won't. I'd just like to claim a little corner of this house. For my gadgets. My guy stuff. Where I can hang out with the guys." He shot her that endearing grin, the one that had won her heart over so many times.

She kissed his stubbly, sweaty cheek. "All right. Are girls allowed inside or is this like 'he-man woman haters club'?" Jack always loved a good *Little Rascals* reference.

"Well, you're allowed." He leered and winked. "I warn you, though—it might get bawdy in there." His brows wiggled in a silly comedic style, and she laughed. His tone then took on a *Twilight Zone* drama and he moved close. "If you dare enter, you can't complain about anything. Cigar smell included."

Brenda pulled a disgusted face and walked away muttering, "We'll see."

Later, after she'd put the kids to bed, she found him sitting on the then-carpeted floor of his new office in the dark, a single beam of light cutting through the room from the hallway. His shoes and socks lay next to him, his back against the wall. He sipped a beer.

"Want company?"

He patted the floor. She nestled herself under his wrapped arm and he offered her the bottle. She took a long sip, then rested her hand on his thigh. Together they shared the drink in the silence after a hectic day. She reached up and twirled a thick curl near his temple with her fingers, and his gaze dropped to meet hers. Jack seemed more content than she'd seen him in months. Brenda stretched her neck to nibble on his earlobe then whispered, "Care to tell me about the bawdy behavior in this men's club?"

They made love in their new house for the first time on the floor, surrounded by boxes.

Brenda warmed thinking about better days, yet the awareness dissolved as her heart flooded with the sadness of how their life together ended. The marriage wasn't perfect. Jack's problems satisfied Brenda's deep-rooted need to save others, her need to keep the ship afloat, her need to be the family problem-solver. The role she had clung to throughout her unstable childhood often caused resentment as an adult. And sometimes Brenda wished somebody would save her for a change.

But Brenda loved Jack. Overall, he was a great provider, hands-on dad, and loving husband. He did the best he could. At least until more recent years.

Had he done his best at work though? Brenda lifted the top book from a pile and brushed off some dust. The title might have made her yawn under normal circumstances. Instead a wave of discomfort rippled through her. *Wiley's Interpretation and Application of Generally Accepted Accounting Principles.* Underneath it, sat the less-than-riveting sequel by Wiley for international business applications.

In past conversations with Jack, he'd told her the book contained the letter of the law for accounting professionals. The remark usually made her mind drift toward thoughts of unloading the dishwasher or folding laundry — both activities being more interesting than accounting rules. Both volumes were marked with Post-it tabs in several places. She flipped to a few of the tabbed sections, then went and got her laptop. The Internet articles in which Jack had been quoted might have touched on these topics. For ten minutes, she played a game of match-the-quote-to-the-accounting-rule. Mining for gold in Connecticut would have been easier.

Pushing the books aside, she pulled open the center drawer. Photos from different periods in their lives peeked out from behind loose papers. She removed items, one piece at a time. A

Father's Day card emerged. A cartoon dad rested on a hammock, sunglasses on, drink in hand. The caption read, "Dad, sit back and relax. If you need anything..." Brenda opened the card. The inside read, "...just ask Mom." She smiled. She remembered the day she had purchased this for Devin and Shannon to give him. After multiple reminders for them to sign the darn thing, they scribbled personal notes of their love, which bore no hint of mom's nagging.

She shoved aside a large bunch of pens. Here they were! She'd often joked that they ran off with the missing socks. A picture surfaced, one of her and Jack taken ten years earlier at the neighbors' Christmas party. On the back, in Brenda's handwriting, it read, "Merry Christmas...I love you." When the neighbor gave her the photo, she wrote the words and tucked it in Jack's stocking on Christmas Eve without much thought.

Tiny pieces of themselves, offered to Jack with little deliberation, told the story of what mattered to a man during his lifetime. Surprised that he had saved the items, tears sprouted and she sniffled but resumed the search. Still, nothing surfaced about work.

The lower drawers on the right side also yielded no results. She tackled the left drawer. A label read Insurance Files. A long-drawn-out yawn slipped out, and she considered giving up. About to stuff the entire pile into the trash, she changed her mind. Instead, she plopped the entire stack on the desk in front of her. One by one she opened each manila folder. Nothing but expired policy notices. The garbage pail at her side gradually filled to the brim.

She almost tossed the last folder without looking inside, but a red tab in the corner stopped her. Brenda opened it and read the words on a bright green Post-it note.

A chill crept over her skin.

Chapter Sixteen

Brenda walked Georgie along a wooded area on the edge of a fifteen-acre nature preserve near her house. The crisp morning air settled on her cheeks, an invigorating sensation after a poor night's rest. The day offered signs of rubbing its tired eyes awake—chirps and rustles in bushes, a car starting in the distance, and a neighbor's bedroom light brightening the window. The rim of burnt orange lining the horizon promised the sun would soon rise.

While waiting for Georgie to investigate a scent, Brenda's thoughts still reeled with the same turmoil that had kept her from a restful sleep. All due to a Post-it note.

The papers inside the folder had contained a series of printed e-mails exchanged between Jack and CEO Bob Manning. She'd read them multiple times and saw that Jack had faced some real problems, but the technical jargon had left her frustrated and confused.

The warning on the lime-green Post-it note in Jack's handwriting, however, shouted a message even a novice number-cruncher would understand: *"BRENDA, DON'T TRUST ANYBODY, EVEN LUC."*

Even Luc? He and Jack had been best friends. Nothing had ever given her reason to see Luc as part of the problem. She needed help, and only one person came to mind who might possess some insights about the note's real meaning: Jack's secretary, Rosie. At that moment, the woman's last name escaped Brenda's memory. She could only think of the name O'Donnell, like the celebrity, but that wasn't right.

Why wouldn't Jack have cautioned her in person? One unsettling reason came to mind—he must have known about her affair with Luc and questioned her allegiance. She shuddered, but not from the chilly air.

Georgie tugged and they moved on. Luc acted as if he wanted to help Jack. Why would he try to help her husband if he had anything to do with this? Brenda wished she'd paid closer attention to Jack's work stories. The diesel engine from a small truck labeled Brad's Best Electric Service disturbed the quiet neighborhood as it made its way to the end of the street and Jack's secretary's name crystallized. "Rosie Bradley—that's it." She glanced around, thankful none of the neighbors were out at this early hour and marveled at the coincidence.

The issue resolved, she now had someone she could turn to for help. Relieved, she gave in to more pleasurable thoughts about the rest of her day. Later this afternoon, she would go to CJ's house for their second and final meeting about his character.

Since Dale's dinner party, she'd anticipated this afternoon's work session with CJ as eagerly as a schoolgirl about to do homework with the object of her latest crush. Every night, as she snuggled under her covers, CJ frolicked on the cusp of her dreams.

She headed home, showered, and dressed for work. The kitchen clock read 8:40. Even though Jack's note said not to trust anybody, he had always held his secretary in high regard. The note probably referred to the inner circle of players higher up. Brenda dialed the main switchboard of GBS. Someone picked up right away.

"May I speak to Rosie Bradley?"

"Hold on, please." The receptionist, bright and perky for early on a Monday morning, transferred the call.

Brenda tried to ignore the pounding pump of her heart and mentally rehearsed her lines. After three rings, a woman answered.

"Hello, Rosie. This is Brenda McAllister." She paused to catch her breath. "Jack's wife."

"Oh, hi Brenda." Rosie's unmistakable voice, gritty around the edges as if rubbed in sandpaper, conveyed her surprise. "It's been a while. How are you and the kids?"

"Getting by. A tough year but we're holding on."

"Well, good. I've thought of you all often. What can I do for you today?"

"I'm calling about what's going on at the office right now." Brenda purposely left it vague to see how Rosie reacted.

Awkward silence hung in the telephone wires.

"Rosie? Are you there?"

"Can I call you back tonight...from home? I think we should talk."

* * *

CJ's attempts to focus on edits of his latest chapter kept getting sidelined. He listened for sounds of Brenda's arrival. After what had happened at the track, he could no longer deny the effect she had on him. Their meeting at Dale's had settled the matter. He hadn't felt this way about any woman for some time.

He tried to quell his anxiety. These days, any little thing seemed to raise his blood pressure to record levels. The doctor had threatened him with a second medication if CJ didn't learn to get it under control.

Yesterday afternoon, while sitting on his deck with a glass of wine to relax, he had remembered an article he'd read about mating rituals among penguins. Writing had always been an outlet for his innermost thoughts, so CJ flew inside and typed an essay titled "Do I Have the Patience of a Penguin?" The article stated that when penguins fell in love, their courting started with the tuxedo-clad couple standing breast to breast, throwing back their heads, and singing in loud voices with outstretched flippers. Later, the male showed his yearning for the female by laying his head upon his partner's stomach. Sometime later, the two waddled to a secluded spot for intercourse, a process lasting about three minutes. Neither then mated again for the rest of the year.

CJ's essay expounded on the lack of both patience and chastity in humans. While writing the story, he recognized a curious fact about himself: he had a strong urge to lay his head on Brenda's stomach.

Friday night in Dale's backyard, he'd come within seconds of kissing her. One thing had stopped him. He worried she might get the wrong impression of him since she seemed well aware of Autumn still lingering in his life. When she returned from her photo shoot tomorrow, he'd end the relationship. Then he'd ask Brenda on a real date, where he'd pursue her guilt-free.

The echoing chime of the doorbell startled CJ. He stood and peeked out the office window. The white Audi he'd seen at Dale's was now parked next to his. He hopped downstairs, a nervous twitter tickling his gut. When he opened the door, Brenda's back was to him. She turned around and the shine of her smile made his nervousness fade.

"Hello." He almost felt a foolish grin appear.

"Hi. I'm admiring your blooming cherry trees." She pointed to the far side of the yard. "What a spectacular view."

CJ did some admiring of his own, the clingy fabric of Brenda's dress providing even lovelier views of her posterior than those he'd enjoyed previously. "Yes. A spectacular view."

"Those dogwoods will flower soon. This is such a beautiful property."

"Thanks. Come in." CJ stepped aside and offered to take her blazer.

CJ had learned a few lessons during his nine-year marriage, starting with how women liked to be complimented when they were dressed nicely. Of course, when a man offered the compliment, it was often about more than the outfit.

"You look nice," he ventured.

"Oh, thanks." The sparkle in her eyes showed the praise had paid off. "I just came from the office. But I hate dressing up. When I wrote my book, I loved working at home one day a week. My attire those days would have been too relaxed even for casual Fridays."

"Trust me" — CJ hung the jacket in the foyer closet — "I take full advantage of that occupational perk. Some days I'm not even fit to answer the door." Today, however, he'd showered, put on aftershave, and even tucked a blue-and-white striped, button-down shirt into his jeans.

He motioned toward the living room. "I had an early lunch, and I've been working nonstop ever since. I'm going to grab us a snack. Take a seat. Want something to drink? Water, soda, wine, seltzer — "

"Wine sounds good."

CJ went to the kitchen. He rummaged through his cabinets for a box of crackers and pulled a wedge of Jarlsberg from the refrigerator. While he arranged everything on a plate, he replayed her beautiful smile at the door, a confirmation of the signals he'd received at Dale's the other evening.

When he reentered the living room, Brenda was leaning over a sofa table examining the photo album he'd left open last night and forgotten about.

She glanced up. "Hope I'm not being too nosy."

"Not at all. Pictures from my Everest climb. Bring it over and have a seat. I'll tell you about the trip."

CJ put the cheese tray on the coffee table, then went behind the bar in the corner of the living room. Brenda picked up the album and walked over to the couch. The soft curves of her hips swayed with each step. He tried to concentrate on dealing with the wine.

He carried two glasses to where she sat. His gaze hiked a trail along her shapely calves, past the tempting curve of her waist, then paused for a split second at the plunge of her neckline, where the peaks of soft mounds teased.

He handed off the drink and joined her on the sofa, shifting sideways and resting his arm along the leather sofa top close to her shoulders. Their knees touched but neither moved.

Brenda took a sip, then placed the glass on the table. "These aren't Everest." She held up several loose snapshots sandwiched in the album, which Larry had passed along to him last weekend at the track.

"A friend gave me those from last season at a race club I belong to."

"Car racing?"

He nodded.

"Do you race a lot?"

"Once in a while, but I mostly like to get out to drive fast."

"I drove fast once." She arched her brow. "Ever have your butt whooped by a girl?"

"Only when you did it at the conference."

She laughed. "Oh, I wasn't *that* bad."

"You were, but I respect a good challenge." He smiled so she'd know any anger from that day was long gone. "You think your Audi can beat my Porsche?"

"Nope, but I take dares seriously."

"As if I didn't know that. Nice car, by the way. I read it's sensible yet sexy and reacts well to challenges." He paused to enjoy her intoxicating gaze and his voice lowered. "Like its owner."

Her ivory skin flushed the color of pink carnations. "Guess I'm sensible."

"What's your top speed?" He assumed she'd say no more than eighty.

She reached for her wine. "I once got a car up to around one hundred."

"You did? Were you late for something?"

She laughed, then sipped her wine. "No. My boyfriend during sophomore year of college drove a 1971 Alfa Romeo GTV. His pride and joy. I bugged him to let me drive. He finally did. I suppose he had ulterior motives."

He nodded. "Smart move on his part."

"He was pretty shocked when he realized how well I handled a stick shift."

"Something not many girls would admit to," CJ teased, but Brenda's devilish grin came as a surprise.

"An old lady like myself can still handle one, in case you're wondering."

He laughed. After she'd blushed at his earlier comment, the bold statement surprised him. "I'll bet you can. Did you live life in the fast lane for long?"

"Nah. Sully, my boyfriend, was one of those bad-boy types. Cheap thrills wear off fast. A month later, I met Jack, my future husband. A more sensible choice, like the Audi." She peered into her drink for a few seconds. "So, how fast do you guys go on the track?"

"I've driven into the one eighties. A few guys at the club have broken two hundred."

"No kidding? I can't even imagine." Brenda lifted one of the racing photos and examined it closely. "Isn't it scary?"

"Not to me."

"What if you were in an accident?"

He shrugged. "I don't let those thoughts cross my mind."

"Never?"

"No." He remembered his loss of control at the track a short week ago, and the strange appearance of Carla's voice. "Allowing the distraction of other thoughts can lead to problems."

She pointed with her chin to the table. "Speaking of risky things, I'm returning the Matthiessen book you loaned me. I can see why it inspired you."

"Do you see a trip in your future?"

"Maybe to a beach resort. I'll wait for them to install the Everest ski lift." She chuckled. "I'm not a big risk taker like you."

She flipped through the remaining album pages, stopping occasionally to ask a question or make a comment. A minute later, she finished and shut the book, then lifted her glass. Leaning back into the sofa, Brenda took another sip of wine. Her lips, the color of faded pink roses, pressed along the rim. He fantasized about kissing her right now, tasting the wine on her full lower lip. When she lowered the glass, she caught him watching.

He cleared his throat, suddenly dry. "Is the wine all right?"

"Very nice." Her words flowed out soft and sexy. Subtly sexy.

He tried to think about something else so he didn't lay his head on her stomach.

* * *

CJ went to the other room to get a pad of paper. Brenda held her disappointment close. His silence after her flirtatious remark made it hard to get a read on him. Either he was sending mixed signals, or she was rustier than she thought.

Brenda put down her glass and reached to the floor to rummage through her bag for her notepad and the book Stephanie wanted signed just as he returned. "I suppose we should tackle the real reason for my visit today."

"Good idea." CJ sat on the couch next to her again. "Why don't you start?"

"Sure. Before we do, can you autograph this for a friend? Her husband is a fan." Brenda handed over the book and pen. "She'd like it to say 'To Don. Happy 45th birthday.'"

He scribbled, then handed the book back.

"Thanks. Now, down to business." She removed her notes and examined them. "Do you mind if we talk this through? Ken's kind of like a patient. I have a few questions for him which I'm hoping you can answer."

"Sure. I'll put my Ken hat on." His eyes squinted with a smile.

"OK, Ken," Brenda played along. "Tell me about Tatiana's death."

"Special Agent Blair meets the woman of his dreams, Tatiana. He leads her into a trap intended to end his life. Instead, it takes hers." The words carried a detached tone. He folded his arms across his chest.

"How did the situation make you feel? After all, you were the intended target."

His gaze fell to the area rug, as if the answers lay beneath the colorful patterns of its weave. "Unfit to be alive. Unfit to love again." CJ lifted his eyes and met hers. His face read like a barometer, shifting to sadness.

"Can you elaborate?"

"Elaborate?" His foot wavered, small uncomfortable movements. Brenda often studied her patients' feet, which never lied and often revealed an unsaid sentiment. "He made a careless decision. Took another person's life. How else could he feel?"

"They're legitimate emotions, but doesn't your character understand things happen over which we have no control?" The words rang true for her own life, yet she pushed the connection aside to concentrate on CJ.

"Sure. He can't forgive himself, though." CJ's voice now had a strained, unemotional tone. "He knew the danger."

"He's not psychic. We leave our homes every day and might run into any number of situations where we might get hurt...or die."

CJ's jaw flexed. "Ken made a choice. He put her in harm's way. He must live with the regret. That's different than what you described."

"OK, let's suppose Ken's not completely unreasonable. Couldn't there be some parameters limiting his self-abasement?"

"His carelessness cost another person her life. A perfect reason to self-abase, in my opinion."

"Still, isn't it irrational to beat oneself up for such a long time?" She waited a few seconds. "I mean, Ken pines over two more books, right?"

"Yes. I do understand that." CJ shifted in his seat. "That's why I'm trying to move forward with the character. Those were my grounds for hiring you."

The outside light showcased tiny amber flecks in CJ's brown eyes. Behind those eyes lay pain. Brenda questioned who they were really discussing.

"Tell me about Detective Saunders. He and Agent Blair have similar paths."

CJ's eyes widened. "You finished *The Hourglass*?"

"Tough book to put down." She took a sip of her wine. "Well done."

"Thanks. And yes, there are similarities between the two characters. They both lost people who mattered a great deal to them. Both believe they could've stopped it." As he spoke, his arms stayed wrapped tight to his broad chest. His struggle to stay detached seemed obvious, leaving Brenda with one conclusion: none of this story rested in pure fiction or pure coincidence.

"Something wrong?" CJ put a stop to her analysis.

"No. Mind if I ask *you* a personal question?"

"You can try."

Brenda spoke softly, less clinically, more like a friend. "How'd your wife die?"

He uncrossed his arms. His flattened palm covered his mouth, then it glided down to his chin. "A car accident."

"May I ask what happened?"

His arms recrossed. "I'd rather not discuss this."

"Oh." The same words Jack had uttered on numerous occasions stung Brenda's old wounds. "Why?"

"Brenda." A sharp edge pierced CJ's tone. "I'm not ready to talk about it."

The refusal released a familiar, irritating flow through her veins, yet this time she pushed forward. "With me or anybody?"

The lines of his face pulled taut. He didn't answer.

"Come on, CJ. You must have discussed what happened with someone over the years."

"Yes. The police and the insurance company. Once with Dale. He was kind enough not to bring the matter up again."

Brenda placed her pad down and leaned forward. "Can I be honest with you?"

He held a long, pointed stare. "Go ahead."

"I believe Ken's inability to move forward is your own."

He lifted his glass of wine and took a long swig. "Then I'm afraid you're confusing reality with fiction." His tone was terse and laced with annoyance.

The answer hit her with the force of a door bumping her in

the rear on the way out. Shut out again. First by her mother. Then Jack. Now CJ.

"Maybe. Or are *you* confusing them?" She lowered her glass. "Your reluctance to answer my question is quite telling."

"Stop pushing. Please."

"Fine." A familiar sensation revved inside her, one present when she couldn't let something go. "Here's my clinical assessment of...Ken." She stopped short of an eye roll but made enough of a face to make her point. CJ drained his glass and plunked it on the glass coffee tabletop with a little more force than necessary. "Your character suffers from the effects of long-term trauma. The primary way the trauma manifests itself is through avoidance. Avoidance numbs his pain, especially when he keeps away from women who remind him of his lover."

CJ's lips moved into a grim twist but he stayed silent.

"He pursues extreme danger, a strange contradiction in my opinion. He'll take risks in other ways but not with his heart."

His posture stiffened and when she stopped he mumbled, "Anything else?"

"Oh sure. The women he selects are far from what he desires. Even though quite sexually appealing, they seem to irritate him. He's come up with this handy form of punishment to ease the guilt over the part he played in Tatiana's death."

CJ stared at his hands. He quietly asked, "How does it stop?"

"How does it stop?" She threw her arms up. "Any of this hit home yet?"

His deep voice crashed like a clap of thunder. "If I wanted you to analyze me, I'd have shown up at your office for an appointment."

"I doubt that." The sarcastic roll of a chuckle carried each syllable. "Hiring a professional to analyze your character is easier than going for help. You're not hiding anything, CJ. The first time I asked about your wife, I saw your agony." The angry burn on his cheeks contradicted the sadness of his expression. She reached out and laid a gentle hand on his forearm. "It's OK to miss somebody, but holding on to the pain for so long isn't healthy."

He shrugged off her touch, then stood and paced to the sliding glass doors where he pocketed his hands and stared outside.

The muscles of his back flexed and, despite his irritation, she persisted. "Are you denying your circumstances aren't tied into this?"

"No."

"Do you think you could have saved your wife?"

"Stop!" He spun around, the pain gone, replaced with 100 percent pure rage. "You don't know what happened!"

She knew she should stop, but getting him to talk suddenly became personal. "Exactly. Because you won't discuss it."

"God, you're like a mallet." A dark cloud shadowed his face. "I can't believe you won't stop talking. Do you treat your patients this way?"

"Well, no. But—"

"Did you do this to your husband?" An angry scarlet burn coated his neck and cheeks.

The question stung like a hard slap.

"That was out of line," CJ mumbled. "I'm sorry."

Did she do that to Jack?

"I didn't mean what I said." His scratchy voice crackled.

CJ's words faded behind the white noise of her thoughts. She'd pushed him. Pushed him hard, the way she'd do with anybody she cared about. CJ seemed like more of a fighter than Jack, but she never dreamed his assault would hurt her this much.

Every argument with her husband ran through her mind.

Every angry retort. Every snippy dig. Now the outcome was so clear; when she'd pushed Jack, he'd pushed the other way. With all her training, how had she missed that?

The answer hit, along with a familiar sick pit in her gut. She pushed her husband because it was what she'd always wanted to do as a kid when her mother drank. Fear prevented her from ever doing that with her mother. Fear of getting in trouble. Fear of making her mother angrier. Fear of her mother becoming more distant.

CJ's words hurt, but she finally saw something. If Jack hadn't shut her out and failed to communicate, things could have been different. Yes, she'd handled Jack in a way that suited her state of mind and ignored what he needed.

"Brenda, I shouldn't have—"

She held out her hand for him to stop. "Every day since I found him dead, I've asked myself how I let his suicide happen. His downfall came at me like a slow train." She shook her head. "I stood in its path. Tried everything to stop it. Until now, I'd never stopped to consider how my hounding might have added to his problems."

"Don't be ridiculous." CJ moved closer to her. "My comment was said in anger."

Brenda didn't care about his explanation. Over his shoulder, she spotted a ficus tree across the room. Around its base lay several dried leaves. Every single time she purchased a houseplant, it died. Repeated replacements became an obsession. One currently nestled in a sunny corner of her three-season room already showed signs of its demise. Did her brown thumb extend to those she cared about? Maybe she couldn't control some things.

Nate's remark on the beach returned. Perhaps his theory was right. Everything that happens is exactly what is supposed to happen. Our actions can't prevent what's meant to be. She didn't want to believe the theory held any truth. But when it came to those she loved, she hadn't been able to help. In fact, helping those she loved was only making her tired. Nobody really wanted her to fix their problems, only enable them to continue, accept, and nurture them through their crisis. Even CJ had only hired her to help with his stupid book. He wasn't interested in finding out that his character was a surrogate for his own problems. Why did she always need to repair the damage anyway?

Brenda stood and began gathering her things. "You know what? Jack never gave me answers. Just like you. So screw you both!"

"What? I—"

"There's one reason I cared about your wife's death." She stopped stuffing a notebook into her bag and faced him. "I give a damn about *you*." She poked her index finger into his chest. "Not your character. You."

"Calm down. Let's—"

"Don't tell me to calm down. You're the one who pleaded for assistance with the book. I'm through. Find someone else to help with your writer's block."

"Come on, Brenda. This is getting away from us."

"I've got news for you. It's gone."

His mouth opened, but when she glowered, it closed. Although her anger often snowed under her better senses, his apology still rang in her ears. She shut her eyes and pinched the bridge of her nose so tight the pressure might leave marks. How did this get out of control? Everything about CJ was now personal. Worse, she'd revealed her hand, told him she cared about him. His reaction, asking her to calm down, left her embarrassed.

When she opened her eyes, a tear rolled down her face. She quickly swiped it away and turned to gather her things. CJ moved close and wrapped her in his arms. She tried to pull away but he held her tight.

"Please don't go." All anger had left CJ's voice, replaced by a gentle tone. "I'm truly sorry. Thanks for caring enough about me to push."

Her head fell to his chest. Jack had never offered that kind of thanks. CJ stroked her hair. She surrendered to the soothing touch.

"No. I'm sorry," she mumbled. "My behavior hasn't been professional at all. Maybe I did it to my husband too."

"Only out of concern." He paused. "Like you did with me."

She lifted her head. Mascara dotted his shirt. "Oh, no. Look—"

"Brenda. I don't care about my shirt." He lifted her chin. "There's truth to what you said. I'd do anything to take back how I just hurt you. I care about you too." His eyes searched hers as if nothing else mattered other than her mercy.

The depth of his request owned her. "I forgive you, CJ."

He leaned close. His lips found hers and caressed them with tender control while he cupped her face. She slipped her arms around his neck. Their breaths mingled and, with each passing second, the kiss deepened. Soft strokes of his mouth mixed with the bristle of his whiskers against her skin.

She moaned, low and guttural. CJ's strong hands traveled the curve of her waist. She pressed herself to him, urging for more. He possessively reached around and pressed his hand firmly to her backside, pulling her hips against his body. Every nerve ending sizzled, untouched for too long. CJ finally pulled back and gazed into her eyes. He traced the side of her face with a single finger, one possessing the power to further weaken her knees. "I've wanted to do that for some time."

"Me too."

The doorbell chimed.

CJ's forehead furrowed. "I'm not expecting anyone." He kissed her softly. "I'll be right back."

Brenda ran her fingers beneath her lower lashes to wipe away any signs of tears. The next words she heard sounded like shattering glass.

"Surprise!" Autumn's high-pitched voice resonated through the house.

Chapter Seventeen

Thank God looks couldn't kill. If they could, Brenda suspected she'd have been the recipient of some serious pain.

Autumn's gaze swung back and forth between them, like a laser. "What's going on here?"

Compared to the last time Brenda saw her, the leggy stunner's skin glistened in a beachy-bronze tone. Placing her slender tan arms akimbo, Autumn glared, but the tight lines of anger on her face didn't mar her beautiful profile.

"We're working," CJ answered firmly, as if he didn't appreciate the allegation. "I mentioned Brenda would be helping with my book."

Autumn motioned to the wineglass on the coffee table. "You call that working?"

Brenda was painfully conscious of the other obvious clues about what they'd been up to. She tried, in a not so obvious way, to smooth her hair and straighten out the slight lopsided tilt to her dress. No sense in giving the perturbed model more kindling to toss on the bonfire.

"I don't appreciate your accusation. I'm glad you're back early, but a call would have been nice."

Was he happy? Brenda tried to keep a neutral face.

"Why?" Autumn snapped. "So you two could stop whatever you've been up to?"

CJ's jaw tightened like a pulled-back rubber band, prelaunch.

"I should leave anyway." Brenda looked at CJ. "We've covered a lot and I have enough background to sum up my analysis."

"I'll walk out with you." CJ glanced at Autumn. "When I come back in, we'll talk."

Autumn folded her arms across her ample chest and nodded but never took her glare off Brenda.

Outside, once they'd reached Brenda's car, CJ slid his hand into hers. "I'm sorry. That shouldn't have happened."

"Our kiss or Autumn's homecoming?"

"Both. I have no regrets about kissing you. I've wanted to ask you out. I mean, only after I end things with Autumn, which I planned on doing when she returned tomorrow." He shrugged.

Brenda sensed his disappointment in what he'd done. "Don't beat yourself up. I let you kiss me and figured you were still dating her." Another minor indiscretion, on top of the major one with Luc, forced her to question her moral fiber. "What will you tell her?"

"The truth. Things between us were cooling down before she left and maybe I was wrong to delay ending things. With her full schedule, I honestly believed the news would be easier when she returned."

"What if she asks about us?"

"Also the truth." He squeezed her hand. "Something's been brewing inside me for you since the day we met."

Brenda tried to conceal her laughter, but a chortle escaped. "My dear Mr. Morrison, I didn't leave the Hyatt thinking you thought well of me. So, did the thoroughness with which I dabbed off the spilled coffee impress you?" She raised an eyebrow.

"Mmm, something like that." He smiled and pressed his lips to hers.

Brenda slid into the car. When she turned to say good-bye, CJ held the same intensity on his face that he'd possessed before the doorbell had interrupted.

"I'll call you." He gently traced her cheek with his finger as his gaze rested on her several seconds longer.

Thirty minutes later, Brenda pulled into her driveway. Inside the house, Georgie greeted her with an enthusiasm usually reserved for pop stars. Even though a neighbor had let her out, Brenda felt guilty about not coming home at her normal hour. She checked her answering machine. The only message was from her daughter. Nothing from Rosie, Jack's former secretary.

Brenda threw on some old jeans, a T-shirt, and an oversized Irish cardigan sweater of Jack's, now stored in her closet. The sweater was purchased in Ireland during their honeymoon, and she always regretted not purchasing one herself, indulging instead in a Claddagh ring, Waterford crystal, and a lace tablecloth. On a chilly winter's night, Brenda often slipped on the thick sweater and waltzed downstairs like it was hers. Jack would remind her, teasingly, that his closet wasn't a secondhand store. She now pressed the soft lapel against her face and inhaled his disappearing, clean scent. For the past year, the sweater was the closest she'd come to feeling his arms around her.

Heading downstairs, she filled Georgie's bowl with kibble and made her dinner, a peanut butter-and-jelly on whole-wheat bread. When finished, the pair went out to the backyard. Georgie sniffed along the lawn while Brenda sat on a weathered teak bench. Stars scattered in the dark sky made it sparkle. The heavenly facade, so simple on the surface, was filled with complexities science had yet to discover. Her journey of discovery felt almost as intricate. She pulled Jack's thick sweater tight around her body, but this time she longed for CJ's embrace.

Brenda remembered Rosie Bradley, the only person she could think of to turn to for answers about Jack's work life. Had her husband's secretary been privy to the inner workings of his day? If so, how comfortable would she be opening up to Brenda?

The two women had seen each other once or twice a year, when Brenda visited Jack for lunch or at the office Christmas party. Jack adored this woman. Once he stated, "Rosie always looks out for my ass." Brenda had replied, "So? I look at your ass too." He gave her the universal "that's not funny" expression. Jack liked to be the one making the jokes.

Georgie came to Brenda's side, poked her leg for attention, and jumped up on her lap. Brenda pressed her cheek against her canine cohort, thankful for her companionship over the past year. A minute later, the phone rang and Brenda ran inside.

"Brenda? Rosie Bradley. Sorry I wasn't able to talk earlier."

"Don't worry. Thanks so much for calling me back."

"In light of what's going on, I'm not shocked you called." The nervousness that had filled Rosie's voice that morning was gone. "The newspaper accounts have left out tons. Behind the scenes, the company executives at the firm are in an uproar."

Jack had always liked his assistant's tell-it-like-it-is attitude. Now Brenda understood what he meant.

"My guess is more will become available to the public when the auditors complete their research." While Rosie spoke, Brenda scurried to Jack's office and grabbed the manila "insurance" folder off his desk. "Plus, the lawyers will go through everything, and who knows what'll come out? So, I'm curious about why you called."

She returned to the kitchen. "I have good reason to believe Jack may not have acted alone in committing the accounting fraud, as Bob Manning suggested to the press." Brenda sat on a stool next to the peninsula. "You spent more time with Jack than anybody. So, I have one question. Do you believe Jack took it upon himself to commit fraud?"

"Not in a million years." Rosie's unequivocal answer sent a wave of anticipation through Brenda.

"Why?"

Silence carried over the phone wires. Brenda worked hard to hold her tongue still.

Rosie sighed, loud enough for Brenda to hear the whoosh over the phone. "I could get in a lot of trouble for sharing this, you know."

"I know. Jack always felt like you watched out for him. His reputation is about to be ruined, and he's not even here to defend himself. I'm trying to do what I can to get to the truth."

"Jack was a great boss." Rosie's voice dipped with obvious sadness. There was a long pause. "I think Bob Manning is behind this."

Brenda remembered his threat at the fitness club, the scared look on his face. "Why?"

"He's done some peculiar things. Like the day Jack died, he came to me and asked me to lock Jack's office door and hand over the keys. And to call you to get Jack's copy. Right away."

"I remember."

"He also told me to keep the cleaning service out, and he said if I needed access, I should let him know." She hesitated for a second. "I didn't tell him I had a spare key."

If Brenda were a dog, her ears would have perked up. Jack used to claim if he were to march into battle, he wanted Rosie at his side.

"I waited." Rosie's grainy voice sounded determined. "Four days after Jack's funeral, Mr. Manning left for a big powwow in the Paris office with several other VPs. After he was gone, I let myself inside."

Brenda remembered that Luc had attended the Paris meeting too. Jack wasn't scheduled to go, which seemed odd.

"Around the same time, I'd heard office gossip about some of the...uh...I guess you'd call them 'techniques' being misused in accounting."

"Like what?" Brenda tried to pay close attention, hoping some of what she'd read in those thick books would make sense.

"A couple accountants on the staff claimed the higher-ups were doing things bordering on fraud. Someone told me Jack might be involved, although I didn't believe them. Adding Mr. Manning's strange behavior to the equation, something wasn't right."

"Did you find anything?"

"Not at first, but while I organized, I found some papers tucked away in Jack's top drawer. A stack of printed e-mails between Jack and Mr. Manning."

Brenda stopped herself from gasping. The contents sounded the same as she'd found in Jack's desk. A duplicate "insurance" set?

"Keeping the hard copy wasn't office procedure. We usually archived important e-mail into a special folder through his e-mail account. Our policy is to keep as much electronically stored as possible. I didn't know if the papers were shoved in back because he intended to hide them or if it was his usual sloppy filing system." Her throaty chuckle sounded like static through the phone. "Your husband was pretty messy."

"Yes. He did those things at home too." His messes annoyed her, but after he died Brenda would have welcomed one of his piles.

"I read the e-mails. I didn't understand the nature of them, but my gut told me they were important, so I put them in a folder and filed them in a cabinet where he kept supplies and some old accounting journals. Here's the weird thing." Brenda held her breath, hoping for a clue. Any clue. "An accountant asked me for a folder stored in Jack's office. I asked Mr. Manning for the key, so he didn't get suspicious if he found out I'd been in there. When I walked in, right away I knew somebody else had gone inside."

"How?"

"The chair was moved away from his desk and left near one of the cabinets." Rosie paused. "Oh, and the closet door wasn't closed tight."

"Are you sure you didn't leave them that way?"

"Mrs. McAllister, Jack always told me I had Felix Unger syndrome. Trust me. I left the chair facing the desk and pushed in and the closet door shut tight. I'd even stored some old annual reports in there and bumped the door closed tight with my hip. That door always got a little stuck."

With those kinds of details, Brenda believed her.

"Everything seemed suspicious after that, so I check other things in the office. The top drawer I'd cleaned was a mess again, like someone had been looking for something. Then I remembered those strange messages I'd filed."

"Had you locked the cabinet?"

"Normally I would have, but I figured nobody would be in there. I went to the spot where I'd put the file and guess what?"

"What?"

"The file was gone."

"Could you have misfiled it?"

"No. I rechecked the entire drawer. Even went through the other three in case I made a mistake, ya know? Other strange stuff suddenly seemed important."

"Like what?" Brenda tried not to sound overly anxious.

"A bunch of times, after Jack returned from Mr. Manning's office, he seemed frustrated."

Brenda's anger at Bob Manning swelled. "Anything else?"

"Hmmm, well…" Rosie hedged. "I'm not really sure if it's related."

"Why don't you let me decide? I need any information I can get."

"Well, keep in mind I didn't catch every word, but about a week before your husband died, he and Luc Pelletier had a huge argument in Jack's office."

The particulars of that week stood out like black against white. Not once did either Jack or Luc mention the fight. In fact, that was the week Jack sent his odd e-mail to Devin. The week he showed unexplained anger toward her but wouldn't say why.

"Did you hear any details?" Brenda's heart beat faster, pulsing with hope that the next statement would send her across the finish line of this race into Jack's past.

Rosie hesitated. "Not really."

"Please, Rosie. Anything might help."

"Bob's name kept coming up. I figured they meant Mr. Manning. A lot of what they discussed wasn't very clear." Rosie stopped. She swallowed loudly a few times, as if she was drinking water. "You know, after he died and I found those e-mails, I figured maybe this was what they fought about." She waited a beat as if she were rethinking the argument. "Toward the end of their fight, I heard your name a few times."

"My name?" Brenda's mouth went drier than the Sahara. "Why?"

"I don't know." Rosie paused. "A short while later, Mr. Pelletier stormed out without saying good-bye. Jack slammed the door shut behind him."

Brenda's body numbed. If Rosie suspected more, she certainly wasn't going to say. Maybe she wanted to save Brenda the humiliation.

"Back to the missing file." Brenda changed the subject. "The only person who could have gone in there was Bob. He had all the keys."

"Except for one. I'd completely forgotten about it until the day I realized the file went missing."

"Who else had a key?"

"Luc Pelletier."

* * *

CJ closed the front door behind Autumn. The breakup had gone poorly. They usually did. He blamed himself. Since losing Carla, his dating life had been a self-sabotaging pursuit, leaving innocent victims in its wake.

The kiss with Brenda had changed everything.

CJ wandered into the kitchen to heat some leftover pasta, suddenly noticing the sparse comforts in the room. The reclusive home, a refuge after the loss of his wife, had been furnished, but was empty of the kind of personal touches that Carla had brought into his life when they had joined households.

He settled at the small kitchen table, positioned to allow a view of the wooded backyard, now shrouded in the settling darkness. CJ let out a long breath, filled with a sense of relief at the end of another empty relationship. The checkered flag had finally dropped, putting an end to his punishing race against his own feelings. The post-Carla choices were all empty liaisons. Choices with obvious flaws. Choices he'd never consider ideal mates.

Brenda's dead-on assessment shocked him. She was right. He and Ken lived parallel lives. He'd known for some time, lately even tried to push Ken forward in the story in the hope that it would help him change his own life. That tactic hadn't worked out for him or his fictional alter ego. With the reasons behind his behavior spoken out loud by Brenda, he'd been granted permission to admit how much he missed what a real relationship had to offer — with any luck, a relationship with her.

The clang of his fork against the ceramic bowl drew attention to the quiet settling over the house. Normally he reveled in the silence, but tonight the quiet left him feeling as hollow as an empty barrel. He turned on the radio and grabbed the newspaper for company while he finished eating.

CJ used to take pride in his toughness, but these days he felt like a piece of fraying fabric, flimsy and soft. The slightest tug on the loose threads left him vulnerable. Earlier, when Brenda became angry and almost left without knowing the depth of his feelings toward her, he thought he'd crumble.

Hearing Carla's voice in his head the week before had shaken him too. The anniversary date of her death was approaching. For ten years now, the days preceding this day were filled with a personal form of torture, inflicted on himself so that he'd never forget what he had done.

CJ was used to suffering. His father, an army lieutenant colonel, ran their household the way he ran his troops. Mistakes and imperfections were met with merciless bullying. The sting of his father's cruel words had stayed with CJ longer than the sting of his hand, shattering CJ's self-confidence. Early on, CJ learned to battle this by striving for perfection. He slipped on occasion, but never as much as his siblings.

CJ loved his mother, but his father stepped all over the family while she remained silent, and all his respect for her withered. Worse and most regretfully, CJ possessed many of his father's bad qualities, which began to become more obvious as he got older. These qualities resulted in the demise of many of his relationships with women.

At age thirty, he'd met Carla.

While stationed at Fort McNair in Washington, DC, CJ and a close friend and fellow officer, Eric Besser, frequented a local diner for lunch. They always sat in the same corner, and always had the same waitress. One day they entered the busy place and managed to find a seat in their usual area. They studied the menu.

"May I take your order?"

A new waitress stood at their table. Right away CJ took in details: the way her soft brown hair rested on her shoulders, the silver glaze of her round blue eyes, how the fit of her uniform revealed a shapeliness that their usual waitress had not possessed.

CJ glanced at her name tag, which read Carla.

"Hello. Where's Gina today?" he asked.

"I'm covering her shift." There was a tired edge to her voice. "Are you ready to order?"

They placed their orders. While waiting, CJ and Eric watched the new employee make a mistake with nearly every table's order in their small section. She arrived with their food and placed a salad coated with Russian dressing in front of CJ.

"I ordered ranch." He pointed at the bowl.

She heaved an exhausted sigh and glanced at her pad. "It says here Russian."

"A little advice for you, sweetheart." He donned a stern demeanor. "Listen more carefully when customers order. As far as my salad goes" — he placed the bowl in her hands — "the customer is always right. Ranch, please."

Her intense gaze pierced with intent to kill. With sarcastic sweetness, she said, "Why, of course, sir. I'll be right back."

Two minutes later, she approached. On her way over to him, she smiled so brightly he detected it from clear across the room. "Here's your salad with ranch dressing." Her voice drizzled like sweet maple syrup.

"Thank you." CJ breathed in the sparkle of her eyes as she moved close to lower the bowl onto the table.

With her face inches from his, she stopped. "Let the boss know I quit because of jerks like you."

She flipped the salad in CJ's lap, turned on a heel, and huffed off toward the kitchen. Eric roared with shocked delight while CJ picked off lettuce, coated with extra ranch dressing, from his army fatigues, thankful for the camouflaged pattern of the fabric.

Stunned, CJ replayed her words. Jerks like him? She was new, and clearly having a bad day. Their regular waitress had insinuated many times that the establishment's owner was tough on them. CJ cringed, thinking of his father.

What was wrong with him? He had hated being treated that way, so why would he treat others like that? Why had he treated this waitress like that?

Outside their booth's window, Carla fumbled with her keys, trying to unlock her car. CJ flew off the bench seat and ran for the exit, leaving chunks of lettuce in his wake. When he reached her car, she sat inside with her hands covering her face and shoulders heaving from crying. He banged on the window. She turned and tears streamed down her cheeks.

"Go away. I'm sorry." Her voice was muffled through the closed window.

CJ smiled to let her know he wasn't angry. He made a circular motion with his index finger so she'd roll it down. "I'm sorry too."

She hesitated but then rolled the window halfway.

"I'm sorry," CJ repeated. "Looks like it's been a tough day."

"A horrible day." Carla pulled a tissue from her purse and wiped her cheeks. "I never should have taken this job. A friend who works the night shift suggested the place. Said she gets great tips." Carla shook her head. "If you're good at waitressing, maybe, but I haven't seen much."

She examined CJ's pants, her remorse now evident, and reached to the passenger seat for her purse. "Let me give you money for the cleaners."

"No." CJ put up a hand in protest.

Carla glanced over CJ's shoulder. "Uh-oh."

The diner's owner, Gus, stood at the top of the stairs, arms crossed against his chest, his burning gaze aimed in their direction.

"Want me to pass along your message?" CJ offered.

She chewed her lower lip for a second. "No. I'll do it."

CJ stepped aside.

The scrawny man yelled, "Carla, where the hell do you think you're going?"

"I quit, Gus."

"Quit? I need a waitress for this shift."

"You'd better get an ad in the paper. Fast." Gus stormed inside and she looked at CJ. "Quitting went better than I expected."

"I'm glad. What's your regular job?"

"Right now I'm getting an MBA at Georgetown University. Before that, I worked a full-time job at an accounting firm. I tucked some money aside to tide me over during my leave but figured I could earn a little extra cash over the semester break."

"Since you're now unemployed, how about I take you out for coffee tomorrow? It's on me." CJ cocked his head at the corny joke.

She smiled and rolled down the remainder of the window. "Sure. I insist on paying, though. That's the least I can do since you won't accept money for the pants." Scribbling her number on a piece of scrap paper, she handed it to CJ and waved as she drove off.

Back at the table, he slipped into the now-cleaned booth while Eric shook his head. "Did she hand you her number?"

CJ nodded.

"If I hadn't seen that with my own eyes, I wouldn't have believed it could happen. Like a production of *Taming of the*

Shrew."

"Yeah. In this case, though, I'm the shrew."

After a three-year courtship, they married. Carla handled him with the finesse of a lion tamer, opting out on the whip and chair, focusing instead on what made CJ tick. She, and she alone, possessed the skills to soothe his anger. In fact, she claimed the lion inside of him was part of his appeal — she just refused to let him scratch her.

Overall, their nine years of marriage were good. Unsuccessful attempts to conceive a child during the last few years of it caused stress. Even though Carla was five years younger than CJ, her clock still ticked and every year added more pressure...

CJ pushed aside his dinner and an ambush of tears blurred his vision. Why did he let this damn ritual of reliving the past start again every year? The answer was obvious: because, after what he did to Carla, punishment was what he deserved. A hard ball of guilt struck his heart, then erupted with atomic fury. He panicked and closed his eyes, inhaling deeply. This time, all he wanted was to commemorate the anniversary day without a bottle of whiskey, without agony.

Reaching deep, he retrieved the feeling of Brenda in his arms, the sensuous touch of her lips, the silky softness of her skin.

CJ put his dishes in the sink and walked outside to the deck off the dining room. He stared into the dark yard and realized how this house had become his cocoon, a refuge away from other people. Looking up to the sky, the blanket of sparkling stars reminded him that not every place in his world was dim.

Brenda's appearance called to him like a beacon. The morning at the hotel when she had spilled coffee on him had instantly reminded him of the day he met Carla. Later, when Brenda stood up to him in the lobby, she rattled his confidence, like Carla had done in the diner.

He had needed rattling. Maybe Ken did too.

CJ walked inside. Ken's misery might finally be put to rest.

Chapter Eighteen

Brenda listened to the message from Luc, his third since their lunch date. His tone gave away obvious aggravation. She remembered the Dale Carnegie quote that Dr. Bernard, one of her favorite professors back in college, used to say: "Inaction breeds doubt and fear. Action breeds confidence and courage."

The reason she hadn't returned the calls was simple: fear. Fear that he'd be angry when she told him she hadn't searched the office. Fear that he still wanted something more from her personally. Fear of Luc, in general, due to Jack's warning and finding out from Rosie that he still had one of the keys to Jack's office. But Brenda knew she was only making matters worse by avoiding him.

Luc always appeared controlled, contented, and temper-free. In fact, she'd only seen him angry once, the last time they were alone together, about two months into their relationship. At that point in their relationship, the physical energy between them had heated to a dangerous sizzle. Both wanted more. One afternoon, Luc called her cell phone. In hushed tones, he shared the news that he'd booked them a hotel room.

Lustful anticipation occupied her thoughts on the forty-minute drive to the Ritz-Carlton in White Plains, New York. Yet as she took the exit off Interstate 287 toward the hotel, a sleazy sensation crept in, forcing her to consider what she was about to do. Guilt disappeared, however, the second she pulled up to the luxurious glass building. The upscale location somehow upgraded her actions.

The sordid thought sneaked into her head again as she walked through the elegant contemporary lobby. The path she walked qualified her for full-fledged adultery. Just because this hotel didn't rent rooms by the hour — or carry the slogan, "For the ultimate in guiltless affairs, do it at the Ritz" — to call this deed by any other name would be a lie.

The elevator lifted her to the fourth floor and she went straight to room 424. Luc greeted her with a gentle kiss, then removed her coat. The chill of the late January day remained in her bones, but it was forgotten when he circled her in an affectionate hug. Taking her hand, he led her into a room with rich, warm wood details and fashionable furnishings. A coffee table held a bucket of champagne and a single rose. He handed her the flower and a fluted glass.

The inviting setting, the attention she desperately missed from her husband, and Luc's unconcealed desire, made her concerns evaporate. They gave the champagne a cursory sip, but the luxurious bedding beckoned. They approached the bed, leaving articles of clothing strewn across the floor.

Luc removed his lips from hers and sampled her neck. While his fingertip delicately pulled aside her bra strap, he whispered, "I paid cash for the room. Nobody will ever know we were here."

His words slammed on the brakes of her lust, but Luc continued his journey toward the exposed area near her shoulder, leaving persuasive reminders of his longing wherever his moist lips landed. Traveling to the soft mound of her pale breast, he gave her more reasons to continue. A tug-of-war ensued between her body's enjoyment and her hovering guilt. He worked his hand to her back to remove the bra.

"Luc. Stop."

When he didn't, she pressed her hands against his bare chest. "Please. Wait."

He hesitated and tried to kiss her. She held him back.

"Give me a second." Brenda bolted into the bathroom.

In her bra and panties, she sat on edge of the cold porcelain tub. A single point ran through her mind, again and again, urgent and demanding, the way a stock ticker tape flashes an important message: *If you do this, there is no going back.*

Tap, tap, tap.

"Brenda, are you all right?"

"Yes. I'll be right out."

Her private tug-of-war continued for close to five minutes. Her needs. Jack's needs. The family's needs. All of these were important. Whose needs came first?

She slowly opened the bathroom door. Luc sat on the bed, leaning against the headboard, shirtless with his pants still on. His refilled champagne glass rested on the nightstand, and he smoked a cigarette. He patted the spot next to him but instead, she sat on the bed farther away.

"You do not want to be near me?" He sounded hurt.

"I'm afraid I do, but I shouldn't. Luc, what the hell are we doing?"

"You ask me this now?" His expression showed disbelief, like she'd told him she used to be a man or something. "I thought you wanted this as much as I do."

"Don't you feel guilty?"

He shrugged, adding a slight frown and raised brows, a dismissive French motion. "*Mon amour*, I care about you."

"I care about you too." She hesitated. "Luc, this isn't right. I'm sorry. I can't go through with it." Brenda stood and picked her skirt off the floor.

Luc crushed out his cigarette and moved to her side. He put his arms around her, forcing her to stop.

"Please, Brenda. These past months, I have been so happy. My marriage to Aimee is not the same these days."

"Please don't go there." Brenda pulled herself away and slipped her skirt over her hips.

"Go where? The same spot you went when you decided you were not happy with Jack?"

"And I feel remorse," she snapped, but he didn't flinch.

"Remorse?" His voice rose. "You Americans. So hung up about sex. An affair is good for a marriage. French women understand."

"Good for a marriage? Are you insane?"

"Oh come on, Brenda. Do not act so naive. In my country, both women and men have affairs."

"Really?" Her voice rose. "How many women have you been with while married to Aimee?"

"None of your business. You have been stringing me along, so do not act as if you are so innocent."

She threw her blouse on and quickly fastened the buttons. "What the hell is that supposed to mean?"

"Never mind. I am merely upset." He wrapped her in his arms and drew her close. "Come on, *ma chérie*. You know you are special to me."

The French sweet-talking almost worked, but she pushed him away.

A dark shadow fell across his face. "Fine. Get the hell out."

She finished getting dressed as he pouted on the bed.

Brenda went and sat at his side. "Luc, I want to stay friends with you. If we were both single, this would be different. In this country, affairs aren't treated so casually. I don't know what else to say." She touched his shoulder. "We've been friends for quite a few years and I don't want to lose that."

He took her hand. "I understand. My disappointment got the better of me. Maybe in the future?"

She reluctantly agreed in order to make a smooth getaway.

Not long after the uncomfortable encounter, Jack died. The night of the funeral, after all the mourners had left her house and she was alone, Luc called. "Brenda, I am yours if you still want me." She'd told him no and asked him to give her some space.

* * *

Brenda hit the button to delete Luc's message. She wasn't calling him back. What would she say?

Changing into sweatpants, she headed to the kitchen to feed Georgie. The phone rang and she sprang to answer, hoping CJ was on the other end. His parting words yesterday were that he'd call. The question of whether he'd successfully ended his short tenure as Autumn's father figure-boyfriend left Brenda edgy and anxious.

Reggie's name flashed across the caller ID.

"Hey, Reg." Brenda answered the cordless phone, disappointed but not letting it show. She walked to the kitchen and Georgie followed. "I was going to call you later."

"How'd things go with CJ yesterday?"

Brenda provided an edited version of Monday night's events. Reggie mmm'd and oh-my-God-ed in all the right places.

"He's a complicated man." Reggie waited a beat. "Do you know what you're stepping into?"

"Do we ever?"

"I suspect he's carrying some baggage."

"So? Who isn't? Although, I'll agree he doesn't travel light." Brenda picked up the day's mail and flipped through the stack, mostly junk. "Late last night, I couldn't sleep, so I snooped around the Internet to find out more about how his wife died."

"Find anything?"

"One article said it was a car accident, which I knew, but there were no details. I found a blog post where a fan speculated his wife's death brought the change in his Ken Blair character."

"What's your take?"

Brenda vacillated. The ridiculous notion hit her that discussing this might be violating a make-believe client-patient confidentiality with Ken and/or CJ. "I honestly couldn't say."

"Hmmm."

"What?"

"Sounds like serious baggage to me."

She wanted to point out that it wasn't only CJ who dragged a past behind him. She suddenly wanted to mention how those problems reminded her of her own, especially his struggle with guilt and forgiveness. Maybe she would even tell Reggie about Luc, a secret which, pent up inside with no place to go, sometimes felt like poisonous gas in a windowless room.

The words began to form, but she clamped her lips tight, remembering how Reggie had slammed Nate over his unfaithfulness. In fact, after the way CJ had carried on about his fidelity to Autumn, she decided that she would have to keep Luc a secret from him too.

* * *

While watching her favorite Wednesday night show, the ring of the phone sent Brenda flying off the sofa once again, her heart fluttering so hard it just about lifted her into the air. She hadn't heard from CJ since leaving his house Monday night.

Disappointment set in when an 800 number flashed across the caller ID. How had she let herself fall victim to the "I'll call you" line? She had ceded complete control over future conversations to CJ. Or was she just being old-fashioned? This was a new millennium. She could simply call him.

Brenda carried the cordless phone handset with her to the couch and plopped onto the soft cushion. Maybe he hadn't ended things with Autumn after all, and was too embarrassed to let her know. Dread wormed through her.

This near-obsession for a man who, at one time, she had disliked with the same disdain she had for cooked liver, left her puzzled. Why the mania for *this* man? But the answer was clear: CJ understood her.

The first time she had become aware of the feeling was at the bar during the conference. CJ had asked, "Are you always this upset when people don't acknowledge you to your satisfaction?"

Wow—he'd sure pegged her. Her first distinct memory of reacting to someone's brush-off happened in middle school. She'd won the Outstanding Student Citizen Award at an assembly. Racing home from the bus with the certificate clutched in her hand, she couldn't wait to tell her mother. When she finally located her in the quiet house, her mother barely lifted her head from the bed's pillow to offer praise. By the time she had sobered up, she didn't even remember the achievement. Brenda cried herself to sleep that night. The incident wasn't the first time she'd been disregarded, but it was the first time she had felt such pain at being dismissed. And it was far from the last. Therapy in college allowed her to recognize her behavior, a behavior which still surfaced in her adulthood at times.

CJ had surprised her again that same night. He had said, "What do you *really* want from me?" At the time, even she wasn't sure, but now the answer flashed before her in neon lights: she wanted someone who saw through her facade, and CJ did just that. The notion that anybody could do so brought Brenda immense relief. Around CJ, she didn't need to keep up the charade of strength she'd carried most of her life.

CJ Morrison figured her out like Will Shortz tackling a complex crossword puzzle. No man she had ever been with had even attempted to climb that particular mountain.

The program she was watching ended, and she picked up a book. The phone rang again. This time, CJ's name stretched across the display window. The loud thumping returned to her chest. "Hi, CJ."

"Hello. I'm glad you're home. I've been thinking of you."

Her heart stumbled over itself, surprised and delighted all at once. "I've been thinking about you too."

"I'm sorry I didn't call sooner. I almost called late last night, but I didn't want to wake you."

"I wouldn't have minded. Been busy?"

"Sort of. After you left, the whole book came together. I've been working on it for the past few days. I get in that zone and sometimes I forget the rest of the world."

"Oh?" Brenda shut off the TV. "So, I'm out of sight, out of mind, huh?"

"No." His voice quieted, almost sounding shy. "You were in my thoughts constantly."

"Maybe you'd like to reel in the fishing line a bit, Mr. Gorton."

He laughed. "I guess it sounds like a line, but it wasn't. You inspired this part of the manuscript."

"Me? How?"

"By forcing me to confront the truth."

"I recall a great deal of conflict but not much forcing. Do you always resist so much?"

"Unfortunately, sometimes. I..." He hesitated. "I hope you won't give up on me."

"Of course I won't."

"Good. Are you free for lunch Friday?"

"Sure. I'm working but can break for lunch. There's a wonderful Italian place in downtown Greenwich called Bacio's. About halfway down Greenwich Avenue. We could meet there."

"Noon OK?"

"Perfect."

"I'd like you to read what I've written." Uncertainty carried in his statement. "Tell me how you like the new storyline."

"I'm flattered you'd ask me to take a look." She decided to ask the question she had been agonizing over for two days. "How'd things go with Autumn after I left?"

"She was angry. No matter what I said, she suspected we did more than work and accused me of lying. Technically, she was right."

Brenda's own lies from the past tapped her on the shoulder and sneered at her. She stuck out her tongue and ignored them.

"Anyway, I told her the truth."

"So, now you're fair game, huh?" she purred. "Better be careful next time we're together."

"Me? You better pay attention to your own advice." His playful tone turned tender. "I can't wait to see you."

"Me either."

They hung up and within a few seconds, the phone rang again. She picked up and crooned, "Can't get enough of me?"

"Brenda? It's Luc."

Chapter Nineteen

On the drive over to Bacio's to meet CJ, Brenda's cell phone rang. Thinking it might be him, she pulled over to the roadside. She didn't recognize the number on the display but answered anyway.

"Brenda?" The unmistakable sandpapery voice of Jack's former assistant questioned her from the other end. "Rosie Bradley here."

"Hi, Rosie. I'm on my cell and headed to meet someone. What's up?"

"I'll keep it brief. My friend Joan is Luc Pelletier's assistant." Noise in the background sounded like she was outside, maybe at a park. "The other day, Joan took a message for him from Bob Manning. Boy, was he cranky, crankier than usual. He demanded Luc come to his office."

Brenda glanced at the car clock and saw she was a few minutes early to meet CJ. She threw the car into park and rested her high-heeled patent leather pump on the floor mat. "Do you think their discussion had anything to do with Jack?"

"Oooh yeah. Joan had lunch with Mr. Manning's assistant, Mary Jo. Sometimes we secretaries chat about what the head honchos are up to. Ya know?"

"Sure."

"Joan asked Mary Jo if something was up her boss's...um..." She paused. "Why he was so upset when he asked for Luc. She confirmed that one of the auditors had just left Bob's office before he made the call. She also said that Donald Wainscott arrived right after Luc."

Wainscott. The image of a plump, snake-eyed man she had once met at Christmas party popped into Brenda's head. "He's chairman of the board, right?"

"Uh-huh. He went in but didn't shut the door tight. Mary Jo heard pieces of the conversation. Jack's name came up more than once." She paused for a short beat. "So did yours."

After Bob's threat at the club, Brenda didn't like that he was talking about her. "Did she get any details?"

"Nothing concrete. Either they missed a deadline or were running out of time, something along those lines. They were pretty angry, though. Luc left in a huff."

"I appreciate the call, Rosie. If you hear anything else, let me know. Thanks."

She hung up and thought about Rosie's find. Without more details, it was unclear how these dots connected, but it confirmed something weird was going on, and that it was related to Jack. What she wouldn't give to have been a fly on the wall of that meeting between the three executives. Had Luc's call the other night been related to that meeting?

Luc had been angry that Brenda hadn't been returning his calls, but his anger eventually dissipated with her repeated apologies. Once he had calmed down, he asked if she'd searched Jack's office. She lied and said she hadn't. He again seemed all too eager to help, but she had refused. While he reiterated how much any discovery could help Jack, her thoughts drifted elsewhere.

She had interrupted him midsentence. "Luc? Did you ever get a sense Jack knew about the two of us?"

Silence on the other end lasted a beat too long. "No. Why?" "Just curious." She sensed a lie. "What were you saying?"

After they hung up, she'd cried. Even thinking about it now, a lump lodged in her throat. The notion that her selfish affair had added to her husband's problems was something she could never forget. A single tear slid down her cheek and plunked onto her lap.

The Audi suddenly seemed stifling and claustrophobic. She quickly pressed the window button. Fresh spring air flowed inside and she inhaled a deep breath. After a minute, she wiped the tear off her cheek, brushed away the mark on her skirt, and left for the restaurant.

* * *

A busy Friday crowd filled the tables at Bacio's. The popular Mediterranean restaurant on Greenwich Avenue was one of Brenda's favorite places to eat. CJ sat across from her at a secluded table near a wall of French doors overlooking the patio. He looked handsome in pressed tan khakis, a white cotton oxford, and a tweed sports jacket.

Brenda ordered grilled swordfish. She watched CJ while he ordered. His very presence made it easier to put the sad moment she'd had in the car behind her and focus on the present. She could smell the comforting scent of his sandalwood cologne. Either it had rubbed off on her after his hungry kiss in the parking lot, or she was simply near enough to smell him.

The waiter left and Brenda leaned forward. "Tell me something about CJ Morrison I'd never guess or read any place. Something that might surprise me."

CJ, who'd just lifted the napkin in the breadbasket, shifted his glance to her. "I've had a lot of interviews and never that question. Let's see..." He removed a piece of crusty bread and placed it on a plate. "So many things." He rubbed his hands together.

"I said surprise, not shock."

"Oh." He feigned disappointment. "Well, even though I went to a military university and then entered the service, I had other dreams."

"Why'd you enlist?"

"My father. He was career military."

"Did you always do what he wanted?"

"In those days. He had very high expectations." CJ spoke lightly, but the blinking of his eyes told her more.

"Were you miserable in the service?"

"No. I respect the institution and being a part of it. Left to my own devices, though, a career in journalism would have been my first choice. There wasn't much money for college at the time. So, the military satisfied Dad and put me through school."

The waiter brought over two iced teas. CJ poured a packet of sugar into his. "Well? What would surprise me about you?"

She squeezed a lemon, aware of his gaze, then wiped her hands on a napkin. "What makes you think I have any surprises?"

"Something big stirs beneath your exterior." He reached for her hand and let his fingertips stroke her palm. "When someone catches my interest, I pay close attention."

Brenda didn't remember the palm being classified as an erogenous zone, but his simple touch felt X-rated. "So, I caught your interest?"

"Right away. Starting with your comment in the lobby. By the end of the conference, you were stuck in my head like a song I couldn't stop humming."

"A bad song?" Brenda's free hand glided over his.

His frown scolded gently. "A song I hadn't planned on listening to right at that moment. I'm glad now, though."

The waiter arrived with salads and their hands slid apart.

CJ kept an eye on her while the waiter put down the plates. When he left, CJ said, "So? I'm waiting for my surprise."

Brenda pushed the lettuce with her fork. "Could I trust you to keep this between us?"

"Absolutely."

"My husband left behind a huge problem. Now it's become mine." The admission brought relief, a little steam escaping from her boiling kettle of problems. "Did you hear about the Justice Department investigation of Global Business Solutions?"

He nodded. "Sure. On the news, maybe a week ago."

"Well, my husband worked there up until his death. He was CFO of North American and European operations."

"CFO?" CJ's brows rose. "Was he involved in the things the Justice Department's looking into?"

Brenda, about to take a bite of salad, lowered the fork. "That's my dilemma. They're trying to pin this entirely on him." She blew out a breath. "I think he acted under somebody's direction."

"Why?"

"My husband had very high principles on matters like this. Plus, I talked to someone who worked closely with him who feels the same way."

CJ nodded, but an awkward atmosphere hovered between them. He tackled his salad in silence, something clearly going through his head.

Brenda wanted to smack herself for raising the inappropriate lunch-date conversation. "I'll bet Emily Post would've advised against discussing corporate fraud on a lunch date."

CJ looked up, forehead crumpled as if confused by her comment. "Oh. I'm thinking. That's all." He rested the fork in the plate and folded his hands. "I hope this isn't too personal. Did his suicide have to do with this work issue?"

"I don't really know. Maybe." She lowered her gaze to the

tabletop, focusing on the clean, white linen covering, wishing her life could be as smooth and flawless.

CJ touched her forearm. "I'm sorry."

She looked up. "It's OK. I've thought about it a lot. Jack slipped away from me over the course of years. I never knew why. The recent news sheds light on work stress I didn't know about."

"You said you don't believe he was involved, but is it at all possible?"

"I suppose. Back in the early eighties, Jack worked for Peat Marwick, one of the big eight CPA firms at the time. He always told me his job was to make sure firms weren't doing anything to deceive shareholders. I can't imagine him acting alone. If someone forced him to take those steps, compromise his values, it would kill him inside."

"Would anything prove he didn't act alone? Maybe something I can help with?"

About to discuss the papers found in Jack's office, Luc's involvement, and everything Rosie told her, she slammed the brakes. Her personal involvement with Luc muddied the waters. "There is one thing. I found two books on accounting principles on Jack's desk the other day. They were marked in some sections, like they were important."

"What'd they say?"

"Chinese would be easier to read, for me anyway. Do you understand accounting?"

He shrugged. "Not really. When I research my novels, though, I need to understand all types of unfamiliar topics. I can't promise anything, but I can take a look."

"Thanks. I'd appreciate it." Brenda didn't accept help easily, yet taking it from CJ felt right. "More than you know."

CJ's eyes squinted as he offered a tender smile. "I'm glad to help. Bring them next time we get together. Besides, you're doing me a favor by looking at the updated chapter."

"Boy, I definitely got the better part of this deal."

"You haven't read it yet." He grinned at his self-deprecating jab. "Let's hope it fits with your character assessment. Be honest. Don't spare my feelings. "

She snorted. "I'd never do that."

"Good point." He chuckled, then his voice became serious. "The storyline might surprise you."

"In what way?"

"Be patient. You'll see." He took her hand and teased the tender spots of her palm. The longing in his expression forced her heart to lunge in his direction.

She tried to figure out at what point she'd fallen so utterly under his spell. Then, for once in her life, she let go of her need for controlled analysis and allowed the sensation to own her.

Chapter Twenty

Brenda sank her head into three pillows strategically squished against the bed's wrought-iron headboard. After today's lunch with CJ, a single question had burned in her mind the entire afternoon at the office: with the bevy of beauties at CJ's disposal, why would he pick her?

After lunch, Brenda sat through three sessions with clients and tried to focus on their problems, while visions of Autumn-like creatures hanging off CJ's arm frolicked in her mind. Even if those gals gave her a ten-year jump start, the race wouldn't be fair. The evolving appearance of cellulite, on top of the stealthy disappearance of breast firmness, happened to every woman as she ages. Jane Fonda could scream "feel the burn" in her face 24/7 and not a darn thing would change. Nature had its own agenda.

CJ's manuscript, however, provided the answer.

Brenda pulled her quilt up to her chest and dropped the stack of pages onto her lap. The chapter opened with a woman accidentally backing her car into Ken's, damaging his beloved vehicle. Running late, Ken overreacts, is rude to her, briskly takes care of insurance matters, then storms off to his meeting. Five minutes later, his parking lot adversary walks into the very same meeting. His boss introduces her as Cassandra. Ken is told they'll be working together on his latest case. Neither is happy. Tensions are high. Angry words are tossed about, but in an instant both the reader and Ken recognize the same thing: Cassandra is a woman who knows how to stand up to him.

The passages reveal a more introspective Ken Blair, a man who at long last admits that the loss of the woman he loved has derailed his life. The special agent wants to move on, but finds it difficult to let go of the strange sense of security his misery brings.

Brenda knew all about such feelings. She had allowed herself to wallow in self-pity after Jack's death. Some days she still did. Misery gave her something to latch on to when everything seemed lost.

The attraction in the draft chapters wasn't one-sided. A second and later chapter showed that Ken understands Cassandra's needs, which fuels her fire for him. The last line of the chapter summed up Ken's feelings with elegance and precision: *More than anything, Ken wanted Cassandra. Her approval, her adoration, her love.*

Brenda reached for the lotion on the nightstand and poured a healthy dose of the lavender-vanilla scented aromatherapy cream into her palm, then rubbed it along each forearm, rounding out at her elbows. She'd winced, thinking about how CJ's young chickadees probably had ice-smooth elbows, board-flat stomachs, and never complained about wearing high heels.

Lifting the bedspread, Brenda bent a leg. Shapely enough for her age, but her thigh jiggled a little more than in years past. She straightened her leg and pointed her toe. Although her calves were smooth, wrinkled skin rounded out the kneecap. Ugh. Clothes hid a lot. One time Jack had painted the living room. Weeks later, when something slipped behind the entertainment center, she went to retrieve it. It turned out Jack had avoided painting a section, which, as he put it, "nobody would see

anyway." The blemish bugged her each time she glanced in that
direction, the same way her hidden blemishes from age added to
her insecurity now.

Maybe CJ didn't notice those details though. Earlier, when
they left the restaurant, he'd opened her car door. Before she got
in, his large hands had circled her waist, turned her around, and
pulled her close. His rich brown eyes captured hers and left her
breathless, speaking a message beyond words. Right there in the
lot, their lips had joined in a long, passion-filled kiss — not the
behavior of a man concerned with a knee wrinkle.

Brenda picked up the manuscript and flipped to the last
page. That was when she noticed the note, addressed to her and
written in CJ's handwriting. She gasped, her heart beating
wildly, and read it again.

Without hesitation, she reached for the phone.

* * *

The wait for feedback always made CJ anxious. Whether
from a friend or a *Publisher's Weekly* review, he worried
incessantly until the news arrived. This time, his anxiety had
little to do with writing skill, and everything to do with content.

He shut off the downstairs TV and trudged upstairs to his
bedroom. Changing into boxers and a T-shirt, he tried to focus
on the details of his speaking engagement tomorrow afternoon.
The thoughts kept getting shoved aside.

Was his note to Brenda too strong?

He grabbed a new book off the dresser and stretched out on
the bed, hoping the material would be good enough to capture
his attention. Halfway through the first paragraph, he stopped.
What if she was still dating the guy from the conference?

How could he have been so stupid? Why did he rush into
things and reveal his feelings to her so soon?

Even though the conference was weeks ago, he remembered

her longing gaze at that man when he had passed by them after his presentation. Jealousy poked out its destructive head, then plopped its weight on CJ's chest and flipped him over for a pin.

CJ pushed with all his might to cast aside the ridiculous emotion. Carla always got annoyed at his unwarranted overprotectiveness. She'd remind him of their deep love for each other, then say that she wasn't going to allow his insecurity to be her problem.

He still missed her. A well-rehearsed pain cracked across his heart.

In three short days, it would be exactly ten years since one horrible decision changed his entire existence.

* * *

He'd been at the hospital the moment he got the news about losing Carla. As he stirred from his unconscious state, he'd scanned the walls of a dimly lit room, a distinctive antiseptic smell hinting right away at his location. Why was he here? Outside the window, a gray sky spit angry drops of rain against the glass. His last memory was of a sunny afternoon driving with Carla...

Then it all started to come back.

CJ lifted his head. His father, Charlie Morrison, sat in a chair near the foot of his bed. His dad's slumped posture and downcast eyes worried CJ, but the details of the accident were blurry.

CJ licked his dry lips. "Is Carla all right?" He reached to rub his throat, sore and scratchy. Pain shot through his arm. A quick look at his side showed it was wrapped in gauze.

His father glanced over and offered only a stare, as cold and raw as a midwinter day. He didn't rise to go to his son's bedside. "She didn't make it." The older man's glare burned CJ's skin like acid. He stood and mumbled, "I'll get your nurse."

That moment changed how he'd feel about his dad forever. His father adored Carla and she him. Charlie Morrison had mellowed somewhat by the time Carla arrived in their lives. CJ's mother was already gone, after a short battle with cancer years earlier. Charlie had retired from military life and spent his days alone and quite content, his edge from earlier years dulled by the passage of time. Carla engaged with him in a way CJ and his siblings wouldn't have dared. Charlie loved her boldness.

While recovering in the sterile hospital room, CJ wallowed in his shame. Whenever Carla's name was spoken, Charlie's crestfallen stare reinforced his guilt—guilt he'd lived with every day for the past ten years.

CJ shook off those terrible memories. This was a time for change. Brenda's arrival in his life made him want to be different, and for the first time in ten years he believed he could be. He analyzed every word of the handwritten note he'd scribbled at the end of the chapter. *Brenda, You brighten the dark, empty corners of my world. You are my Cassandra. CJ.*

He had wanted to tell her the depth of his feelings at lunch today but chickened out. Years of avoiding deep attachment made the idea of rejection unbearable.

The sudden, shrill ring of the phone next to his bed startled him. "Hello?"

"It's Brenda. Sorry to call so late. Did I wake you?"

"No, I'm up. I'm reading." Relief washed through him at the sound of her voice.

"Too tired to talk?"

"Not with you."

"I finished what you gave me to read. I loved the storyline, CJ. Really great. A wonderful way for Ken to regain a piece of himself."

"Then it seems realistic from your professional perspective?"

"Sure. Sometimes a new person enters our lives, and they're

a catalyst for change. Cassandra might be all Ken needs to get perspective on his life."

"Good." He tried to still his fidgeting hands. "Guess I know how Ken feels."

"You two have a lot in common, but I'm curious about one thing." Brenda's tone shifted, now soft and sexy. "How did you know the way your real-life inspiration for Cassandra felt?"

"I didn't." CJ's heart eased, the weight of worry scurrying away. "I based the writing on pure hope. Then Cassandra's feelings aren't mere fiction?"

"Oh, they're very real. I can't stop reading your beautiful note."

For a moment, CJ was sure he could feel her warm breath on his cheek. "I wanted to tell you at lunch."

"I wish you had. I'd hoped this connection between us wasn't in my imagination."

"The characters are imaginary. You're very real to me."

"You're a clever man. Sending me a message through the story. That's a first for me."

"First for me too. After I gave you the package today, I realized you might still be seeing the guy you dated from the conference."

"We only went out a few times. Besides, the last time he and I were together, I couldn't get you out of my head."

CJ's heart lifted. "When can I see you?"

"I'm with my daughter in Hartford all weekend, and Monday I have appointments all day, into the night. How's Tuesday? I'll be in Westchester from one to four to speak to a college class. Not too far from Chappaqua. I can come over afterward."

He remembered the date and almost said no, but changed his mind. "Tuesday is perfect."

They hung up. Their conversation lifted him up in a way he

hadn't latched onto in years. What a strange coincidence Brenda would be with him on Tuesday of all days. Perhaps another sign his life needed to change.

Chapter Twenty-One

CJ's eyes fluttered open. The skylight above his bed revealed a cloud mass the color of aluminum with a dull shimmer to its finish. The sun was lost somewhere behind, but the brightness spilling around the edges of the clouds filled him with something new on this fateful day: hope.

He sat on the edge of the bed and rubbed his face awake, then switched on the TV with the remote. Matt Lauer joked around with the weather guy, who forecasted scattered showers but a possibility of sun later in the day. The time at the bottom of the screen read 9:05.

The phone on his nightstand rang. He shut off the TV.

"Morning." Dale sounded chipper and was probably at the office by now. "Did I wake you?"

"Nope. Just got up."

"Thought I'd check in. How's the book coming along?"

He didn't believe Dale's concern was about the book, but he played along. "Great. Finally made some headway on the section we hired Brenda for. In fact, I stayed up late last night to finish the second-to-last chapter. She's made a real difference."

"Sounds like the consulting arrangement worked out well."

"Yup. We're through, but I'll be seeing her today anyway. I'm taking her to dinner."

"Dinner? Today?" The ring of approval echoed in Dale's words. "Good. I like her."

"Me too."

"I'm off to a meeting. Don't forget—call if you need me."

"Thanks. I will." CJ hung up the phone.

Dale still phoned or stopped by every year on this anniversary day, even though CJ had come a long way since the first year following Carla's death.

That first year was the worst, but it was always bad. A darkness crept in past his defenses and he retreated into a cocoon of self-loathing. He stayed inside, racked with pain and torment, and ignored the world. Isolation let the mood marinate. He always ended up at the liquor cabinet, seeking something to ease the ache.

That first anniversary, he had nose-dived straight to the bottom of the ditch. By ten a.m. he'd arrived at the liquor store and purchased a small arsenal to resupply his cabinet. By eleven, he'd twisted off the first cap. After that, the day became a blur.

At some point, he had woken up flat on his back on the sofa. The dampness of his shirt gave him a chill, although he couldn't remember how it had gotten wet. The second his eyes started to open, an intense glare, probably from a lamp, sent a sharp pain to his head. He shut his eyes tight. The last thing he remembered was standing on the deck in the drizzling rain, drenched in miserable memories. The rustle of paper startled him. This time he opened his eyes all the way to see Dale sitting in CJ's favorite chair, a black leather replica of an Eames lounger, reading a book with his feet propped on the ottoman, as if he was in his own living room.

CJ lifted a hand to ward off the light. "What are you doing here?" His mouth was dry, like cotton had soaked up every drop of saliva.

Dale stopped reading. "I let myself in. Good thing you gave

me a key for emergencies."

"Why didn't you ring the bell?" CJ mumbled.

"I did. For a while. I even called from my cell on your front stoop." Dale was calm and unruffled. "Your car was here so I checked inside from the deck. You were passed out on the living room floor. Seemed like a good time to use the key."

CJ spotted a fifth of bourbon, well on its way to being finished, on the coffee table. He rolled over, turning his back on Dale.

A moment later, CJ cleared his throat. "How long have you been here?"

"A couple hours." Dale thumped the book shut. "I figured today would be tough."

CJ didn't answer.

"You were out cold. Since you still had a pulse and got ticked off when I shook you, I hoped for the best and dragged you to the couch. I figured a 911 call wasn't the type of publicity you wanted."

Embarrassed, CJ snarled, "You didn't have to come over. I'd have been fine."

"Maybe. We need to talk."

CJ wanted to be angry, but the anger he had directed at himself every day, for the past three hundred sixty-five days, had left him with nothing more to give. He rolled over and managed to sit up, causing a wave of nausea.

Dale pointed to a glass of water and a bottle of Tylenol. "You might need those." He waited a second while CJ rubbed his cheeks. "Listen, buddy, this has to stop."

"What?" CJ lowered his hands. "I'm entitled to feel this way, especially today."

"It's not only today. Carla would hate you acting this way. No matter what happened, she loved you and wouldn't like this road you're headed down."

Removing two tablets from the bottle, CJ popped them in his mouth and gulped the water. Carla wouldn't have tolerated this behavior. She'd have whipped him right back to reality, something he hadn't considered in the midst of his self-pity.

"You're right." Despite the water, his mouth still felt dry. "She wouldn't."

Dale lifted his feet from the ottoman and leaned toward CJ. "You're damn lucky this hasn't hurt you professionally yet. Listen, my friend, if you don't get your act together, it could have an impact." Dale's voice rose, a rare occurrence. "Right now, your name is a hot commodity. The publisher is waiting for another book in the series — any book, for that matter. Customers will buy it simply because your name is on it. That won't last forever."

The comment stung, but CJ wouldn't say so out loud.

Dale sat back and, more gently, added, "Carla would want you to keep writing."

In the early days of CJ's career as an author, Carla had supported them. If he let his progress sink now, her efforts would have been for nothing. The conversation with Dale kick-started CJ's slow climb back into the real world.

Within a week, CJ had started his third book, which became *The Hourglass*. The violent, dark topic suited his mood in those days. The anger he carried somehow dissipated through writing. He established a daily routine around his work. He resumed jogging and joined a gym. He had the occasional bad day, but nothing compared to that first year.

Then the second anniversary hit.

He hid away at home, a bottle by his side. Self-pity surfaced like an old friend. The one day of misery served as a form of punishment, remuneration for his unforgivable actions. This time, however, he got right back on track with his work. Dale didn't have to intervene.

Years passed. His life improved. *The Hourglass* became a best seller. His status as a successful author made meeting women easy. When the movie rights to the first Ken Blair novel sold, the producers asked him to write the screenplay. Once the film hit the theaters, he became a minor celebrity.

His life became something he'd never expected. Young actresses flirted with him, gorgeous models pursued him. Being forty-something didn't matter; fit, nice-looking, with celebrity status and few financial concerns made him desirable to these women. They satisfied him in the bedroom. Other men looked on with envy when he entered a room with one of these beauties. He never grew emotionally attached to any of them. He never wanted to love so deeply again.

Yet each year, on the anniversary of Carla's death, he mourned her in the one way he knew how. The drinking became a ritual, the only way he knew how to cope.

But today would be different. The sun burst from behind the gray clouds and brightened his bedroom. He brightened with it, anticipating Brenda's arrival this afternoon. CJ knew he would have to hand Brenda the darkest part of himself today. Today he would tell her how Carla had died.

He sorted through the layers of his tale, the events of that day. Out of nowhere, his dad's reaction to what CJ had done returned. What if the truth disgusted her? She might blame him, like his father had. She might say he didn't deserve forgiveness. His chest tightened. Panic cornered him, and suddenly he felt as if he were being buried alive. He tried to inhale, but he struggled to breathe.

Brenda might walk out of his life, forever.

The optimism with which he had woken vanished. Now he felt fragile and unsteady, as if walking on a thin sheet of ice.

* * *

"Thanks for taking care of Georgie, Jessica." Brenda spoke into her Bluetooth headset. She had just left the small college in Purchase, New York, where the head of the psychology department, a long-time friend and colleague, invited her to speak once a year. "Georgie's treats are on the counter near the fridge."

"I've already given her two, Mrs. M."

"Two? No wonder she loves your visits." Brenda chuckled and couldn't get mad. The thirteen-year-old loved Georgie almost as much as she did. "Oh, Jess, did the Dumpster get dropped off?"

"You mean the big metal thing in the driveway?"

"Yes. Sounds like it's there. I'll call you when I'm on my way home."

Tomorrow was Brenda's day off. At long last, she wanted to face the painful purge of Jack's office. Reggie was right that reengaging with the world had revived her zest for life. She had spent the past few days on a high induced by the nonnarcotic, but quite habit-forming, attentions of CJ Morrison, and she was on her way to get her fix. She trembled in anticipation.

At the end of CJ's long driveway, Brenda parked next to his Mercedes and grabbed a canvas bag with the accounting books from Jack's desk, which CJ had promised to translate into understandable English. She pressed the doorbell, adjusted her skirt, the pleats askew from the car ride, and smoothed her fitted top, a dressy black V-neck.

All weekend, she'd fantasized about her arrival kiss. Her heart pranced with a few extra beats, anticipating his touch any second now. No answer. She rang the bell again. This time movement sounded from inside.

The door swung open. CJ squinted at her. He motioned for her to come in and massaged his face, redder on one side than the other. "What time is it?"

"Almost four thirty. Were you napping?"

"I guess I dozed off." He seemed confused. His eyes opened wide, as if he'd only just realized she'd arrived. "I've been waiting for you all day." With both hands on her waist, he pulled her close and his lips landed on hers.

The smell of alcohol lingered on his breath. Brenda tried to enjoy the long-awaited contact, but an alarm sounded inside her mind. She loosened his hold.

"Are you OK?" She leaned back and surveyed him. The whites of his eyes held a pink tint.

"I am now that you're here." His voice carried an ever-so-slight slur.

"You've been drinking."

He wrinkled his forehead. "So?"

"Did you drink a lot?"

"I don't know." He nearly growled, his mood menacing, but not enough for her to back off. "Jesus. I had a few drinks. Who counts?"

"I do." Familiar disappointment pounced on her chest.

When her mother would do this, Brenda would hide in her room, waiting for the mood to disappear. With Jack, she'd coddled his anger, not as frightened, but wishing to keep peace in the house. Today, however, she didn't hold back.

"Why don't you go splash some water on your face?" she snapped. "It might help you wake up a little."

He shot her an annoyed glance but did as she asked, gripping the railing to steady himself on his way upstairs.

Brenda considered walking out the door, ending this before anything started. Every childhood memory of dealing with her mom's confusion after binge drinking tumbled to the forefront of her consciousness. A knot formed in the core of her stomach, but a force propelled her into the dimly lit living room to search for clues. Some people excelled at crossword puzzles or the daily word jumble; Brenda could figure out how much someone drank through simple observations.

Soft jazz music flowed from two small speakers located on an entertainment center. She crossed the room and pulled open vertical blinds. Bright light streamed in through the glass doors and she scanned the surroundings. On the coffee table next to the sofa rested an open fifth of straight bourbon whiskey, A.H. Hirsch Reserve. Sixteen years old. Good stuff.

She walked over and took stock of the situation: a half-full bottle with the cap off and an empty glass nearby. On the floor between the sofa and table were scattered sheets of paper. She picked them up and recognized the manuscript she'd read the other night, now marked with red on a few pages. Pushed against the arm of the sofa were two round pillows, pressed together as if somebody's head had rested on them.

Maybe CJ had been working, decided to have a drink, got sleepy, lay down, and fell asleep. She studied the half-empty bottle and the incomplete work. No. He'd had more than one drink.

With her mom, one drink always led to more. The evening at Dale's house, CJ had stopped at two drinks and switched to seltzer because he had to drive later. Even at the conference, where he appeared to imbibe quite a bit, his wits seemed intact. His nastiness that night stemmed from his interactions with her, not from drunkenness. Why the drinks today?

Footsteps sounded on the wood floor. She turned around. CJ walked toward her, still disheveled, but he appeared slightly more awake.

"Why are you drinking in the middle of the afternoon?" She worked to keep her voice firm but not hysterical.

"A couple drinks isn't a big deal. Jesus, Brenda. People do that."

"Don't patronize me. I know people drink, but they're

usually having a good time. They don't look like you do right now."

"I just woke up!"

The knot in Brenda's gut tightened. "I'm concerned." She softened her tone. "That's all."

CJ stared for a long moment, his thoughts unreadable. He walked over and turned off the music. Quiet draped the room like a parent's silent reprimand. He sat on the couch, poured himself another short glass, and tipped it back. Her insides burned as if the liquid had slid down her throat instead of his.

"You're not making this any easier." He pointed at the couch. "Sit. Please."

Surrounded by her past, Brenda suddenly felt vulnerable and scared. She sat down on the sofa, but perched on the edge like a sprinter in start position, prepared for a quick getaway.

CJ put down the glass. His gaze raked across her, then he placed a hand on her knee, an inch below her skirt hem. With an appreciative touch, he went underneath the fabric. Warmth from his smooth palm traveled to the top of her thigh. Small movements of his thumb caressed her.

"I've missed you." His low, husky tone made her breath shorten.

Physical desire for him roused, but she reminded herself of his condition. Her hand slipped beneath the skirt and stopped on top of his. She led both hands down her thigh, then placed them on her lap, brushing the skirt back into place.

"I've missed you too. Did something happen?"

CJ's face contorted into a frown. He fell against the sofa back, releasing their hands. "My wife died ten years ago today. At five thirteen. The witching hour." He lifted his arm and tipped his wrist to see the time. His sad expression tumbled further and he whispered, "Almost there."

A chill rippled along Brenda's neck as the ghosts of CJ's past stepped into the room and the warmth fled. The pain hidden behind his sullen gaze, the pain she'd caught glimpses of on several occasions, now stood before her naked and unconcealed.

Her anger shriveled.

"I want to tell you how she died." CJ looked away and ran a fingernail in a pattern across the soft arm of the leather sofa. "On the anniversary date, this is what I do." He motioned toward the bottle with a quick tip of his head. "Drink. Rehash the details. When you asked to come over today, I almost said no. I decided this year things would be different." Their eyes met. "I'd be with you."

"So, why are you drinking?"

A dark shadow crossed CJ's face. "Because I know you'll leave after I tell you."

"I promise not to go." She reached for his hand, which stiffened but didn't pull away.

He looked off to the wall. "I don't care what you do. I'm telling you anyway."

She suspected he did care or he wouldn't have been drinking. Tense lines near his mouth showed his determination to tell her the truth. "The day my wife died, I was being honored by the Suspense Writers of America. My writing career had finally started to take off. I wanted her by my side." He dared to glance at Brenda, as if he was afraid she'd left. "We were running late. Carla always kept me waiting. She made me crazy. I asked her to be ready on time, just this once. Once again, she made us late." A red hue rose up his neck, the start of his blossoming anger. "If she hadn't, none of this would have happened." He pulled away from Brenda and reached for the bourbon.

"CJ." Brenda touched his forearm. "Please. No more."

He stopped and stared at her for a minute, then settled back against the sofa.

"We got in the car, started to argue. Her lateness always caused fights, but that day was the last straw." He winced. "We lived in a rural part of Dutchess County. On the way to the highway, we got stuck behind a horse trailer on a curvy road. Between the fighting, being late, the damn slow truck…" His fist balled. "Jesus, I thought I'd explode. We were arguing and I saw a chance to go around the trailer to pick up a little time. I waited. Once I made an attempt but pulled back into my lane. She asked me not to pass, said it made her uncomfortable."

CJ took a steadying breath and eyed the bottle. "I ignored her. Near the end of the passing zone, I got another chance."

The loud chirps of several sparrows perched on the deck's bird feeder disrupted CJ's train of thought. The cause of the commotion turned out to be a threatening crow that landed nearby. In a Poe book, Brenda thought, this would be her warning to get out of there before it was too late.

CJ shifted his gaze to Brenda. She suddenly felt unimaginable pity for him. She couldn't leave him in this condition.

"Go on. Please," she said.

"I saw a second opening and swerved out." His next words tiptoed out, like a secret he didn't want anybody to hear. "This time she begged me not to go."

Brenda looked at her lap, remembering the many times she and Jack had shared the same words about passing, an act which always made her nervous.

"See?" CJ's expression illuminated with the glow of rising anger. "I knew you'd act this way."

"It wasn't a judgment on you. Sometimes when my husband attempted to pass a car, I had a similar reaction. I think women drive differently than men."

He twisted his lips in skepticism. "Maybe. Anyway, I ignored her and yelled back that I needed to pass because she'd made us late. I floored it around the trailer." A tear escaped, flowed along his cheek and stopped at his chin.

Brenda took his hand in both of hers and he didn't resist.

"I got past the horse trailer," he continued, "but not the truck. The passing zone neared its end. I pushed down on the gas pedal..." His lips quivered and she squeezed his hand. Behind his lifeless eyes hid remorse, guilt, and shame.

"There was a second car in front of the truck. I never would have..." He swallowed "I wouldn't have tried to go around them both." More tears slipped through the cracks. "The rest happened so fast. A pickup truck headed for us in the oncoming lane. I swerved to the left. There was nowhere else to go. I wasn't fast enough." He freed his hand from Brenda's and wiped away the ever-increasing tears. "The truck slammed into Carla's door."

He closed his eyes and turned away, but before he did, she saw that his face had become a mask of agony.

"She died instantly," he whispered.

CJ's pain seized Brenda. She held his shaking body in her arms, nestled her head in the crook of his neck, and cried along with him. They sat that way for several minutes. As his tears subsided, the trembling of his body slowed.

She lifted her head and stroked moisture off his cheek. "Thank you for telling me. Now I understand why it's been so hard for you."

"There's more."

CJ removed her arms, and stood. A bit unsteady at first, he walked toward the sliding doors. He crossed his arms and stared outside, his back to Brenda.

"When the coroner did the autopsy..." His voice cracked. "I...I didn't know she was six weeks pregnant. We'd been trying for years to conceive. She'd had many miscarriages. Carla's mother later told me she wanted to wait a little while to tell me the news this time."

Brenda's hand flew to her mouth. She understood the joy of pregnancy, of desiring a child. Dragged into the despair of a man who believed he'd lost his entire family due to his reckless actions, heaviness settled in her chest. She started to cry again. For his lost loved ones. For his guilt. For his sadness.

"I never should have taken such a chance…she was everything." CJ lowered his head. His shoulders drooped.

Brenda walked over to him, pressed herself against his back, and wrapped her arms around his waist. "I'm so sorry."

His body quivered. After a long minute, he stopped and sniffled. Quietly he said, "Please leave."

Brenda couldn't budge. She'd held up many fractured souls in her day. But this soul mattered now, more than ever. CJ had done something neither Jack nor her mother ever did. He'd trusted her enough to discuss the matter.

"I don't want to leave." She tightened her hug, then placed a kiss on his shoulder.

He lifted her hand and pressed it to his lips. "Go."

She stayed put. "You shouldn't be alone right now."

His back muscles became rigid. "Go. I'm embarrassed. I want to be alone."

He pushed her away gently and moved toward the sofa, his longing gaze glued to the bottle.

"You want to be with that" — her finger aimed for the bourbon and she cocked a brow — "more than you want me?"

He narrowed his gaze but stayed silent. Then he walked over to the table, poured another drink, and left the room.

Brenda winced. So much for him being different from the others. Countless times she'd received similar snubs from her mother and Jack, but they were weak — weaker than CJ anyway. Brenda had always suppressed her anger, not wishing to hurt them further.

CJ had had the courage to talk to her tonight. CJ showed her his strength, proved it to her. Coddling him wasn't even an option. Years of anger, pent up for far too long, finally erupted out of her.

Marching to the coffee table, she grabbed the neck of the whiskey bottle and stormed into the kitchen. At the sink, she removed the drain plug. Countless times, she'd dreamed of performing this act with her mother's drink, with Jack's. She glanced up at the doorway. CJ stood and watched, the slight tilt to his head and wrinkled forehead marking his confusion.

With a slight tip of the glass container, the golden-amber liquid disappeared down the drain. Satisfaction and relief swept over her.

"What the hell are you doing? That cost three hundred a bottle!" He came at her fast. His outstretched hands caught hold of the bottle as the last drops trickled away.

"Here." Brenda shoved the empty bottle in his direction.

His glare burned into her. CJ slammed the glass container on the counter and grabbed her wrists. "How dare you!"

"How dare *you!*" She struggled in his hold. "I'm trying to help, but you'd rather sit here drowning your sorrows in bourbon. Let go of me."

His hold on her wrists loosened and she shoved him away. CJ stumbled. Brenda returned to the living room, grabbed her purse, and flew toward the front door. He followed her.

She spun around and hissed, "Keep the hell away from me."

"You weren't going to stay anyway." The statement, filled with desperation, seemed more for his own benefit than hers. A shadow eclipsed his expression. He moved close. "Don't lie to me."

"I didn't lie." Brenda took careful steps back but hit the hallway wall. "I understand…people make mistakes." Her angry confidence returned all at once. "Good Lord! Stop blaming yourself and move on. Would your wife want this? Let it go."

His expression transformed, as if reality had just come into focus. The anger evaporated, replaced by a look of pure longing. "Brenda, this wasn't what I wanted. Please don't leave."

CJ pressed her back against the wall. Hungry lips brushed along her jawline, then trailed down her neck.

"Let me go." Her request sounded futile and forced. She gave in, too exhausted to fight, too fond of him to refuse.

The warmth of his mouth melted over hers. Hungry and wanting, her resistance weakened further. He skimmed underneath her skirt and caressed her thigh. Betrayed by her better senses, she wrapped a leg around him, drew him close. The pressure of his body filled her with desire.

Spicy bourbon, still strong on his lips, gnawed at her. She tried to ignore the feeling, but some part of her was shouting, "Stop allowing people like this to enter your life!"

Prying her mouth from his, she mumbled, "Stop."

He kissed her throat.

Louder, with more force, she said, "CJ. Stop." She pressed her hands to his chest and pushed. "I can't deal with another drunk." She scooped her handbag from the floor and bolted for the front door.

"Brenda, wait." CJ grabbed her arm.

She twirled around. The slack-jawed confusion of his expression made her anger stir again. "No. I'm tired of helping people like you. I've done it my whole life." Pulling her arm away, she headed straight for the door. "If you knew anything about me, you'd *never* have let me come here today to find you this way."

She swung the door open and tried to slam it shut, but he pushed through the doorway, after her.

When she reached the car, she spun around. CJ stood on the bottom step.

"Think about someone besides yourself for a change," Brenda shouted. She got in, then backed up fast. Slamming the car into drive, she pressed the gas pedal with a heavy foot and pulled away. A glimpse in the rearview mirror showed a crushed, confused man watching her departure.

Even in her adrenaline-filled daze, Brenda managed to find the highway and avoid an accident. Her hands clenched the steering wheel so tight, the Jaws of Life would have found their removal a challenge. Five minutes later, she shifted in her seat, loosened her grip, and let out a long, liberating sigh.

Something suddenly occurred to her: this was the first time she'd ever walked away from someone else's problems. She'd taken the first step in defeating the monsters that had pursued her all her life.

She slipped the Bluetooth headset over her ear and called Reggie, thankful to find her at the office. Details of the scene at CJ's house poured out in one long, hysterical outburst. When Brenda finished, Reggie remained quiet.

"Don't you have anything to say?" Brenda paused. "Maybe I told you so?"

"Nah. I'll bet that's the last thing you need to hear right now." Reggie had used the same sympathetic tone during their childhood whenever Brenda had offered details about her mother's problems. It greeted Brenda like an old friend.

"Thanks, Reg. I'm so confused about CJ. His car accident story ripped my heart. Last time I asked how his wife died, he told me he had only discussed it with Dale and the police. Telling me was huge."

Reggie stayed silent, which meant a negative comment was on the tip of her tongue and she'd opted to exercise some rare diplomacy. "Well...I do understand what you're saying. But he's really hung onto it for so long. That doesn't seem too healthy."

"Think about what happened. Wouldn't you feel horrible in

his shoes?"

An audible sigh whispered through the phone. "Probably. Why would he let you see him in that condition? Didn't he know about your Mom? Or Jack?"

The question pushed some culpability in Brenda's direction. "No. I've never mentioned either one." CJ's behavior might not have been the same if he'd been aware.

"Oh? I'm surprised. You're usually pretty open."

"Not the best way to entice a man. You know, baggage?"

"Hmmm." Sometimes Reggie's lack of comment hurt worse than her jabs.

"Hey, Jack turned to drinking fully aware of my mother's problems." Brenda's anger skidded in a new direction. "At least I understand why CJ turned to the bottle. My husband never did me that courtesy."

"True. Look, Brenda, I'm proud of you for walking out. As long as I've known you, you've always tried to fix everyone's troubles."

It was true. Her entire life she'd been the family seamstress, mending and repairing everybody's tears. "You're absolutely right. I did walk out, walked away from someone's mess. I'm damn proud of myself."

"Hold onto that feeling. Promise me you won't start to second-guess yourself."

Brenda didn't answer right away. Did she really want to give up on him entirely?

Reggie, the mind reader, stepped in. "I know you like him, Bren. In a way — oh boy, I hate to admit this after his behavior at the conference — I think he's good for you. Promise me, though, you won't sell yourself short."

"I won't." With Reggie's support, she felt a slight boost to her resolve. "It's up to him to make a move. If he doesn't show me he's capable of dealing with his problems, well, then he and I are through."

At that moment, the words he had written to her popped into her head: *Brenda, You brighten the dark, empty corners of my world.*

His presence brightened the darkness in her world too.

Would she be able to stay tough if he failed to redeem himself?

Chapter Twenty-Two

It wasn't the crash that woke her. On the night that Brenda's mother threw a lamp against the bedroom wall, Brenda was already lying awake, listening to her parents argue. A minute later, her younger sister, Marianne, crawled into Brenda's bed, scared and in tears.

They fell asleep together. The next morning, the front door slammed, waking Brenda. Outside, daylight peeked through the gap in the curtains. Her nightstand clock showed the middle school bus would arrive in an hour. Marianne didn't budge when Brenda slipped out from under the covers. She crept to her parents' bedroom, where the door had been left ajar.

"Mom?" Brenda dared to raise her voice a little higher than a whisper. "Are you sleeping?"

No reply. Brenda pushed open the door. The elegant bedroom was dimmed by closed roller shades, pulled tight to the windowsill. Her mother lay curled in a fetal position on the floor next to the mahogany four-poster bed. Dressed in a sleeveless baby blue nightgown, her honey-colored flip hairdo, usually perfectly coiffed, held none of its normal bounce. To her side sat a bottle of vodka. A handful of shots remained. Raspy, drawn-out breaths suggested her mother was asleep and not hurt.

The sizable ceramic lamp from their nightstand lay in the corner, smashed into three large pieces with smaller chunks and a displaced shade. Brenda tiptoed toward the bed. Taking the vodka, she hurried to the kitchen. At the sink, she twisted off the cap, then removed the drain stopper. Underneath the smooth white porcelain was a pipe that led to a place far from here. Starting to tip the bottle, she stopped. There would be repercussions. She replaced the cap and left the bottle on the counter.

* * *

Awake for the past half hour, Brenda watched the rising sun take her bedroom from dim to bright. She couldn't shake the childhood memory as she tried to fall back to sleep. In place of sleep, she participated in a wrestling match with her blankets as she tried to pin down her feelings about CJ. His anger over the emptied bottle didn't concern her. So many times during the course of her life, she'd dreamed of doing that. Not only with her mother, but with Jack too.

Yesterday's elimination of CJ's bourbon was a catalyst for change in Brenda's life. But could that life include CJ, after what had happened? CJ's shame over the role he had played in his wife's death tugged at her heart.

She understood that shame.

Her own shame over Jack's suicide followed her as closely as the dog most days. She willed the phone on her nightstand to ring, willed it to be CJ. She willed him to apologize and assure her that he'd work on his issues. All she got was silence.

After a shower and breakfast, she took a long walk with Georgie and contemplated the enormous task at hand: purging the unneeded remains of a once busy, thriving household. Over twenty years, the four McAllisters had gathered a ton of belongings. Few items ever left the house, each person clinging to their goods as if the fate of mankind depended on them. As the only person left in the house, she'd be the judge and jury about what could stay and what would go.

The only person in the house.

The words plunked at Brenda's feet and she tripped over them. Life alone in this large place was often burdensome. Simple things Jack would have fixed without difficulty, by grabbing a tool from the basement or taking a trip to the hardware store, often turned into big productions. The need to move was about more than that, though. Memories of the life she had shared with Jack followed her every day. They made it difficult to embrace her new status as near fifty and single again. The household cleanse represented a step toward a new life, and she didn't need her degree to recognize why it mattered.

Once home, she went upstairs. Working her way through various rooms, the hours passed. Every closet, drawer, or cardboard box she rummaged through became a portal to the past: old games in the family room closet, Devin's first pair of Rollerblades and his worn-out baseball mitt, clothes with the kids' sports teams displayed on jackets, and dated screen prints on T-shirts reminding her of Shannon's Backstreet Boys phase. Some of these items found their way to the Dumpster; others were tossed onto a pile for Goodwill or a pile for the homeless shelter.

When she pulled out a torn and tattered box containing Monopoly, the family's favorite game, a dull ache in her heart screamed out. Tears welled. Over twenty years of her life remained trapped in these walls, hidden in closets or stored in the attic, a life that had vanished with the loss of her husband.

She went downstairs to the kitchen sink, splashed water on her face and dried it with a paper towel. After making a turkey sandwich, she sat at the peninsula and ate while flipping through a magazine.

The wall clock showed it was close to one. A second wave of gloom rolled in with the realization that CJ hadn't tried to make amends. She checked for any missed calls while she had been out at the Dumpster or scouring in the deep recesses of a closet. No message.

This time the urge to call him didn't surface. The cleaning project had kick-started a feeling of renewal as if she manned the control panel of her destiny for a change. She wouldn't call him.

For once, Brenda had shed her usual skin. No more fixing. No more shoving her needs aside. No more playing the victim of circumstance.

Chapter Twenty-Three

"Come on, big guy. You climbed a 29,000 foot mountain. You can do this."

CJ's internal pep talk did little to calm his nerves, but he pulled into the driveway all the same. The number 16, to the right of the front door, confirmed that the white colonial with black shutters was Brenda's.

He stepped out of his car and looked around. Rounded shrubbery huddled in a neat row along the brick foundation, and mature trees towered over the rooftop like large stalks of broccoli in the early stages of bloom. He inspected the surroundings. Very suburbia. The nearby scenic preserve offered a back-to-nature neighborhood touch.

He leaned into the car and pulled out the bouquet of white tulips. Butterflies stirred to life inside his belly, but he tried to ignore them and rehearsed his apology, unsure how long Brenda would grant him an audience. Based on yesterday's exit, he hoped she didn't have a carton of rotten tomatoes on hand.

A shrill bark came from inside the garage. No sooner had he remembered Brenda's Web site picture with her terrier, than the same dog flew out of the open garage in a barking fury. The wiry dog stopped several feet away, but exhibited the seriousness of a Swiss Guardsman manning the gates of the

Vatican. Its guttural growl sent CJ a warning.

CJ kneeled and extended a hand to the furry security guard. "Hey, pup. Come here."

The dog tipped its head in a quick assessment, then backed away. If this was a sign, it told CJ that unexpected visitors weren't welcome.

After a restless night reliving the previous day's events and a solemn morning, mulling over ways to make amends, he was no closer to knowing how to make amends for what he had done to Brenda. At last, he had phoned her friend Reggie for help, the junior-highish act a sign of his desperation. Reggie's response was chilly. He offered a toned-down version of what had happened the night before, focusing on the anniversary date and his dark mood.

"I suspect you're not telling me everything." Reggie had said, sounding ticked off.

He flinched at the blunt jab. Brenda must have spoken to her already. "You're right. I'd been drinking."

An icy silence lasted for several seconds. Then Reggie said, "Possibly the worst thing you could do. There's history there."

"I had no idea." Now some of Brenda's comments at the height of her anger — or what he remembered of them — made a little more sense.

"Why are you calling me, anyway?"

"I need help fixing this. I need suggestions."

"She's my best friend. Why should I help you?"

He felt his last, best hope — her best friend — begin to slip through his fingers. He blurted out the truth: "Brenda is the person I've been waiting for. I don't want to lose her."

"She's spent a lot of her life picking up the pieces for people like you." Reggie took a scolding tone.

"I'm trying to pick up the pieces of this one. That's why I called you." Desperate, he shared something he'd only planned to tell Brenda. "I need help. And I'm willing to get some."

Reggie didn't reply right away. Her deep sigh crackled through the phone line. "Make the first move. Help her for a change."

"OK. I thought about going to her office for a surprise visit. I'm not sure she'll take my calls."

"Brenda doesn't go into the office on Wednesdays. She's home today." After a long beat, she added, "Her address is Sixteen Jacobs Lane in Greenwich, which I'm only handing over since these days everything's on the Internet anyway."

He scribbled down the information. "Thank you, Reggie. After a conference call at two I plan to head over. If you two talk before then, please don't mention my visit. After what I did, she might not answer the door."

"You've got until five." Reggie hung up.

The overseas work call had taken close to an hour. It was now four.

Brenda's voice echoed from inside the garage. "Georgie."

CJ stood and the small dog backed up. Brenda stepped out of the garage. Nervousness rushed at CJ, tackled him, stalled his breathing. She held an old wood-framed tennis racquet, still pressed tight in a four-sided wooden bracket with rusted wing-nut screws. Georgie ran to her side and offered yippy comments about CJ's arrival.

"Shhh!" The dog quieted but stayed by her side in a protective stance. Brenda's glower possessed the power of a Marvel Comics superhero, and landed on him with a sharp zap. "You have some nerve showing up unannounced."

"I thought if I called, you'd hang up on me."

"No. First, I'd say there's no room in life for people who abuse alcohol. Then I'd hang up. What do you want?"

"I'm here to apologize."

"Apologize?" She walked to the Dumpster and tossed the

old racquet inside. Turning to him, she crossed her arms and tilted her head. "I've received plenty of apologies in my life. They've never fixed a thing."

"Here." He held out the bouquet. "Did you know tulips symbolize that the cold and dark of winter has ended and better times are ahead?"

Brenda examined the flowers. "No." Her arms remained wrapped, secure as a straitjacket.

"They're also offered as a plea for forgiveness." CJ paused, but Brenda didn't budge. "Brenda, I am truly sorry."

She uncrossed her arms and reached for the bouquet. The stiff lines on her face relaxed — ever so slightly — for the first time since he'd arrived. "I'm cleaning and could use help with the heavier boxes." She headed for the garage and cast a glance over her shoulder. "That is, if you have time. Then maybe we can talk."

For the next twenty minutes, Brenda instructed CJ in various tasks with the compassion of a disgruntled DMV employee. Conversation was limited to the tasks at hand. CJ had gotten this far and was smart enough to not try to guide the conversation back to the reason behind his visit.

The second she had led him into the study, it became clear that what she was doing went beyond spring cleaning. An empty brass curtain rod remained over two double-hung windows. Several pieces of framed artwork sat propped against a wall. Unused nails remained exposed on white walls. Based on a large desk pushed into a corner with unplugged lamps on top, CJ guessed that the space used to be an office. A cardboard box labeled Jack's Books sat open next to a near-empty built-in bookcase. Jack's office.

After he had carried a heavy box of worn shoes out to the Dumpster, she said, "Almost done. These pictures go in the basement." She leaned over and lifted three of them. "Follow me."

CJ took the remaining pictures and they marched in silence down the hallway. The dog followed behind Brenda. A steady click of its nails sounded on the hardwood floor, keeping pace with Brenda's steps. One huge section of the hallway contained a collage of family photos, but Brenda's brisk stride didn't give CJ a chance to study them. They came right back upstairs and Brenda stopped at the stove, where a tantalizing aroma escaped from a red cast-iron pot, its lid jittery.

CJ noted the details of the room, after rushing through many times earlier. White cabinetry, a tiled floor of light gray squares, and vibrant red, blue, and yellow ceramic plates with Tuscan patterns. The white tulips he gave her jumped out against the speckled black marble countertop, where she'd dumped them on the way in—along with his apology.

"Smells good." CJ made his first attempt at small talk. "Expecting company?"

"No. I made beef stew." She lifted the lid and stirred the contents in the pot with a wooden spoon.

Her curve-revealing yoga pants, worn with a man's oversized oxford shirt tied in a knot near her hips, stirred his interest, but he tried to ignore his longing. She lowered the burner temperature and motioned with her index finger for him to follow. Back in the near-empty office, CJ felt warm, so he removed his sweatshirt. Underneath, he'd thrown on a black T-shirt. He lifted the last heavy box and caught Brenda inspecting his biceps. Flustered, she quickly looked away and asked him to take the carton to the Dumpster. On the way from the room, he gave her a knowing grin but wiped it away fast when she stared back, every facial muscle frozen in displeasure. God, she was the toughest nut he'd ever had to crack. But that was one of the things that made him like her.

On his way back from the Dumpster, he vowed to get this

conversation going, break through her tough facade and get her to talk. Brenda stood in the middle of the room with her hands on her hips and a troubled expression.

"What's wrong?"

"All that's left is to sort through those items." She blew out an exhausted breath and pointed to a large plastic bin on the floor next to a sofa. "I've been avoiding this all day."

"What's in it?"

"Special things that Jack, my husband, saved over the years." Her mouth sagged. Deep sadness behind her gaze showed the agony was about more than the added workload.

The day CJ had cleared Carla's items from the house, Dale and Vivian had been at his side the entire time. The memory still carried the sting of a paper cut, a pain he'd never forget.

She watched him for a beat. "I'm sure you know how hard this is."

"I do."

"When we moved here, Jack had things he insisted on keeping, some of them from his childhood." Brenda went to the bin and removed the lid. "I thought about tossing them, but they meant so much to him. So I drove to the hardware store and got him that bin. It's been shoved in the back of the closet for so many years, I hate to toss things he cared about. The kids might want something of his."

"I don't save much, but when I do, there's always a good reason." CJ suddenly felt dumped into the middle of her private world. "You're right to go through it. Would you prefer I leave?"

Without hesitation, she shook her head and grabbed him with her worried eyes. "I don't want to be alone right now."

"Then I'll stay." He wanted to pull her close in a hug to lessen the pain—the way she had tried to do for him yesterday. His limbs went heavy with regret over what he had done to her.

"Thanks." She almost smiled. Brenda plopped on the floor,

leaned against the sofa, and pulled the bin closer. CJ lowered himself to the floor on the other side of the container, his back also against the sofa. Georgie went right to Brenda and cast a suspicious glance in his direction.

"Hi, Georgie." He smiled. The dog's ears went back and CJ chuckled.

"Go say hi." Brenda encouraged Georgie with a motion of her chin toward CJ. Georgie stepped over Brenda's legs and padded over. While CJ stroked her back, she studied him with caution. A caution he figured she'd learned from her owner.

The phone rang. Brenda reached for a cordless headset on the sofa, giving a quick look at the caller ID before answering. "Hi, Reg."

She cradled the phone against her shoulder and reached into the bin, lifting out an old trophy. "Uh-huh." A long pause. "Really? Yes. He's here." She paused again and CJ heard Reggie's garbled voice on the other end.

Brenda put the trophy down and listened. "Glad you told me. No. I'm not mad...not at you, anyway." She stole a look at CJ. "Thanks. Call you later." She hung up.

"Wow." Brenda pulled a postcard from the bin and read the back. "You must have something pretty important to tell me if you contacted my friend."

"Brenda, there's no excuse for what happened yesterday." CJ dived for the first crack in the door since his arrival. "Telling you about the day I lost Carla, well, honestly, it scared the hell out of me."

She lowered the postcard and looked him in the eyes. "I know telling me was hard." There was sympathy in her tone.

"I'm ashamed of myself. Old habits die hard, I guess."

"Come on, CJ. Let's start by ditching the horrible excuses."

"You're right." He reached over and touched her arm. "The way you found me, I promise, it won't happen again."

The promise hung in the space between them, exposed and vulnerable. Her eyes narrowed. "Famous last words."

His arm dropped.

She tossed the postcard in a nearby trash can with the same ease with which she had dismissed his promise, and then returned to rummaging through the bin. Her disregard nudged him like a schoolyard bully, but he didn't cower. He rose to his own self-defense.

"Brenda! Look at me."

She lifted her head.

"I never talk to anybody about the accident. Only Dale." CJ never forgot Dale's lowered eyes, the slow shake of his head as the details spilled out or the shame of divulging them. "Even his judgment was obvious. Brenda, I...I care for you, want you in my life. Jesus, if you only knew how much I worried about confessing to you."

She didn't answer but lowered her gaze to her lap. Her mouth turned down. His fingertip traced the grain of the oak floorboard. Based on the strong lines, the wood probably came from an old tree. It had stood strong before being chopped down for use. The car accident had drained CJ's strength, even after the physical injuries had healed. He knew that he'd never fully recovered. Talking to Brenda, though, freed his former spirit, made him feel stronger.

"That accident, my lack of concern for someone else's safety...it's the most shameful thing I've ever done. If I told you and you walked away..." CJ stopped, unsure what might happen, although the possibilities consumed him with dread.

"Telling me was big." Brenda looked at him, her expression transformed to compassionate. "You were brave to open up and trust me. I understand shame. It comes in many different forms. We've all done things we're not proud of." The pain returned and clouded her face. They were no longer discussing his problems.

"I can't imagine you've done anything to be ashamed of."

"We're *all* capable of doing things to hurt the people we love." She pulled an item from the bin—a certificate—and acted overly interested in the find.

Reggie's short history lesson about Brenda's past returned, but something seemed incomplete.

"Did my drinking yesterday mean anything more to you?" CJ asked.

The certificate went into the trash. Brenda nodded, then quietly revealed the circumstances of her childhood and problems in her marriage. The matter-of-fact manner in which she spoke didn't deceive him. Every once in a while she removed an item from the bin or touched her face or tucked a few hairs behind her ear. Most of the time, she avoided his gaze.

He wished he could have given her a hug to make it better, but he didn't dare. "I'm sorry you went through all that."

"Me too." She scrutinized him for several seconds. "If you'd known my story before, would I have found you drunk yesterday?"

CJ didn't know but wanted to be honest. "I sure hope not." When she pursed her lips, he added, "I plan on getting help. A couple of years back, Dale recommended someone I should talk to. It's time I went. In fact, I've already left a message to set up an appointment."

She stared at him, measuring the statement as though she possessed an internal truth meter. Without a reply, she returned to the bin. Her face brightened when she removed a photograph, one with the distinct paper size of an instant camera shot.

"I can't believe Jack kept this." She studied the picture as the glaze of a memory filled her eyes.

"What?"

"Oh, Jack and I lived together for a year before we got

married. That year we were invited to a Halloween party, so I bought a witch costume." She lowered the picture. "I also got another outfit he didn't know about at a lingerie shop, for the anniversary of our first year living together. The night of the party, when he came home from work, I wore the lingerie but told him it was my costume. Back then, quite a risqué costume. Nowadays you'd find an outfit like that prepackaged and worn by girls in high school." Brenda shrugged. "Times sure have changed."

"May I see?"

"Sure." She handed CJ the picture.

He held it at arm's length since he'd left his reading glasses in the car. A bit younger-looking and slightly more slender, Brenda wore black stockings, a garter, and a tight corset. A black feather boa draped her shoulders and her hands grasped the furry object on both sides. She posed, twisted at the waist.

"Very sexy." CJ grinned and arched a brow. "You could've gone as Gypsy Rose Lee."

She chuckled. "Gee, thanks, Gramps."

"What'd Jack do?"

"At first, he was deliriously happy with the outfit. Then he said 'Wait, *this* is for the party?' I let him believe it for a while and worry about his girlfriend walking out the door dressed so provocatively."

"If I were in his shoes, we'd have been late for the party."

"Oh, we were." This time she raised a brow at him. "He insisted on taking this photograph with our Polaroid so he could have a reminder of what waited at home during his trips. He worked as an auditor for a CPA firm and traveled a lot."

CJ studied the picture. "You haven't changed much since then."

She chortled. "I notice you're not wearing your glasses, but I'll still take the farsighted compliment. Twenty-five years ago I found all sorts of flaws with my body. Now my Miss October days are looking pretty damn good."

Their hands brushed as he handed the photo back. In a tender voice, he said, "You're still very beautiful."

Their eyes locked. He sensed a momentary weakening in her barrier.

She returned to her hunt through Jack's items without commenting.

CJ understood why Jack had saved the photo. Women underestimated how a small act, like buying a sexy outfit for a special night with their guy, could go a long way. When Carla had done something like that, CJ had repaid her in multiples with model husband gestures for the next couple of days. Brenda showed she was the kind of woman who made things special for the people she cared for.

Regret over his pathetic actions the day before swelled. "I read the accounting books you left behind yesterday." After the call to Reggie, he hoped to use them like an ace in his pocket if the game got tough. "I understand the tabbed sections."

"You took that slow form of torture over doing something better with your free time, like cleaning the bathrooms?"

He grinned. "I hoped doing so might keep me in your good graces, or at least prevent you from throwing me out the door on my ass the second you saw me."

"Do I seem like the kind of lady who'd throw someone out on his ass?" She grinned, and her eyes sparkled for the first time since CJ's arrival. The first sign he might be forgiven.

"Only to someone who deserved it."

Her lips wiggled as she fought a smile. "As you did?"

"Did? Am I forgiven?"

"Weren't those books boring?" She ignored his question.

"Not the stuff compelling drama is made of, but they serve a purpose."

"Thanks." Her face warmed. "I appreciate it more than you know."

The statement carried weight and left him curious about her marriage. After such a tragic and painful loss, he really didn't know how Brenda viewed her future. He sure wanted her in his, though, and wasn't going to let this opportunity slip away.

Taking her hand, he flattened the palm against his chest, right near his heart. "I know your husband had problems, but I can't imagine how he could have left all this behind." His voice softened. "I'd give anything for this life, to be with you."

Their eyes locked. Each second she didn't respond carried the weight of a minute.

"Would you like to stay for dinner?"

"I'd love to." CJ's entire body relaxed, awash with relief he hadn't felt all day.

Chapter Twenty-Four

Georgie poked her head into the lower cabinet where Brenda searched for a wide-mouthed crystal vase. She found one and, after adding water, slowly lowered the large bouquet into the container. They settled into a perfect arrangement, as if they already knew their places. She wished life were so easy.

Even though she had hidden her delight over the flowers, CJ had impressed her. He could have simply swung into the local grocery story and run out with a $9.99 mixed-bouquet special. Plus, even if reading those accounting regulations was all about scoring points, at least he showed a willingness to help her. Brenda seldom asked for assistance. When she did, it was a last resort, a fact that Jack had seldom grasped.

The late afternoon sun streamed into the room, casting a band of brightness across the bouquet. The random act of nature seemed to be trying to tell her something.

The phone rang and she grabbed the kitchen wall phone. "Hello."

"Brenda. It's Rosie. I'm sorry to bother you again."

"It's no bother." She stretched the cord to the window and saw CJ leaving the garage and heading toward his car to get Jack's accounting books. "I've only got a quick second. Company is over."

"Sure. Sure. Listen, I hate to be blunt, but did you tell Luc Pelletier we'd talked recently?"

"No. Of course not. I know that if anybody knew about our conversations, it could compromise your employment at GBS."

After several seconds of silence, leaving Brenda uncomfortable, Rosie said, "He came up to me at work today as I was packing to leave. Wanted to know if we'd talked lately. I told him no, but he acted like he didn't believe me." Rosie sounded worried. "He looked like hell. Stressed, tired eyes. Wanted to know if I was close enough to you to go over and help you look for some papers in Jack's home office. When I asked what he was talking about, he got all huffy and stormed off. Do you know what he's talking about?"

The question made Brenda feel cornered. "Look, Luc's obviously having some problems with his bosses. Maybe that's why he's stressed. Stick to your story. I'll never tell him we talked. And Rosie, the less you know about my conversations with Luc, the better. You never know if you'll be subpoenaed if the Justice Department takes this thing further."

A noise made her turn around. CJ had put down the books on the counter and watched her on the phone. She forced a smile and held up a finger.

Rosie sighed deeply. "Good point."

"Thanks for the heads-up. Really, Rosie, thank you for all you've done. I've gotta run, but call me again if you need to." Brenda walked to the wall to hang up. It brought her close to CJ.

"I see you're enjoying the flowers," he said.

"They're beautiful. Thank you." Brenda gently touched his forearm and the corners of his eyes softened. "Have a seat." She motioned to the stools next to the kitchen peninsula. "Can I get you something to drink?"

"Some water, thanks." He sat and slipped on half-framed

reading glasses.

After grabbing two bottles from the refrigerator, she slid onto the stool beside him. "Are you about to tell me everything I ever wanted to learn about generally accepted accounting principles but was afraid to ask?"

"It's not so bad. Nobody ever died from boredom." He grinned and twisted off his bottle cap, more relaxed than earlier. After a sip, he opened the book to one of the tabbed sections. "These books state the rules publicly owned companies are required to follow with their financial record keeping, to prevent them from doing things on paper which misstate their true performance."

"Firms sometimes do that because of pressure to have their numbers appear better, right?"

"Yup. You could teach this stuff."

She chuckled. "To be honest, when Jack went into more detail than that, my mind went numb."

"The contents can be pretty mind-numbing. Actually, reading these books got me curious about accounting fraud in general, which isn't a new issue. Most fraud nowadays is related to overstating revenues. One of the most famous accounting fraud cases happened in 1938. A company took advantage of the lack of rules about inventory accounting. They claimed to own ten million dollars' worth of inventory, but the stuff didn't exist, which understated their cost of goods sold."

"I'd say 'what?' but don't really want you to repeat it." Brenda cracked a smile to match the dry comment.

"It's another way to manipulate earnings. Everything seems to come back to earnings."

She remembered everything Luc had told her. "OK, smarty-pants writer guy. Does any of this relate to the sections Jack marked in his books?"

"Yup. In fact, all of the places he marked have to do with

rules about revenue recognition."

"In English, please."

"All the places Jack marked relate to proper handling of revenue items, like sales. Sometimes firms manipulate their books by making sales seem better than they really are."

"How can you fib about a sale? You sell something and add it to one of those green accounting sheets, right?"

"Not really. More than one line on a financial statement flows into sales. Like returns or bad debt, for example. You can deceive people by timing when a transaction is truly defined as" — CJ made air quotes — "a 'sale' versus something else."

Brenda pretended to hold onto a fake cigar and wiggled her brows in Marx-brothers fashion. "Somebody should write rules for this stuff."

His lips curved upward. "Good idea, Groucho." His eyes lifted over the tops of his glasses.

She suddenly became aware of the closeness of their seats, the closeness of his arm next to hers, and the closeness of his face. Neither of them looked away. She wandered in the pull of his gaze, lost, unable to leave. The stroke of his lips stalked her memory, and she wished for a repeat performance.

CJ shifted on his stool. "Jack marked off several FASB, Financial Accounting Standards Board, rules on this topic." He flipped the pages. "There's 'Revenue Recognition, when right of return exists,' standard number forty-eight, and…" — he turned several more pages — "number forty-nine, 'Accounting for Product Financing Arrangements'…"

Brenda listened closely, recalling several comments in the e-mails between Jack and Bob discussing sales. They were innocuous the first time she read them, but now they took on new meaning. "Hold on." She walked over to the kitchen drawer and removed a manila folder. "I found this in Jack's office here at the house. I think they discuss things from those rules. It was tucked away in his desk, almost hidden."

"What's inside?"

"Several e-mail exchanges between Jack and the firm's CEO, Bob Manning." Brenda opened the folder, scanned the first few pages, and handed one to CJ. "This one discusses sales. Maybe the topic applies to one of those accounting rules you mentioned."

He examined the paper. The vertical crease at the pinch of his nose deepened with his scrutiny. "Do you mind if I take a peek at the rest of those?"

"No. Did you find something?" Her heart took a lively step, the first flicker of hope she'd had in weeks that Bob Manning might not have complete control over the situation.

CJ removed another e-mail. "Maybe. Give me a minute." He sorted through the folder, quickly absorbed in the contents.

Brenda busied herself making a salad for their dinner. For the first time in years, she didn't feel like a lone woman going up against an army, thanks to CJ. She glimpsed at him shuffling between the book and the e-mails. This afternoon he had lavished her with gifts, attention, and assistance in multiple arenas. She wanted to believe in magic, believe this to be real. At the refrigerator, she reached deep in the back for a bag of tomatoes.

"Who's Luc?"

The cool air inside the refrigerator collided with heat rising along her cheeks. "Jack's work colleague. Why?"

"There's a Post-it note in the back of the folder. Did you know that?"

"I did." Brenda wanted to stay hidden in the trenches with the food, primarily to avoid looking CJ in the face. Instead, she grabbed the tomatoes and a block of cheese, then came out of hiding. "It's pretty ominous." She fled to the safety of the sink, where she kept her back to him. "There's more to this than those papers."

"Oh?"

"Days before news of the prosecutor's case against Global Business Solutions, I got a call from Luc Pelletier, the 'Luc' Jack warned me about." She rinsed the tomatoes and paused long enough to carefully select her next words. "He's the VP of technology but was also a close friend of Jack's. We met for lunch and he warned me about the SEC charges a day before they were in the papers. He also informed me the CEO of GBS, Bob Manning, would be fingering Jack as the mastermind behind the fraud."

"So much for the buck stopping at the top." CJ's voice dripped with disgust.

"I've never liked or trusted Bob. Call it a gut read." She faced CJ and reached for the cutting board. "At lunch, Luc suggested Jack may have left something at home to prove he didn't act alone. That's why the note doesn't make any sense. All the things Luc has done make him seem like an ally. But that note..."

"How well do you know him? Is that the Luc I heard you mention on the phone just now?"

She twirled to face the cutting board and chopped to hide any giveaways in her expression. "Uh-huh. He spent a lot of time here. From time to time we went out with Luc and his wife."

"Sounds like you were close."

"The guys were." The heat of the lie burned brilliant in her mind, probably on her face too. The trained eye of an admitted people-observer like CJ would certainly notice. The act of cutting the tomato suddenly took on the concentration of brain surgery.

"Anyway, Luc's suggestion to search Jack's home office was a good idea, but I put it off for a while. The room made me uncomfortable. Too many memories. Especially of the day I found Jack's body. The police asked me to search there for a suicide note." She dumped the chopped vegetables into the salad.

"*You* found him? He died here?"

She nodded, adding in a quiet voice, "The garage. Exhaust asphyxiation." Her chest tightened. She swallowed and reached for the cheese.

"Did you ever find a note?"

"No." Crumbling the feta, she glanced over at CJ. The muscles of his eyes wilted with concern.

"Was his office the room we cleared today?"

"Yes. Luc's request pushed me to find out what Jack left behind." Brenda rinsed her hands and dried them with a dish towel as she turned to meet CJ's solemn stare. "I don't want my husband's name dragged through the mud."

CJ lifted the Post-it note. "Did Jack write this note?"

She nodded. "I was shocked. I wish I knew what he meant."

CJ studied the paper. "There were no signs the two men might have had problems?" He looked at her. "Any secrets between them?"

Brenda suddenly felt like a witness in a courtroom drama contriving a carefully worded response. She walked over to the peninsula and faced CJ. Rosie's comment about Brenda's name surfacing during the argument replayed. "None I'm aware of." She forced herself to maintain eye contact. "The warning note gave me the idea to call Jack's assistant. I figured she had a front-row seat to his workday."

Brenda repeated Rosie's story: Bob's demand that she lock Jack's office, his confiscation of the keys, the e-mails that she uncovered and which then went missing. She told CJ that Luc also held a key to the office and how Rosie had overheard a fight between the two men, but she omitted the mention of her own name in the argument. CJ listened quietly, drumming his fingers on his lips the whole time.

"The folder Rosie believes went missing appears to be another set of what we have here." Brenda tapped on the manila folder. "Based on who held keys, either Bob Manning or Luc took the original set. And if I can't trust Luc…"

"Has he contacted you again?"

"Unfortunately. He's been hounding me to check the home office, even offered to help. He seems unusually anxious."

CJ rubbed his chin and pursed his lips. "After looking at these e-mails, it appears Jack played a role in some highly illegal transactions." CJ's grave expression made her worry. "But, they also prove Bob's involvement. In Jack's defense, he cautions Bob in writing about the legalities, but was threatened when he did so."

"Threatened? How?"

CJ lifted a page. "In an e-mail from Bob, after Jack tried to dissuade him from several transactions, he writes 'your unhelpfulness is about to fall into career-limiting territory.'" He looked up. "That's a job threat, if you ask me."

"Jesus." Brenda sat next to CJ, stunned, but at last grasping onto a piece of real evidence against Bob. The reality pooled in her mind, seeped in with slow effort like rain on dry dirt. Did Luc know about these e-mails? Is that what he wanted?

"You OK?" CJ removed his glasses.

"How's this possible? Jack worked for years to police this very sort of activity. Participating in these acts must've been torture." A switch flipped inside Brenda, and she slapped the marble counter. "God damn him. If he'd just told me, I would have insisted he quit and find another job. Why didn't he trust me? I could've helped."

"He'd already committed the crime. Bob might have been holding the actions over his head to keep him there."

"So?" Her anger toward Jack escalated. "You don't

understand. Jack could be complacent with problems — at home, too. I didn't try to change him. But on something this huge — I mean he was coerced into breaking the law — I can't believe he let it eat him alive rather than try to find a way out. He could have reported Bob to the SEC, shown them the e-mails."

CJ slid his hand over hers. "Brenda, that would have been a huge boat to rock. Was Jack the type to take on such a huge fight?"

"No." The truth in his comment made her anger deflate. "Not at all."

They both sat in silence, staring at the countertop. She enjoyed the feel of CJ's warm hand over hers.

"Why is Luc in the middle of all this?" CJ tipped his head. "You said he works in their computer department, not finance."

"He claims his concern is about Jack. It seemed legitimate at first — at least until I found the Post-it note with Jack's warning."

"How is he hounding you?"

"A lot of phone calls asking if I've cleaned the office. Wants to come over and help. That's all." Uneasy going down this path, she still wanted to be somewhat truthful. "I keep putting him off. He even called again yesterday, but I didn't return the call."

"Doesn't his persistence seem over the top?"

CJ was right. Luc's overwhelming concern didn't make sense. Did this have more to do with rekindling their personal relationship? Or was it something else?

CJ waited, his dark brows bent. The day they first kissed, he'd expressed shame in his disloyalty to Autumn. How would he react to the news that Brenda wasn't a model spouse? Or that Luc's behavior might, in fact, be about her?

* * *

Georgie yipped at the French doors to go outside. Brenda ignored her. Seconds earlier, with dinner finished, CJ had slid his palm across the tabletop, taken her hand, and placed a gentle kiss on the tips of her fingers.

A flickering flame in the middle of the kitchen table sparkled in CJ's dark irises as he watched her, waiting for a reaction. The Three Tenors serenaded them in the background, like cheerleaders for his advances.

"Do you always distract the hostess before the dishes are cleared off the table?"

"Only the pretty ones," he replied softly.

Georgie yipped again.

"Thanks, mood breaker." Brenda looked at the dog, who was wagging her short tail impatiently.

CJ chuckled. "Is she smart enough for that interruption to be intentional?"

"Sometimes I wonder. Duty calls." Brenda stood and their hands slipped apart. "While I clean up, would you mind taking the dog out back?"

"Sure." He got up and patted his side. Georgie followed him and the pair walked out the door.

After clearing the table, Brenda loaded the dishwasher, then filled the sink with soapy water and watched them from the kitchen window while she washed a few items. Dusk fell on the property, one step away from darkness. CJ tossed one of Georgie's favorite toys, a neon tennis ball, across the yard. Georgie bolted like her survival depended on the catch. CJ called to her and learned fast that Georgie liked the game of "retrieve and keep."

Things between them throughout dinner had returned to preproblem levels. In fact, the prior day's crisis had fostered a new openness. When she offered him wine, he opted out, claiming he wanted his wits about him with her today. The unrequested gesture gave her hope in the possibility of a relationship.

CJ talked about how he had met his wife, his family, and the tumultuous relationship with his father. She discussed the better days of her married life, glossing over the later years. Although she came within a millimeter of telling him about her transgressions with Luc, the words never left her mouth. Knowledge of their involvement wouldn't help solve their current problem.

A moment later, CJ and Georgie came inside. CJ excused himself to wash his hands in the half bath down the hall. He returned, grabbed a dish towel off the stove handle, and dried the wooden salad bowl.

"Thanks again for the delicious meal. Did your mother teach you to cook?"

She laughed. "I learned to cook like this *because* of my mother. A family meal is hard to make if you're passed out. I got tired of eating cereal for dinner." She shrugged. "I did OK for a teenager without much direction."

"Oh." His mouth dipped into a frown.

Brenda returned to her washing but observed his pensive expression in the reflection of the darkened window above the sink. "Don't be sad. I'm not. Those things happened a long time ago."

"Yeah, but kids shouldn't have to fill the role of a parent."

"No, but if you have no choice, then you do it. Plenty of kids have endured far worse." She held up a dripping pot, which CJ swathed in the dish towel. "Family problems can make a kid grow up fast."

He nodded and continued to dry. The atmosphere shifted once again. There wasn't quite an elephant in the room, but something was skulking in the corner.

Handing CJ a washed wine goblet, Brenda pointed to the corner. "Those go in the cabinet over there." Staring out the window into the night, the dark glass reflection allowed her to look at CJ while he dried and put away the goblet. He turned around and approached the sink, studying her, unaware that she was also observing him. He moved close behind and when he looked up, he caught her gaze in the glass.

"Jack's drinking must have been like reliving the past." CJ's tone was careful, a balance of concern and sympathy.

"At times." Her hands rested in the soapy water.

"Yesterday must've seemed that same way too." He watched her reflection. "I'm truly sorry, Brenda."

"I've already forgiven you."

"I would never hurt you on purpose. I don't want to be another person who creates problems in your life."

Although inches apart, she already felt his energy throughout her entire body. She stilled, waiting for and wanting his touch. Their gazes remained locked, reflected by the window, and she knew that the connection she felt for him wouldn't disappear.

Quieter, near a whisper, he said, "Sometimes the past clings to you. Mine did."

She nodded. Her past adhered the way a leech did, often feeding off her for survival.

He circled his arms her shoulders. His warm cheek settled next to face, and from behind his body pressed against hers. Removing her hands from the soapy water, he dried them with the dish towel, then dropped it on the counter. In one swift movement, he turned her around and took her into his embrace. His closeness, the faded scent of sandalwood cologne, the secure hold to his chest—all assured her that anything in the world could happen and she'd be safe.

His mouth moved close to her ear. "Thank you for giving me another chance."

Before she could answer, he set his mouth on hers. She drank in the soft and tender attentions of his hips. His large hand traced her side, stopping on her hip and holding her steady. The other caressed her nape, then slid upward to cradle her head. Holding her in place, he deepened the kiss.

When they finally parted, she wasn't about to let him go. "Any chance you'd like to join me upstairs?" Her mouth brushed lightly against his cheek.

"I'd be a fool to say no to you."

"You would. Oh, and for future reference, you were ninety percent forgiven with the flowers. Nice delivery."

"I meant every word." He tenderly kissed the top of her head. "What got me the last ten percent of the way?"

"Drying the dishes."

"Duly noted." CJ kissed her again and left her so unsteady that only his hold kept her upright.

* * *

The edges of an erotic dream gradually faded. Brenda squeezed her eyes tight and willed herself back to sleep. Loving lips sampled her neck, and a warm hand circled her abdomen. Then she remembered that it wasn't a dream. CJ had spent the night.

The kiss in the kitchen had led them to her bedroom where they satisfied their passion, engaged in intimate pillow talk, and allowed themselves to fall asleep entangled in the tenderness of each other's hold. Now, his touch roused her, making her thankful that her first appointment at work wasn't until eleven.

A slow lift of her eyelids revealed the morning light, sneaking past cracks in the tab curtains. For a millisecond, she feared that in the light of day, the reality of sexual contact with someone his own age might create nostalgia for his perky-breasted, younger companions. Most men were blind enough to their own flaws to believe they deserved better than they could offer. But as the warm hand resting on her stomach inched down and stroked her thigh, turning her internal burner to high, she reminded herself to stop dwelling on her flaws.

She spooned closer. His arms circled her, then secured her in place. "Good morning. Don't you ever rest?"

"Not with you so close to me." His voice still carried the husky sound of sleep.

"Why's that?" Brenda curled farther into his body.

"Mmmm." He nibbled her earlobe, leaving delicate tickles from his facial hair. "Like you don't know."

He cupped her breasts but she wiggled free, then flipped on her side to face him, adjusting the patterned quilt in the process. She propped herself up on her elbow so that her face hovered above his. He slipped a hand behind his head and chuckled.

"What's so funny?"

"The very first time I ever saw you, you looked like this — sleepy eyes, messy hair." He fondled a few strands of her hair. "You're cute."

Brenda groaned. "Cute? I hoped you'd forgotten my appearance. If I recall, the look you gave was closer to disgust."

"No." His brows furrowed. "I questioned why you'd come to the lobby looking like you'd just rolled out of bed."

"I *had* just rolled out of bed." Brenda swirled her index finger through mixed gray and white hairs on his chest. "Primping is a low priority when making an emergency cup o' joe run."

"That was my lucky day, even with the spill." CJ ran an appreciative hand along her shoulder and sent warm tingles to all the right places.

Brenda lifted the covers and peeked under them. "OK, mister. Where's CJ? He's waaaay more skeptical than you."

"Every now and then I see the light. That flying cup of coffee hit me like a brick. I couldn't get you out of my head all day." CJ rolled onto his side and slung his hand over her hip. "When I bump into a good thing, I know it."

The unhurried movement of his hand traced her backside and sent a wave of heat to her core. Brenda's concentration was split between their conversation and his hand movements. She shifted her leg and rubbed it against his thigh. "Aha. So you admit *you* bumped into *me*."

"A figurative bump, my dear."

She flattened her hands near his shoulders and enjoyed their muscular firmness. The conversation no longer held interest. She leaned close to kiss him just as his gentle massage of her bottom stopped.

"Hey, what gives? I was enjoying that."

His deep gaze filled with intensity. "From the very first day we met, I've been following a path to your heart."

Her chest swelled with reciprocal feeling. "I'm glad you stayed on that path." The tip of her finger traced his full lips. He caught it with a soft kiss. It brought back the loving forages he had taken over her body many times during the night.

As if he had read her mind, he teased her bare shoulders with tender, moist nips and worked his way around her body. Strong hands held her as his mouth began its exploration. Brenda, bathed in the sea of sensations, put herself at his mercy and let him own her until she could take it no longer. Her blissful sigh sent him a signal. CJ moved on top of her, capturing her mouth with a thorough kiss and pressing his arousal close. Brenda shifted her hips to allow their bodies to join.

Through eyes blazing with passion, he whispered, "I hope this is the first of many mornings I wake up next to you."

She did too.

Chapter Twenty-Five

CJ accelerated on the I-95 ramp toward Greenwich but groaned when he hit the bright taillights of Friday afternoon commuter traffic. Even though he had a lot to do before leaving for Paris on Sunday morning, he'd called Brenda the second he got home from her place on Thursday morning and asked for a Friday night date. Reason argued that he could survive ten days away from their blooming relationship, but the memory of Brenda's tender kisses, her soft skin, and the elation in his heart pushed for one more date before his departure.

His cell rang and he tapped his Bluetooth headset. "Hello?"

"Hi. It's Brenda."

"I was just thinking about you. Did you get in touch with Hugh?"

"Yup. In fact, one of his partners is a criminal defense attorney, specializing in high-profile, white-collar crimes. Hugh's going to have him call me. He thinks the SEC would be quite interested in those e-mails Jack saved but doesn't think I should approach them alone. Thanks for the name."

"Glad he could help. I've hit some traffic but I should be there in time for the movie."

"About that, I got home later than expected. Would you

mind staying in tonight? We could get takeout and watch a movie at home. Tomorrow's forecast is for rain. Maybe we can catch a matinee before you leave."

"I'm yours to do whatever you'd like."

"Anything? So Bingo's not off the table?"

He chuckled. "Nothing will get me to turn this car around."

"Good." Brenda paused. "I can't wait to see you."

"Me too." CJ hung up.

The electric guitar sounds of Led Zeppelin played low in the background, the song, "Ten Years Gone," an ironic coincidence. Years ago he had read that the songwriter, Robert Plant, penned the tune after a woman gave him a choice: her or his music.

When CJ wrote *The Hourglass,* the story idea stemmed from his own three lost chances at love in the course of his life. The last and most devastating loss was Carla. The book's theme had suited his mood. Time had run out for him, the same way it had for his character. He had believed that he would never love again.

Yet now the possibility dangled in front of him, and his choice was obvious. He hummed along to the radio, happily.

A short while later, he turned off the crowded highway and navigated the Greenwich roads toward Brenda's neighborhood. Near the nature preserve, he slowed the car to turn into her driveway. A metallic red BMW caught his eye, backed into the corner spot at the far end of the preserve's parking lot. It had been parked there the other day too. He'd taken special note because he'd always admired the sleek lines of the 328i xDrive Coupe. At one time he'd considered the model for himself.

Through the tinted glass, a shadow of a man's silhouette sat behind the wheel. Probably some guy doing something behind his wife's back or looking for a minute of escape from a busy household.

CJ pulled into Brenda's driveway, grabbed his overnight bag

from the passenger seat, and trotted to the front door. The BMW left his thoughts, replaced with the knowledge that he was seconds away from holding Brenda in his arms.

Chapter Twenty-Six

"Guess the forecasts for rain on Saturday were right." Brenda motioned toward the dark clouds in the distance as she and CJ walked down her driveway to his car. The twenty-four hours they'd just spent together had passed far too quickly. "Let's hope you get home before it starts." She tried to sound optimistic, concealing her disappointment over the end of his visit. Their Friday night together had been low-key and lovely. It had felt like simple, long-overdue companionship.

Saturday morning, they'd lolled in bed, eaten a late breakfast, then taken a romantic walk in the nature preserve. The day had concluded with a busy afternoon at the movies and an early dinner at a nearby restaurant. The unexpected grand finale, an encore performance in her bedroom, further delayed CJ's return home to pack for his early morning flight.

"I'd be in Chappaqua already if you didn't keep tempting me." CJ's face pulled into mock reprimand.

"Me? The problem isn't my prowess as femme fatale but your lack of willpower."

"Hey, I managed to get through the meal without sprinting from the table and dragging you back into bed. That last round was all your doing."

She snickered, then smoothed the inside of his palm with her fingertips. "You didn't seem to mind."

He pulled her close and planted a tender kiss on her lips. "It'll be a miracle if I get to the airport tomorrow."

Opening the car door, he tossed his bag and denim jacket on the passenger seat. He pushed up the sleeves on a thin V-necked sweater, and gazed at Brenda. She leaned against the Mercedes, enjoying the view of his muscular forearms.

Mid sleeve-roll, he stopped. "What?"

"Are you sure you need to leave?" She arched a suggestive brow, then looked him up and down hungrily.

"Like I said." He took her arm and drew her close. "A miracle."

* * *

When CJ finally got in his car and pulled away, Brenda watched his taillights disappear down the street. The sight left her feeling empty in a way she hadn't expected. She shivered from a cool breeze as the dark clouds overhead inched closer. Once inside, she went straight upstairs to get a sweater. A messy bed greeted her, the sheets tangled as if a wrestling match had taken center stage on her king-size Sealy Posturepedic.

Tired, she plopped onto her back and her lids drooped. CJ's cologne wafted over her, invisible proof that he'd lain there not too long ago. Brenda pulled the sheet close and inhaled, stirring memories of their passion. Outside, a low rumble of thunder made her wish he hadn't left. After a minute, she forced herself up and began to make the bed. As she pulled up the top sheet, she spotted CJ's cell phone on her nightstand.

Once through with the bed, Brenda slipped on a cardigan and tucked the cell phone in the deep pocket. On her way downstairs to feed the dog, she decided to call his home phone and leave a message. He'd need this for his trip. Maybe she'd drive to his house, sneak in one last kiss.

Approaching rain clouds darkened the house. She flipped on several lights. The doorbell rang and Georgie flew into her usual barking rage.

"Shhhh!" Georgie quieted after one final bark and followed behind her to the foyer. A welcoming expression planted in place, she pulled open the door. "Forget someth..."

Brenda stared wide-eyed at Luc Pelletier.

"Hello, Brenda." Luc stared back, straight-lipped and serious.

"What a surprise." Brenda offered a weak smile, hoping to soften his obvious irritation over all the unreturned calls.

"May I come in?" His face remained stony.

"Sure." Brenda held the door open but immediately wished she hadn't.

The odor of cigarette smoke came with him when he stepped inside. "I see you've found yourself a new boyfriend."

"What do you want, Luc?"

"Why aren't you returning my calls?" he snapped with the force of a whip.

"On second thought, you can leave."

He snorted and brushed past her toward the living room, an envelope clutched in his hand. "We need to talk."

An internal alarm sounded and triggered a tightening in her stomach. Jack's note flashed in her mind: *Don't trust anybody. Even Luc.* Trust or not, she couldn't get rid of him now. She followed him to the living room.

"Looks like you've cleaned out Jack's office." Luc took an uninvited seat on the sofa.

Brenda rested her hands on her hips. "How would you know?"

"While you were out earlier, I let myself in." His self-satisfied expression made her want to lunge at him. "With the key you have hidden on the patio."

"Jesus, Luc! You broke into my house? What's wrong with you?"

He held up a large golden envelope. "It's time you understood what's going on. Let's start with you telling me what you found in the office."

Anger at his arrogance trumped curiosity about the contents of the envelope. "How dare you break in here and act as if I owe you answers."

He held up his palm. "Save the drama. Did Jack leave anything in there related to this SEC investigation?"

She took a deep breath to clear her thoughts. She had to be sure she didn't slip and tell him anything. "No. He didn't. I only cleaned a few days ago. I planned on calling to tell you once I wasn't so busy."

"Busy screwing your new boyfriend. Must be serious since you're doing sleepovers already."

"How the hell do you know? The reason I didn't sleep with you was because we were both married. Or did you forget?"

His cold stare would have made ice shiver. "What did you find in the office?"

"Nothing. There were work papers, but nothing I found proved Jack's innocence."

He shook his head. "I know he left something in this house."

"How do you know? Besides, why are *you* so obsessed with locating those documents?"

Luc leaned back and removed a pack of Gauloises. "This isn't about Jack's innocence. It's about making sure Bob Manning isn't found guilty." He removed a cigarette from the pack. "Ashtray?"

"I don't allow smoking inside. Besides, I thought you quit."

"Get me an ashtray or I will find one myself." He crossed his legs and confidently leaned into the sofa. "There's more you need to know. I am not leaving."

She definitely didn't want him snooping around, especially in the kitchen. She walked off to get an ashtray.

Had she heard him right? This was more about Bob not being found guilty than about helping her husband? She glanced to the kitchen drawer. The folder containing the evidence Luc demanded hid inside. Better hiding spots crossed her mind, but just as she was about to move the documents she remembered CJ's cell phone in her sweater pocket. If someone else knew Luc was here, she'd gain some small measure of peace.

She took out the phone and started to dial Reggie's number, forming the brief words she planned to whisper about his arrival in her mind. If Luc became violent and hurt her, at least someone would know.

"Hurry up, Brenda," Luc hollered. "Or do you need help finding an ashtray too?"

A nervous churn rolled in her stomach. Brenda pocketed the phone. The ashtray would take some digging and she didn't want Luc coming in here. She began to search for one, stretching to reach an upper cabinet where she stored rarely used items. After pushing aside a warehoused-size box of artificial sweetener and a can of WD-40 she found a ceramic ashtray. She returned to the living room. Luc already had a lit cigarette dangling from his mouth.

After a long drag, he studied her through the stream of exhaled smoke and patted the sofa next to him. "Take a seat."

She moved to a chair across the room. The cracked lines of his face revealed his tenseness, his displeasure.

"What the hell is going on, Luc? You're here to help Bob?"

"It's not that simple. This has been going on for years."

"Years?"

"Yes, Brenda. Jack's problems started long ago, the day Bob asked him to make an adjustment which wasn't a sound accounting practice."

"Jack would never do that!"

"Well he did. Maybe you didn't know everything Jack did in his day." Luc's curt response rang true, and she thought back to all the times Jack had come home distracted and reaching for the bottle.

"Bob demanded more," Luc continued. "By the third request, Jack's guilt got the best of him and he refused. That's when Bob threatened Jack with his job."

The words "career-limiting territory" from the e-mail flashed in Brenda's mind.

Luc took a drag then flicked the ashes. "Jack had to oblige. He did not want to get fired. Keeping up with the Joneses in Greenwich requires a pretty hefty salary." Luc lifted a brow. "Over the course of time, the bigger threat to Jack became Bob's ability to implicate him in the illegal actions—the ones he had been forced to take in the first place. Jack had no way out and Bob's orders became bolder over time."

"Wasn't anything put in writing?" She toyed with the one piece of knowledge in her possession.

"Not much. Bob was smart enough to make sure Jack's prints were on the gun. He was always careful nothing pointed to his own involvement." He twirled the ash head of the cigarette against the edge of the ceramic dish. "However, something slipped through. Something I believe you have in this house."

"Why are you so intent in helping that sleazebag?" She didn't even bother to hide her disgust. "Jack was your friend."

"I do not have a choice." Luc snarled.

She snorted and said sarcastically, "Someone's forcing you?"

Luc's face hardened. "Three months before Jack died, he made the mistake of threatening Bob. There had been several e-mails between the two showing Bob's involvement. Jack had the foresight to save them. One day, Bob placed another demand. This time, Jack refused and revealed that he still held a few good cards. That shocked the hell out of Bob." Luc nodded, clearly impressed by the act.

"You haven't answered my question. Bob's forcing you?"

Luc's jaw muscle tightened. "Try to be patient...as I have been with you." He took another drag off the cigarette, then crushed it out as he blew a slow stream of smoke. "Anyway, for a short time the threat forced the bastard to leave Jack alone, but our CEO is not a man who responds well to threats. He looked for new ways to browbeat your husband." Luc held up the envelope he'd arrived with. It suddenly carried a menacing glow.

"What's in there?"

"A private investigator was brought in to dig up dirt on Jack...or his family."

Brenda withered. Jack didn't have anything dirt-worthy going on; however, *she* sure did.

"Guess you have realized where Jack had a weak link." Luc didn't even attempt to hide his smugness.

Fear circled her, but she asked, "What happened next?"

"Around a week before Jack died, Bob called him in and presented a proposal to distort figures for the first quarter. Jack said no, reminding Bob about the e-mails he had saved."

"The week before?" Brenda recalled their fight after Jack's strange comment to Devin. "Are you sure it was that week?"

Luc nodded.

"What'd Bob do this time?"

"He showed Jack these."

Luc flipped open the tab of the envelope and pulled out a stack of photographs. She avoided eye contact as he handed them to her.

The pictures displayed a sunny fall day at a farmers' market several towns over. Brenda remembered the place and the exact Saturday they had been there. She and Luc had stopped to pick up apples during one of their rendezvous.

In the first photograph, the pair gazed longingly at one another while Luc's hand cupped Brenda's cheek. She flipped to the next. Luc held open her door and their lips brushed while she stepped inside. With great reluctance, she moved to the last. The photographer must have had a very strong lens and an exceptionally good hiding spot. At a more secluded hideaway, Brenda and Luc pursued their passion with fervor not appropriate in public, touching places reserved for serious romantic business.

"Jack knew," she said softly. Luc nodded. A slow chill stalked up her spine and stopped at her scalp, leaving her numb.

Luc shifted in his seat. "Jack confronted me right away, told me how Bob had vowed to ruin your career if Jack didn't continue to do as he requested."

"*My* career?"

He motioned to the photo and his gaze dropped to the floor. "Marriage therapist with a popular self-help book caught in this compromising position? That would not bode well for your career."

Rosie's comment about the argument the two men had had in Jack's office now made sense. That was why her name had come up.

"Oh my God." The horrible reality of the situation felt as if it would choke her. Tears trickled down her cheeks. She tossed the pictures onto the coffee table with disgust, as if spiders were crawling over them. "It's my fault he committed suicide."

"I'm as much to blame." True sorrow resonated in Luc's voice.

Brenda wrapped herself in a hug, closed her eyes, and dropped her chin. "Did you discuss our relationship with him?"

"Yes."

She looked up.

Luc leaned forward in his seat. "He was furious. I tried to explain…explain how the pictures made it seem worse, explain that we hadn't slept together." He shrugged. "He didn't believe me. Even when I said you turned to me because of your deep frustration with his silence about his problems." Luc's shoulders drooped. "Right before Jack threw me out of his office, he said he'd never trust me again." He snorted a quick sarcastic grunt. "Even speculated that I was working with Bob to hurt him." Luc paused. "Jack's stress seemed to be making him paranoid."

"Paranoid? He'd seen pictures of you making out with his wife."

"Yes, but thinking I would align myself with Bob? A ridiculous notion."

"But you're doing that now!"

He threw up his hands. "Come on, Brenda. I have been forced to do so. Bob assures me he will lose no sleep if he shows them to Aimee." Luc's chin trembled. The speech he had given her in the hotel room, about how relaxed the French were about extramarital liaisons, was exposed as merely a ruse to get her into bed. She couldn't say she was entirely surprised. "Brenda, I begged Jack to tell you everything. He did not wish to lose face in your eyes."

"Lose face?" Every nerve in her body went numb. "He worried I'd judge him?"

Luc nodded. "He also said he'd never stop loving you."

The details of those final days swirled in Brenda's mind: the day she confronted Jack about Devin's concerns; the last time they made love; the desperation in his eyes when he'd told her he loved her. All were still etched in her memory, the details as tangible and real as if they'd happened yesterday.

Luc's next admission was spoken quietly, as if he were

afraid to admit it out loud. "He said we were done as friends." The downturned tips of his frown tumbled farther.

The cold front she'd displayed toward him thawed a little. The last words her husband spoke to her returned: *Sometimes people are forced to make choices and do things they never thought they'd do.* Tears spilled and Brenda buried her head in her hands.

If she hadn't rushed off to work, if she'd stayed and talked, would her life be different? Had Jack been about to discuss the illegal activities he'd been forced to undertake? Would he have confronted her over her affair with Luc? Maybe he'd been about to admit that he needed help for his excessive drinking. Or maybe he had wanted to discuss all three things.

Brenda went to the kitchen and returned with a box of tissues. Wiping under her lashes with one, she tossed the box on the coffee table.

Luc leaned forward, studying the photographs of the two of them and looked up. "I'm sorry, Brenda." His voice was filled with regret.

"Sorry? You should have told me this long ago. At the very least, if you were trying to stay loyal to Jack by keeping silent while he was alive, the day we met for lunch would have been a good time to come clean."

"You dumped me." Luc's words were laced with bitterness. "I did not view you as a friend. Besides, I had no choice."

She shot him her best judgmental glare. "We all have choices."

"Look, I tried to help Jack. Before his funeral, Bob had Jack's office secured. I could not figure out why. Then I remembered how, months before he died, Jack had Rosie make me a key to his office. He claimed it was in case he lost his." Luc shook his head. "Very strange. After his funeral, I wondered if there was more to it than that. One Saturday, many weeks after the funeral, I snuck into his office. There had to be something in there, anything, to explain why Bob wanted things kept under wraps." He sighed. "I found nothing."

All along Brenda had figured that Luc's key had been the one used to remove the missing copies Rosie mentioned, but she sensed he was telling the truth.

"So Jack didn't tell you about any evidence he hid?"

"No. I learned of that recently, when the SEC investigation got Bob nervous and he reused those photos to blackmail me this time. He claims Jack hinted that there were more copies of the e-mails hidden outside the office." He snorted again. "Thanks to those pictures, Bob knew exactly who he could blackmail to look for them."

"You could've said no." About to call him a traitor, she stopped, knowing the comment was unfair.

Luc stared at the floor and folded his hands. "I had my own life to think about."

Brenda recalled the day she'd found Jack in the garage. Within seconds of finding Jack dead, a question had occurred to her, one that thrived on guilt, thrived on her lack of any real answers about what had made him kill himself. That question gnawed at her soul like a deadly parasite: had her actions caused the man she loved to end his life?

The ache in her heart swelled until it reached a bottleneck at her throat. Mercy, from beyond Jack's grave, arrived through Luc, a man who had broken into her house earlier that day. Bob might have backed him into a corner, but how did she know she could believe him?

Would his words be enough to allow her to forgive herself?

Chapter Twenty-Seven

CJ drove down Brenda's street and neared her driveway. He cursed his absent-mindedness, but was pleased that the forgotten cell phone would give him one more chance to kiss her good-bye. He'd miss her while he was gone.

Surprised to see another car in her driveway, he pulled up to the curb in front of her house. Upon closer inspection, he realized it was that same model BMW he'd spotted in the nature preserve yesterday. He recalled the shadowed silhouette of a man behind the wheel. It had seemed a bit out of place for the setting, but it hadn't bothered him until now.

The dark sky plopped two large droplets onto his windshield, as if sending him a warning. He laughed out loud. Jesus, had he been writing suspense for so long that he had become suspicious of everything, even the weather?

He let go of his paranoia and trotted to the front door. A friend had most likely stopped by. As soon as he tapped on the door, the dog began to bark. Footsteps approached from inside, then the door slowly opened. As soon as he saw Brenda's face, he knew that he'd been right to be concerned.

"Are you OK?" He stepped inside.

She nodded but her usually bright eyes were dim, as if a storm had knocked out their power.

"Whose car is in your driveway?"

A man's voice came from the other room. "It is mine."

CJ's stiffened.

"Luc's here." Brenda's voice, barely above a whisper, carried a lifeless sound.

"Has he hurt you?"

"No." A tear slid down her cheek, which she dabbed with a crumpled tissue. He put his arms around her and she collapsed into his embrace. She whispered in his ear, "He wants those e-mails, but I told him I didn't know anything about them."

CJ nodded and she took his hand, leading him to the living room. CJ studied the stranger, who leaned forward on the sofa and returned his stare with scorn-filled eyes.

The first time CJ had entered this room, its warm autumn tones, oak floors, and comfortable furniture had made him feel instantly welcome. Now a cold spell had settled over it, the cigarette odor a further violation of the space. A crescendo of rain droplets shattered the stillness, the downpour striking the windows like small pebbles. A clap of thunder rounded out the symphony of sounds.

"I finally get to meet the man who won Brenda's heart." Luc's words were lathered in resentment. He stood and extended his hand. "Luc Pelletier."

Luc's accent sounded French, but the sound didn't match with the long-sleeved, striped polo shirt, faded jeans, and running sneakers. CJ reminded himself that the French didn't walk around in berets all the time.

"CJ Morrison." CJ ignored Luc's outstretched hand. "What are you doing here?"

"I cannot visit a friend?" Luc's questioning brows rose at CJ. He plopped down on the couch and took out a pack of cigarettes, removing one. "Brenda and I have known each other for years."

"You've been lurking outside her house. I saw your car across the street yesterday." Brenda gasped but he continued. "Care to explain what you're up to?"

Luc lit the cigarette, slowly dropped the match into the ashtray, then leaned back and crossed his legs. He stared back at CJ in silence.

The cavalier dismissal pushed CJ's fury to the brink of an explosion. To avoid escalating the tension, he started to count to ten; however, at three, he detonated. "Listen, pal. I want an answer!"

Luc blew out a long trail of smoke while his vision drifted to Brenda. "You didn't tell me your new lover was such an impatient man."

"Cut it out, Luc." Brenda's voice sounded tired.

The words "new lover" pounded in CJ's ears. He waited for a response from the confident Frenchman but impatience took over. "Well? I asked you a question. What are you up to?"

"How about having your girlfriend fill you in?" He leaned forward and flicked his ashes. "This is as much her problem as mine."

CJ's gaze followed Luc's hand to the ashtray on the coffee table. Several photos lay scattered at the end of the table. The photos were of Brenda, yet when he focused on the details, he almost couldn't believe them. He dropped Brenda's hand and walked over, lifting one of the pictures.

"They're not what you think, CJ."

He stood transfixed by the first photo. Her words sounded as if they were coming from a long way away. In the image, Luc's fingertips stroked Brenda's neck, her closed eyelids. His head was tipped back as his mouth neared her parted lips.

Jealousy pounced on CJ and ripped its claws directly through the center of his heart.

CJ reached for another picture. Brenda wanted to lunge out to stop him, but she stood frozen in place. He picked up the next photo, the one in which Luc touched her cheek, his spellbound gaze fixed on her while she entered his car. The moment carried a surreal glow, like a bad dream, the kind when you find yourself naked in front of the classroom, exposed in unimaginable ways.

"I can't believe this." CJ's face pinched into an agony-filled grimace while an angry flush rushed his cheeks. "When were these taken?"

"Over a year ago. But I'm not involved with him now."

"When your husband was alive?"

Brenda's gaze dropped to the floor as she nodded, wishing she'd told CJ the true nature of her relationship with Luc earlier.

"You say that, but how can I...?" He stopped and pressed his lips together.

"What?" Her cheeks numbed as the blood drained from her face. "How can you trust me? I'm telling you the truth."

CJ's lips pressed tight and his fists clenched. "You lied to your husband."

The backs of her eyes burned, one step from spilling tears. "I had my reasons."

Luc sneered. "What? You didn't tell him you dated another man while you were married?" His smug expression seemed intended to provoke CJ. "Guess she's not the woman you thought she was."

"Shut up, Luc." Brenda yanked the photos from CJ's hand and stuffed them into the envelope. Tossing them on the table, she yelled, "Take your damn pictures and get out."

CJ watched her, his face pale. "You said Luc and Jack were friends?"

"They were."

CJ glanced from one to the other. "I don't believe this. I knew there was something you weren't telling me."

Brenda felt as though she were battling on two fronts at once, and her will to fight left her. She walked to the window to face the storm outside, preferable to the squall in the room. Nobody spoke, yet silence clamored in her ears. She dared to glance at the two men. Luc's arm was slung over the back of the sofa and he held a superior expression, obviously pleased with the quarrel. CJ rubbed at the middle of his forehead, eyes closed, as if trying to decide between true and false on a test.

"CJ," Brenda said. Both men looked in her direction. "My husband had problems but wouldn't let me help. I tried." Her voice struggled against the exhaustion that she felt. "Being with someone else...I guess it made me feel a little better. I didn't plan to betray my husband. It always seemed wrong. We stopped before Jack died."

CJ's face tightened, drawing his brows together. He shifted his weight and stared at the floor. Brenda returned to the view outside as her tears mimicked the pounding rain.

CJ moved toward her but kept a safe distance. "Why were those pictures taken?"

She sniffed. "As blackmail."

"Blackmail? By whom?"

"Bob Manning."

"I wouldn't discuss this with him if I were you," Luc threatened.

"Oh? Why not?" She spun toward him and his eyes opened wide. "Why should I listen to a liar like you? A man willing to ruin his friend's reputation to save his own neck? A man who got angry when I refused to have sex because my marriage vows mattered?"

"You led me on!" Luc spewed venom with each syllable. "Now, there is no choice but to help Bob."

"We all have choices. Get out of my house."

"We have unfinished business." Luc crushed his cigarette and stood. "I need those documents. If they're not in this house, then Jack left them someplace else, maybe a safe deposit box. *You* need to help me find them."

Brenda marched toward Luc, then planted a finger at the center of his chest. "I will *not* help you with anything to hurt Jack. Now get out."

Luc didn't budge. "Your professional reputation will be ruined if Bob leaks the pictures. So will my marriage."

"Get! Out!"

Luc smirked. Brenda dared to glance at CJ, whose cheeks burned as red as a fire engine. His jutted chin and firm stance made his pose look like that of a warrior.

"She's asked you to leave twice." He almost growled the words, his voice deep and imposing. "Now *I'm* ordering you to. Get the hell out."

Luc snarled. "This is not your problem."

CJ stepped to Brenda and gently pulled her away from Luc. "Tell Manning to think twice about releasing those pictures. The e-mails are stored in a safe place with an attorney."

Luc's jaw fell and he blinked several times. "Is this true? You are lying to me. Brenda?"

"You heard him." She played along. "Tell Bob not to do anything stupid."

Luc's shock quickly disappeared, replaced with eye-bulging rage. "I cannot believe you lied. Dragged this out. Manning has been all over me for weeks."

CJ moved in on Luc fast and close. Real close. Right up into his personal space. He stood several imposing inches over Luc, who peered back at CJ, his nostrils flaring, his skin pale.

"Nobody has contacted the SEC. Yet." CJ kept his manner calm. "If anything slanderous is said about Brenda, you can bet they'll get a call. Time to take your photos and leave." Luc stepped back and CJ didn't budge. "Do me a favor too. Pass along our message to Mr. Manning."

Luc snarled like a dog with his tail tucked between his legs. "You keep them." He motioned with his chin to the envelope with the photos. "Bob has more copies." He moved away but gave one last threatening snap of his snout. "You've made a big mistake, Brenda."

Luc all but ran out.

* * *

Splashing cool water on her face refreshed Brenda's tired eyes, but her heart lay limp, exhausted from the events of the last half hour. Still there remained unfinished business.

Returning to the living room, CJ sat on the couch with his arm stretched along the top. His preoccupation with the empty wall led her to fearful speculation.

"I guess I was lucky you forgot your cell phone, huh?" She pulled it from her pocket and handed it over.

He shook off his distant gaze and pocketed the device without a word.

"Thanks for the quick thinking too." Brenda would have said anything to fill the silence. "Bringing up the lawyer saved the day."

"Every so often, I'm quick on my feet." CJ leaned back against the sofa. "You're the only one who throws me off balance." Disgust registered on his face.

Brenda walked to the window and stared outside again, so he wouldn't see how much the comment hurt. Rain trickled at a slower pace, leaving water stains on the glass.

CJ cleared his throat. "That day in the kitchen, when we discussed the accounting books, as soon as Luc's name came up you acted strangely. I knew you weren't telling me something."

She turned around, tired of defending herself. "I told you. We're not involved any longer."

He snorted. "From where I stood, Luc still has some strong feelings for you. You must have some for him if you were willing to cheat on your husband."

"Yes. I did. Not do — *did*. That's past tense. Christ, a best-selling author like you should know the difference."

He waved a dismissive hand. "You know what, Brenda?" His neck reddened. "I'm not sure I buy it. If you'd told me from the start, maybe I'd believe it's over. But you hid it. That sends an entirely different message."

Frustration pulsed through her veins. She gritted her teeth, one step from exploding, when she stopped and forced herself to stand in CJ's shoes. Those photos were probably as hard to see as if he'd walked in on the act. Her omission of her history with Luc, after he had bared his soul to her, only made it worse.

She swallowed. If there was any time for honesty, it was now. "The other day, I almost told you everything…about my involvement with Luc."

His shoulders stiffened. "And you didn't. Why?"

She overlooked his derisive lilt. "I didn't want you to think I was that kind of woman. The day Autumn walked in on us, you were mortified by our kiss. What I did was far worse."

CJ had been studying his hands and winced at the comment.

"The last years of my marriage were tiring," she plunged on. "So many days were spent trying to fix a man who only pushed me away. I felt unloved, unappreciated." She closed her eyes to stop her tears, then swallowed. "Luc and I joined forces to help Jack. Our relationship evolved from that. It filled a void. I always knew it was wrong." She waited for him to say something but he stared at the floor while a judgmental silence hung over them. "For Christ's sake, CJ! I walked out of a hotel room on the guy to stop myself from breaking my marriage vows. At least give me some credit for that."

CJ lifted his head and met her gaze.

The sadness in his eyes gave her hope that the truth had helped her case. But she knew she had no way to prove all her feelings for Luc had disappeared. "I ended it that night. I asked him not to call me again. He's not the man for me." She paused. "You are."

His shoulders relaxed and his lips parted.

Before he could say a word, she added, "You know, the day you came over here after the anniversary of Carla's death, you promised me you were a changed man. You asked me to trust you. I did. All I can ask now is for you to trust me in return."

CJ held out a hand. For the first time since Luc's arrival, her guard lowered. She took his hand and joined him on the couch. Their knees touched while they stared at each other for a long moment.

"It's actually a relief telling you," she confided. "When we talked about Luc the other day, I almost said something. Here we are, starting this relationship and I kept worrying about what you'd think of me if you knew what I'd done with him..." She stifled a tear. "I thought you'd no longer want to be with me."

CJ pulled her into his arms and held her tight. "Don't ever think that," he whispered. He released his hold and cupped her cheeks, grazing her lips with a gentle kiss. "It's typical of me to let jealousy get in the way of clear thinking. I..." He hesitated, and frowned. "The idea that I'd lost you to Luc was unbearable."

CJ cradled her head in his large palm and his mouth covered hers. Tender movements sent a message—this kiss wasn't just about desire; it was about how much he cared for her. He slowly pulled away and pulled her into a hug. She dropped her head against his chest and her eyes shut. Never again would she keep anything from him.

The image of Jack having a front-row seat to her infidelity in those photos appeared out of nowhere. Imagining his pain at merely hearing the news was bad enough. Knowing that he'd been a witness to her acts made the hollow of her chest ache. She burst into tears.

CJ stroked her hair. "We're OK. Please don't cry anymore."

"I know. I always worried that Jack would learn about what I did with Luc, but I never dreamed he'd seen me in action." She sniffled and lifted her head. "How can I ever shake the idea that what I did may have caused him to end his life?"

CJ frowned. "You could start by listening to your advice to me. Things happen which we can't control. There have to be limits to self-abasement, remember?" He tipped his head.

"It's hard to be objective about ourselves. Even for people in my field."

"Sounds to me like Jack struggled handling his problems. He made a huge mistake not confiding in you sooner. It could have made a difference."

"It's possible." Brenda sat more upright and CJ wiped the wetness on her face with his fingertip. "Jack told Luc he still loved me, but it ended their friendship."

"So, Jack forgave you."

"Yes, but—"

"Brenda. Your husband had other options."

She shrugged. "Logic doesn't always trump emotion."

"Preaching to the choir, sweetheart." The corners of his mouth lifted.

She nodded and accepted the wisdom of a man who'd spent a decade caught in his own traps.

"I wish I didn't have this damn trip." CJ's brows furrowed with concern. "I'm worried about you."

Worried about you. Those simple words left her speechless. Most of her life, she'd performed an act as a strong, capable person who didn't need anybody's help. But she was getting tired of that act. Her head dropped to his chest. With silent understanding, he gathered her into his embrace.

After a minute, CJ said, "Maybe you should call the police. Have them make a few trips out here tonight, in case Luc comes back."

She lifted her head. "I don't even know how I'd explain it."

"Tell them a car has been hanging around the parking lot and the guy seems suspicious."

Brenda smoothed his cheek with her palm. "To make you happy, I will. You know I'm so glad you still feel the same about me...even after what I've done."

"I handed you the most shameful part of my past and it didn't change how *you* felt toward *me*."

"Yes it did."

"What?"

She cocked the corner of her mouth into a teasing tilt. "It brought me closer to you."

"Exactly, wise guy." He searched her face. "That's how I feel right now. We should both learn to forgive ourselves. So it doesn't get in the way of where *we* might be headed."

"Sounds like a plan." Brenda kissed his cheek, but a nagging doubt persisted. Her life was filled with opportunities to pardon the sins of loved ones. Why couldn't she completely forgive herself?

An idea popped into her head about a place she might be able to turn for help, but she wasn't sure she'd be welcome there.

Chapter Twenty-Eight

Brenda had driven by St. Mark's many times since Jack's funeral, but not once had she stepped inside. Today, however, she parked at a nearby lot and made her way toward the church's wide steps.

Last night's storm cast debris along the downtown sidewalk. Brenda shivered; the thin cardigan she wore over a short-sleeved shirt had been too optimistic for the early morning spring temperatures. A yawn slipped out of her mouth. Last night, CJ had stayed a bit longer, then reluctantly left to pack and get ready for his five a.m. limousine pickup. They had parted on a perfect note, and by the time he left, she was sure that he believed her about the photographs. Those snapshots, however, set the stage for an agonizing night's rest. Jack filled her thoughts, her dreams and, eventually, her prayers.

Today's visit to the church was for him.

Muffled organ music flowed from the building, a sign that the service had started. Brenda's shoulders relaxed. She felt a tiny burst of relief, knowing she wouldn't have to engage in small talk with the other parishioners. As she closed in on the Gothic structure, she recalled several sad hugs at these steps after Jack's service. The memory was one of the reasons she hadn't returned in so long.

The Episcopal church, built in the 1870s, boasted a tall tower set atop stone walls. A rich, ruby wooden door welcomed visitors. Brenda had once asked Father Reynolds why the door was painted that color. He'd said that nowadays it served to remind us of the blood of Christ, and how we are always safe in God's care. He added, though, that the origins most likely carried back to ancient times. In those days, no one could pursue an enemy past red doors into a church. Brenda considered the reason behind her visit today and wanted to ask the pastor about what would happen if you were your own enemy.

She stopped and stared at the structure, begging for a sign that she'd made the right call in coming here. Jack used to insist the entire family attend Sunday services at least once or twice a month. The kids groaned but were lured by the promise of brunch at a nearby diner when church ended. Her husband had always been more devout than her. So why hadn't Jack turned to this place in his moment of desperation? More importantly, why did she stand here now?

The little voice, which had coaxed her to those doors, poked an elbow. The Father's sermons had always offered great insight. She took a deep breath and stepped into the building. A loud click from the side entrance door opening made her pause. Anita, her neighbor, rounded the corner. She must have attended the earlier service.

"What a surprise." She eyed Brenda from head to toe, pausing a second too long at her jeans. "The service has started already."

"Thanks. I'm running late. Nice to see you." Brenda forced a neighborly smile and continued up the steps. Brenda had hoped to enter the church undetected; Anita had ruined her plan. The woman held the unofficial title of neighborhood Judge Judy combined with gossip queen extraordinaire. Only those in her inner circle, especially the ones who treated her latest tittle-tattle and opinions with the reverence of their *People* magazine, were safe from her commentary. Brenda was glad that she had an excuse to hurry away.

Pulling open the large wooden door, a creak announced her arrival. An usher stepped out of nowhere and held it the door open. She mouthed "Thank you," walked around to the rear of the sanctuary, then slid into an empty pew.

Father Reynolds watched a parishioner read at the lectern. He hadn't changed. Still a round man with thinning hair and gentle blue eyes, his soft-spoken, calm demeanor and unexpected sense of humor always struck the right chord in Brenda's heart. He spotted her. His face brightened, the small gesture making her glad she had come; the surroundings, however, did not.

Sadness slipped into her heart and took it prisoner. Reminders of Jack's funeral were everywhere — her front row pew, the area where his casket had rested. Even the rows of now-empty pews near the back reminded her how those same pews had overflowed at Jack's service.

The choir sang a hymn and, halfway through, a tear leaped from Brenda's eyelid. Brenda dug deep for a distraction and suddenly found the stained glass of the windows more intriguing than ever before. She focused her attention on the colorful panes of glass, and managed to dam further tears.

When the song finished, she let herself get swept up in the service. Halfway through, the pastor stood and studied some papers on the pulpit, then scanned the crowd, appearing to take a barometer reading of his audience before the start of his sermon.

"I'm an old guy who admits to embracing a lot of things from the past." His voice boomed over the microphone. "But one thing I love about today's world is my computer." Light laughter skipped through the crowd, presumably at the visual of the seventy-year-old clergyman in his long worship vestments checking his e-mails or making an online purchase. "Actually, I find all the technology we have at our fingertips amazing. BlackBerrys, cell phones, computer tablets. Gadgets to help us keep track of everything. I store my sermons, phone numbers, finances, and pictures of my family on these things. For me, the best part is if I make an error or come across something which I no longer need, I don't have to cross things out or use Wite-Out. With the stroke of a simple key, it's eliminated. Vanished as if it never existed in the first place. Like a computer, we store a lot of information in our heads. So in some ways, our brains resemble these modern day devices."

He scanned the audience as heads nodded in agreement. "What we store inside us can be both good and bad information. A huge difference between the technology and our minds is the ability to delete things we no longer want to keep. I've often wished I had a key which would allow me to erase some of my thoughts. Erase my mistakes. I wish my mind came with a built-in recycle bin, like the one on my computer, where I could dump all the things I no longer want to hold onto."

He lifted his fingers in air quotes. "When my thoughts ask, 'Are you sure you want to permanently delete this memory?' I would simply click yes."

Caught up in the pastor's sly grin, Brenda laughed along with the congregation. She felt the same way. If she had a recycling bin for her mind, she would delete every encounter she had ever had with Luc. She would delete the day she had run off to work and ignored Jack's final plea.

A serious shadow fell over the clergyman's face. "Today's first reading was from Ecclesiastes. In this, we heard 'For there is not a just man upon earth, that doeth good, and sinneth not.' Guilt poses an interesting reality for us humans. We've all felt it at one time or another. Blame leaves us believing something is wrong with us. It can be caused by any number of things. It can be because we believe we've failed someone or broken a rule, either religious or man-made."

Brenda reflected on the verse, especially in light of her own failings. Had she been in a classroom, she might have raised her hand and asked him "but doeth that make sinneth OK?"

"Seeking pardon for our sins can make us feel alone." The clergyman paused for a beat and waited for the words to sink in with the parishioners. "Yet we're not really by ourselves. In Ernest Hemingway's short story, 'The Capital of the World,' he writes about a young man who wrongs his father and runs away from his home to Madrid. The father searches for his son and eventually takes out an ad in the Madrid newspaper. It says, 'Paco, meet me. Hotel Montana, 12 noon Tuesday. All is forgiven. Love, Papa.'" He tilted his head. "Paco is a common name in Spain. When the father arrives at the hotel, he finds eight hundred young men waiting for their fathers. Yes..." The preacher raised his voice. "They were *all* seeking forgiveness."

The words dangled in front of the crowd. He tipped his head to study his notes, offering another view of his sparse hairline during the long, deliberate pause.

The pastor's comments went beyond hitting close to home for Brenda; they entered her premises with overnight bags and moved into the guest bedroom. How had she been so blind? Of course she alone didn't corner the market on transgression.

"We all make mistakes." There was tenderness in the pastor's voice. "We all long for forgiveness. We cannot easily forgive ourselves. And even with God's forgiveness, many of us hang on to a belief that we have failed at something."

Brenda swallowed and blinked to stifle her tears. Clinging to failure, in a strange way, had kept her afloat. In reality, though, the notion sat like stuffed stones in her pockets, forever threatening to pull her under.

Father Reynolds cleared his throat. "I think the Lord has given us a clear button made only for forgiveness. The problem is that we forget it's there. We don't think to use it. However, when we do, we accept His forgiveness, paving the way for us to forgive ourselves. Through God's grace, we are then able to forgive others."

Brenda remained numb throughout the rest of the service. The words "God's grace" repeated over and over in her mind. The forgiveness she had offered to others over the years — her mother, Jack — seemed like a form of God's grace. If Jack were here, would he forgive her? Had he already done so by telling Luc he still loved his wife, despite what she'd done? Was that a sign?

The service ended. She stayed in the pew and waited for the church to empty. The last person filed out. Father Reynolds made his way over to her. He extended his arms wide so she stood and gave him a hug.

"I'm so happy you're here, Brenda. How are you?"

"I'm OK."

"Devin has been e-mailing me from Rome. He seems quite happy there."

"He does. I'm glad he stayed with his plans after what happened with his dad. It helped him get through a difficult year."

"Yes. We've shared many wonderful e-mails about God and life."

They stood in awkward silence for a few seconds. Father Reynolds finally said, "Does anything in particular bring you here today?"

"Damned if I know."

His soft laugh relaxed her.

"I suppose in a weird way, Father, Jack got me here today."

"I'm the last one to say anything is weird." The older man's eyes twinkled as if he were about to share a secret. "God works in strange ways."

"I guess he does. Your sermon really spoke to me."

"Good. At least I reached one person today." He pointed to the pew. "Would you like to sit and talk?"

She nodded and they took a seat.

"You're having forgiveness issues, Brenda?"

"I have been for some time."

"Family members often blame themselves when a loved one commits suicide. In your field, I'm sure you know that."

"Yes. Because of what I do for a living, I blame myself even more. I think Devin does too. I did everything in my power to help Jack, but he never seemed to notice. Or notice how miserable I was." She searched for her next words with caution. "I pushed aside my commitment to our marriage. I wasn't the best wife." Brenda studied the maroon carpeted floor, not wanting to look at the pastor's face.

He took her hand and she met his eyes. "I knew Jack pretty well. I don't believe he'd want you doing this to yourself. No matter what you did." Sincerity reigned in the preacher's kind face. The words presented, as if from Jack's perspective, possessed a redeeming quality. "I see a lot of families and get a sense about people. Jack cared about you. I believe he'd want you to move on."

Those few words, coupled with the sermon he had just given, were like a sickle clearing a path through a field. A thousand pounds of grief floated off her shoulders. For the first time since Jack died, she felt hope.

"Then maybe Jack would want me to reboot my system right about now." Her newfound relief sparked the giddy remark. "Hit Control-Alt-Delete on the keyboard and start over?"

"Very clever." Father Reynolds beamed in return. "Yes, I think that's exactly what he'd want."

She squeezed his hand. "How can I ever thank you?"

"Hmmm." His brows stretched upward. "If I ever reuse this sermon, may I use your line?"

"You bet." Brenda smiled. "A small price for what I got here today, Father. Very small."

* * *

Brenda rested her arm on the ledge of her open car window, and crisp air swept across her skin. Through her open sunroof, the sun bathed her in warmth while she inhaled the sweet smells of spring.

Besides the beautiful Sunday, the strong presence of invisible hands supporting her helped elevate her mood. Those hands took the form of CJ's compassion the night before, of the gift she'd been handed today by Father Reynolds, of her renewed optimism, bubbling beneath the surface. At last, some difficult times in her life seemed behind her, so far back, in fact, that they were a mere speck in the rearview mirror.

Turning onto her street, she checked the parking lot in front of the nature preserve. Three cars were there, none of them Luc's car. She didn't believe he'd return after CJ's threat.

Approaching her driveway, she did a double take. A familiar black car was parked out front. She pulled in and stepped out of her Audi. CJ's Cheshire-cat grin showed his pleasure at surprising her. "I thought you'd be over the Atlantic watching a movie and eating peanuts."

He sat on the top step, his long legs stretched out and crossed at the ankles. "Nah. I decided to get you coffee instead." He lifted two Dunkin' Donuts cups. His untucked, wrinkled oxford shirt hung over his jeans, messier than she'd ever seen him.

She laughed and sat next to him on the landing. "Seriously, folks, how'd I get so lucky to have you delivering me coffee right now?"

"I switched my flight to Tuesday morning. They'll start work without me. Two days later isn't a big deal." He lowered the cups onto the steps, took her hands, and gave her a quick kiss. "I tried to call earlier, but you didn't answer. I got nervous and decided to drive over."

"I went to church."

"I know. Luckily, your neighbor passed by right as I arrived. She stopped to tell me where you were. She told me the service ended at eleven, so I got us coffee, then went to the hardware store and got you a new lock for the back door." He reached behind and lifted a plastic Ace Hardware bag. "Last night I began to worry that Luc might have made a copy of your house key."

"Oh, I never thought he'd do that, but you might be right."

"I'll install it today."

"Thank you." Overwhelmed by his thoughtfulness, she leaned close and placed a soft kiss on his lips. "Come inside. Anita might have a listening device pointed at us from her window."

He handed her the hardware store bag, then stood with the two coffee cups. "She was nice enough to stop and let me know where you were."

"Yes." Brenda slipped the key into the knob and bumped it open with her hip. "I suspect your unplanned arrival will be the topic of great speculation at tomorrow's coffee klatch."

CJ stepped inside, shaking his head. "Women are so confusing."

They walked toward the kitchen. "Am I?"

"You can be, but the bewilderment you create has enough side benefits to make it worthwhile." CJ rested the drinks on the kitchen island, reached out, and drew her close. "Speaking of benefits…"

He leaned close and kissed her, the tickle of his mustache soft and familiar. Brenda enjoyed his secure embrace, nuzzling against his solid frame.

"I'm so relieved you're all right," he whispered.

She hugged him tighter.

"I called Hugh Schmidt this morning." He let go and handed her one of the cups. "I know you spoke to him a few days ago, but after I left last night, I kept thinking we should talk to an attorney as soon as possible, before Bob does anything else. Hugh is going to contact Tom Simmons, his partner, about us coming in tomorrow. He'll let me know the time later."

She swallowed a sip of coffee. "*Us?* Are you going, too?"

"Yes."

Her mouth opened to protest, but before a single word slipped out, he put a finger on her lips.

"I know you're capable. I thought you'd like some moral support."

She closed her mouth and took his hand. "Thank you."

He gave her a satisfied smile. "So? How was church?"

"Good. Better than good."

"Carla went pretty regularly, but it wasn't for me. Do you always go?"

"No. Jack was more of a churchgoer, but I'd get there with him often enough. Something told me I should go today. Then the sermon turned out to be exactly what I needed to hear. A strange coincidence, I suppose."

"Really?" CJ sipped his drink. "You know what Albert Einstein said, right?"

"No, but I have a feeling you'll tell me."

"Coincidence is God's way of remaining anonymous."

"Do you believe it?"

He shrugged. "Makes me think."

"Me too. Anyway, I'm glad I went. I found something I

needed."

"What?"

"A voice from the past." She paused. "And a little lesson on computers."

"They're talking those up in church now?"

"In a manner of speaking. I've decided to archive a few old files and open some new ones. In here." She pointed to her head.

"If God's got a new kind of operating system making transformation *that* simple, I'd like the details."

"God doesn't do it. You do." Brenda put down her drink and took away his cup. She slipped her arms around his neck. "I've cleared space on my hard drive to make room for you."

His face lit up. "This is beginning to sound promising." He pressed his lips against hers, his tender movements escalating into a deeper kiss.

Her hands skimmed his chest, stopping inches above the waist of his pants and prying her lips away from his. "Speaking of hard drives..." She did her best leer and dropped her voice to a seductive hush. "Maybe I could take a peek at yours."

"Mmmm. It's possible." His hand fell to her bottom and made slow movements, chipping away at what little self-control she held onto. His tone became serious. "There's one condition."

"A condition?"

He nodded. "No more computer references."

"Listen, pal. If I dated Bill Gates, this techie dirty talk would be exactly the type of thing to get me furs, jewelry, exotic trips..."

CJ covered her mouth with his. His palm pressed to her lower back and pulled her against him, the gentle command rousing her, shifting her need for him into overdrive.

He stopped and smirked. "Deal?"

"What's a computer?" she murmured and took his hand.

Chapter Twenty-Nine

The Manhattan Securities and Exchange Commission offices were located in the financial center of New York City. Decked out in standard office decor — with its glass coffee tables holding neat stacks of magazines, palm floor plants growing out of their normal element, and neutral-colored furniture — the surroundings screamed "boring government office." Tom Simmons, Brenda's attorney, sat across from her on a beige sofa in the quiet waiting room outside SEC Director Leon Moretti's office.

Tom concentrated on an issue of *Forbes*. His calm manner did little to ease her nerves. High inner brows and a wide chin gave him a trustworthy appearance. His expensive suit, gold Rolex, and side-parted haircut, much like the four-hundred-dollar style John Edwards touted, exuded confidence. A man who could afford such pricey articles must do his job well.

Over a week ago, she and CJ had met Tom for the first time at the law offices of Schmidt, Barrows, and Simmons. They had shown him everything. The documents Jack saved, the accounting books he tagged, and the secrets they'd learned about the inner world of GBS. Tom had recommended they contact the SEC immediately, with himself as the go-between. CJ left for France saying he considered her in good hands but called her every other day anyway. His concern made her miss him all the more.

Brenda tossed the *Newsweek* she'd been flipping through onto the side table. Her crossed leg jiggled, so she placed her palm on her knee to stop it before the black pump on her foot could fly off and knock Tom unconscious.

"Nervous?" Tom had stopped reading and watched her.

"Nervous would be the understatement of the century."

He smiled, puffing his cheeks. His trustworthy factor rose. "Don't worry. I'll do most of the talking."

The office door clicked open. A man with thick black hair and round tired eyes came out. A woman with a short, sensible haircut, sensible shoes, and a plain navy suit followed. Gloria Steinem would never accuse her of playing the girl card.

The man extended a hand. "Tom? Brenda? I'm Director Moretti. This is our Regional Trial Counsel, Sarah Burnett."

The counselor offered a greeting. She appeared to need some rest, as well.

"Follow me." Moretti motioned with the flick of his wrist.

A trip down two antiseptic white hallways led them to a small windowless conference room where Tom and Brenda sat across from the director and trial counsel.

"Mrs. McAllister, thank you for coming forward." The director's voice sounded sincere. "The e-mails you found related directly to the charges we've been investigating against GBS."

"We thought they might." The tension in Brenda's shoulders disappeared and she allowed herself to relax.

Director Moretti folded his hands on the table and ping-ponged his focus between Brenda and Tom. "We have reason to believe, besides the CEO's direct involvement in these fraudulent events, that Donald Wainscott, the vice chairman, may have been involved. Two of the e-mails your client saved mention him. It may be enough to charge him too."

Moretti turned to Brenda, narrowing his eyes. "You do recognize your husband committed a crime, Mrs. McAllister?"

"Of course I do."

He leaned forward. "Then why didn't you come to us sooner?" His tone was suddenly sharp and accusatory. "I mean, Mr. McAllister must have talked to you about his work."

The small room shrunk, becoming a windowless cell. "I never knew about it." She felt defensive and nervous, as if she herself were being prosecuted. "Jack kept it hidden from me. We never discussed—"

"How about the e-mails?" Moretti interrupted. "When did you first know of their existence?"

The first day she'd stumbled upon them was several weeks ago. Weeks ago sounded horrible. Brenda's heart began to hop in place, and she felt an urge to sprint from the room. The director's intense look suggested every move she made mattered. Nothing would be overlooked.

How could she tell him she'd held these e-mails for so long?

The dryness in her mouth made her wish for water. She tucked in her lower lip while she thought, then realized the simple facial gesture might count as a strike against her. "I told you—"

Tom held out a hand, a signal for Brenda to stop. "Mrs. McAllister had no knowledge of her husband's involvement until recently. Jack McAllister was blackmailed into committing these crimes. We have a witness who will corroborate her statement, as well as attest to the recent recovery of the e-mails."

"Blackmailed?" Sarah Burnett glanced up from the stack of papers she'd been sifting through.

"Yes." Tom glanced at Brenda. "In the months before his death, my client's husband tried to stop Manning. Jack McAllister told him about the documents you now have. Manning played pretty dirty, though. He hired a private investigator, dug up a new tool for him to exploit."

Brenda wished she could disappear. Her breath stilled and her muscles froze.

"The stress of having to perform illegal acts put a lot of strain on the McAllisters' marriage." Tom dropped the details as if he were discussing a corporate merger. He reached into his briefcase and handed Moretti the envelope with the photographs Luc had left behind. "Jack McAllister's troubles were not his alone. Some incriminating photos were taken of Mrs. McAllister with a man she became close to during this difficult time. Those pictures were used to blackmail her husband."

The two prosecutors glanced in Brenda's direction. Moretti opened the envelope and removed the photos, slowly studying each one and passing them off to Burnett. Both had the decency to not look at Brenda during the process, yet the hot burn of humiliation scorched her soul. She forced her chin to stay high, as if their perusal of such intimate moments didn't matter to her.

"See the man in those pictures?" Tom continued without reference to the content. "He's Luc Pelletier, who also works at GBS. Bob Manning used the pictures to coerce Mr. Pelletier into helping him locate those e-mails."

Tom had made Brenda go over all the details with him, starting with the friendship between Jack and Luc, right through to the face-to-face confrontation with Luc at Brenda's house one week earlier.

Tom opened his briefcase and removed a letter. "I have a signed letter from Mr. Pelletier stating that he is willing to speak to you to help your case against Manning and Wainscott. Both my client and Mr. Pelletier want these pictures to go away. We need your help."

Moretti's face, tired when they had first met, came to life at this new development. "I'm not sure how we can help you."

"Well, we're hoping you'll agree to communicate this

message to Mr. Manning. If those pictures are made public, they'll be used against him, too, to further prove his involvement as a blackmailer and mastermind behind the corporate crimes."

Moretti's palm covered his chin and his gaze traveled to Burnett.

"We're offering this to you in good faith," Tom added. "We don't want the photographs to get out or to be used against anybody at this point."

Burnett made a near-imperceptible nod toward the door and Moretti stood.

"Excuse us for a moment." The director went to the door.

Brenda studied both their faces, blank as clean, white sheets. These two should quit their jobs and join the professional poker tour. What were they thinking?

* * *

The lively murmur of dinner conversation at Le Bouchon hinted to the size of the Friday night crowd. The maître d' spoke on the phone but held up a finger when CJ and Brenda walked through the doors.

CJ's last two days in Paris had been busy and they hadn't talked much. Brenda was anxious to fill him in about the SEC meeting and the call she had received this afternoon from Tom Simmons, but decided to wait until they'd ordered.

The maître d' hung up and his round face broke into a broad beam. "Mr. Morr-ee-son!"

"Hello, Andre. I have a seven thirty reservation." CJ placed a delicate hand on Brenda's lower back.

"Euuhh." Andre scanned his list. "Ah, yes. Come zees way."

While he gathered the menus, the phone rang again. He rolled his eyes. "*Une minute, s'il vous plaît.*" The accent almost sounded phony. It was so much more exaggerated than Luc's.

Brenda leaned into CJ. "You must be a regular. Only my dry

cleaner greets me so happily."

"It's one of my favorite restaurants." His palm took subtle liberties along the curve of her side.

Brenda moved closer. "I missed you." She stretched on her tiptoes and whispered in his ear, "If you keep touching me that way, I'm going to suggest we do takeout."

"Hmmm." His mouth relaxed into a playful rumple, something he always did right before he teased. "They don't do takeout here. I suggest we stay and eat." In a low, husky tone, he whispered in her ear, "Besides, once I get you in bed later, I plan on staying there for a while."

Warmth spread through her, from the top of her head to her toes. Brenda now knew how it felt to be a piece of melting chocolate.

Andre hung up and motioned for them to follow. The dining room was lit by a warm glow from dimmed antique chandeliers. Tan walls with a gold hue were complemented by rich mahogany moldings. Their table sat in a row near large windows, topped with arched Palladian curves, which overlooked a topiary garden decorated with small glistening white lights on each bush.

CJ pulled out half-framed reading glasses and perused the menu, then put it down and lifted the wine list. His expression turned to one of serious concentration, as if their wine choice were the most important decision of the day.

After the waiter took their order, CJ reached across the table and took her hand. "Tell me about the SEC meeting. Did Tom earn his fee?"

"He did. Thank God he was there. The director who's heading up the case against GBS suggested I'd been holding out on them." She shook her head. "As if I knew Jack's every move in the office, but Tom jumped right in and stopped them."

"Jesus, what's wrong with these guys? You're on their side."

"Don't you watch TV? Prosecutors are very suspicious people. Tom gave them Luc's letter and asked them to relay our message to Bob Manning about the photos. In fact, Tom called with some good news just this afternoon. According to Director Moretti, we don't need to worry about the pictures surfacing again."

"Great!" CJ squeezed her hand. "Now you can put all of this behind you."

"Yeah." She took a deep breath before delivering the next piece of news. "I called Luc to let him know."

A slight pause, then CJ said, "How'd he react?"

"Relieved." She was relieved too. CJ showed no signs of jealousy over the contact. "Luc's really not a bad guy. More a victim of circumstance." In hindsight, a great deal of Brenda's resentment toward him had to do with anger toward herself for straying from Jack.

"Backed into a corner, people are capable of surprising things," CJ agreed.

"He asked if you and I were serious."

"Oh?" His lips pressed flat, showing concern mixed with mild jealousy. "What'd you tell him?"

"Well." Brenda hesitated, suddenly shy. "What would you have told him?"

He cracked a grin, and any hint of jealousy vanished. "Are you always going to answer every question with another question?"

"Not always. This one I am."

He leaned closer. "I'd have told him I'm very serious about you, sweetheart."

"Oh good." Her thumb massaged his hand. "That's how I answered him."

The waiter arrived with their wine and they pulled apart. While the waiter uncorked the bottle and poured, they eyed each other.

After the waiter was gone, CJ reached into his pocket. "Speaking of how I feel about you, I got you something." CJ removed a miniature silver Eiffel Tower and placed it in front of her. "I know you wanted the original, but this is the best I could do."

She lifted the souvenir of the famous landmark. "Between this and the waiter's accent, I'm practically there."

"I have a question." CJ's face held a look of hope. "In a few months, I have to return to Paris. I'm hoping we can visit the real Eiffel Tower together. Will you go with me?"

His gaze hit her with the warmth of a summer breeze. Brenda placed the souvenir in the center of the table and took both his hands in hers. "I can't wait."

Epilogue

Brenda and CJ maneuvered through the crowds at American Airlines' terminal at JFK Airport. They stopped at the end of a long line of travelers waiting at the security check-in.

"You might want to start looking for your passport." CJ unsuccessfully fought a playful smirk. "You'll need it when we reach the front, and I expect you don't want a replay of last time." He'd just witnessed, with some amusement, Brenda empty her entire handbag to retrieve her passport when they had checked their luggage.

"Already on top, wise guy. I learned my lesson."

"I was going to ask you to put the boarding passes in your handbag once we got through security, but maybe I'll keep them here." He tapped the pocket on the lapel of his sports jacket and right away slipped an arm around her shoulders to give her a quick hug.

"I'll defer to your judgment."

He gave her an appreciative inspection, from head to toe. "You look cute, but did you ever consider an outfit with pockets when traveling?"

Brenda's sundress, worn with a short cotton jacket and flat ankle-wrap sandals, was an attempt at comfort combined with a little European style. "I don't need them. That's the reason women carry purses."

He eyed her skeptically but didn't reply.

Their arms drifted apart and they moved forward in line, toting their carry-on bags. They neared the metal detectors and X-ray machines. A long conveyor belt held large plastic bins where travelers were instructed to place their belongings, including their shoes.

CJ moaned. "For God's sake! I hate these new procedures." He leaned over, pulled up the leg on his jeans, and removed a loafer. "One crazy guy puts a bomb in his shoe and now I have to take mine off every time I want to board a plane." He took off the other.

Brenda was used to CJ's harmless grumbles. She stretched up and whispered into his ear, "Maybe this'll make you feel better. I plan on giving you one of those new TSA pat-downs once we get to the hotel."

When his frown transformed into a tolerant smile, she felt satisfied that she had done her part to keep his blood pressure in check.

"I'm going to hold you to that." He placed the shoes in the tray without another complaint.

Once they were through security, they headed to the Admiral's Club to eat.

At a newsstand near the restaurant, Brenda spotted a headline on the front page of the *New York Times* and stopped. "The Buck Stops Here: Global Business Systems CEO Arrested Despite Claims of Innocence." A picture of Bob Manning being led to a car by two men in dark suits accompanied the headline.

Bob didn't look nearly as smug as he had the night he had threatened Brenda at the fitness club. In fact, he seemed downright scared. CJ purchased a copy along with the *Wall Street Journal*. Once in the Admiral's Club, they ordered a late lunch, then buried their noses in the articles. The details were even better than Brenda could have hoped.

Bob Manning would be charged as the mastermind behind years of misrepresented earnings at GBS. Donald Wainscott, chairman of the company's Board of Directors would be investigated for having knowledge of the acts taking place. The newspaper also recanted some previous reports, specifically, those quoting Manning as suggesting that Jack had single-handedly acted to create and execute the fraud. More important, the assertion that he took his life because of his crimes was deemed to be unfounded. Brenda's heart leaped with relief when she read that the SEC had exonerated Jack of all charges. Tears welled and she lowered the paper. She shut her eyes and said a short prayer to Jack, hoping he knew and somehow heard the news.

"This article mentions Jack's name has been cleared," CJ said. Brenda opened her eyes and realized that CJ was still reading his paper, unaware that she had stopped. "Does that one?"

"Yes."

His eyes met hers over the top of the newspaper. He slipped his hand over hers. "Jack would be proud of you."

"I hope so. I'm relieved it's over."

"This paper also says that Luc's testifying."

"Really? That's brave of him."

CJ nodded. "Against Manning and Wainscott. Luc claims they both tried to get him to destroy evidence."

"Jack's e-mails."

"Probably. After he gives his testimony, this says he'll be returning to the office in Montpellier, France."

"Oh." Another unpleasant piece of her past was about to be erased, but the news carried bittersweet emotion. "His wife wanted to move back to France pretty badly, so that should put their lives back on track."

The waiter brought them two iced teas and CJ folded the newspaper. "There's something I was going to give you when we got to Paris, but I can't wait." He rummaged through his carry-on bag, then placed a gift on the table in front of Brenda.

The signature white bow and aqua box could only have been from Tiffany's. She drew the gift closer, pleased at his gesture. "What's this for?"

"Just because." He smiled. "Before you open it..." He hesitated, folding his hands. "I want you to know something." He blew out a breath. "Sorry. Sometimes words come easier to me in writing."

She could tell that whatever this was, it meant a great deal to CJ. She smiled, to make him more comfortable. "Take your time."

He studied his hands. "I've never discussed my writing of *The Hourglass* with you." The words came out slow. "I wrote the book during a very dark time in my life...right after Carla died." His eyes lifted to hers. "All I could see were endings. Bad endings. The idea of using the hourglass as an image seemed perfect, given my frame of mind in those days. It seemed my time had run out, and I wasn't ever going to get another chance at the happiness I had with Carla. I thought I didn't deserve another chance. I let some bad things own me for a long time."

Brenda understood that the words didn't come easily. He wasn't used to offering that much of himself. She put her palm over his clasped hands.

CJ's face brightened. "I missed the obvious back then. Not anymore." He pointed to the gift. "This may seem a little corny, but..." He shrugged. "I'm a writer. It's symbolic for me. Go ahead. Open it."

Brenda undid the flawlessly tied bow on the Tiffany box. Removing the lid, she took out a black case and tipped open the top. A shiny gold hourglass charm, perhaps a half inch in size, rested against a smooth velvet backing. The tiny figure dangled from a sparkling gold necklace chain. The tip of her finger caressed the smooth spindles surrounding the crystal casing.

CJ reached across the table and took her hand. "Meeting you has given me another chance. Until we met, I failed to see how an hourglass can be flipped over to start time again. You're the reason I see it now."

"How beautiful!" Brenda removed the necklace from the box. "Will you help me put this on?"

CJ's eyes twinkled, noticeably pleased she liked the gift. "Of course."

He went behind her and hooked the necklace. On the return to his seat, she wrapped her fingers around his forearm to stop him. "Thank you. You've brought something to my life too."

"Have I?" He searched her face.

She nodded. "Your support means everything to me." She motioned with her finger for him to come closer and, when he did, pressed her lips lightly to his. "I love your gift...and you."

His affectionate gaze settled on her. "I love you too."

He returned to his seat and she lifted her iced tea. "A toast. To the end of Jack's mess and to...to our new beginnings. *Santé.*"

"Studying up on your French?" He lifted his drink and they clinked glasses.

"Just 'cheers' and 'where's the ladies' room?'"

Their food arrived and they ate in comfortable silence. Brenda looked forward to the trip ahead — five days in France with the film's producers and the next four in Rome visiting Devin. The last leg of their journey would consist of five days in Tuscany.

Brenda stared out at the runway as a plane accelerated. The jumbo jet lifted from the pavement and soared into the sky. She reached for her throat and fondled the hourglass charm, contemplating the depth of her feelings for CJ and their future. One thing was certain: CJ wasn't the only one for whom the sands of time had started to flow again.

Acknowledgments

The journey to write a book is a long (sometimes lonely) road. Luckily, I found Dawn Dowdle and the Blue Ridge Literary Agency. A thousand thanks to Dawn for believing in my story. The supportive environment and camaraderie you've created and fostered at BRLA makes me thank my lucky stars that I submitted my work to you.

I'd like to thank Annie Melton for the opportunity to publish with Etopia. To my editor, Julian Mortimer Smith, thank you for putting the finishing polish on my words. I truly enjoyed collaborating on edits with you and have walked away a better writer. And special thanks to the Etopia Art Department, for a cover beyond my wildest dreams.

To Bill, I thank God every day for such a wonderful husband. Your hard work and support are always noticed and appreciated. Now you can read the entire book.

To Linda Chiara, everything I need to know about writing I learned at Molten Java while sitting across from you and drinking my coffee. What would I do without you?

To Nicole and Katie, my two beautiful daughters, your journey into adulthood inspires me every day. I am blessed.

A loud and hearty shout-out to my test readers Lisa Buccino, Janice Stevenson, Rebecca Strang, and Rita Uylaki. Limitless thanks for your time and support.

And a heartfelt thanks to all my wonderful friends, who have shown support, curiosity, and excitement about my writing. You are too numerous to name, but I remember each and every kind word.

~ About the Author ~

Novelist Sharon Struth believes you're never too old to pursue a dream. The Hourglass, her debut novel, received first place in the Dixie Cane Memorial Contest and second place in the Golden Heart. She writes from the friendliest place she's ever lived, Bethel, Connecticut, along with her husband, two daughters and canine companions. For more information, including where to find her published essays, please visit http://www.sharonstruth.com.

Discover more about Sharon Struth here

Blogs at "Life in the Middle Ages"
http://www.sharonstruth.wordpress.com

Website: www.sharonstruth.com

Shares in group blogs at "Tempting Romance"
http://www.temptingromance.blogspot.com/

Facebook Author Page
http://www.facebook.com/pages/Sharon-Struth-Author-Page/139641182749036?ref=hl

~ Available Now from Etopia Press ~

Blueberry Truth
Ute Carbone

Beanie MacKenzie and her husband Mac have led perfect lives, with perfect families and perfect jobs they both love, he a leading cardiologist, she a teacher at a school for troubled children. Now they have the perfect home, a big house on a quiet Albany street, just perfect for raising a big family. Only the babies they've been trying so hard to conceive just won't come.

Stressed in her marriage and fearing she may never bear children, Beanie throws herself into her work, surrounded by society's throwaways. Enter Beanie's new student, seven-year-old Blueberry Truth Crowley, a fiercely independent child whose life had been anything but perfect. Abused, neglected, and mistrustful of everyone around her, Truth throws a monkey wrench into the perfect order of Beanie's classroom--and into her very life--challenging Beanie's notions of motherhood, commitment, and family. But their unlikely bond may be just the thing to teach them both about love.

~ Available Now from Etopia Press ~

Let Angels Fly
Noelle Clark

Life's full of surprises the second time around.

Arriving in Cambodia to volunteer at an orphanage, Abbie finds a warm welcome with the owner of her hotel, the handsome Craig Nelson. Craig is everything her ex-husband wasn't—warm, compassionate, and a generous humanitarian dedicated to helping the local people. But after raising a family and being devastated by the end of her bad marriage, the last thing Abbie needs is complications. She's on her own for the first time in many years, and it's time for her to spread her wings and fly free amid the people and culture that have always fascinated her.

But while exploring the ancient temples of Angkor Wat, Abbie overhears odd noises and sinister conversation that raise her hackles. Turning to the only person she thinks may be able to help—Craig—she realizes she's witnessed tomb raiders—art thieves stealing frescoes to sell on the black market. Unable to let the pillaging of the beloved temple continue, Abbie goes back to investigate and finds evidence that proves her theory. And in the mean time, she finds herself falling for Craig.

Yet change isn't easy for either of them. Both carry scars, and neither is ready to let go of the past. When Abbie is attacked in the market place, it's clear her presence in the temple wasn't overlooked. When Abbie agrees to help the police stage a sting operation to catch the thieves, things go from bad to worse. And Craig might be powerless to help…

~ Available Now from Etopia Press ~

Gone
Barb Han

How far would you go to find a child that never existed?

Elizabeth Walker awakens in a mental institution, the aftermath of a nightmare in her veins. All she can think of is saving a little boy — her son. But the orderlies who rush in and jab her with needles assure her she has no son. So does her mother, who demands her doctors keep her calm and prevent her from these troubling delusions. But Elizabeth's nightmares are so real, and her arms still feel the memory of holding her son. And her instincts tell her to trust no one. Her child is gone. Her memories are gone. Everything is just…gone.

Ex-military medic David Kerrigan will never stop blaming himself for the childhood tragedy that took his younger sister's life. Working on assignment at the facility, he's drawn to Elizabeth, and he's not sure that everything about her case is on the up and up. David knows full well he can't change the past, but what if he can save this one person? And maybe helping Elizabeth might just save them both…

CPSIA information can be obtained at www.ICGtesting.com
Printed in the USA
LVOW08s1511251113

362758LV00002B/433/P